# The Wild Azerii

A sudden breeze in the treetops caused Morgana to glance skyward again. The moon's aura appeared brighter, and as she gazed at its silver-edged beauty, a glittering veil spiraled out from the shining sphere. She watched in awe as the spiral grew larger and slowly descended until it reached the distant treetops. A sound shimmered amongst the trees, like crystal raindrops as it fell slowly through the forest. Within the sound, she could hear the tinkling voices of the Others, the Azerii 'mist ponies' of her childhood, laughing in playful delight. Cloaked in glimmering mists, they appeared in the forest, lighting the path with their glowing voices.

Morgana stood at the edge of the trees. All of her past spoke to her of the dangers that lay ahead. Her teachings said she should run back to her family where life was ordered and secure. If she followed these beings there would be no safe home that she could return to.

A moment's decision that seemed like a lifetime swept through her. Shifting her pack once more, she firmly stepped onto the path and was joyously welcomed by the dancing Azerii.

Also by Alii M. Bek

**_Be-Dazzling!_**
Hand Beading Techniques for Clothing
and Costumes

*Published by Outrageous Temptations*

# The Children of the Anarii

by

## Alii M. Bek

**Full Circle Press**
Marysville, Washington

A Full Circle Press Book
Marysville, WA

ISBN: 0-9651543-1-9

First Edition: June 1996

Cover painting by: Emery Bear
Cover design by: Emery Bear
Map design by: Alii M. Bek
Book design and typesetting by: Alii M. Bek

Manufactured in the United States of America
Printed on recycled paper.

# Acknowledgments

Whom do I have to thank...

Emery Bear, for the cover art and his encouragement; Pamalah McNeiley, for her proofing; Taia Stewart, for her gentle editing; Mary Anne Mauermann, for her wisdom; my brother, Scott, for his unconditional acceptance of my art; and the jewelry lady who 'saw' this book published when I had barely started it.

## Thank You!

# Biography

Alii M. Bek, a Seattle native, currently resides in Marysville, WA, with her two cats; Zenith and Serroi, a dog named A. B. Normal, and a large stash of fabrics and costumes from her 20+ years of professional dance and costuming. She began her working life with a B.A. in graphics from Central Washington State College, then worked for several years in that field until boredom set in and she discovered the creative liberation of Middle Eastern Dance. Through her involvement she created her own theatrical dance productions and began her writing career, writing articles on costume design for national dance publications and eventually self-publishing a how-to book called *BE-DAZZLING! Hand Beading Techniques for Clothing and Costumes* in 1992 under her stage name, *Tahia Alibeck*. She had her own business called *Outrageous Temptations by Alibeck,* where she created extravagant costumes and wearable art and taught beading classes to other aspiring costume designers, professional seamstresses and avid sewers.

In 1987 she began her metaphysical explorations. A year later, while on her spiritual quest, she began writing **The Children Of The Anarii**; a metaphysical fantasy that expresses many spiritual truths as the story unfolds, and provided many coincidental experiences while it was being written for the authoress. Alii views the book as the first of a trilogy that mirrors her own journey to finding her own truth and a sense of peace that each person struggles to find inside themselves.

To Shannon, who believed in me.
To Ken, who loved me.
To Emery, who heard me.
To my Dad, who made me fight for my dreams.

And to Raphael and the Anarii,
who made me laugh and cry, and showed me
the magic upon this wondrous journey.

# Don't just dream it–
# Do it!

# The Dream

The horses went by in marvelously colored trappings; red, green, blue, gold and more red. The colors seemed to call out to each other. In tropical dizziness they called. And beckoned. Screamed outright. The horses seemed not to notice, nor did their riders. Solemn gray they wore, their faces hooded. Mists seemed to follow them as they rode. None looked right or left, just forward. Still the colors called. But they were not listening.

Then I noticed. The colors were not the trappings of the horses. The colors were the horses! Blazing in their glory they changed with every step, every muscle movement! And the horses were no longer walking solemnly along. They were prancing—no!—dancing! A playful little trot here, a sidestep there! Each seemed to be enjoying their game of a dance. But their riders did not notice this. How could they not? I tried to tell them, but I am only a shadow in this world. I am not real.

Or am I?

# The Children of the Anarii

*the journey begins...*

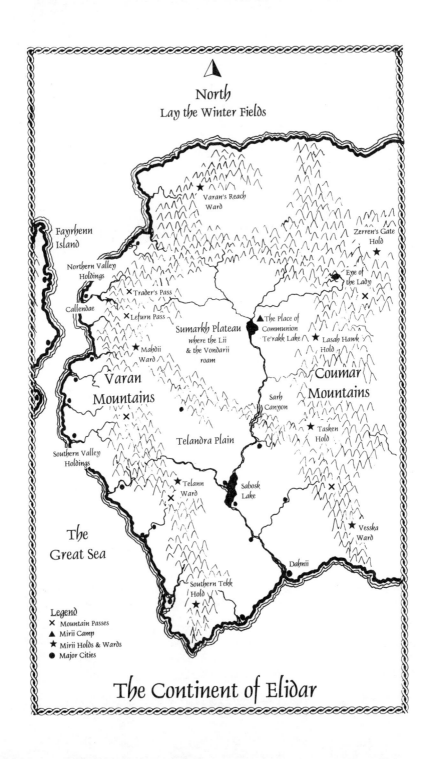

North
Lay the Winter Fields

Fayrhenn
Island

Varan's Reach
Ward

Zerren's Gate
Hold ★

Northern Valley
Holdings

× Trader's Pass

Eye of
the Lady

×

Callendae

× Lefurn Pass

Sumarkh Plateau
where the Lii
& the Vondarii
roam

▲ The Place of
Communion
Te'rakk Lake ★ Lasah Hawk
Hold

★ Mahdii
Ward

Varan
Mountains

Coumar
Mountains

×

Sarh
Canyon

★ Tasken
Hold

Telandra Plain

Southern Valley
Holdings

★ Telann
Ward
×

Sabosk
Lake

×

The
Great Sea

★ Vesska
Ward

Dahnii

Southern Tekk
Hold
★

Legend
× Mountain Passes
▲ Mirii Camp
★ Mirii Holds & Wards
● Major Cities

The Continent of Elidar

# Prologue

"They're gone, Stil." Rejat breathed her words through clenched teeth as she pulled her inner-sight back from distance scanning the trail behind them. She opened her eyes and abruptly closed them again as another dust-laden gust cut into her face. The wind died briefly and she squinted back into the eastern forests they had just crossed. A dry early summer left the trees covering the sharply rising slopes of the northern Varan Mountains looking starved, the branches of the long-needle pines and cedarjinn brittle and edged with gray dust from the higher cliffs. Her Azerii companion, Stillyth, in his horse form, turned around carefully on the narrow path at the edge of a slide nearly obliterating the old trail, his hooves clattering amongst the loose rocks that littered the ground. He surveyed the open face of Traders Pass, seldom used now that most travelers preferred the lower southern passes.

Against the wind's insistent breath Rejat tugged at her dark red coat, then silently urged Stillyth across the crumbling path. "It's not much worse than when we crossed before, what—five years ago?" she mused aloud as she pulled her flailing hair from her mouth.

1

*It has been used,* he sent, his thoughts ominous in her head.

Leaning forward, she patted his neck affectionately, watching his sure steps along the roughened path where it curved outwards around a steep slope. The trees below danced in the brisk winds. *Mostly by us, and the few who remember or dare this way,* she returned, stroking his mane, then fell silent as the memory of those for whom she journeyed rose in her mind. With half-closed eyes she lifted her gaze toward their destination, while her thoughts scattered like the tossing particles in the wind.

When they gained the wider ground at the end of the pass, a movement in the trees ahead of them caught their attention. Stillyth halted as Rejat began searching the clinging forest. As she drew a long dagger from her belt, her thoughts quickly created a protective light barrier around her, then expanded it outward to surround both herself and her mount. From the edge of her vision it shimmered faintly at arm's reach like the inside of a silvered glass bowl.

"Kill her! Kill the Mirii Witch before she uses her magic!" a maddened voice shrieked as a man dressed in the green and brown of a Forester burst from the trees, a dark sword held aloft over his head. Stillyth reared back and Rejat flung herself hard against his neck as the man's blade came crashing down, slicing through her flaring shield and into Stillyth's ribs. Stillyth bellowed in pain.

*Stars! They've got Keethra!* Rejat shouted inwardly as her mount stumbled away from their attacker. Mentally she cursed the dark oily blade that slipped through her shield where cold steel would not. As the man came at her again she grabbed her saddle horn with her free hand and kicked the Forester's sword hand away as he attempted to strike again, then pushed her shield to visible brightness. At a sudden pain in her shoulder she jerked forward, swinging her dagger up as she turned to face another man's sword darting through her shield. She parried his blade mid-length and shoved it away, kicking out again before he could draw back to strike. Clinging tenaciously to her mount with her knees, she released her saddle horn to create a blazing ball of light in her closed hand, then flung it at her attackers. It burst with the sun's brilliance, forcing the Foresters to jump back, their clothes and hair smoking from the consuming heat.

Ignoring his injury, Stillyth reared again under her and struck out, his hooves slashing the jaw and chest of another Forester who reached for the discarded reins. As the man fell, the Azerii struck again, meeting another Forester and sending the man sprawling onto his companion while Rejat clutched her saddle to stay on.

"Filthy Mirii Witch! Aza-Whore!" their curses filled the air as another fireball reached them from Rejat's hand. Her shield flared like lightening against each thrust made with their dark oily weapons, her barrier only stopping their hands from penetrating further. Another blade snaked past her hip as the stallion danced beneath her and she slammed her dagger hand in a wide arc, cutting the man's forearm to the bone. His bellow answered her as he suddenly dropped his sword. She lashed out with her dagger as another Forester stepped into his place and nearly fell when Stillyth abruptly bucked, kicking at a man behind them. She clutched his mane to regain her balance, losing her dagger.

*"Still! Run!"* she shouted, clasping her hands

3

together while she held on with her legs. As she inwardly cited the First Law, *The Mirii shall not kill*, she frantically gathered up her shield energy then flung her hands apart, releasing fireballs that engulfed everything with dazzling light as they met their targets. Horrid screams filled their ears as they bolted through their attackers and plunged into the depths of the enclosing forest beyond.

# Chapter 1

Morgana Brejjard stood alone by the river and watched, her gaze reaching across the ever-changing waters. She had returned many times to this place, seeking answers to the restlessness that plagued her soul.

"Today, the Lady must call me today," she whispered, looking out over the misty flow. She felt the inner voices sweep through her awareness— words without words. When would she understand? She had felt this nameless calling all her life, especially as a child...when she believed she could fly. "Only in your dreams," her mother had said. "Not just in my dreams, it was real!" she had cried. Her mother had only frowned and said every child had these dreams. But when had they all forgotten how to fly?

A defiant thought rose suddenly in her mind as a tear clouded her vision, "It was real, I did fly!" she whispered to the river. From the far bank a bird cried out, as if to agree.

A light morning breeze brushed the chill from the river and she hugged her shawl around her tighter, remembering the previous day's heat. She turned and began walking along the narrow path towards her

secret place under a large cedarjinn tree. It was her
favorite hideaway where she stole as much time as
she could, away from her tedious hold duties; watching the river, listening to the voices; waiting and
dreaming. She loved the stillness of the forest, the
endless murmur of the river and the wild creatures
there. She remembered her childhood, spent in
games of solitude at the river and the freedom she felt
as she skipped beside the dancing waters, exploring
pools of scooting fish and calling after the birds that
hunted among the shining rocks. She yearned for that
freedom again, with a passion she kept hidden from
everyone she knew. Once, a few summers past, she
spent a night alone under her tree and upon her return had been frightened by her father's rage at her
night's venture. He threatened to confine her to the
dark upper rooms of the main house if she ever con-
templated repeating her foolishness and would have
done so instantly if her mother had not intervened.

She approached the cedarjinn tree. The great
evergreen was one of the larger ones on her father's
lands, with a trunk nearly twice her arm span and a
crown seeming to reach endlessly for the sky. The
lower branches hugged the earth on all but the water
side where it stood bedded to the rocky bank. It had
nearly been washed away several times for much of
its huge roots were exposed, but still it clung to the
bank, daring the river to pull it to its doom. In summer the river was low enough so she could sit
amongst the largest roots facing the river and not be
seen, not even by the wildest animals who came to
drink.

Morgana reveled in the brisk air as she settled
into her hideaway. The morning's vapor left everything cold and damp, but the day promised to be very

warm. She told herself she would come again before the first stars appeared, but her father kept a close watch as of late. She huddled deeper into her shawl as a breath of wind brought the water's chill around her once more. I should return, she thought as her gaze followed the glistening waters. Her mother expected assistance for her sister's betrothal feast, but defiantly she stayed, even knowing the anger that would be waiting. The river's call was stronger than her fear.

Tillan strode heavily from the large gathering room down the main hall and into the kitchen at the rear of the house. His anger was stretched taught across his lined face. "Where is Morgana?" he demanded of his wife.

Brea paused from her tasks, focusing on her hands. "I don't know," she said evenly, "I told her last night I needed her help early." She glanced at him, keeping her face still. "Maybe she's gathering flowers for the tables." She continued with the feast preparations, knowing her calm words would not soothe her husband any more than her own anger.

He slammed his hand on the table before her. "She's at the river again, isn't she?"

Brea looked into his face. There was fear behind the anger in his eyes again. She wanted to embrace him, to tell him Morgana was just walking ahead to meet their guests. But she lowered her eyes and remained silent. She feared for her eldest daughter, but much as she prayed and scolded, nothing seemed to keep Morgana from the river.

Tillan abruptly turned and stormed out of the

kitchen, angrily muttering that he would punish their eldest for her disobedience this time. Brea watched him go, then returned to her preparations, her heart aching over the discord in their family. Morgana had tried to tell her of the mysterious feelings that drew her to the river, but it was all wrong to her. A woman should not feel those longings. Those feelings belonged to men and the creatures of the wild. A woman should feel her place was at home, not out there. Only a few in her memory had felt that call, and they were lost to everyone now. They had answered and followed the river's mists to a place none could understand, only fear.

She looked up as her youngest child came running in. Siann announced that the Rinon family had arrived and reported how much food they had brought to add to the evening's feast. Her son fairly burst with pride over his sister Kina's promise to the Rinon's son, Dain. The Rinon LandsHold was the largest in the valley and Dain was the best rider and hunter in the world as far as he was concerned. Siann idolized the young man and though Brea thought it a bit much, she was always amused by his excitement and glad enough for any distraction from her worried thoughts of Morgana.

The vision began slowly, rising with the mist from the river's crystal surface. A world of clouds began to slip around Morgana, enshrouding the late morning sun as it lay on the water. Pale ghostly figures of unnamed shapes moved across her mind like smoke rings from her father's pipe. Then, with a change, a solid form appeared. A tall shadow moved toward her, at first indistinct, then evolving into a darkened horse and rider. The rider was cloaked in deep red, the same color as the heavy trappings of the horse. Blood red, Morgana thought. How odd, no one wears red, except the Mirii.

She watched the figures move closer. The rider's hood was pulled far over the shadowed face concealing who or what this person was. Something pulled at the back of her mind; a forgotten memory of this one.

When the horse was a few steps away, it stopped and with a shudder, the rider threw the cloak's hood back. A woman's face appeared amid darkened flame-red hair, the face deathly pale with exhaustion, her dark copper eyes shadowed and lined. "Morgana Elissii," the figure spoke in a tired low voice. "Morgana Elissii," she repeated stronger, leaning forward over the horse's neck.

Morgana stared at the woman, her fear slowly twisting about her. "Who are you?" she whispered, her voice shaking.

"Rejat," the woman replied. The horse pulled at the reins, jerking her arm and she grimaced in pain. She looks so tired, Morgana thought, and found her fear slipping away as concern for this stranger replaced it. She raised her hand to soothe the nervous animal, but the horse snorted a warning at her hand.

The woman closed her eyes and leaned back. "We need your help, Morgana Elissii. Please help us," she said, her eyes tightly closed in obvious pain. "They have hunted us for four days through the western Varan. We can't outrun them much longer. Stillyth is failing. What you see now is my mastery over him, not his true self." She gently stroked the horse's shoulder.

"Who is hunting you?" Morgana searched the woman's face for some clue to her identity and how she knew her name. And what did her words mean; mastery, over who?

"Come to the island, near the fisher's dam," Rejat said urgently as the mist swirled higher around her. "I can't hold this Shadow any longer. Stillyth must rest or he will die. You must come soon or it will be too late for us." The two forms were veiled once more as Morgana stood and reached out to them, wondering why she could not help them now. A sudden touch of wind swept the mist aside and they were gone.

Morgana looked down at the empty shallows of the river. The rocks and sand appeared undisturbed. She pulled herself up the bank and looked out over the now clear surface. It was so real, could I have dreamt this? The air around her was as still now as when she had arrived. She looked up at the shadows in the trees, then with a gasp of surprise, realizing the lateness of the morning, turned and ran from the river.

The Brejjard LandsHold lay amongst the rolling foothills of the coastal region of Elidar, on a south-to-east turn of the Kesh River as it fell from the upper Varan Mountains on its way to the sea. A vast forest fringed and pocketed the LandsHold which was fair in size and standing amongst the holds of the northern valleys. As Morgana hurried through the summer-crisp woods and fields of her father's lands, endless questions raced through her mind. Who was that strange woman? She knew my birth name, but why did she add the name Elissii? And how did she know my name in the first place? Was it real or just an illusion? She had heard the voices in her dreams before but none had felt so compelling.

She walked through the vegetable and herb gardens toward the kitchen storeroom at the back of the house. She could hear several voices stirring from inside, some of their guests having already arrived. She heard her sister Kina's pleasant laughter at the attention she was receiving. A blessing to her, she thought with some sadness. She did not wish to see her sister leave home. Kina was the only one she could talk to of her loneliness and longing for something she could not name.

Morgana slipped into the storeroom and peeked around the inside door to the kitchen. Her mother and sister were talking to Dain's mother Salahn and his younger sister Adala. Adala was showing something to Kina and talking excitedly, while the two mothers looked on in amusement.

She stepped back in dismay. Adala. She had forgotten she would be here. Bitterness surged in her as she remembered Adala's betrayal of her special place at the river many years before. She was the same age as Kina and was always trying to please everyone around her. She was small and slim with pale golden hair that turned nearly white by summer's end. "A natural beauty," Morgana's father had called her, comparing her delicate features to his eldest daughter's taller stature and stronger build.

She clasped her own long wheaten hair in one hand and leaned back against the storeroom wall, wishing to run back to the river. Looking down at her dust-covered shoes she suddenly realized how discordant she looked in contrast to everyone wearing their

11

best clothes, while she was still in her old ones. She turned toward the outer door, wondering if she could slip away unseen to her room when Brea entered the storeroom.

"Morgana, where have you been? The Rinon's are here," she asked in a low voice. Morgana turned to face her mother and answer, hesitating when she saw Adala step in behind her.

"I—left my shawl out on the fence yesterday and went to get it. I guess I was enjoying the morning and forgot to come right back," she said lamely, knowing her mother would not argue with her in front of their visitors.

"Well, you'll have to change quickly and then help me in the kitchen. I really wish you would pay more attention, Morgana. I told you I needed your help early this morning." She picked up a basket and started placing fruit into it. Adala quickly offered to help and received the basket from Brea's hands.

Morgana slipped into the kitchen, quietly greeting Salahn and meeting Kina's knowing glance, then hurried down the hall, listening to the voices from the gathering room where her father was talking to the rest of the Rinon family. It was going to be a difficult day for her later, but she decided she would return as soon as she could to the river for its comforting solitude. With a sigh of relief she swept into her room and closed the door softly behind her.

She changed quickly into her best pale blue skirt and tunic and was combing her hair when her brother came bursting into the room, pausing barely long enough to knock.

"Gana, Gana! She's here!"

Morgana held back an angry retort to Siann's unruly entrance and froze, her brush caught in mid stroke. "Who's here?" she demanded of her excited brother. A flicker of apprehension crossed her face.

Siann pounced on her bed and answered easily, "Aunt Elas is here, and cousin—what's her name. Don't you know anything?" He rolled back and stared at the ceiling, making lazy circles with one hand held high.

"Don't you know anything yourself? Mia's her name and please don't forget it." Relief slipped through her as she continued brushing her hair. Her brother's initial excitement began to affect her. She was always glad to see her aunt. Elas was forever an intriguing and pleasant mystery.

"Mi-ya, Mi-ya, Mi-ya," he chanted, wiggling his hand with each breath. "Momma says hurry up 'cause you're late. Everybody's showing up now and she doesn't want dinner to be spoiled 'cause you were dreaming at the river..." Siann mumbled on, then jumped to his feet and skipped erratically out of the room.

Morgana eyed her brother's disappearing back. He knows too, she thought absently. She quickly adjusted her belt and slipped on her shoes. With a last look in the mirror she stepped out to the hall.

Voices danced from the front rooms of the house and, much as she wanted to greet her aunt, she hurried to the kitchen. At the great hearth her mother was roasting a large haunch of meat over the fire while another aunt, two cousins and her grandmother were preparing more dishes for the feast. Salahn, Adala and another Rinon cousin were setting out the food they had brought while Siann ran in and out with reports of who was doing what throughout the house. With a sigh at the frantic orderliness she went to help her mother.

A laughing voice drew her attention. "I see they have put all the women to work in here again, while they sit around and gossip." In the doorway stood a tall woman of early middle years, her golden bronze hair worn loosely to her shoulders. A dark-haired girl of twelve stood beside her. A mocking scowl crossed the woman's lightly tanned features.

"Elas! How good to see you! We did not know if you and Tagar would be able to come," Brea exclaimed, leaving Morgana at the fire to give her sister-in-law a warm embrace. "It has been too long since we last saw you, you must come more often." She turned to the thin girl beside her. "Mia, look at much you have grown!" She gave her a quick smile.

Mia whispered a shy reply and Elas hugged her foster daughter for her response, then turned back to Brea. "I see Tillan has not changed at bit; he's sent you to the kitchen to do the dirty work as usual. Even though it's against my better judgment, where would you like our help?" She grinned broadly and began to roll up the sleeves of her copper-colored dress. Brea introduced Elas to her guests and sent Siann out of the kitchen for more wood.

Elas approached Morgana and the two embraced. "How is my favorite niece? Still watching the river?" she said softly and clasped Morgana's shoulder, gazing directly into her face.

"How do you always know?" she whispered, then added, "I'm fine, Aunt Elas. I'm so glad to see you again."

"We shall talk later." Elas gently squeezed her shoulder then turned away to help Brea. Morgana watched her for a moment then returned her gaze to the fire, her mind wandering over her aunt's words. Elas always had an air of knowing, a calm she held

14

behind a mask that was as changeable as the shifting flames before her. How does she always know? Morgana wondered again as her attention drifted with the flames while the excitement in the room continued to build around her.

The garden tables were bountiful with delicious and aromatic foods brought for the betrothal feast, the many dishes wonderfully created by the loving efforts of the families and their invited guests. Flickering lamps hung from the eaves of the main house and amongst the shade trees of the Hold's gardens. Hired musicians and singers entertained the joyous throng with playful and sometimes mischievous banter, calling on all to celebrate the betrothal of the two young people. All eyes were on Dain and Kina as they strolled through the gathering, welcoming each with open smiles and eyes full of their happiness.

Wistfully Morgana watched her younger sister. Kina's long fair hair was twisted back and braided with small lavender flowers which perfectly matched her slender cut dress. She was so happy, her face radiant with anticipation of her spring marriage to the handsome man beside her. Dain was a few years older than Kina. His trim frame stood a hand-breadth taller than her, his dark curly hair cut short over his broad shoulders, the darkened color of his tunic and trousers complementing his chosen's gown.

Morgana turned her eyes to her plate, suddenly unable to eat more than a handful of the delicious fare. She looked up and met her father's gaze, then quickly looked away. Even though his face did not show it, she could see the anger in his eyes. Her glance fell on her aunt. Elas was also watching, but her gaze was thoughtful. Morgana stared again at her plate, lost in her musings until her mother called for her help to finish preparing for the evening's late fare. Suddenly feeling tired, she rose from the table and followed her mother into the kitchen.

At Brea's request she went to the storeroom for more fruit. As she stepped inside, she saw that the outer door was open and walked toward it. Standing on the threshold, she gazed longingly at the darkening sky toward the distant river. The cool of the coming evening was inviting after the warmth of the kitchen. She leaned back against the door frame, still feeling the unexplained fatigue. As she closed her eyes, the voices started again, still indistinct, but urgent this time. Once more the dark mists began to surge within her inner sight.

Red fire and pain suddenly flashed through Morgana, leaving her gasping for breath on her knees. She opened her tearing eyes and heard the voices again, this time clear and precise. *Morgana Elissii! Morgana Elissii! Morannon, Morgan, Morgu Elissii, Varayanii, Mordlyth! Mordlyth!* they screamed at her. She scanned around her as the voices took on confusing forms that swirled through the fog cloaking her sight. Golden eyes seemed to float in and out of her vision as the voices repeated their strange words. Then as abruptly as the vision started it was gone, and she was left kneeling on the grass behind the storeroom.

"I see it has started," Elas said calmly from the doorway behind her. Morgana looked up at her aunt's face and saw her eyes shining faintly. "It was something like that for me too. You cannot deny them when they call you." She stepped forward to help her niece to her feet.

Morgana leaned back against the wall and took several deep breaths. "What do you mean?" Her fear clawed at her throat. She clutched her arms as a chill rushed through her. "Did you hear them? Do you know what it means? Do you see them too?" she asked, her voice shaking with every word.

Elas gave her hair a stroke. "They spoke to me for the first time many years ago." She slowly closed the storeroom door behind her. The falling night crept in around them. For once Morgana wished for a lamp instead of her usual reveling in the darkness of the evening. She shivered as she stared at her aunt.

Elas spoke again slowly, watching Morgana's face in the failing light. "I have known them and still do. But I chose not to follow. Their path is not to my liking."

Morgana's eyes widened. "What do you mean? Who are they? What do they want with me?" Her confusion filled her words. She was frightened by the pain of her vision, but wished to understand.

Elas saw this in her searching eyes. It is well she questions the fear, she thought. "I cannot tell you their names for I do not know them. However, I do know who they are and their purpose in calling you." She held Morgana's arm to steady her and quietly scan her. Her niece was in her twenty-third year, a tall young woman of fair coloring in hair and eyes. She was as yet unwed, answering to no man except her father; a lonely life in this society. She knew of Morgana's visits to the river and what drew her there, and of Tillan's opinion of his daughter's elusive activities.

Elas was not fond of her brother-in-law, for Tillan had a heavy hand with his family and his hold members at times. As the eldest male of his father's children, he expected obedience from all. His younger brother Tagar was amused by Elas' occasionally heated arguments about Tillan's parenting. The two brothers were as unlike as bird and fish, the one quick-tempered and overbearing, the other calm, self-assured and playful. Elas remembered her first meeting with Tagar when his first wife was ill. He had married young and the woman was not strong. She had died a few years later, giving birth to their son Brient. Those were Elas' traveling years and she didn't stay too long in any one place. *The people were so very afraid of Healers, even though they need our help,* she thought sadly.

"Aunt Elas?" Morgana shifted uneasily beside her.

"I'm sorry, I was just remembering something." She shook her head. *She is strong, but not prepared,* she mused, her thoughts returning to the present. She started to withdraw her scan from her niece when a brief flash of a red-clad horse and rider caught at her awareness.

Elas' gaze became electric. "Tell me of your Vision at the river this morn!" She tried to mask the urgency in her voice. She did not wish to frighten her niece anymore than the Others already had.

Morgana returned her surprised stare. "How did you know? I told no one."

"Never mind how. I know. You must show—tell me!" Elas' words shifted into her controlling Voice. *I'm out of place, I must be calm,* she thought, cross with herself.

"I—was at the river, just daydreaming," Morgana faltered, "and this woman on horseback appeared in the mist. She was hurt, all in red, and I thought—well, she said my name. How did she know

my name? But she called me another name too. 'El—
Elissii', that's it! She said 'Morgana Elissii'. Her name
was Rejat and she said someone had been chasing
her for four days through the Varan and she was master of someone named Stillyth and he was dying. I
don't understand, Elas, what does it mean?" She had
tears in her eyes again. Was it concern she now felt
for the woman of her vision?

"Show me, Morgana," Elas said calmly now.
"Show me what you saw." Her Voice gentle and yet
compelling, she gazed into her niece's dark face and
held her eyes in union. She feared Morgana would
remember this later but it was too important to know
what she had envisioned.

The vision became real again for Morgana as
her memory replayed it for her aunt. Elas held her
shoulders and if any saw they would have thought the
two lost in deep conversation and would not have remarked upon it. But within Morgana's mind she saw
the pale glow of Elas' eyes in the darkness and felt the
strength of her aunt's mind within her own.

# Chapter 2

Rejat placed the cup to her companion's lips. *Where is that cursed girl?* she fumed, angrily trying to steady herself.

*You probably scared her half to death and she'll never come to the river again,* Stillyth's thoughts intruded upon hers. He would have smiled but was too exhausted to do more than drink from the cup she held for him.

She scowled at her injured Azerii, lying before her in his hu'man form. "You can joke even though you're—" Her throat caught at her words as she helped him to another sip of water, then cradled his head in her lap. Brushing his dark bronze hair from his face, she gazed down into his faintly glowing copper eyes. "You must sleep, Stil, if we're to leave by moonrise." She carefully smoothed her journey blanket around his shoulders for the third time. "The moon will be up in a few hours and those bastards will be on our trail again."

*I know, Laa,* he returned, using their endearing name, *but you cannot wait for me. You must find the girl yourself. I cannot travel any farther.* A shudder swept through his lean frame. They had run too long, too far since the attack. His injury from the Keethra blade would not let him go any more distance without help. They had not found the assistance they so desperately needed to get through the northern valleys of the western Varan.

Rejat caressed her companion's shoulder. "How ironic, a Healer cannot heal her own Azerii!" she stormed, tears of rage and frustration at their situation, wincing from her own injury with each movement.

*You really must learn to control that temper of yours, Laa.* Stillyth's calm surrounded her like a warm embrace. Even in his weakened state his mind link was strong.

She echoed his calm back to him, remembering her anger made him suffer more. "Rest, dear Laa, and I'll try to becalm myself." She stilled her mind to scan, sensing the shelter they had found on the island was still safe and they were alone for the time being. She pushed her awareness out beyond the island to seek any recognizable minds, remembering her morning's contact with Morgana. Where is that girl, she thought irritably. Dayana said she was the one; she has never been wrong in her visioning before. Why isn't she here?

Rejat's mind wandered over the darkened valley, touching here and there; a soaring nightbird, stalking cat, sleeping cattle. No hu'mans did she mind-touch, for the distance was too great to control them and only a mind she knew, or another Mirii, could she link with. When Stillyth's breathing became more relaxed and she knew he slept, she shifted her awareness to scan for their followers. Unable to pick them up, she set her guards and tried to rest for the wait until moonrise, when they would have to move once again.

Morgana awoke and dreamily gazed at the dark ceiling above her. She briefly wondered where she was and as her awareness returned, how did she get here? Slowly she recounted the previous day's events...the river, the afternoon's preparations and the evening's festivities for her sister and her be-trothed. She thought about the great amounts of food which she had eaten little of, and of her aunt, talking behind the kitchen. What did we talk about? What happened after that? She dimly remembered telling Elas something important, but then nothing, a blank. She was in her bed, the house was quiet. She could hear her sister's soft breathing across the room.

She rose quietly and crept to the window to open the shutters. Outside the moon was rising above the trees and filling the back garden with its luminous grace. It was very late; the sky filled with flickering stars.

Morgana leaned against the window ledge. She felt strange, as if something was going to happen. An immense tension seemed to fill her body. She strained to hear the soft flowing of the river through the trees, the nightbirds in their silent hunts, other creatures of the moonlight moving about; their day, her night.

She gazed at the moon again, it's cold beauty stirring something nameless within her soul. The moon seemed to beckon to her, "Come out, come out and run with me! I'll show you a world you have only dreamt about but never dared! Come ride the winds with me, Little One! Daughter of mine, come play in my gaze..." she seemed to hear it say.

In creeping succession the voices started once more. Then like a sparkling stream they were cascading all over each other. *Come out! Come out! Morgana Elissii! Morgana...Morannon...Morgan, Morgana Elissii!* She watched in awe as a mist seemed to roll out of the garden earth before her eyes. Clouds foamed upwards and within each were blazing colors and shimmering shapes that became the forms of ponies. Small, delicate, fleet of foot and tail, they pranced before her in myriad coats of aurora. A delight to behold in their magical dance, they called her to come and play in the moonlight. *Come and dance with us, Lady of many Talents! Come and play in our Lady's Mantle of moonlight graces! Come and join us, Morgana Elissii! Morgana! Come! Come and be Mirii!*

She stepped back from the window, a cold dread twisting within her mind. Mirii! The accursed ones! Evils of the night, sorcerers and demons! Death and sickness were their craft! All the stories she remembered from childhood came flooding back to her. She shut her eyes against the terror of these creatures and closed her mind to their cries. "Evil be gone! Evil be gone!" she cried softly to herself, tears welling up from within her heart. She suddenly found she could not stop crying and slipped to the floor before the window. Outside, the voices faltered, matching her sorrow in soft wailing's for their own longings, then ended in a rippling fashion, leaving the garden silent once more.

Morgana raised her head and looked out the window. The garden was as before, empty in the moonlight. A shudder swiftly passed through her. In the stories of old, the Mirii were to be cursed! And their dreaded companions, what were they called? Azerii. Yes, that's the name, that's what those creatures in the garden were!

"Azerii," she whispered, "How can something so beautiful be evil?" Tears flooded her eyes again as she felt a strange and sudden longing to see the mystical creatures again. Her mind told her of the danger of these beings, but her heart longed to join them. How could this be?

A soft rustle from across the room claimed her attention. She caught her breath, her heart pounding as she stilled herself. Her sister stirred in her bed and with a pleasant sigh, rolled over and drifted into deeper sleep.

Morgana wiped the tears from her face. With a last look outside, she quietly closed the shutters and slipped back to her bed. Sleep did not return easily. She remembered her childhood, the lessons she had been taught and the fearsome tales of the Mirii sorcerers and their Azerii demons. Shapeshifting, mind control, disease, murder; their evil was endless according to her elders. No one wore red because of the Mirii. It was their color. It was an evil color. *The color of blood,* she thought sleepily.

*Blood is the Life,* a voice rattled behind her eyes. *We have no Blood without you and the Mirii. We have only the Light, Morgana. You have the Blood and the Light.* The voice flowed around her mind in wispy trails. *You have the Life, Morgana. You are the Life, Morgana Elissii. You are the Life.* The voice trailed away into the depths of her sleeping memory.

Rejat's guards chirruped a warning to the drowsing Mirii. She sat up stiffly and scanned the island for the approaching intruder. The moon was full and rose brilliantly over the sleeping forest. As her scan crossed the intruder's path she was surprised to be recognized and welcomed by another Mirii. She heard the other's Azerii crossing the river's ford to the small island, and guided them to the thicket where she and Stillyth were hiding. Producing a small light sphere, she checked her Azerii's sleeping form and waited. A few moments later two women, Elas and her Azerii Brealyth appeared, stepping through the thicket's opening.

Elas knelt facing Rejat, the two women placing their hands palm to palm. A soft glow slipped through their fingers, lighting up their faces. Rejat's tired eyes gazed into Elas' concerned ones. "I'm sorry, my sister, I was not here earlier to help you," Elas said softly. "The young woman you contacted is not prepared. She has no knowledge of us." She lowered her hands, the shimmering light still cascading from her palms, her eyes falling on the man lying beside them.

"But she does now, doesn't she, Elas?" A half amused smile crossed Rejat's lips. She lowered her gaze, her smile fading quickly as Stillyth woke and slowly opened his eyes.

His face was cloudy with sleep, exhaustion and pain. His eyes greeted Elas, then he turned his gaze to her silent companion. *Greetings, Brealyth,* he sent.

Brealyth returned her unspoken welcome, then touched Elas' shoulder. *We must hurry, Tagar is worried.*

"I know, Brealyth." Elas turned to Rejat. "Is Stillyth able to travel?" She raised her hand to his forehead, only touching him after a quick nod from his Mirii.

"I don't think so, Elas. He needs your skills before we can move."

"Show me his injuries." She placed her hands on her knees and sat back as Rejat pulled the blanket back from Stillyth's body. The gentle light revealed a blood stained cloth covering a long gash down his left side from mid-rib to waist.

Stillyth closed his eyes in pain. *An unfortunate thing a body can be,* he sent to Rejat.

She nodded in agreement. *But worth the experience?* she returned as she stroked his cheek.

*Yes!* he sent firmly, gazing up into her face.

Elas placed her hands over the wound as Brealyth knelt beside her, the Azerii shifting into formless light, then merging within Elas' body. The glow from her hands became stronger. "There will be pain, Stillyth. This is a bad wound. You have journeyed too long in this condition. This is from a Keethra blade, isn't it?" She lowered her head and became silent.

Rejat placed her hands on Stillyth's shoulders. Both Mirii became lost in concentration; Rejat absorbing and blocking some of his pain, Elas healing his torn body.

Stillyth closed his eyes and tensed. The pain became terrible, his form trembling in the flow of their energy. Just as he became accustomed to the throbbing discomfort, a new warmth replaced it. Not the fire of his fever, but a summer sun. Comfortable, as cooling spread while the pain left, his fever vanishing as the wound became healed.

Elas snapped her head up and leaned back,

sweat beading across her brow. "Brealyth, Be Thanks!" she said breathlessly as her Azerii shimmered around her body.

Rejat raised her head, her eyes filling with tears. "Elas srii Brealyth, Be Thanks!" she echoed forcefully.

A horse's nicker carried across the river, demanding their attention. "We must go quickly." Elas stood, her Azerii slipping behind her, shifting into horse form outside of the thicket. They pulled Stillyth to his feet. "You can ride behind Tagar, once we cross the river," she said to Rejat as they helped him to Brealyth's back.

Stillyth grasped Rejat's hand. *I will be well now, Laa. You still need assistance.* He smiled tiredly down at her.

"All right, Stil." Rejat turned to her sister. "I shall trust your man's help, Elas," she said as she picked up her belongings. The two women and the Azerii stepped out of the thicket and quietly crossed the island to enter the river's shallows. They rejoined Tagar and Mia, who waited with their restless horses on the northern bank of the moonlit river.

Morgana rose with the first light of dawn, dressing quickly in her outdoor working clothes. With a glance at her sleeping sister, she quietly moved out of the room and through the still silent house to the kitchen. After the grand feast of the previous day, none of her family was stirring. She gathered some of yesterday's bread and a ripe yellowenn fruit to tie into a scarf, then stepped through the storeroom to the back garden. As she walked amongst the orderly rows of vegetables and herbs, she noticed there were no traces of the night's visitors. With a backward glance at the house, she quickly slipped through the gate and headed for the path to the river.

Walking along the outer fields she thought about the day before and all of its events. And the night; was it a dream? The Azerii, no one had spoken of them for many years it seemed. Her elders told their tales and rumors were whispered of lone Mirii traveling about as Healers from time to time, but no one really saw them did they? Was it real what she had seen? There were no tracks; nothing in the garden had been disturbed during the night. But she remembered clearly what she had witnessed and was now full of questions with no one to give her any answers.

She pulled out the piece of bread and began to nibble hungrily at it as she walked. Almost aimlessly, she headed for her tree, watching to see if any of her father's holders might be about. When she was sure she was alone, she turned to the narrow path through the brush leading to the cedarjinn tree. As she started to slip down to her place amongst the exposed roots, a flash of vivid color caught her eye. Dangling from a single strand, a red tassel waved in the slight morning air rising from the river. She froze, then slowly reached out and touched the feathery softness of the tassel, then carefully picked it off the low branch. Staring at its brilliant color, she studied it closely, as she absentmindedly stepped to sit amongst the roots. With the forgotten bread in one hand and the forbidden tassel in the other, she slowly raised her eyes to the river.

It was real! She was here! Then her memory fully returned as the vision came flooding back to her.

"The island! I was supposed to go there to help them!" she cried to herself, her dread rising at her unwitting betrayal. Quickly she stood again, plunging the tassel into her skirt pocket, and climbed out of her hideaway. She began to walk briskly along the descending river toward the island near the fisher's dam.

By the time Morgana reached her destination she was nearly out of breath from the rushed hour's walk. She glanced around at the edge of the river, then seeing no one about, waded into the ford without stopping to remove her shoes and struggled toward the island. Clutching her skirt to keep from tripping in the current, she reached the gravelly bank, soaked to her waist from the cold waters. She paused at the edge of the island's growth, looking again across the river, then tramped into the brush toward the center of the small island. She finally stumbled onto a narrow path and followed it, eventually coming to the other shore. She turned back and tried another direction. The small trees and brush gave no indication that anyone had been there for some time. Nearly dizzy from the cold and running back and forth, she finally sat down near the island's downstream side and gazed dejectedly over the water grasses flowing lazily in the current. Her sight lifted to the tall reeds waving in the wind. Low branching trees nearly covered the opposite bank, almost concealing the southern trail along the river's edge.

With her chin on her knees, her eyes followed the path upstream as she thought about her vision. "She said to come here. Where is she?" she muttered to herself. The tassel was real, but there were no signs that the stranger had been there. Maybe something had happened and she didn't get here. She pulled the tassel out and placed it on her knee. "Where is she?"

she asked it in frustration. Nothing but the rushing voice of the river and the morning's birds answered her. She closed her eyes and rested her chin once more on her knees, hugging her arms around her dampened legs.

A rumble from her middle reminded Morgana of her half eaten breakfast. She pulled the bread out of the scarf she had tied to her belt, but it was now a soggy lump. She wrinkled her nose and tossed it into the river. For the fish, she thought hungrily. The fruit would have to hold her until she returned home. Its sweetness reminded her of yesterday's plentiful fare of which she had eaten little. She wondered why she had been unable to eat, when her normal appetite had fully returned with the morning's light.

As she slowly bit into the fruit, her gaze was caught by a movement across the river. Looking up, she saw two men on horseback riding along the southern bank. From their clothing they appeared to be Foresters. Dressed in brown, gray and green, they seemed to be hunting something as they rode northward along the trail, their eyes watching the ground before them. At a sudden urge to hide, she backed into the underbrush of the island's canopy. With some difficulty she watched them as they proceeded along the trail. Their lean horses were both muddy brown in color, one with a brilliant white blaze down its long face. Its rider had beard and hair to match, falling from under the man's cap. The second was younger with dark bronze hair that waved softly with the rocking movement of his horse. Both men were intent on their tracking and for a moment she thought they would pass the island by, but with a sudden cry from a soaring bird the two stopped and gazed across to the island. The men began talking and the younger pointed to the island and started to turn his horse in its direction. Holding her breath and pressing herself deeper into the earth, she silently prayed that they would not approach. The elder shouted something to his companion then started to ride forward on the trail again. With a look of anger, the younger man stopped and turned his horse after the elder.

Morgana thought she would never breathe normally again as she watched the two continue down the far side of the river until they were out of sight. Slowly she stood, brushing leaves and dirt from her clothing and hair, and cautiously made her way back toward the center of the island. A scrap of bright color caught her eye as she wound her way through the thick underbrush. She stopped to see what had drawn her attention to the tall grass and brambles. It was a piece of torn cloth. Bright red, no more than a single finger's span wide, it beckoned to her from the crushed grass of a nearly hidden thicket of bramble vines and small trees. She stepped into the thicket and knelt before the bright strip, eyeing it as if it might disappear before her. When it did not vanish she gingerly picked it up to give it a closer look. Bright red and neatly woven, the narrow strip looked like it had been torn for a specific purpose, rather than just ripped from someone's clothing by the brambles. She looked around the small clearing. It was not large enough to bring a horse through without causing more damage to the surrounding brush, but one or two people could easily hide from searching eyes. *Mirii,* she thought, as excitement began to push her fears aside.

She looked around the thicket again, searching for any other sign of who had been here and where they may have gone, but the grass gave no answers beyond the piece of cloth she clutched in her hand. She placed the cloth with the tassel and noted the exact match of the brilliant color. Obviously from the same clothing, she thought, and tucked both back into her pocket. She looked skyward, noticing the morning was nearly gone. With a last glance around, she made her way back to the path leading to the river's ford to return home.

# Chapter 3

Rejat glanced uneasily around the darkened loft. She hated being tied to any one place, particularly when she had to rely on others for her safety. Her Azerii, in horse form, slept below in one of the enclosed stalls. Elas said Stillyth would need to rest for a few days before they could travel again, and Rejat had her own hurts to be tended to, though they were minor next to her Azerii's.

They had ridden swiftly to this place during the night, and in the pre-dawn hours Elas had spoken with the LandsHolder, Kaill Brenan. He was a friend to Mirii, she said. His family had been helped by Mirii Healers in times past and had known Elas and Tagar for several years. Rejat was not convinced, but she was not in any condition to turn down proffered help. Even though his outer wound was healed, Stillyth still needed to rest in order to heal his spirit from the physical pain and exhaustion he had suffered. So she agreed to let Elas be their guide and she spent the rest of the evening in the loft overlooking her companion. Elas' Azerii stayed with them also, while Elas, Tagar and Mia stayed in the main house with the family. Brenan was a generous man, offering to put Rejat and her Azerii in his home as well, but Elas felt the two should show themselves to as few as possible, particularly since Rejat had made the foolish choice to wear a prohibited color.

"You were looking for trouble by wearing Mirii red," Elas had commented while caring for Rejat's injured shoulder. She had replied something about being Mirii, not a Forester, and being in a hurry anyway. She now realized she would have to hide her clothes and wear something safe, which Elas would undoubtedly provide for her.

Elas was always right, it seemed. Rejat rubbed her still sore shoulder and thought about her early journey years with her half-sister. She was lost in fond memories of their youthful games when the darkness of the loft was broken from below. Brilliant morning sunlight poured in through the stable's main door with a small child creating a pillar of shadow in the brightness. Rejat watched from between bales of straw as the dark-haired child boldly walked into the stable to the stall where her Azerii still slept. The boy stood before the stall's gate and peered through the gaps at the dark copper form lying on the straw within. Then he looked straight up to the loft at her hiding place and smiled. A smile of knowing, her senses told her, the child recognized the horse as Azerii. Then, without a word the boy walked out of the stable in the same bold manner, closing the large door behind him.

Rejat watched the small form leave and thought wildly—*He knows! Will he give us away?* A moment later she knew the boy would not. With a sudden yawn she lay back amongst the bales and cast her mind out after the child. No, he would not tell. It was his secret. The special smile played before her inner eyes again. He was someone to watch though, this child had the gift of knowing. I will remember him to the Elders. He may join us one day, she thought sleepily.

She smiled to herself. It was time the Mirii made their presence known again. The Unnamed Azerii were restless, there were not enough youths from the Mirii Holds to meld with them. They had remained hidden too long, the People were forgetful of their shared past. It would be well to come again... carefully...before...Rejat's thoughts dissipated as her mind opened to the vision before her. Slowly—like the snow falling before her eyes; cold, bitter cold all around, the darkness of the loft was replaced by the blinding white of snowfall. She sensed smoke; dark, choking, and death, near but fading, then returning. The Dark Azerii—*the Madness returns!* Her mind recoiled at the touch of the Madness. Around her were others she did not know; some Mirii, other valley people. She stood before them amongst the winter-grayed structures of the LandsHold, and faced the coming terror. Blindly it came, crashing through the destruction it had caused, lusting after more. The Madness screamed in her mind, demanding freedom through the killing. Enmeshed in pain through forcing meld, it had only one hope for release—by the destruction of its ill-fated host!

Suddenly a child ran before her eyes toward the dreadful duality that lurched before them. A child, the boy in the stable! Dark hair falling back, the boy ran toward the Madness. Rejat found her Voice crying a desperate *Stop!* but the child only ran on. The Madness appeared in hu'man form, its features twisted in agony and rage. She stared in horror—it was the LandsHolder Brenan, the energy of the Dark Azerii possessing him, shadowing around him like a black fog. The boy stopped before him, standing as if offering to be sacrificed. The man/Azerii towered over the boy, nearly falling forward over the child in its path. The Madness raged at the small obstacle, but moved no closer. As if held at bay by the child, the raging Madness halted with a howling shriek, directed at those gathered beyond its reach. A male voice, pleading in her mind reached her, *Take the boy away! Take him away! No one is safe while this child is here! It will take them all if you do not take this child away!* The Dark Azerii screamed beyond the man's anguished thoughts, *No! He is the One! I must have this One! He is Mine!*

The overlapping voices screamed in her mind. Rejat faced them both, preparing to attempt to master the invading Azerii when suddenly the vision broke, and with a jolt left her sitting in the loft, drenched in sweat. Stillyth was kneeling beside her in hu'man form, holding her in his arms.

Emotions flooded through her in crashing waves as she returned to her present, the dreadful vision leaving its painful mark. Below them Brealyth stood and listened as Elas spoke to her through meld. *Stay with them, I will come soon. Let Rejat rest, the Vision has served its purpose. We shall mark the child.*

\*

Elas stood in the kitchen doorway of their host, her hands wrapped around a warm cup of tajiz. She had been listening to Kaill Brenan's wife Siva, speak of the hold's activities while she stood at the table kneading a batch of bread dough. Kaill and his eldest boys had gone to their tasks, with Tagar volunteering to lend a hand for their hospitality. While Brealyth relayed what Rejat had visioned, Mia played with Siva's two youngest children in the holdyard, drawing Elas' attention away from their conversation.

Siva fell silent as she continued working the dough, refraining from asking what was wrong when Elas' face became abruptly still for several minutes.

Shaking her head, Elas released her link with her Azerii and smiled an apology to her hostess. "I'm sorry, Siva, my mind is elsewhere this morning. Tell me about your children, are they well?" She moved to assist her at the table.

Siva smiled nervously in return and resumed speaking about her eldest daughter's new baby and how well her son-in-law fared on his father's lands. Her guest listened politely as she began to talk of her youngest son Jeven, and his wild imaginings. Her voice took on a note of concern as she spoke of the four-year-old's make-believe playmates, the 'mist ponies' as he called them.

Elas instantly recognized what Rejat had sensed. The boy was a Talent and would meld easily with an Azerii when he was old enough. The 'mist ponies', or wild Azerii as the Mirii called them, would seek him out for he was open to them and yet strong enough to prevent a meld unless by his choice. She thought over what Brealyth had told her of Rejat's vision while Siva rambled on. The child would have to be marked. The vision had shown the season to be deep winter, but the boy looked much the same age as now. She was wondering how she was going to mark him without his parent's knowledge, when Siva stopped talking and touched her hand.

"You know Jeven is gifted, don't you?" she said, her eyes intent on Elas' face.

She returned Siva's gaze with a look of surprise. "Do you believe what Jeven says?" she countered her question evasively.

Siva's eyes held a shadow of apprehension. She sat down at the table, her hands white with flour. "Elas, I know you are a Mirii Healer, and your people have befriended Kaill's family in the past. I have no cause against the Mirii, but I'm worried about Jeven." She twisted her hands before her. "I want my children to be happy and safe. Jeven has seen the Azerii. I know that's what they are. So does Kaill. We have talked about this. I feel your coming was a gift. Please tell me what you see for my son. I know the Mirii have visions, is that what you saw? Some vision about my son?" Her eyes pleaded for an answer.

Elas sat down next to her. "Siva, what I did or did not see, it doesn't matter. I do not tell the future through my Visions. We only receive them as a possible future, not a definite one. Anything can change the outcome. If we were to live only by our Visions, we would never progress, never take our journeys to who we are. We would close all our futures to stay in the past. The Visions can be a wonderful gift or a grievous curse."

Elas paused to think. Siva sat beside her, looking forlornly at her flour covered hands. She glanced down at her own. *Even in our differences, how similar we are. Each of us worrying about our children.*

"Siva. Do you wish my help for Jeven?" she said carefully, using the Voice to get her full attention.

Siva looked up, hope flickering in her eyes. "Elas, I want my family safe and happy. If Jeven is to become Mirii, then yes, I want your help."

"I must speak to Rejat, but I want you and Kaill

to be a part of this. There has been too much hidden from your people in the past. You must know the risks as well as the rewards of your child's talent. I cannot explain more of this now, only that it is ultimately Jeven's choice." She took Siva's hands in her own. "I promise you this, no harm will come to Jeven. If it is in my power and it is meant to be, he will be safe and happy with the Mirii."

✳

Morgana quickly walked back to her home, her stomach rumbling its annoyance at her lack of a proper meal, but she was more intent on how she was going to explain her absence and the state of her clothes. She would have to hide the tassel and the piece of cloth. If anyone found them they would ask too many questions that she did not wish to answer.

Her skirt was dry by the time she slipped through the back garden gate. She heard her mother calling after her brother from the kitchen for something she did not quite catch. When she did not see anyone about, she raced alongside the house for the window of her room.

The shutters were wide open and the room was empty. Morgana pulled herself up and through the window into the room then quickly hid her prizes under her bedding. She pulled out a clean skirt and tunic from the wardrobe, kicking off her wet shoes, then started combing the tangles and leaves out of her hair when her sister walked in.

"'Gana, where have you been?" Kina whispered loudly, startling her. "Mother's been worried all morning and Father's out looking for you. What happened to your clothes?" She put down the linen basket she was carrying to pluck a twig from her sister's sleeve.

Morgana glanced out the window, then back at Kina. "I woke up early, I couldn't sleep, so I went out for a long walk and didn't notice how late it was getting." She tried to sound calm but the look on her sister's face said she wasn't convinced.

Kina pulled a leaf from Morgana's hair. "Father was very angry; I think he's gone to the river." She started to help her clear her hair of the tangles.

Morgana abruptly stopped her hand to stare at her. "Why do you do this?" she said softly.

"Do what?" Her sister turned and picked up the clean tunic.

"Pretend nothing is wrong. Protect me from them." She suddenly felt tears in her eyes and looked away.

Kina turned back to Morgana. "Because you are my sister. Because you are so strong to everyone, and yet I know how lonely you are." She handed her the tunic. When Morgana didn't take it, she continued. "Remember the stories you used to tell me? About those wonderful creatures you saw in your dreams and how much you made me laugh? Remember how Father used to listen and laugh too? I remember, 'Gana. And I remember when you stopped, when Father made you stop. You were so sad, I wanted to make you happy again. I know Father can be difficult, but he doesn't understand you, that's all. I want you to be happy again, like I am. You made me happy for so long, so I just wanted you to be happy too." Kina paused to listen for their mother for a moment.

Morgana studied her younger sister. Kina appeared so mature for her seventeen years. She seemed so happy, her life was going exactly where she wanted it to go. Why can't I feel at peace like her? she thought sadly. She brushed her tears aside and started to change her clothes.

Kina helped her with her tunic. "I know how important the river is to you. I've seen how much happier you are when you have been there." She took the mud speckled tunic and skirt and tucked them into the bottom of the basket. She turned back to Morgana again. "I don't know where you are going, 'Gana, only that you had better go soon. I don't think you should wait any longer for your dreams to come to you. You have to go find them. You have to make them come true." Her eyes were suddenly bright.

"Kina, how could I ever leave?" Morgana blurted, shocked by her sister's words. "You are my best friend, my sister! How could I leave my family, my home? I don't have anywhere to go—" her voice tumbled and she sat down with a thump on her bed. In misery, she looked at her now bare feet. Her shoes would be damp for some time. Kina came over and sat next to her and took her hand.

"I'm sorry I wasn't much fun at your betrothal feast," Morgana said softly, trying to hold back the loss she felt for her soon to be wed sister.

"We missed your dancing, but you can still dance at my wedding." Kina squeezed her hand. "Leyan was asking about you. I know you don't care for him, but he does seem pleasant enough to me."

Morgana nodded and silently thought about Leyan. Yes, he was a likable man, but she felt no real interest in him or any other man in the valley her own age. He was an older cousin of Dain's and had a good sized holding of his own. Her father approved of him, but she just did not care. She remembered someone she had met when she was fourteen. Too young to wed but old enough to be interested, the youth had been passing though with his family. They had only stayed in the valley over the winter and then moved on. His name was Nygel, and he had black hair and copper eyes, with an intense smile he had cast her way. They had barely known each other, but somehow their brief friendship had left a lasting bond in her memory.

Her silent thoughts were broken by her mother's voice from the doorway. "Morgana! Where have you been?" Brea shouted her frustration at her eldest daughter.

As if one, the two sisters jumped to their feet, still holding hands. Morgana started to speak when Kina squeezed her hand in warning. "She's explained everything to me, Mother. She was so upset about yesterday that she woke up early and went for a long walk. She didn't notice how late it was getting and she walked clear over to the winter stables." She squeezed her hand again. Morgana looked unhappily at her mother.

Brea threw her daughter an exasperated look. "Well, your Father is furious with you. You had better hope he calms down before he returns. I have work for you in the garden, so put on your old clothes and hurry." She turned and left the room, her anger momentarily soothed by Kina's explanation. Morgana watched her leave, then gave her sister a warm embrace.

Kina smiled brightly. "Let's hope Father does calm down or dinner's not going to be pleasant for any of us."

*

Rejat cautiously opened her eyes, breathing deeply as she struggled to relax. The vision was gone. There was no snow, no raging Azerii, no Madness. Stillyth sat beside her in the straw, holding her in his arms, his dark copper eyes staring intently into her face.

"You saw?" Of course, a stupid question, she thought crossly. One's Azerii always experienced what their Mirii visioned.

Stillyth smiled and brushed a lock of hair from her face. *Of course, a foolish question. Are you well?* The concern in his thoughts was mirrored in his eyes.

"I'll be all right, in a moment," she said, trying to regain her awareness of their surroundings. Her visions always left her disoriented for some time after they had passed. She wished they would not dump her so abruptly. Dayana said it was because she tried to hold them back instead of letting them run their course. "Brealyth, does Elas know?" she said aloud to the other Azerii waiting below.

Stillyth answered for her. *Brealyth says she relayed the Vision to Elas, and she said she would come soon, but that you should rest. She knows about the child and is speaking to the mother now.*

Rejat leaned against his shoulder. He had rested some, but they both needed more. She wished she could have blocked the vision, for it was draining to both of them, but it had come so unexpectedly that she had been caught up before she could stop it. It had been a difficult one too; she could still feel her horror of the Madness that the vision prophesied. The raging Dark Azerii had been a powerful one. She did not wish this vision to run its course. To face that one could mean madness for them both.

"The Azerii are breaking away," Rejat said sleepily, her head slipping under Stillyth's chin.

He cradled her against his chest. *I am not going away,* he replied, even though he knew she was not listening. Carefully he lowered his exhausted Mirii to the straw and lay down beside her, pulling her worn journey blanket over her and watching her till he knew she slept.

*Brealyth, tell Elas, Rejat sleeps,* he sent to the other Azerii.

Brealyth appeared in the loft above them as a softly glowing light. *Do you know this Azerii?* she sent as she drifted next to his sleeping Mirii.

*No, this one is not of my knowing. It is very strong and I feel it will destroy many of the Hu'mans in its desire for meld, until it finds its Mirii.* He pulled the blanket up around Rejat's shoulders.

*You do not think it will pass in their destruction?* Brealyth sounded alarmed. An Azerii who forced meld on a hu'man always sought it's own destruction along with it's host.

*I feel this one is different. Rejat has much fear of this Vision. She would not willingly be a part of this path.* He gazed at his sleeping companion. They had been in meld for many of her years. He did not wish her to face that which she feared. He and Rejat had mastered the Madness of an invading Dark Azerii before, many years past. But this one of the vision was somehow different. He was not sure why he saw this. The Azerii did not have visions; only the intuitive Mirii had that talent, although it was strengthened by their meld with their Azerii.

Brealyth mover closer to Stillyth. *I know the wild Azerii that frequent the valleys. I will seek them out for their voices in this. But I too feel this one is somehow different. I shall speak with Elas of our concerns.* Her soft light glimmered and then vanished.

Stillyth watched her depart then joined his Mirii in their much needed rest.

# Chapter 4

Dusk had shadowed well over the Brejjard LandsHold when Tillan returned from his daily concerns. After giving his horse over to the stable hand, he stomped through the holdyard into his home, speaking to no one. Silence roared around his broad frame like a storm; his taut face holding the rage seething within, his eyes revealing his temper.

He entered the large gathering room. Brea and Kina sat at the table, under the light of two oil lamps, stitching on the fine lace that would become his daughter's marriage gown. Behind them, Siann played on the floor before the fire, building vagaries with small sticks.

Carefully laying the lace on the table, Brea rose to greet her husband. Seeing his face she froze. Tillan seemed to look straight through her as he stared into the room, then abruptly he turned and strode out into the hall. As she quietly followed her husband down the hall to their daughter's room, she felt the color leave her face. Never had she beheld so much anger in his eyes. She had become familiar with his displays of temper over the years. He was a proud man and his emotions sometimes ran high, but the silent anger that now raged was frightening.

Morgana was lying on her bed, reading by the light of a solitary candle. She looked up and was startled to see her father standing in the doorway, his dark eyes grim. "I see you have finally come home." His voice was low and ice-ridden.

"Yes, Father," she replied, lowering her gaze as she put her book down to sit up. She could feel his anger across the room. Fear slipped around her, anticipating the punishment he had chosen for her. For a brief moment she thought of her carefully hidden prizes, then hastily looked back at him as if he might read her thoughts and find more cause to be angry with her.

"Listen very carefully to me," he said, his voice low and clear. "Since you have chosen not to obey my wishes concerning your frequent idleness at the river, and your unwomanly denial of the suitable men in the valley for a husband, then I am forced to make the responsible decisions for you." He paused, his eyes never leaving her face. "You will remain here at all times. You will be locked into a room at night, to prevent you from further irresponsible trips. You will stay here with your mother until I have chosen a husband for you. You will then be married as quickly as is proper. If you try to disobey me in this I will disown you, Morgana. You will have nothing, and I will make sure that no one will assist you. Do you understand?" Tillan's eyes were bright with triumph.

Morgana felt her world fall away. To be denied her freedom, the sweet solitude of her river visits, to be forced to marry! She felt her heart close to this man who would do these things to her.

"I understand, Father," she replied softly, lowering her eyes to hide her pain.

In stunned silence Brea watched her husband. She knew Morgana was silently disobeying their wishes with her visits to the river, but she rarely gave them any other difficulty. She did not understand Tillan's demand that she marry. Morgana just wasn't ready to settle down, she thought with some sadness. Kina was such a contrast to her sister and she did not miss the younger girl's devotion to her older sister, or Kina's subterfuge.

Morgana's bedding was moved to the spare room up over the kitchen. The room was used mostly for storage of winter clothing and was small and cramped with a small window overlooking the garden. Though all were visibly upset, no one voiced their protest to Tillan's harsh demands, except Kina who started to offer some resistance on her sister's behalf, but with a cold look from her father, she too became silent.

Morgana withdrew into her self, meekly surrendering to her father's orders. Without a word to any, she allowed herself to become as a prisoner. No one saw her tears when the door was closed and locked, separating her from the rest of her family for the night. At the window, she stood with a small candle as her only light and surveyed her surroundings. With little hope of brightening her silent misery at her loss of freedom, she decided to move her bed under the window, where she could at least feel the freedom of the night's air and see the glancing moonlight over the garden. Then with sorrow enfolding her into its dark robes, she released her tears into the lonely room.

She spent the next two days in silence, only speaking politely when a response was required, completing every duty that her worried mother gave her.

Brea watched her daughter for some sign of rebellion, but all fight seemed to have gone from her. Even Siann tried to break into his sister's world, but she would not allow anyone to reach her. A grim determination to give her father no cause for additional harshness seemed to have taken hold in Morgana. When Tillan returned from his hold duties, he requested a report on her from Brea, who finding no fault with her, pleaded with him to release their daughter from his demands. But Tillan would not change his mind. He locked Morgana in the little room at nightfall.

On the morning of the third day, Elas and Tagar rode into the holdyard. Brea came out to greet them, inviting them inside. Brea noticed that her sister-in-law looked tired, but spoke of other things. Tagar asked after his brother and was told he had gone early to handle an exchange of horses with one of their neighbors to the west and that he would not be back until after dark.

Brea led them into the kitchen for a fresh pot of tajiz at the large central table. While she and Siann bantered with Tagar, Elas scanned for Morgana and found her in the herb garden behind the kitchen with Kina. She excused herself and left her husband to keep Brea and Siann occupied. Once outside, she watched the sisters for a moment before approaching them. The two sat on a bench under the eaves of the large house. Morgana's face was pale and drawn; her sister spoke to her but seemed to get no response

At Elas' arrival Kina looked up and smiled. "Oh, hello, Aunt Elas. I didn't know you were coming today." She rose to greet her, glancing back at her sister who did not seem to notice their visitor. She spoke quietly to Elas, "Please talk to Morgana, she will not listen to me." Her face was full of sadness. With a warm embrace, she went into the house, leaving Elas with Morgana.

Elas sat next to her despondent niece. "Tell me what's happened, Morgana." She gazed out over the garden.

For a long moment the young woman remained silent. "I am a prisoner in my Father's Hold," she said coldly, staring past the gardens towards the river. "I really don't want to talk about it."

Elas marked her niece's strength. Morgana's mind was firmly closed. It will be difficult to pull information from her in this state, she thought.

"Morgana, can you put your small troubles aside for a moment and listen to me?" She decided there was no point in waiting for her niece to stop sulking.

Morgana turned a stony face towards her aunt. For a brief moment anger blazed behind her blue-gray eyes.

"I want you to come with me to the Brenan LandsHold. Their daughter is ill and I want your help."

"Why? I am not a Mediciner," she said evenly.

"No, but I think you could be." Elas' eyes held Morgana's gaze.

"You think—I could be a Mediciner?" Morgana suddenly found hope beating within her heart.

Elas held back a smile. "Well, I have knowledge that I can give you, if you truly are interested, and I think you might have the gift for it."

"Are you a Mediciner?" Morgana looked at her aunt in a new light. She dimly remembered childhood ailments and Elas' tender remedies which were given when her mother's own failed.

Elas looked out over the garden again. "I can teach you my methods, Morgana, that you may be of service to our people. It may allow you more freedom than your present situation has. Or would you rather remain here?" She turned back to her niece.

Morgana jumped to her feet. "Aunt Elas, if you think I have some small ability then please teach me! I have no wish to remain a prisoner of my Father, or marry his choice of husband for me!" She stood tall and glowing with excitement, all past hurts pushed aside for the moment. But they will not be forgotten easily, Elas thought as she stood to embrace her.

"Now listen, Tagar is speaking with your mother about this. If I know her, she will not be willing to let you go against your Father's wishes. You must be strong in your intent, Morgana, but do not bully her. She will face your Father's wrath before you. Remember that." Elas looked her squarely in the eyes. Morgana nodded her understanding, then the two walked back into the kitchen.

Brea sat beside the kitchen hearth. Tagar, with Siann on his knee, sat at the long table across from Kina. All looked up as Morgana and Elas entered. Her mother suddenly seemed so fragile, Morgana thought, watching her anger and fear flitting back and forth in her eyes.

Brea stood before her. "Your Father will not permit this, Morgana."

"I know, Mother." She waited, facing her solemnly.

Brea looked at Elas, then Tagar. "Are you sure she has the gift?" She challenged each with her gaze.

"We are sure, Brea," Elas answered her as Tagar nodded his affirmation.

She looked at the hearth. "I do not wish you to

leave this way, Morgana, but I will not forbid you if it is your desire to go. If you truly have the Mediciner's gift, then you must use it." She turned back to her daughter, tears brimming in her eyes. "I will not force you to a life you do not desire, even though I desire it for you." She stood stiffly before her eldest daughter, trying to maintain her composure.

Morgana reached out and wiped a tear from her mother's cheek. "I will not go if you forbid it, but I do wish to know where my gifts truly lie. They certainly don't seem to be in my hold-work."

Brea tried unsuccessfully to flash a quick smile, but she suddenly embraced Morgana, tears flowing from her eyes. Kina and Siann were soon included as Tagar and Elas watched. When they began excitedly talking at once, Brea suddenly put out her hand for silence.

"Very well, Morgana. Go, quickly, prepare yourself. Kina, you help her. Siann, go have the black mare saddled, I will not have my daughter walking towards her destiny!" She resumed control of her kitchen and ordering her children out, turned once more to Elas and Tagar.

"Promise me she will be safe, Elas." She took one of Elas' and Tagar's hands in her own. "Promise me, Tagar. I have much misgivings about this." Her worried eyes met their calm ones.

"I shall teach her well, Brea. She will be fine." Elas spoke with the Voice to calm her sister-in-law.

Tagar squeezed her hand. "I will talk to Tillan about her, if you wish."

"No, I shall speak with him. He would not listen to me before, but he will have no choice now. Morgana would not have fought him before this news, but she will now. It is better that she go now, before he returns. He does not fare well to have his wishes refused," she smiled sadly, then brightened, "but I love him anyway!"

"One of us shall return by nightfall, Brea," Elas said suddenly, an inner feeling prompting her on. "Tillan must be told and made to understand. You must both understand." Tagar looked at Elas, his eyes questioning her silently, but she could not answer further.

✳

Elas, Tagar and Morgana rode easily across the Kesh River Valley to the Brenan LandsHold which lay several miles south below the river's fording, past the fisher's dam. Morgana was eager to speak to Elas about the mediciner's life, but her aunt's thoughts seemed elsewhere. Tagar also appeared preoccupied and lagged behind as if he were looking for something. She wondered if their behavior had anything to do with the vision she had experienced or the mysterious red tassel and cloth strip she had carefully tucked into the pocket of her riding skirt.

The Brenan LandsHold was on the southeastern side of the valley, a good two hours' ride from her home. She remembered the hold being larger than her father's, having visited the Brenans' once many years earlier, when her father had traded horses with them. She had been about ten years old, and had played with the eldest daughter who was roughly her age, but she did not remember much else about the hold except for the many fine horses they owned. The mare she now rode was from their stock.

As they approached the hold, she began to feel a strange prickly sensation at the top of her head.

She thought she heard a voice call to her from behind, but when she turned to look to her uncle, he
was nowhere to be seen. Turning forward again, she
found Elas had stopped and was looking at her
strangely, then abruptly turned and urged her horse
into the holdyard.

A woman in a green skirt and tunic came out
to greet them, followed by Mia and two small children, a dark-haired boy of about four and a tow-
headed girl of about two years. The girl clung to Mia's
skirt, while the boy walked straight to Elas' horse and
put his hands onto the proffered nose of the silver
mare. A wide grin lit the child's face and Elas laughed
in delight as she slipped to the ground.

"Greetings, Siva! This is Morgana, my niece;
Brea and Tillan Brejjard's daughter. Morgana, this is
Siva, wife of Brenan LandsHolder, and her youngest
children, Jeven and Dariel." Elas clasped Siva's hand
warmly and hugged Mia in welcome. Jeven and Dariel
ignored Morgana, Jeven still intent on Elas' horse,
Dariel having switched to her mother's skirt.

Morgana smiled her greetings, suddenly feeling
shy and out of place, the strange sensation still with
her.

"Yes, I remember you, Morgana. It has been a
long time since you were here." Siva welcomed her
and invited them into her home. She started to offer
the use of their stables for their horses when Morgana
heard herself ask if she could care for them. With a
surprised smile Siva gave her consent, then she and
the children started towards the main house.

Elas handed the reins of her horse to Morgana,
a puzzled look on her face. "Don't be too long, we
must talk." She studied her niece's face briefly, then
turned and followed Siva.

Morgana started towards the stables, leading the two horses. She thought over her sudden offer to care for their mounts; though she was familiar with horses, she usually left this duty to the horsekeeper of the hold. She swung open the large wooden stable door and began to lead the two into the cool dimness, then stopped for a moment to let her eyes adjust to the darkness within.

The black mare let out a nicker of impatience for the food and water she wanted and nudged Morgana's shoulder. Elas' silver mare stopped just inside the doorway. She dropped the silver's reins and led her horse to an empty stall where she found a full bucket of water. As the black mare began to noisily drink, she turned back to the silver. Standing in a pool of sunlight in the doorway, the silver mare's coat seemed to shimmer before her eyes. Then with a dazzling flash, the mare suddenly disappeared.

Morgana blinked, staring at the empty doorway, the sunlight spilling before her.

"Well, it's about time you got here," a woman's husky voice spoke from behind. She spun around, nearly losing her balance. No one stood behind her. Wildly she threw her gaze around the stable, then raised her eyes to the loft. A shadow moved and became a figure. In the faint light that reached the loft, she saw the red-clad woman of her vision, her fiery hair framing her face. Behind her, another form took shape, shimmering into the taller figure of a dark haired man dressed in similar manner to the woman.

Morgana stepped back in fear as the images of the two figures and the vanishing mare clouded her mind. The black mare forgotten, she turned and fled out of the stable's darkness to the comforting daylight of the yard.

She stumbled outside and ran headlong into Tagar. He caught her before she could fall, noticing the panic in her eyes. "Morgana, are you all right?" he said as he grasped her shoulders.

Morgana closed her eyes, relief flowing through her from his presence. There was something very strange going on here and her uncle was a comforting figure at the moment. She tried to slow her rushing breath to speak. "I saw—something—someone, in the loft. I'm sorry—it, she—startled me. Elas' mare—where is it?" She looked at Tagar for a reasonable answer to the horse's disappearance.

"I haven't seen the mare. Who was in the stable?" He started to walk towards the open door, leading his bay stallion. Morgana hesitantly followed him and stood by the door after he calmly went inside.

Tagar gazed around the stable to see what could have frightened his niece. The black mare whinnied at being left so abruptly, still saddled and without food. He led his bay to the stall next to her and started to remove his saddle. "It's all right. There's no one here now," he called to Morgana as she hovered near the door.

She took a deep breath and walked inside, nervously eyeing the loft. Tagar was right, no one stood there now. She went to her horse and began to remove the saddle, then brought the mare a pail of grain and some hay.

Tagar was adjusting the halter on his stallion and spoke quietly, "Visions can occur in strange and familiar places, Morgana."

She froze, staring at her uncle in surprise. He turned his back to her as he placed his saddle on the stall rail between the two horses. Thoughtfully, she picked up her saddle and placed it next to his. "Uncle Tagar, I saw Elas' horse disappear. How? Was that a vision?" She watched her uncle for any reaction.

Tagar turned back to face her. He leaned against the stall post and returned her stare, a flicker of amusement in his russet eyes.

"Let's go talk to Elas."

# Chapter 5

"You did what? Rejat, how could you!" Elas hissed angrily at the red-garbed woman before her. Rejat sat in the window seat, looking out over the kitchen garden behind the house, her long legs propped up against the frame. Siva had taken the children to the kitchen and left Elas alone in the gathering room before her abrupt appearance.

"I was tired of waiting. I thought I'd make my presence known. I'm sorry, I was wrong, all right? The girl isn't ready, is she?" She continued staring out of the window, avoiding Elas' angry eyes.

"She only knows the tales of her elders, Rejat. The Mirii are an evil to her, and the Azerii..." Elas mentally yelled at her own Azerii for frightening Morgana by disappearing in front of her.

*She was being scanned,* Brealyth replied defensively.

"Scanned? By who? Azerii, or Mirii?" Elas shot her question to Rejat and Brealyth.

"How do I know? I didn't pick up the scan," Rejat growled in reply, crossing her arms in irritation, then grimacing as the unwise movement brought pain from her recently healed shoulder.

"No, you were too busy making an entrance!" Elas stormed towards her, then stopped as her Azerii reached her again.

*There are Unnamed Azerii near.*

"Unnamed? I thought you were familiar with all the wild Azerii in the valley," Elas voiced her concern. An Unnamed Azerii could mean the vision that Rejat had experienced was progressing more quickly than they expected.

*I do know all the Azerii in the valley,* Brealyth sounded disappointed, *but this one blocks all scans. The others are open, this one is closed. The intentions are not open.*

Elas looked at Rejat. Her face showed her concern also.

"Stil told me what Brealyth said. We must move quickly, whether the girl is ready or not. We can't wait any longer." Rejat stood, still rubbing her shoulder.

"Very well, but let me talk to Morgana first. You have no sense of diplomacy," Elas scowled at her sister.

Rejat nodded in agreement. "All right, I'll come when you call. I'll be waiting in the loft." A shimmer of light began forming around her. Her body took on the light, shifting briefly, then sliding into the shape of a large red cat. With a quick leap, she was out of the window just as Tagar brought a pale-visaged Morgana into the room.

✳

As Morgana followed her uncle into the gathering room, she saw Elas standing by the open window looking out at the garden behind the house. She turned at their entry and smiled, a trace of distraction on her face. Tagar embraced her and spoke a few words too low for Morgana to hear, then stepped across the room to sit in a chair by the hearth.

Elas turned back to the window and spoke in a weary voice, "Sit down, Morgana. You are not used to a long ride, you must be tired."

Morgana glanced around the room, wondering where Siva and the children were as she settled into a chair near the hearth across from her uncle. She watched him for an answer to her aunt's strange manner, but his mind also appeared some distance away; he gazed into the darkened hearth between them. After a respectful pause where no one had spoken, she decided to ask her puzzling questions. She turned to her aunt. "Why have you brought me here? Have I met all of Siva's children? None of them seem ill to me, where is the one you spoke of?" She pushed the incident in the stable aside for the moment, that question too preposterous to hazard asking.

Elas turned from the window, her face showing signs of strain. "Tell me what you know of the Mirii and the Azerii." Her eyes locked on her niece and held her from any outburst of fear.

Morgana stared back, startled by her words. "I—only know what I was taught, of the Mirii, the stories of their treachery. The Azerii are demons," she said, then paused, remembering how drawn she had been a few nights before, after witnessing the Azerii 'mist ponies' playing in her mother's garden behind their home. "They steal the souls and minds of people," she finished cautiously.

Elas crossed her arms before her and sat on the window ledge, lowering her gaze to the floor. "It is time you knew the truth, Morgana. My truth. I will not hide it from you any longer." She looked up at her niece again, her pale blue eyes appearing to glow from within, a powerful effect Morgana suddenly remembered from their conversation after Kina's betrothal feast.

"I am Mirii. What you saw as my horse is my Azerii, Brealyth, who surprised you without my knowing," she grimaced. "The woman you saw in the loft is Rejat, my Mirii half-sister, and her Azerii, Stillyth. They were tired of waiting for you, it seems." She paused, waiting for her words to take effect. When her niece did not speak she drew a long breath and continued.

"Hear me, Morgana," she said, the command grabbing her listener's attention completely. "Hear the Legend of the Mirii." She stood slowly as a shimmering haze began to outline her body.

"Before time began, before all knowing, before the People, before Us, before all Life, they were here," she chanted, the words sharp in their falling. "Before all. The Ancient Ones. They dwelt here in the light of their own choosing, all memories now lost. Then the People came. The Ancient Ones saw the People and were curious, but they did not meet. *They seemed so fragile to Us, they know not the Way, our Way of Being.* So they watched and waited."

"A generation of the People passed, and they waited. Then the first contact was made between the Talents of the People and the Ancient Ones, the Azerii, the Beings of this world. The Meld was formed with the Naming of the Azerii, and the Life Experience was given to those Azerii who had forgotten the Knowledge of Life. The Mirii were created in that joining, and their talents were expanded in their union with their Azerii."

"The Meld Azerii rejoiced for the shared Life Experience, but it was not enough. Few in number were the Talents, and the Unnamed Azerii were many. *We have waited so long, let Us share the Life Experience,* they said. *We do not have enough Talents among the People to meld, you must wait,* replied the Mirii. So the Azerii waited."

"Many generations passed among the People. With each Talent born the Azerii rejoiced, for another meld was possible. The children of the Mirii were all Talents, and the Mirii and the People prospered. A new way was opened for the beings of this world."

"Then some of the Unnamed Azerii became impatient once more. One by one they began to force the meld on the People and the terror of the Madness began. The People cried out in fear, *The Azerii have gone mad! They will destroy us!* The Mirii spoke with the Unnamed Azerii, *You will destroy the People if you force the meld!* they told the Azerii. But they would not listen."

Elas drew a deep breath, her eyes shimmering in eerie brilliance. "The time of devastation began. The People struggled to defend themselves from the Dark Unnamed Azerii. The Mirii sought to protect the People and their Meld Azerii and to stop the Unnamed who would force meld. The Azerii themselves were in conflict." A flicker of emotion passed silently over her face. "More generations passed and the strife continued, each Being intertwined in the other's path."

"Then the Dark Azerii struck in force. In less than one life-span nearly a third of the People were destroyed. In desperation they pleaded with the Mirii for their help. The Mirii agreed; they would stop the invading Dark Azerii or perish in their efforts. A great

Communion was held between the Mirii and their Meld Azerii. Few paths were laid before them. They all chose the One. The Covenant was created with a great tearing of the Life Force, and the invading Dark Azerii were stopped."

With another quiet breath she continued, her eyes impassive to her lengthy accounting. "For a few generations the Mirii were called 'Saviors' and great honors and privileges were given them. But the Mirii became arrogant and the People forgot their heroic past. A violent rebellion against them finally drove the Mirii into hiding. Their name became a curse and the Azerii became horrific tales to frighten disobedient children with."

A measure of life returned to Elas' eyes. "And still the Mirii hide, and the Unnamed wait. But the tearing free has begun. The Unnamed Azerii will not wait much longer." She stopped speaking and for a brief moment seemed frozen in time. Slowly she closed her eyes, as if it took great effort to do so, and carefully slipped into the chair that Tagar quickly provided for her.

Morgana was stunned, then suddenly her thoughts became frantic. *It's not real,* she heard her mind cry, *it's all lies, do not believe these lies!* She watched her exhausted aunt as Tagar looked on anxiously. All of her childhood teachings came crawling up behind her, scratching and screaming; *Listen to me! I am the truth, not this! Not the cursed Mirii!* She closed her eyes and the scowling image of the red-haired woman was before her for an instant. She jumped to her feet, knocking over her chair. Elas and Tagar looked up at her with startled expressions.

Her strangled words broke free. "You lied to me! You lied—all those years—*all a lie!*" she shouted. "How could you do this? How could you lie to your family? *How could you lie to me?*" she cried, her anger and fear drowning her senses. She began sobbing and was enraged at her tears. She turned away as her distress flooded through her.

"Morgana, I'm sorry," Elas said gently, "We had no choice. Your family would not understand. They still live by their fears. You were not ready to know the truth."

"The *truth?*" Morgana hissed, turning to face her aunt. "How can what you say be the truth, when all my life I have been told what the truth was?"

"Each person knows their own truth, Morgana." Tagar stood calmly beside Elas. "Do you know what your truth is? Listen to your heart, not to what others tell you. Find your own truth."

"No! I will not listen to either of you!" she shrieked, her anger overtaking her fears. Recklessly, she ran from the room and out of the house, her mind racing—where can I go? Where can I run? As she stopped in the holdyard, confused and alone, she heard the black mare whinny softly from within the open stable. She ran inside, heedless of the past incident, and freed the mare from the stall. Quickly she saddled the questioning horse and pulled herself onto the broad reassuring back. Then, in frantic haste, she drove the horse out of the shadowy stable and into the bright afternoon sun and without a backwards glance, rode away from the Brenan LandsHold to the open forest beyond.

*

Weariness clung to Elas as she sat with her head in her hands, her heart anguishing over Morgana's painful words. Tagar stood beside her, his own regrets apparent as he held a comforting hand on her shoulder. Rejat strode in from the hall, her anger flashing across her narrow face.

"She has gone?" Elas asked without looking up.

"She went flying out of here like a host of Kir-Latts was on her heels," she replied sourly.

"What happened? What did they give her?" Elas passed a tired hand over her face.

"The Legend, Elas. They gave her the *wrecking Legend!*" Rejat swore, a disgusted look replacing her anger. She pulled a chair over and sat facing her sister and her mate. "They read her the Legend and scared her but good. Where is she going to go now? Back home? From what you've told me, her father will terrorize her even more after this." She leaned back in the chair, folding her arms gingerly in front of her.

Elas' face was pale as she looked up. "They gave her the Legend? Why? Why now of all times?"

"You don't remember?" Tagar said as he knelt beside her. "Who spoke through you? Can you identify the link?"

Elas shook her head. "No, I can't remember. The link was very strong, but they will not identify this One." She gazed dejectedly at her sister.

Rejat leaned forward. "Was it the same as my Vision?" Could it be this Azerii?" She tried to keep her voice calm, but her eyes betrayed her anxiety.

Elas' expression abruptly shifted. "We must

65

mark the child, then go find her. She will be waiting at the river," she said firmly as her gaze bore into Rejat's.

"How do you know?" Rejat saw in her sister's eyes the distant shine of scan. Something odd was happening, she thought as she called her Azerii back from his pursuit of Morgana. "Are you sure?"

Elas sighed and turned to the window. "No, I'm not sure, Rejat, but we must do this, now." She looked back at Tagar. "Would you please get Siva? We need to move quickly."

✻

Morgana pushed her horse relentlessly across the valley, retracing her earlier ride, slowing only to cross the river's ford. She tried to close her mind from her thoughts, focusing on the pounding movements of the animal beneath her as she raced through the forest on the northern river trail. *It was not real...it is all lies...believe in our teachings...believe... believe....*The words rattled through her head, shaking at her like dead branches in the bleakness of winter. She could see her father's face before her as he told her his Truth's; of life, of death, and of the Mirii and the Azerii. Had it all been a lie? Who could she believe in? Where could she go to find the right truth?

As her horse tired from its exhausting run she numbly allowed the mare to slow to a quiet walk. Around her the great trees of the Varan Forest loomed majestic and serene, undisturbed by her troubled passing. She inhaled their richness, their green becoming a warm calm that flowed over her. She began to relax again in the comfort and solitude of the forest. She would seek the truth, her own truth, as Tagar had said.

She considered her uncle. Had he always known Elas was Mirii? How could he lie to his family about her? She tried to remember when she had first met Elas. It had been early in her youth and the memories were unclear now. She loved her mysterious aunt dearly, but this knowledge was too much to bear. Could Elas be one of her people's enemies? How could she accept this truth? How did Tagar? He must have known and somehow it did not matter to him. Tagar was always so calm about life, but to marry a Mirii? She breathed aloud her turmoil.

It was late afternoon when she brought the mare to a halt. She had topped the last hill along the river. Before her were two paths; one to her family's hold, the other continued north along the river. She remembered her father would not be returning until well into the evening. She had time. She would follow the northern trail to her place at the river, to think about the events that had brought her to this cross-road in her life.

✳

A dusty haze was rolling through the forest as Morgana approached her tree. Her thoughts quiet now, she listened to the river's murmuring heart as it flowed on its endless path. Again she thought of that path. Where did it lead? From what place did it begin? Why was she always drawn here and why did she only feel at peace in the forest? But the river did not have an answer to her soundless questions.

She turned her horse to the narrow path off the main trail, the dust cloud shifting in and out, veiling her sight from her destination. She puzzled at this strangeness in the heat of the day, but her tired mind took little notice in her desire to arrive at the shelter of the cedarjinn tree. At the last bend in the path she stopped and dismounted, dropping the reins to the ground to let the mare graze in the long grass. As she stepped forward the haze suddenly engulfed her, stilling her in sudden coldness, then with a breath of wind it vanished.

Morgana looked up, blinking at the sudden brightness. Her tree was gone.

*

Gone! Savaged to the roots, the great tree lay stretching before her stunned eyes, its length drowning in the cold shallows of the river. Its girth had been severed by the maniacal hacking of broad axes. The deep cuts where the blades had missed their mark were like wounds, revealing the unhandy labor behind each strike. But the tree had finally surrendered to its quickened fate.

Slowly she knelt beside the great ruined trunk, her hands touching the shattered form. She felt as if she had lost her most precious friend, and felt her world falling apart around her. Gazing hopelessly down the length of the tree, she suddenly embraced her old companion and with despairing cries, released her sorrow into the stillness of the surrounding forest.

# Chapter 6

Brea stared pensively into the kitchen hearth, her thoughts wandering aimlessly like the small flames that danced over the gleaming coals. Across the room Siann was helping his sister clear the table of their evening's supper, Kina cautioning him to be careful with the larger dishes. Trying to be as quiet as possible, the two children occasionally glanced at their mother's passive form, waiting for a sign of her usual briskness.

A loud crash brought Brea's attention back to the kitchen. She turned as Siann looked up guiltily, a towel in one hand, the other still holding the broken handle of a cup. Kina stood looking vexed beside him, her hands on her hips in her mother's fashion.

"What are you two doing? Removing my dishes the easy way?" She rose and walked around the table to Siann.

"I didn't mean to break it!" he blurted out, sorry brightness rimming his blue eyes.

She looked at the remnants of the cup, now scattered across the floor. It was Morgana's favorite, a brightly painted cup that Elas had given her. She knelt and began to pick up the pieces, Kina quickly helping her.

"It's all right, Siann," Brea said quietly. "It was an accident, Morgana will understand. Just be more careful." She stood again and placed the broken pieces on the table.

Siann suddenly burst into tears and wrapped his arms around his mother's waist. Kina put the pieces she had picked up onto the table and watched her mother soothe her little brother. As she turned back to finish with the dishes she thought warmly of the children she would have someday.

A horse's whinny from the holdyard caught their attention. Brea looked up over her son's head, her eyes questioning.

"Father? I thought he wasn't due till late," Kina remarked, then started for the hall. Before she had taken two steps she abruptly halted. "Morgana— what's happened?" she exclaimed.

Brea turned, gasping in surprise. In the doorway stood her eldest daughter, wretched trails of dust streaking her face and layering her clothing. Her tears were gone, but they had left their mark. Despair filled her eyes. For a moment no one moved, for she appeared as a frightening stranger to them.

Brea stared at Morgana's disheveled condition, Siann turning in her arms to gaze solemnly a his sister. She released him and walked silently to her daughter. Morgana's eyes met her's, but she did not speak. Brea touched her cheek, the movement mirroring Morgana's gesture from what now seemed eons past.

"Momma," her daughter said, her voice barely above a whisper. She gently embraced her, feeling the stillness that matched the stony way she stood. Fearful of her strangeness and absent tears, she pushed her apprehensions aside to care for her stricken daughter.

"Kina, go and prepare Morgana's bed. Her old one, in your room. First, get some clean towels. Siann, go take care of the mare, see that she is stabled properly. You know what to do."

Kina and Siann hurried out of the room, while Brea guided Morgana to sit at the table, preparing to care for her and get some food into her. She did not ask anything of her silent daughter. Her questions would be answered later.

Siann returned, stating that Morgana's horse was already in the stable, though he had to remove the saddle and bridle and feed the mare. He watched his sister quietly as Brea heated a kettle of water, Kina soon arriving with a bundle of towels. His mother then shooed the questioning boy out of the room so they could care for his sister.

Morgana sat unmoving, allowing everything to flow around her, offering no resistance or response as her mother and sister gently washed her stained face and hands. She ate sparingly the food placed before her, but only after Brea's pleading eyes met her distant ones.

Brea watched her eldest absently nibble at a piece of bread as Kina carefully brushed a tangle from her hair. She glanced out the window over the garden. The evening was well on them and Tillan would be returning soon. She did not want him to see Morgana this way. She would make sure her daughter was in bed before he arrived. In silence she vowed she would not let Tillan hurt Morgana anymore.

When Tillan returned late that evening he was tired to his bones. His day's journey had been long and hard, but he was satisfied with the outcome. He did not notice Brea's tension when he asked about his children. "All are in bed asleep, they too have kept busy this day," was her reply. After a quick meal, they went to bed also, Morgana's restrictions placed out of his memory in the evening's forgetfulness.

✳

Morgana slept. A sleep of emptiness, of renewal of body, but not of spirit. Her emotions scattered and displaced, she dreamt of utter blackness circling around her. She was the beginning, but where was the end?

A path revealed itself in the darkness. Gleaming stars led her to a place of familiarity, warm and embracing, beckoning to her. She found herself standing before her home, the front door swinging open at her touch. She walked inside and called out her mother's name. Only silence answered her. Again she called and began to search, adding her names of the rest of her family. Where were they? Where had they gone? The house looked the same as it always had, nothing was out of place.

Suddenly the voices began, calling her in whispers, urging her, *Away...Away...Leave this place...*the words becoming louder until she found her hands at her ears, pleading with them to stop. Shouting wildly they called her again, *Morgana! Morgana Elissii! Be gone! Be gone from this place! Beware! Beware the Dark One!*

The once warm house became cold like the heavy darkness of winter. The voices ranted on, their words becoming chaotic. She began to run through the house trying to escape their ravings. At the front door she froze. The heavy wooden door was shut, but somehow she could see through to the other side.

Beyond it waited her family; they looked ashen; their skin, hair and clothing a lifeless gray. In a tight cluster they called out to her, but she could not hear their words, their voices lost beneath the deafening cries of the Others.

Morgana stood before the door, unable to open it and watched as a shadow embraced it and started consuming the house. She could feel its aliveness, its energy touching her senses. As she watched in terror, the Shadow began to extend a long plume of blackness toward her family, engulfing all it touched. She tried to call a warning but her voice died in her throat. *Morgana Elissii! Morgana... Morgan, Morgu, Morannon, you are mine...you are Mine!* the Shadow's voice roared at her. She felt her mind recoil from the darkness that pummeled at her being, her fear threatening to drown her. Unable to move, she watched the Shadow slip inward from the door, the dark vapor creeping around her, the voice echoing endlessly, *Morgana Elissii! Morgana... Morgan, Morgu, Morannon, you are mine... you are MINE!*

A small spark of anger struck her inner being and flared alive under her fear, pushing another voice before it. *Find your own truth...* it whispered, small at first, then moving persistently against her fear, it spoke again. *Find your own Truth...* Louder now, the voice repeated, becoming a shining flame, pushing the Shadow back. *FIND YOUR OWN TRUTH!* Her mind grasped the words like a torch before her and she thrust back the Shadow that would conquer her soul. "My Truth!" she shouted at the black wall that loomed before her. *"TRUTH!"* she shrieked and the wall suddenly shattered like ice.

She opened her eyes and found she was sitting in her bed, a frightened Kina staring across at her in the flickering candlelight of their room.

\*

Morgana stared across the dimly lit room at her sister, sitting wide-eyed in her own bed. She looked at her clenched hands held out before her. No torch did she hold, no black fog swirled around her. As she lowered her hands, Kina slipped towards her, carrying her candle which sent erratic shadows dancing around their room.

"'Gana, are you all right?" Kina whispered as she sat next to her, her eyes full of worry.

Morgana opened her cramped hands and touched her dampened cheeks. She had been crying. The dream had been so real! Or was it just a dream? She looked at her sister. Kina reached out and wiped a tear from her face.

"I had a dream, it was awful!" she said, her voice a quavering whisper. "I dreamt that you and Siann, Mother, Father, the house, everything was being smothered in a black cloud, and that it was going to take me too! I couldn't move to help you, you were calling me and the Voices kept shouting and this other Black Voice said my name and that I was—it kept saying, 'You are Mine!'" she choked, remembering her fear.

Kina embraced her. "It's all right, 'Gana, it was just a dream, that's all. It's all over now."

Morgana clenched her eyes shut and tried to clear her emotions. "No, it's not just a dream. It was too real!" she said breathlessly as Kina released her. She brushed her tears away then caught her hands together at her chin. I must go see Elas, she will know what it means, she thought frantically.

"What do you mean? Of course it's a dream, what else could it be?" Kina searched her sister's face for an answer she could understand. "What happened to you today?"

"Oh, Kina, I wish I could tell you!" Morgana burst out, her tears threatening to return again. I will not be afraid, she thought, angry at herself and stilling a sob of anguish. "I can't tell you," she said slowly, trying to calm herself. "Only—I can't stay here any longer. I must leave. I must find my own truth." She reached over to her bedside for a candle and touched it to her sister's. Its sudden brightness hurt her tired eyes.

"What do you mean? Now? Where will you go?" Kina's voice suddenly sounded like a small child.

Morgana slid out of her bed and stepped to the wardrobe door. She struggled to remain calm as she began searching through her clothes.

Kina repeated her questions. "Morgana, where are you going? How can you?" Perplexed and frightened, she stood and raised her hand to her sister's shoulder, attempting to make her listen.

Morgana turned to her, appearing calmer that she felt. "Kina, I have to go. I will not marry whomever Father chooses for me, nor will I be shut into that room and locked away like a beast at night. I must go. You have found your happiness, now I must find mine." She turned back to the wardrobe.

In sudden tears Kina sat once more on her sister's bed. Silently she watched Morgana remove a small amount of clothing from the wardrobe, taking only her outdoor working clothes, grabbing a few other necessities, then stopping to quickly change her clothing. She couldn't believe her sister would leave

her. Not now, not at this time, right after her betrothal. She felt a twinge of anger, then guiltily looked
up at her sister, now quietly watching her.

Morgana stepped over and sat beside her and
took her hands in her own. "Kina, if there were any
other way I could stay I would," she said softly. "But I
can't. Father will be terribly angry with everyone once
he finds out about today." She looked at her hands. "I
wanted to help you plan your wedding, I wanted to be
your Honor Maid and see your new home. But I
can't, Kina. I just can't stay here anymore." She fell
silent, then hugged her sister close. Kina clung to her,
suddenly needing her elder sister's comforting embrace.

Morgana slowly released her and stood. "I
don't know what I should take, besides clothes. I've
never done anything like this before." A faint smile
crossed her face.

Kina sniffed, then said brightly, "Well, I certainly haven't done anything like this either!" The two
stared at each other in silence for a moment, then
burst into hushed laughter. Kina jumped to her feet.
"You need to take some food. You could have a long
journey ahead of you." In childlike humor, she
grabbed her candle and slipped to the door. "You
finish packing, I'll get some food for you." She tiptoed
out of the room, Morgana watching her leave, then
turning back to her preparations.

A short time later Kina returned with a bundle
in her arms. "I found an old day pack in the cup-
boards; there's room in here for your clothes and the
food I packed."

Morgana pulled up her heavy felted blanket.
"It's too bad my winter cloak is in storage, it could be
necessary." She rolled up the blanket and tied a cord

around it, then sat down and began to put her clothes into the pack.

Kina walked to her own bed for a moment then returned and sat next to Morgana again. She held up a tiny object in her fingers. Morgana looked closer; it was a small silver bell. Kina handed it to her. "I found this in the garden a few days ago. I didn't tell anyone, I didn't want Father making me throw it away. You know how he is about things like this," she smiled knowingly. "I see them in my dreams, 'Gana. The mist ponies. I think they gave it to us. They were so beautiful, how could they be evil?" Kina's voice sounded almost wistful.

Morgana stared at her, then at the silver bell in her hand. Kina dreamt of them also? Or did she really see them and believe it was only a dream? "Kina, you should keep this. If it was a gift, it was given to you, not to me." She started to give the bell back when Kina closed her hand over hers.

"Then it is now a gift I give to you. For your journey to find your truth."

Morgana felt her heart swell with love for her little sister. With tears in her eyes, she embraced her again. "It is a gift I shall treasure above all others." For a silent moment the sisters held each other, then Kina released her.

"You must go now, 'Gana. I think it will be light in a few hours." She wiped her tears from her cheek. "Are you going to take one of the horses?"

"No, I don't think I'll risk it. I'd love to take the black mare, but Father would come after me even faster if I did," she sighed, then picked up her pack. "I'm going to head for the river. I don't know why, but I feel someone will meet me there." She stood and shouldered the pack and headed for the window, then turned again to Kina.

"Everything that is mine I leave to you. I won't
be needing anything else here. If I can, I will come
back for your wedding. I shall love you always, Kina."
She turned and opened the shutters. Her sister rose
and they held each other one last time. Then Morgana slipped out of the silent house of her childhood
and into the moonlit garden.

# Chapter 7

A crystalline moon rose high above Morgana as she shouldered her small pack and carefully followed the well-traveled pathway through her father's holdlands towards the river. The dark forest loomed silent and eerie before her, the tall grasses around her still as ice in the moonlight. She felt insignificant before the great trees, as if they were the guardians of an ancient temple which she must pass through to seek her answers.

She paused to look back. The follow-lights of her home were no longer visible, only the silent fields and wooded thickets of midnight could she see. No breeze stirred the air. It was as if time had stopped and now waited for her so it could begin anew.

Morgana faced the dark forest. What was so inviting in the brightness of day now appeared impervious, as if daring her to enter its depths. Beyond the trees lay the river; the passage to the sea or the stairway to the mountain skies. Which way would it lead her? With a sigh she adjusted her pack again and started into the forest.

She had barely taken two steps when she found she could no longer see the trail before her. Dismayed, she turned to gaze back at the fields she had just traveled. How was she to find her way to the river? She could hear its endless rushing within the domain of the forest, but she had no desire to walk blindly through the dark to meet her destiny.

"Destiny," she said softly. What a curious thing to think of now. She set her pack in the long grass at her feet and looked up at the sky. The stars glimmered against the black of the night, the moon's brightness creating a dancing halo as she watched its delicate splendor. "Destiny, where is the path to my destiny?" she asked the pale moon. A remnant of the dream spread before her eyes, a void that moved of its own will misting her sight. She shut her tearing eyes against the terrible memory, willing her fears away. "No more crying!" she scolded herself and retrieved her pack.

A sudden breeze in the treetops caused her to glance skyward again. The moon's aura appeared brighter and, as she gazed at its silver-edged beauty, a glittering veil spiraled out from the shining sphere. She watched in awe as the spiral grew larger and slowly descended until it reached the distant treetops. A sound shimmered amongst the trees, like crystal raindrops as it fell slowly through the forest. Within the sound, she could hear the tinkling voices of the Others, the Azerii 'mist ponies' of her childhood, laughing in playful delight. Cloaked in glimmering mists, they appeared in the forest, lighting the path with their glow-ing voices.

Morgana stood at the edge of the trees. All of her past spoke to her of the dangers that lay ahead. Her teachings said she should run back to her family where life was ordered and secure. If she followed these beings there would be no safe home that she could return to.

A moment's decision that seemed like a lifetime swept through her. Shifting her pack once more, she firmly stepped onto the path and was joyously welcomed by the dancing Azerii.

*

Elas sat at the table in the center of the gathering room; Tagar and Rejat stood silently behind her. The LandsHolder Kaill Brenan and his wife Siva waited across from her, their youngest son Jeven stood between them. Jeven smiled at the two Mirii.

He knows this is for him, Rejat thought, smiling back at the dark haired child.

Elas sighed and brushed a tired hand across her face. Morgana was out of her reach for now, but she would have to be found later when they had time to look for her. She pushed her concerns for her niece out of her thoughts in order to focus on the task before her. Studying the boy, she found his mind open to hers and fully aware of her intentions. *Jeven is open to all Azerii,* the knowledge suddenly flashed before her. He was like an open book available to any who cared to look. He would have to be strong, he would attract many wild Azerii and could become a victim of the Dark Azerii should Rejat's vision prove to be true.

*It was true enough for me!* Rejat's mind voice interrupted her. She grimaced at her sister's intrusion, then looked at the boy's father. His thoughts were a mixture of apprehension, concern and skepticism. He did not quite believe in his son's unseen talent. As he had told Elas earlier, none of his family had ever had the ability to see the wild Azerii. But Siva had convinced him of the necessity of this meeting and he trusted her judgment enough to allow this 'ceremony', as the two Mirii termed it.

"Kaill, Siva, I thank you for allowing this Protection Ceremony for your son," Elas began slowly, wanting them to be aware of what they were about to do. She agreed with Rejat, the time for secrecy was passing. They would need more of the People's help in the future and it was best if they understood her intentions from the start. "The purpose of this ceremony is to mark and protect your child from any Azerii who might try to meld with him before he is prepared."

"What is 'meld', Elas?" Siva asked softly, her eyes full of her anxiety for her son.

"It is a word we use to describe when a Hu'man and an Azerii merge awareness. They have complete knowledge of each other's thoughts. They become as one; the Hu'man gives the Azerii the ability to take on a physical form, such as the horse you saw me ride here on, Siva. The Azerii gives to the Hu'man by enhancing their talents, such as seeing the thoughts of others—when they allow it," she added quickly, noting the look of surprise on their faces, "and the visioning of possible futures, plus other abilities, depending on the Hu'man's talents."

Siva glanced nervously at her son, then back to Elas. "What are Jeven's talents?"

Elas sighed again. She did not wish to spend what little time they had explaining the whole of the Mirii's abilities to one nervous mother. "I believe he has several talents, though his strongest now is his ability to see and hear the wild Azerii."

"Mist ponies!" Jeven said suddenly, his eyes firmly challenging her to correct him.

She smiled in response. "Mist ponies, yes, Jeven, you are right." She became serious once more. "Siva, Kaill, I cannot explain everything to you right now. Much of what we do will seem strange or appear as if nothing has happened. The work we do does not always appear physically. Much is done on the unseen levels, like the Azerii. I cannot prove to you that these levels exist, for they are not visible to all eyes. But know this, they do exist," she stated firmly, meeting their eyes. "You and I share but one world, one level of life. The Azerii dwell in another, all around us." She studied their expressions. Kaill still looked skeptical, Siva now looked confused. She continued, using the Voice to relax them both. She could not wait for their understanding this time.

"Rejat and I will mark Jeven. He will carry this mark so all Mirii and Azerii will know him as a Talent. You will not be able to see this mark, nor shall any other who does not have the ability. He shall not feel any pain, Siva." She smiled at the surprise that crossed the other woman's face.

"What do we have to do?" Siva bravely pushed her worries aside. Her husband took her hand and began to rise from the table. Jeven remained at the edge, excitement in his shining eyes. Elas, rose and nodding to Rejat and Tagar, moved away from the table to the middle of the room. She turned to face the boy and dropped to one knee, spreading her arms out wide at shoulder level, palms upwards.

"Jeven, son of Siva and Kaill Brenan." Jeven laughed and walked around the table to stand before her. Rejat stepped behind the child, kneeling as Elas and opening her arms.

Elas spoke the Voice to calm the excited boy. "You must stand very still, Jeven. Nothing will hurt you, but you must keep perfectly still. Close your eyes and pretend you are a tree, a great green cedarjinn tree. You have strong roots that go all the way to the center of our Mother's world. You have many wide branches that catch Father sun's life-giving light." He became very quiet between the two Mirii's outstretched arms. Elas scanned his mind. He was ready. As one, she and Rejat rose to their feet.

"Brealyth srii Elas, Become!" she called her Azerii to join her. A shimmering white light unfolded from around her body and slipped to her right to stand in a woman's form, mirroring Elas' features and posture.

"Stillyth srii Rejat, Become!" Rejat said, her Azerii appearing in similar fashion in his hu'man form, to her right. The circle now complete, four figures surrounded the silent child. From their open arms a wall of golden light radiated, arching up over their heads and descending to the floor.

From Elas' inner eye she saw the golden wall close beneath their feet, encircling the five in a glowing sphere. "Jeven, Hu'man, see me." The boy opened his eyes and smiled up at her. "I, Elas srii Brealyth, Mirii, mark and welcome you." In her mind she heard her Azerii speak, *I, Brealyth srii Elas, Azerii, welcome you.*

Jeven's smile brightened. Over the boy's head, Rejat spoke, "I, Rejat srii Stillyth, Mirii, mark and welcome you." Her Azerii completed the circle with his mind response, *I, Stillyth srii Rejat, Azerii, welcome you.*

Elas closed her eyes, envisioning a brilliant light before her inner sight. As she opened her eyes once more, a small star appeared over Jeven's head. She slowly lowered her gaze with the star following, resting finally on the child's forehead, above and between his dark eyes. The star blazed for a brief moment, then dimmed to a soft glow.

"Jeven, Hu'man, you now carry the Star of the Mirii. All Mirii will know and honor your boundaries. All Azerii will know and honor your boundaries. Until the time of preparation, abide here with your family in peace." She paused and looked past the boy to her sister.

*He will need more. The one I saw is strong.* Rejat's thoughts were filled with whispers of her vision. *We must make the Protection Ring.*

She nodded and prepared herself. Drawing the others inward, she knelt before Jeven once more, the circle now held by Rejat and the two Azerii. "Jeven, show me your hands," she said softly. He held out his hands, uncertainty in his face for the first time. She gently took his hands in her own and then closed her eyes. Two shining silver rings appeared around her wrists, then as Jeven watched in wide-eyed fascination, the rings slipped over her hands to his own to rest upon his wrists. She released his hands. "Hold out your arms."

Jeven stretched his arms wide. A silver thread spun out from the rings, connecting them wrist to wrist before him, then expanding into a glimmering mist that quickly encircled him.

"Lower your arms, Jeven," Elas spoke again and as the boy complied, the mist quickly faded leaving only the silver rings on his wrists. "You now bear our protection. Should you ever need help because of an Unnamed Azerii seeking to force meld, the rings will shield you and the Mirii will come to your aid."

Jeven stared at Elas, his face troubled by her words. She scanned his thoughts and placed understanding in his mind. The boy's face relaxed. He would remember.

Elas stepped back from him into her place in the golden sphere. A tired look crossed her face as she began to release the shield circle. As one the two Mirii raised their arms up and over the boy, drawing the sphere inward, then opening it above them, as their Azerii shifted back into their light forms. The golden wall of light slowly began dropping to the floor where it vanished, leaving the two women facing each other over a smiling little boy, their Azerii shimmering around them.

✳

With dizzying antics, the wild Azerii led Morgana through the blackness of the forest, their tinkling voices playfully calling her onward. On occasion she glanced nervously back the way she had come, but each time one of the Azerii would produce a brilliant light before her that was impossible to see beyond, so she turned forward again towards the river. The wild Azerii slowly began to take shape as she followed them, their myriad colors shifting into the mist ponies she had witnessed in her mother's garden. Aurora mists swirled around their bodies and their dancing feet never seemed to touch the ground.

Her eyes misted at the beauty of these magical creatures. Why had she not remembered them from her childhood? Where were they leading her now?

She thought of her family. What would they do when they discovered her absence? She hoped Kina would not be punished for helping her leave. Her father would be so furious with her. She had defied his plans to be rid of her, and yet, now he was rid of her, she thought sadly. Why had he been so angry with her? She had always completed her duties to her family, she just did not desire to be tied to a husband at this time. Her visits to the river had not harmed anyone; why did he destroy her tree?

"Why did he cut down my tree?" she suddenly said aloud, her tears threatening to begin anew. She stumbled over a hidden root and would have fallen, but something caught her outstretched hand. She looked around as she regained her balance, but she could see nothing in the dark underworld of the forest but the shimmering mist ponies before her.

*Come, Little One, the Lady will soon be gone,* their voices whispered around her.

"Where are you taking me?" She stopped and gazed at their shifting forms. She was tired and the path was beginning to seem endless.

*To your destiny, Great One,* their voices rippled back, and for a moment she saw a robed figure standing in their mists.

"What is my destiny?" She grabbed at their words, searching for their meanings.

*Destiny, destiny, destiny...*the Azerii echoed back at her, moving forward again, their laughter filling the night. Morgana shook her head, their ringing voices making her dizzy. She adjusted her pack again and started after them.

The rushing of the river became louder, and abruptly the trees opened up before her. The river looked black and boiling in the darkness, the moon having descended below the tree tops, its light filtering through the upper branches in shallow beams. She dropped her pack and gazed out over the water, the Azerii flowing around her. "Where are we?" she asked, her voice revealing her fatigue.

*You must wait here for the One,* they sent

with excitement in their words. *You stand before your destiny, Morgana Elissii. Now you must wait and prepare.*

She looked down at their shimmering forms. "Prepare? Wait and prepare for who?" she asked, puzzled by their words, her fear slowly rising within her. She did not wish to face more of the unknown in the darkness by the river.

The Azerii suddenly crowded close to her. One by one, their shimmering forms brushed her hands and their voices rustled through her mind. Words flitted through her that had no meaning, but as each voice touched her they began to slip away into nothing, until all but one had vanished into the night.

Morgana looked at the swirling mist pony before her. Golden eyes met hers and she could almost feel its soft warm muzzle stroke her open hand. *Rest here, Morgana Elissii,* the Azerii's voice brushed her tired mind. *You will be safe here. We shall watch over you.*

She knelt before the aurora creature. Freeing the blanket from her pack, she wrapped it around her and sat on the cold earth beside the river. She turned to the mist pony and asked, "What is your name?"

The Azerii seemed pleased, but shook its glistening head. *Sleep, Light One. The Naming is not yet to be.* The mists began to rise and swirl around its body till she could only see shifting lights dance before her sleepy eyes. She rolled deep into the blanket and with her pack behind her fell into a dreamless sleep.

In the early morning darkness she was jolted awake by the urgent voices of the wild Azerii. She opened her eyes to their frantic movements over her head and groggily asked, "What is it? What's wrong?"

*Morgana Elissii! Awake! Awake! You must*

*go! Now!* They repeated their cries, ignoring her questions. Brushing her face and hands, their voices pushing and pulling at her to move, she only felt a faint tingle at their touch. She sat up stiffly at their insistence, still wrapped in her blanket, then rose unsteadily to her feet. She searched around her through the dark forest not yet lit by the wildly moving Azerii. Dawn was still not on the horizon; it seemed darker than before. She wondered how long she had slept; not long enough, she told herself and began to reach for her pack.

A strange cry from the wild Azerii made her hesitate. Looking up, she saw them suddenly stop in mid-air as if held motionless by some unseen force; then with a rush of chattering voices they vanished into the forest.

She stared open-mouthed at her glittering escorts' abrupt departure. A wave of abandonment flooded through her. She had no lantern, guide nor idea as to which way she should go or whether she should wait for them to return. She suddenly remembered her father's teachings from her childhood. The night was a dangerous time to be alone and lost in the middle of the forest.

She knelt and reached for her pack, her mind flying. Should I wait for someone? I can't see anything here anyway; if I move I may end up in the river. Better to wait for the one they said was coming to meet me. Her thoughts rolled on as she clung to her pack. The closeness of the dark wrapped itself around her like the great black cape her Aunt Elas wore in winter.

The thought of her aunt caused her regret. "Why didn't she tell me before? she whispered to the forest. "Why did she hide the truth all these years?" Tears began to slide down her cheeks, she wished she had not run so recklessly from Elas now. She remembered the tired look in her eyes and Tagar's hurt expression. She offered me a chance for a different life and I ran from it. Now look where I am, stuck in the dark by a river I've known all my life and I can't find my way! Angrily she sat down and pulled the blanket close around her shoulders, staring blindly into the forest.

The rushing murmur of the river began to lull her to sleep when a sharp crack startled her. She strained to see what had caused the sound. A sense of unease began to fill her as she breathlessly waited for another sound to reach her ears beyond the endless noise of the river. Still clutching her pack, she quietly rose to her knees. The silence of the forest was deafening next to the rushing of the waters. Her heart pounded in her ears as her panic crept through her body.

A rustle in the brush before her brought her instantly to her feet. A low growl reached through the darkness. She clutched her pack in front of her like a shield, the blanket slipping to the ground behind her. In the darkness she glimpsed a pair of yellow eyes. *Kir-Latt,* she mentally told herself, and tensed to run. She had never heard of the large dog-like beasts coming down into the lowland valleys in summer. They roamed the high mountains nearly all seasons. Though they avoided hu'mans, she had heard stories of a few attacks on the huntsmen and foresters who worked in the high mountain valleys.

The beast huffed a short growl and her feet began to feel for the trail behind her. Another sharp bark and her panic erupted. She threw the pack at the unseen animal and turning, flung herself blindly down the trail. A screaming cry broke from the Kir-

Latt's throat as it began to pursue her.

The trail rose and fell beneath her pounding feet, the branches whipping her as she fled. Unerringly, as if something led her, she ran alongside the river, her steps missing the holes and tree roots of the forest floor. The Kir-Latt's scream reached for her again and again. She ran, her terror pushing her on, never pausing to notice that dawn had begun to lift the night from the woods around her.

A rearing horse appeared before her, bringing her to an abrupt halt. Confused, she struggled against the strong arms that quickly grabbed her away from the flailing hooves. Amidst the shouting of many voices she fought, then collapsed, sobbing with relief when she finally realized her captor was her Uncle Tagar.

# Chapter 8

"It's all right, you're safe, you're safe now," Tagar said to Morgana as she sobbed into his chest. In the rising light of day that filled the small clearing by the river he held her close while Elas and Rejat calmed a nervous gray horse. His stallion snorted in irritation behind them. "You're safe," he repeated again as she began trembling in his embrace. He looked up over her head. The two Mirii women met his gaze, their tired faces rigid with concern.

Rejat scowled, releasing the gray's head and turned to the trail from which Morgana had just appeared. Walking up a brief distance, she stopped to crouch down in the narrow path, closing her eyes to scan. They had all heard the Kir-Latt's hunting cry, but it had sounded odd to her. She pushed her distance scan out seeking the elusive animal, her Azerii Stillyth searching beyond her reach.

Elas watched Tagar comfort their niece for a moment, then stepped away from the now quiet horses toward Rejat. She stopped behind her. "Do you feel it? Is it the same one as your Vision?" she said lowly.

Rejat forced a sigh as she drew her awareness back. "No. If it was Kir-Latt, it's disappeared. Stil says the wild Azerii are in the hills. They must have led her upriver."

"But we all heard it. What else could it be?" She took a step past her and stubbornly pushed her own scan out.

Rejat stood slowly, glancing toward Tagar and Morgana, then turned again to her sister. "Well? Did you find it?"

Elas opened her eyes and shook her head, pulling her scan back. "Maybe, I'm not sure. There is something, but it seems to be less than a Kir-Latt. A much smaller animal, I think." She turned to trace her steps back to their companions.

Morgana sat on a broken log in the clearing. She was wrapped in her uncle's cloak, her hair all a tangle, her face and hands bleeding from dozens of scratches from her desperate flight. Tagar stood beside her, watching his niece visibly shake under the heavy cloak, her hands clasped around the waterskin he had given her. He looked up as Elas and Rejat returned, then stepped up to his mate. "She's terrified, Elas. What did you see?"

"There was something, but we're not sure what," she said quietly, her eyes on Morgana's face. "Did she say anything?"

"Not much, except she's sorry she yelled at us." A wry smile crossed his face.

Elas shrugged. "It was to be expected, I should not have waited so long." She approached her niece. Morgana raised her streaked face to her aunt, then lowered her gaze. She took a deep breath to speak, Elas stopping her with a touch.

"No words now. There will be time later. Come with me." She took the waterskin, handing it to Tagar, then led her niece to the river, directing her to sit at the water's edge. She knelt beside her, producing a small cloth from a dark gray pouch tied to her belt. She soaked the cloth in the cold waters then began to gently bathe Morgana's hands and face. Rejat followed, stopping to stand at Morgana's shoulder and silently pick the brambles out of her hair.

Morgana glanced up at the strange woman from her vision. Rejat returned her gaze impassively, her narrow face guarded. A swift rush of lightheadedness brushed across her forehead, then the painful scratches on her hands brought her attention back to her aunt kneeling beside her.

Elas held her hands between her own. "Morgana, listen to me. We must ride on. You are coming with us?" At the silent nod from her niece she continued, "Good. But your face and hands are badly scratched. We may cross others' paths before we reach our hold."

"What Elas is trying to say, Child, is you look awful," Rejat said impatiently. Morgana glanced up at her as she scowled at Elas over Morgana's head.

Elas' expression was controlled when Morgana turned back to her. She smiled and shook her head. "I'm sorry, Rejat is correct. You do look rather battered. What I was going to say is we shall take care of your injuries if you will allow it, so they won't bother you as we ride."

Morgana looked puzzled. "How?" she asked, her voice sounding small.

"We are Healers," Rejat said briskly.

Elas glared at her sister again. "Just close your eyes. I can't explain it now. Just relax, don't be afraid. You have nothing to be afraid of now."

Elas' voice dissolved Morgana's unease. She closed her eyes, relaxing on the sandy riverbank. A coolness began to surround her stinging hands and face and she was briefly aware of other thoughts flitting amongst her own.

"Open your eyes." Her aunt's voice seemed to echo from some great distance. She drew her heavy eyelids apart and gazed at her hands. Rosy from the coldness of the river, they greeted her clean and un-blemished. She touched her face, her cheeks cold and wet also, but the stinging pain was gone. In silent awe she turned to her aunt's gentle smile.

"Teach me, Elas. I want to know the ways of the Mirii."

\*

The chza fled noisily down the awakening mountain, crashing frantically through the low bram-bles lining the forest floor. Blindly the creature ran, straight as an arrow's path, never turning except to narrowly miss the trees threatening to end its head-long flight. Eyes wide with an unknown sight, the doe headed towards the valley.

Rejat picked up the chza when she scanned again for the elusive Kir-Latt as she, Elas and Mor-gana walked back to rejoin Tagar. She stopped for a moment to intensify her scan and see what caused the animal's panicked flight. Her companions turned back to her. Elas motioned for Morgana's silence and step-ped beside her sister.

Morgana patiently watched her aunt and the strange woman, their faces lifted to the wooded hills beyond the river valley. The red-clad woman's eyes were hooded, her gaze seeming withdrawn, while Elas' eyes appeared unfocused even though they were open. She felt a strange absence in their presence as if she were alone once more.

Elas pulled back her brief scan and laid a hand

on her sister's shoulder. The other Mirii shook her head, blinking her eyes as she returned from her scan. "I couldn't reach it, its mind is closed to me."

Rejat appeared disturbed by her scan. "The chza is blind. It's being driven by something—" she broke off, her face crossed with an unpleasant memory. "We must be cautious. Let's go, now." She regained her stern composure and strode off, leaving Elas and Morgana to quickly follow.

They joined Tagar as he waited with the horses, the two Azerii appearing suddenly in horse form behind his stallion and the gray. "Are you all right, Morgana?" he said and held out the reins of the gray horse.

"I am better, Uncle," she replied and stared first at the horses, then at the proffered reins. Tagar smiled at the unspoken question in her eyes.

"The mare was a gift. Her name is Kahja. We had thought to find you at your tree." Her sudden pallor at the mention of her tree stopped his hand. He glanced at Elas who had caught the young woman's fallen expression. She shook her head, indicating "no questions now", and placed a comforting hand on her niece's shoulder.

"We must go. Brenan gave the mare. You must ride, we have a long distance to cover." She took the reins from Tagar's hand and placed them in Morgana's.

Morgana raised her head and blinked the brightness of her tears from her eyes. Taking a deep breath, she whispered her thanks and with Tagar's help, pulled herself up onto the mare's saddled back.

When the four were all astride their mounts, Elas turned and began leading the way, following the north trail along the river. Once started, she spoke over her shoulder to Morgana, following close behind. "We must keep to the river for awhile, then we shall cut back toward our hold. We must be cautious, we do not want anyone to follow. Your father may be out looking for you, so we shall Veil if Rejat and I scan him or any others near our path. We must be silent when in Veil. Do you understand?" she said, turning in her saddle to see her niece clearly.

Morgana nodded, even though she did not fully understand her aunt's strange words. Elas smiled.

"As soon as I can I will teach you the meaning of my 'strange' words." She smiled again at the startled expression on Morgana's face. "Yes, you will learn this also. It does save much time."

"And breath," Rejat muttered lowly.

Morgana stared at her aunt as she turned to the trail again, noticing the Azerii she rode. The silver mare walked strong and steady along the rugged path that the dusky gray she rode tread unevenly. She looked back at her uncle's horse behind her. Tagar's bay stallion seemed to be almost clumsy compared to the Azerii. Behind him Rejat's copper-colored Azerii seemed to float through the forest rather than walk, its head held high as if this were a wide valley road instead of a narrow wooded path.

A thought suddenly crossed her awareness. Where was Mia? She had not noticed her young cousin's absence until now. She stared at Elas' back, her thought echoing her wonder at the girl's unknown location. Mia had been at the Brenan LandsHold the day before, was she still there? Why would Elas leave her with them? She thought to ask her aunt, then remembered her words of caution and remained silent.

They rode along the river keeping close to its ever-changing banks. In the undergrowth alongside the trail they found Morgana's pack and blanket, looking none the worse for the manner in which they had been discarded. She silently repacked the blanket after Tagar handed it to her. A short distance later she recognized where she was in relation to her home, having traveled this path many times before her early morning flight. She had fled the Kir-Latt downriver, towards the fisher's dam. Were the mist ponies leading her upstream, towards the foothills of the Varan? She wished to speak to her aunt to question her as to why they would lead her towards the mountains and away from anyone she knew. They spoke of my destiny. She nursed their words as the forest slipped by. But where were they leading me? Who was I to wait for?

As they followed the trail an inner tension began to fill her, now that she knew where she was. They were crossing her father's lands and riding closer to her fallen companion. The silence of her escort became heavier. She wanted to turn away, throw herself into the downward rushing river, anything to escape the painful sight of her tree. Her hands clenched the reins tightly and the gray began pulling at the harshness of her grip. She stared at the river, willing her mind to look on its passing beauty, pushing away the memory of her tree.

Tagar's hand on her own startled her. She stared at her uncle and saw the concern in his eyes as he glanced down at her hands. Guiltily she relaxed her hands and let the gray's head drop.

Elas stopped them behind a thicket that overlooked a large clearing along the river. Beyond lay another grove. Rejat joined her, the two speaking quietly at the edge of the trees, then turning back to Tagar and Morgana.

98

"We must Veil here," she spoke softly, moving to her husband's side. "Rejat has scanned some of your father's people about. We do not wish to be seen here, but we must cross Tillan's lands." She turned to face the clearing again, Rejat's Azerii stepping to Morgana's side.

"What if you just Veil Morgana and Rejat? Tillan would not pay us much notice. His people know us well enough." Tagar looked from her to Rejat. The red-haired Mirii frowned.

"No, I think it best if none see our passing. With Morgana's departure, Tillan will be suspicious of all who cross his lands. Besides, if crossed, it would give me great pleasure to tell him exactly where we are taking his daughter, and why, and for your family's sake, I don't think you really want me to do that right now," Elas said, a quick smile playing across her face.

Tagar returned her smile. "Tillan would never forgive me and would probably disclaim me as his brother."

"From what Elas has told me I'm surprised you claim him as yours," Rejat smirked, calmly returning her sister's glare.

Tagar smiled at her words and reached over to pat Elas' knee. "I don't think my brother has ever forgiven me for pledging your sister, Rejat."

"Well, I never forgave her for that either," Rejat laughed, catching her outburst in feigned surprise as Elas hissed "Enough!" at their banter.

"Are we agreed then?" She leaned forward to see Rejat clearly past Tagar and Morgana.

"Agreed," Rejat smiled in reply and stepped her Azerii a pace away from Morgana's horse, as Elas did the same from Tagar's. In unison, the two women raised their arms wide in the morning light filtering through the trees. Whispered words crossed their lips, the meaning unknown to the two waiting between them. A silver haze shifted before and around them for a moment and then was gone. Out of the corner of her eyes, Morgana could see a silvery mist flow by, but when she looked directly it was not to be seen.

Elas lowered her arms and her Azerii stepped forward toward the clearing. Tagar urged Morgana after her, then followed with Rejat once again behind him. They slowly crossed the wide clearing without a word and passed into the forest on the other side.

Once again the thoughts of her tree returned to plague Morgana. As they resumed their quickened pace, she felt her heart close up inside, withdrawing from the renewed memory of the destruction before her. I will not cry before anyone again, she vowed to herself and somewhere beyond her the silent voices wept for the lost tears within her soul.

✳

The cedarjinn tree lay silent in the flashing river, the remaining upright branches waving sadly above the waters for rescue from its unwelcome fate. Elas and Rejat still held the Veil over their company when they came upon the tree. They stopped to survey the destruction, Elas dismounting and walking to the ruined trunk, bringing the Veil with her. She stared out over the sprawling length, then knelt to lay her hands on the open scar of its heart. The tree cried of its fate to her soul and sang of the abandonment by its protector. She listened to the heart of the tree, saying nothing in return. Her own heart ached for this useless destruction and she inwardly raged at the man responsible.

Unable to answer the cedarjinn's song she rose and turned to her companions. Tagar's face revealed mixed emotions; he was against such waste and knew of the importance of this tree. Rejat wore a cold mask. Elas recognized the fire that raged behind those copper eyes. But Morgana—*Ah, Morgana!* That's what happened after she left us. She knew of this. Her niece's face also wore a mask, but her eyes betrayed her pain at this sight. She sat stiffly upon her horse, not daring to move lest she give away the sorrow she held inside.

Elas walked up to her and held out her hand. Morgana stared down at her then slowly dismounted, taking her hand. She led her niece to the cedarjinn tree and placed her hand on its heart. Morgana snatched her hand back in surprise as the tree's agonized cry suddenly filled her senses. Frightened, she looked at her aunt who nodded silently and placed her hand once more on the tree. Again she heard the cry from her beloved tree, but placed her other hand beside the first and began to listen.

Strange words rang through her, words that had no meaning but somehow she knew of their intent. A greater sadness flowed through her and she became one with the tree in a way she had never experienced before; sadness at the loss that was different from her own. The betrayal by someone who was the tree's protector. She felt herself drawn into the life of the tree as if she were connected to its life in some unknown manner. The world around her suddenly changed, as the merging of the tree's soul and her own became stronger. She struggled to understand it's song, the final chorus that was given to her and to remember all that it was.

Deeply she listened to the tree, the outside world falling from her consciousness, until a small voice began calling her back. Reluctantly she followed, saddened that she could not stay and learn more from her old friend. The voice became urgent; she could not linger. With a great sigh she opened her eyes to the sight of her aunt bending over her.

Morgana stood and pulled her hands from the cedarjinn's trunk. She felt different, as if for a brief moment she had become one with the tree and felt its life flow through her veins. She looked at her aunt who shook her head to her questions, then followed her back to her horse. Wordlessly she pulled herself onto the gray and took the reins from her uncle. Elas returned to her Azerii and led them back to the river trail and their journey.

As they left sight of the tree, Morgana closed her eyes and felt as if a great weight had been lifted from her heart. She suddenly realized that she was the tree's protector, but that the tree had forgiven her by giving her its song. With a last glance at the tree's final rest, she gave her farewell in soundless words to her childhood friend.

# Chapter 9

They followed the Kesh River north until they were well past Tillan's hold, Elas and Rejat keeping the Veil over them until they were sure they had not been seen. Occasionally Rejat would send a short scan out for the vanished Kir-Latt and the panicked chza, but both seemed to have disappeared. When they stopped to release the Veil it was well past noon, the day's heat crept in through the trees, competing with the cool breeze flowing off the river.

They stopped to rest at a small clearing beside the river a few paces from the trail. As Morgana dismounted she nearly fell from her saddle. Elas exchanged worried glances with her sister.

Rejat's thoughts touched her mind. *She needs rest, she has been through too much in too short a time.*

Elas glanced back at her niece, sitting in front of her horse with Tagar beside her. *I know, but we cannot stop for long. We must move quickly, I need to know her mind, to question her about her Visioning,* she sent in reply. At her silent prompting, her Azerii disappeared to scan their path ahead. In like manner Rejat's mount followed, to continue his search for the Kir-Latt and chza. The two sisters join-

ed Tagar and Morgana, Tagar handing Elas his waterskin.

"We cannot stay here long. I wish to be on our
own lands before nightfall." She took a long swallow
from the skin and handed it to Rejat.

"Brient will be wondering what has happened
to us," Tagar commented, rolling a small object between his hands. "I told him we would return two days
ago. He'll think Tillan kept us over to talk of hold-
joining again."

"Who's Breint?" Rejat said, sounding only
slightly interested as she took a long drink from the
waterskin.

"He's my son, by my first wife," he replied,
palming the object again. "He's in his twentieth year,
and as much like his mother as like me. He cares for
my hold when I travel."

"He worries too much when you are gone."
Elas plucked the object out of his hands and flicked it
between her own. Tagar pretended dismay, then
slow-ly reached over and held out his hand. Elas
smiled, fingering the hidden object, then placed it in
his palm, closing her hand over his.

Tagar squeezed her hand. "Breint worries
about you too."

She smiled and turned to Rejat. "Why are you
interested?"

Rejat shifted uneasily and handed the waterskin to Morgana who seemed ready to fall asleep.
"His name, something familiar about his name. I don't
know why."

Elas smiled wickedly, "I know why," with smug
anticipation in her eyes.

Rejat glared at her. "Why?"

"Don't you remember? The one with the big

blue eyes? The southern borders? The one with the cat?" Elas held her breath, watching the puzzlement that crossed her Mirii sister's face.

Rejat suddenly laughed and threw her hands in the air. "Oh, that one! Now I remember!" She laughed again and slapped the dust from her knees. "How could I forget his name! Or his eyes."

"Or his cat. I remember that cat was very well, ah, trained, at picking out young, unsuspecting..." Elas stopped, laughter replacing her words.

"Enough, Elaa! Let me keep some mystery from your Chosen. Besides, that was a long time ago." She smiled again at the memory.

Morgana listened to their playful talk, struggling to keep her eyes open. She felt relaxed in their company, safer than she had felt around anyone in what seemed a long time. She watched Tagar play with the rolling object in his hands, heard Elas and Rejat's sparkling laughter and watched the Mirii toss her flame dark hair.

Suddenly a nervous snort rushed from the two horses behind them and a shadow seemed to pass through her. From the brush appeared a great black Kir-Latt, with two escorting Azerii as brilliant columns of light on either side. Heavy black fur surrounded its face and shoulders and crested along its broad back to the bushy tail. Silver eyes glowed above a fierce muzzle, Morgana imagining that the closed jaws contained many dagger-like teeth. The beast waited quietly before them, the light columns glowing like silent suns beside the creature.

Elas and Rejat rose slowly, their hands open, palms forward. "Welcome, Brother Kir-Latt," Rejat said.

*Welcome, Sister Mirii,* the beast's mind voice

boomed through them. Morgana started—she too heard its voice!

*Welcome, Little Sister.* The Kir-Latt looked straight at her and a shiver of unknown emotion flowed through her body.

"Welcome—Teacher," she uttered in return, surprise flitting across her face at her words.

The black creature gazed at Tagar. *Welcome, EarthKeeper.*

Tagar stood slowly. "Welcome, Lord Hunter," he said shakily. When Elas turned a startled glance to him he smiled uneasily.

"You can hear him?"

"Yes, very well." He shook his head distractedly. "A bit unsettling though."

She turned again to the Kir-Latt. "Welcome, Brother Kir-Latt. How may we assist you?" She took a step forward.

*There is another of my Tribe who is in need of your skill, Sister Healer.* He also took a step closer, his escort keeping their positions beside him.

Elas glanced at Tagar, then faced the Kir-Latt again. "I shall gladly help in any way I can, Brother Kir-Latt. Can you take me to your companion?"

*He is not my companion,* the Kir-Latt sent flatly. *But he is of my Tribe. I sense he has allowed the company of one not chosen. He now lies near, his body is in dis-ease.*

Elas cast a sharp look to Rejat. "Has the One left him?"

*Yes. I sense none of the Others near. Only his foolish mind greets mine.*

Rejat called her Azerii to her. Swiftly one of the columns of light shifted and became the copper stallion beside her. "Lead us to your Tribe member, Brother Kir-Latt," she said as she swung into her saddle.

Elas called Brealyth into like form. "May our companions attend?"

The Kir-Latt turned to Morgana. *Little Sister shall come if she chooses. I sense the Earth-Keeper does not wish to be a part of this.*

Tagar looked uncomfortable. "I mean no offense, Lord Hunter. I'm not accustomed to your—presence, or your great mind voice."

*Be calm, EarthKeeper. Remain here if you choose.* The Kir-Latt sounded almost amused. He turned suddenly and started off away from the river. Rejat grabbed Morgana and hauled her up behind her and they quickly followed.

They rode swiftly after the dark beast, Morgana holding tightly to Rejat's waist until the Mirii loudly complained, "You'll squeeze the breath out of me!" She found riding on an Azerii was not quite like riding on a horse. The ride was smoother, even at a swift gallop through the heavy wood the Azerii never stumbled in the thick undergrowth. She watched Elas over Rejat's shoulder. She could barely see the Kir-Latt bounding ahead of them.

What seemed moments later they abruptly stopped before a dense bramble thicket. Morgana felt a strange tension around them as they slipped from their mounts to face the Kir-Latt who waited before the dark wall of green.

*My Tribe member lies within,* the gruff mind voice said. She saw a small opening in the thicket near the right edge.

*Come, Sister Healer.* The Kir-Latt stepped forward to nuzzle Elas' hand and led her to the opening.

Elas paused before the bramble wall and called Brealyth to her. The Azerii horse vanished and a shimmering halo outlined her body. She knelt and peered into the dark hole, then cast her hand into the opening. A prism of light flew from her hand into the hole, gently lighting up the interior. Morgana watched, fascinated by her aunt's talents and leaned down to see what lay inside the bramble thicket. Rejat stepped forward as Elas beckoned to her.

The Kir-Latt stepped to one side of the opening and sat to wait. Elas, followed closely by Rejat, slipped into the opening and out of sight. Nervously, Morgana stepped closer to the passage, curious about what the two Mirii were doing to help the unseen Kir-Latt, but still fearful of the great beast who waited silently before her.

The Kir-Latt turned his luminous gaze to Morgana. *Why do you wait, Little Sister? Do you not wish to help?* The silver eyes closed slowly, then looked upon her once more.

Morgana felt overwhelmed by the Kir-Latt's gaze. "I do not know how to heal, Lord Kir-Latt." Her voice sounded lost speaking to this great creature.

*Your words are not needed. I hear your mind voice.* The Kir-Latt blinked again and raised his head high. *Come to me,* he commanded, rising to his full height.

Morgana heard the power within his voice. Fear held her in place for a moment, then swallowing hard, she stepped to within an arm's length of the Kir-Latt.

The beast shifted his massive head to look fully at her. *What do you feel?*

She stared into his eyes. "Fear," she whispered.

*But you came,* the voice echoed within her.

"Yes, but I still feel afraid." Her legs twitched to turn and run, but she held her ground.

*Good. You know your fear, but remain.* The Kir-Latt took another step closer and thrust his head up, revealing the dagger-like teeth she had previously only imagined.

Morgana suddenly laughed. The posture of the Kir-Latt reminded her of the Rinon's show horses when they were at festival. She caught her breath when the Kir-Latt dropped his head and seemed to glare at her with an almost pained expression.

"I'm sorry, Lord Kir-Latt, but the way you stood just now reminded me of our neighbor's horses when they are on show." She held her breath as the Kir-Latt placed his head under her upraised hand. She carefully stroked the dense black mane on the beast's head. The Kir-Latt purred like a cat, the sound higher, like a vibrating song in its throat.

The Kir-Latt looked up at her. *What is my name?* the voice commanded once more.

"Darkness," she replied, her hand resting on the black head. The name shifted around her memory, the word echoing from some unknown past. "Why do you call me Little Sister?" She sat beside the Kir-Latt, suddenly feeling an understanding between them.

*You have named me truly, Little Sister. Now I name you. Elissii, Child of Knowing. When you are Mirii you shall run with me. You shall learn Kir-Latt speak and be one with us. You shall be a Speaker of Truth. You shall know the Winds, Elissii.*

Morgana gazed at the dark face. "How do you

know I will be Mirii?"

"The Kir-Latt are Visioners," a voice spoke from behind them. She looked up to see Rejat standing outside the bramble wall, a soft glow around her body. She quickly glanced to where her Azerii had been standing and was surprised to not have noticed his departure.

She turned back to the Kir-Latt. "Why did I call you Teacher?"

*Because you have known me before.* The Kir-Latt turned to face the Mirii as Elas crawled out of the passage, a tired expression held in her eyes as she stood.

"Your Tribemate will need rest and protection for some time, Brother Kir-Latt." She rubbed her hands over her eyes, the glow of her Azerii still around her. "He has allowed much disease from the meld he accepted. We do not know how soon before he is truly whole again." She lowered her hands from downcast eyes. Morgana thought she saw tears beneath her dark lashes.

The Kir-Latt quickly slipped into the thicket. Morgana rose to ask about the other Kir-Latt when Darkness reappeared from the opening.

*My Tribe thanks you, Sister Healers, Sister Mirii!* The deep mind voice boomed at them. *We shall sing your praises to the Lady! We shall honor your names to our memory! We shall open our hearts to your songs!* He roared his thanks to them with his awesome howl.

Elas, Rejat and Morgana covered their ears at the Kir-Latt's true voice which cut the air like glass. When his song fell away Elas returned the Kir-Latt's thanks. "We honor our Brothers of the Kir-Latt Tribe as before and always. It is our privilege that we have been of assistance to your great and wise people."

Rejat echoed her words and added, "My thanks to your Tribe for their help in my journey through the Varan Mountains. We would not have survived without it."

The Kir-Latt suddenly stared intently at her. *We do not usually interfere with the Hu'mans, but we were forewarned of your journey and knew of your danger. Be warned again. The Hu'mans still follow your path and desire to prevent your journey from completion. We shall assist you should you need us when you cross the Wildering Ways.*

His voice became gentle once more as he turned to Morgana. *Farewell, Elissii. Remember your journey. Follow your path to your Truth, Child of Knowing. We shall meet again when you are Mirii. Remember Darkness. Embrace your fear, then stand before it. Farewell, Little Sister.*

The Kir-Latt turned and entered the thicket. Elas and Rejat began walking away from the bramble wall, back in the direction from which they had come. Morgana stared at the dark passage, her thoughts dancing. I wonder what happened in there. Was that the Kir-Latt who chased me along the river? Rejat's voice cut sharply through her speculations and she turned and hurried after the two women waiting for her astride their Azerii.

"Come, Morgana. We still have some distance to go before nightfall." Elas offered her hand and pulled her niece up behind her. "Tagar will be worried. He is not overly fond of the Kir-Latt."

"Must have been quite a shock for him to talk to one," Rejat said.

"I don't understand," Morgana said over her

aunt's shoulder. "the mist ponies called me Elissii, so did the Kir-Latt, but he said it as if he gave me the name. How did the others know? How did the Kir-Latt?" she said thoughtfully. It was getting difficult to think about anything, she sleepy remarked to herself.

"The Kir-Latt are Visioners," Rejat replied, her voice seeming to echo as if from a distance. "They see beyond the normal limits of Hu'mans and remain separate. It is because of this separation that they can see. If they become involved in other's paths, they lose their ability to vision. They are the Ageless Ones."

Morgana watched the red-haired Mirii. Her face appeared drained, as if the healing had taken some of her vitality. Elas too seemed much more tired than before. She held her aunt's slim waist, careful to keep a secure hold without causing her discomfort. She struggled with her own exhaustion as she fought to remain alert. The rocking motion of the Azerii was comforting, while a horse would keep one jarringly awake. Time slipped past her unnoticed and then she heard Tagar's voice welcoming their return. He helped her down, then greeted Elas as she slid off her Azerii into his warm embrace.

"We missed you," she murmured.

"I missed you too. Are you all right? You look worn out." Tagar held her close and glanced over her shoulder to smile reassuringly to his niece.

"Come on, you two. We've lost much time," Rejat's voice cut impatiently.

Morgana turned to glance at her. She sat on her Azerii with one hand rubbing the copper neck affectionately, but her eyes revealed her tension and unrest. She looked away from Morgana's gaze and her Azerii moved toward the trees.

Morgana turned and walked to the gray mare and hauled herself into the saddle as Elas and Tagar separated and returned to their mounts. Without a word, the four moved back to the trail and resumed their interrupted journey once more.

\*

Sunset had long since passed when the four rode into Tagar's LandsHold. They were greeted with much noise from the excited barking of the hold's dogs in spite of Brient's efforts to silence them. He finally gave up and warmly greeted his father and stepmother, then more formally welcomed Morgana and Rejat. As the HorseKeeper led their tired mounts to the stables, with Rejat leading Elas' and her own Azerii in their assumed forms, the others followed Brient into the main house.

Brient was full of questions about their overly long absence and was finally put off with a promise from his father to tell him everything in the morning. When he asked about Mia, Elas replied she was spending a few days with the Brenans and would return soon. Morgana noted Brient's concern for his young foster-sister and wondered what her own father's concern would be for her. She missed her sister and hoped again that she would not fall under their father's anger.

They headed for the kitchen, where Brient and Stara, the house steward, began preparing a meal of breads, smoked meats, cheeses, fruits and watered wine for the late travelers. Rejat joined them as the food was laid out on the room's large central table. The elder woman eyed her dark red clothing but said nothing; she was well aware of the Mirii's position in this hold. Rejat smiled coldly at her glances and pulled up a stool next to Morgana.

"The horses are well cared for here," she said firmly, a hint of approval in her voice.

Tagar smiled from across the table and handed her a cup. "My HorseKeeper is well-learned in his craft. It's even better that he loves the horses more than his own family, but only for me and the horses."

"And well he should love them beasts," Stara said from the bread cupboard. "He spent more time with them than the family who deserted him." She brought another loaf to the table; the first was nearly gone.

"He was abandoned by his family? Why?" Rejat asked, grabbing a thick slice of bread as Brient cut the new loaf.

Stara eyed the Mirii with a curious intensity, then glancing at Elas and Tagar spoke on, "His family said he was touched by them wild ones."

"The mist ponies?" Morgana said wearily, her eyes slightly enlivened by the food and conversation.

"Ah, yes, young lady, them wild ones. They said he talked to them, so they left him in the Varan."

"Who found him?" Rejat glanced at Tagar. "You?"

He refilled his cup, then filled Elas'. "Yes, when I was working with the Huntsman Tor. We found Jess with a small herd of mountain horses. He was half starved, just a child, about ten years old. The horses seemed to protect him from any travelers. They almost wouldn't give him up." He offered a refill to Rejat who gladly accepted.

"Where was he from?" Morgana asked softly, struggling to stay awake while she nibbled on a piece of bread.

114

"He wouldn't tell us, but I think he's from the southland valleys. We never found out how long he was with the herd. Several months, I believe, but he won't talk about it." Tagar nudged Elas to look at her niece, nearly asleep at the table.

"I'll take care of her," Stara spoke up as Elas started to rise. "You finish with yer supper." She helped Morgana to her feet, while the young woman was trying to apologize for her sleepiness.

"Go to bed, Morgana. Stara will look after you well enough," Elas said, smiling at her niece's protestations.

"Sleep well, Morgana. We shall speak again tomorrow," Rejat added over her cup. She glanced at Elas. "Maybe we should set our guards around her in case 'them wild ones' come looking for her again."

Elas continued staring at the door well after Stara and Morgana were out of sight. "No, I don't think that will be necessary tonight. She is too exhausted to hear them anyway."

"I think she's blocking." Rejat glanced at the door, then turned back to her sister. "She seemed to close up shortly before we came to that tree. I think she's still closed."

Tagar shook his head, a puzzled look on his face. "I can't believe Tillan would do such a thing."

"Morgana has been closed for a long time," Elas said and turned back to the table before her. "I should have spoken sooner."

"She wouldn't have heard you. She wasn't ready to hear anyone till now." Rejat stared tiredly at the cup in her hand.

"What makes you say that?" Elas stifled a yawn.

"Her reaction to your, or rather, their speech,

about us." She glanced sideways at Brient, who listened with some interest.

Elas stared at Rejat, then at her stepson. She set her cup down carefully and asked, "Brient, what am I?"

He looked startled, then answered her. "You are Mirii, a Travelaar Healer."

"Do you know what this woman is?" Elas glanced across at her sister sitting beside him.

"She is Mirii also. Travelaar Healer?" He turned his gaze briefly to his father. Tagar smiled, his cup paused before his lips.

"Aza Har, Travelaar." Rejat locked her eyes on Elas.

"We do not keep secrets from Brient." She released her gaze from her sister and spoke gently, "He is as my own son, I will not keep my truth from him."

"And the others in your hold?" Rejat turned to Tagar.

"We have always welcomed the Mirii into this LandsHold, I would not have it any other way. Though in private. Our neighbors, including my brother, would be very difficult to deal with if we made our choices known."

Rejat snorted. "I'd say you were making small of that fact." Her eyes challenged his words.

"My people are taught the truth of the Mirii, not the frightened old lies of the elders," he continued, returning her cool gaze until she looked away.

The Mirii lowered her sight. "My apologies to you, Brient," she muttered, then looked up. "I have long avoided the people of the western valleys. In the past, I was not so fortunate to have met such a wise LandsHolder who educated his people as to the Hu'manity of the Mirii. Most prefer to believe their elder's talk." She turned to Elas and Tagar. "And my apologies to both of you for my skeptical and irritating ways. I shall try to keep a more open mind in the future."

Elas smiled. "Nonsense, Rejat. We love your irritating ways. It keeps us so amused." She laughed at her sister's renewed scowl, then offered to refill her cup. Rejat rolled her eyes and held her cup out, a tired smile at last returning to her face.

Tagar noisily placed his cup on the table and stood. "Well, I'm for bed. Will you join me now, wife? Or will you gossip more with your long-missed sister?" His bright smile was drawn by the fatigue in his face.

Elas leaned back wearily. "Let me show my long-missed sister where she can sleep and then I shall join you, husband." Her smile was also faded by the rest she longed for. She stood slowly as Brient started to clear the table and with an arm around Rejat's shoulder, led her out of the kitchen behind Tagar, to find her a bed for the night.

# Chapter 10

Untroubled by the dark dreams of the past, Morgana slept soundly, and far into the rising of the morning sun. Soft words caressed her awareness in the hazy light filtering through the small room's open window. She stirred slowly, enjoying the warm comforts of her bed and dreamily rubbed a hand across her eyes. The voices played above her again, flowing in and out of her mind, pulling her into wakefulness. She opened her eyes and gazed up at the ceiling above her. Sudden rainbows of light sparkled across the dark wood-beamed surface and danced around the room as a soft breeze stirred through the window. She turned to study what had created this marvelous display when she heard the door open and Stara shuffled into the room.

"Oh, I see yer awake now, are ye?" The old woman nodded at her smile and deposited her pack on the foot of the bed, then walked over to the window and pushed the shutters open wide. "I'll be bringing some washing water and towels, right quick. Yer Aunt and Her is waiting fer ye below, ta' have some breakfast with them," she said and turned to study her guest for a moment, then started for the door.

"Wait, Stara—why don't you like Rejat?" Morgana spoke up cautiously, watching the house steward's face. She had appeared to accept the Mirii's presence last night; why would she not use Rejat's name this morning?"

Stara halted and faced her at the foot of the bed, her hands firmly planted at her hips. "That woman is the coldest I've met. She means ye business, I expect, business that means none ta' me." She shook her head, her soft gray hair brushing her cheeks. "She is yer concern, not mine, but don't look fer na' tears from that one."

"Have you met her before then?"

"I've met that one before. Good she is, at what she chooses, but cold, that's all. We should na' be so cold. It's our place ta' feel, ta' know. She knows, but na' feels." She folded her arms before her. "She's one to be leaned on, but only so far as she chooses. She will see ye through the times good and bad, but she will na' allow yer heart to touch hers. She has closed hers to all, sometimes even to yer Aunt. I should na' be telling ye this, but I see the tired bones in ye, ye need yer sleep. She would na' give it ta' ye if Elas had na' spoken." She turned again to the door, then glanced back. "Don't worry, Elas'll take care of yer tears, even if Her won't."

Morgana watched her leave the room, disturbed by her words. What had made Rejat close her heart? And was she to be fully trusted? She started to pull her clothes out of her pack when Stara returned with a basin and pitcher of hot water and some towels flung over one shoulder. She placed them upon the small table next to the bed, then turned and handed the towels to Morgana.

"Hurry, Child, they're na' waiting well." Then

she shuffled out once more, closing the door behind her.

✳

"Let me talk to her first." Elas locked her pale blue eyes on Rejat's evasive copper ones. "She knows me, Rejat. She doesn't know you."

The red-haired Mirii stretched her long legs out from under the garden table and took another sip from her cup of lukewarm tajiz. Leaning back in her chair, her rangy body at ease for the first time in days, she gazed out over the tranquillity of her sister's garden. Small butterflies flitted over the radiant flowers and herbs of the kitchen garden, obviously a favorite place for her hostess, she noted, for her sister's psychic energy was everywhere. "You should have been an EarthSinger, Elaa."

"I don't have the talent. Stop changing the subject."

"Of course you do. You heard Morgana's tree, and your mark is all over your garden." She dropped her gaze into her half-filled cup.

"My garden is physical work, not psychic work. Besides, that cedarjinn tree was an Ancient; you would have heard it too if you'd come closer."

"Trees are not my talent," she replied, picking up a sweet roll to dip it in her tajiz and take a bite.

"You're still changing the subject." Elas poured herself more tajiz, then pushed the pitcher across the table to her sister as she looked up from her nearly empty cup.

"All right, Elas, you talk to her. But do it quickly, will you? Dayana won't wait forever." She filled her cup and took a long swallow.

"Dayana's sure it's Morgana?" Elas absently twisted a dark red garnet ring on her left hand.

"She showed me her face. It's her. I knew it the moment her vision was shared."

"But you haven't seen Morgana for years, since she was a child. How can you be so sure?"

"I just know. Dayana showed me more than just Morgana. She visioned her, you, the cedarjinn tree and that fool of a father of hers."

Elas looked out over her garden, silently contemplating the home she had made with Tagar. The place of Communion was so far away; she was not happy with the thought of being absent for almost a year. If only he could go with her.

Stara plopped a hot tray of spiced fruit bread on the table. "The young lady will be down shortly, Elaa," she said, breaking into her musing.

"Thank you, Stara. Has Tagar moved yet?"

"Na' that I've seen." The elder wiped her hands on the apron over her skirt. "Do ye wish me ta' move him?" A wry grin creased her aged face.

"No, let him sleep. Brient was all ready to go after him when I got up. Let me know when he wakes, though." She watched Stara rearrange the table then stroll back into the kitchen.

"She still doesn't like me." Rejat cut a piece of the hot bread and offered it to Elas, a wicked smile on her face.

"Sometimes I'm not too crazy about you either." She took the offer, then laughed at her sister's frown. "Remember last night's conversation?"

"After four cups of your Cladarian wine?"

"It was half water!"

"Still good stuff. Yes, I remember last night. Now who's changing the subject?" she smiled and cocked her head at the kitchen door behind Elas. *Morgana.*

She came through the door carrying a fresh pitcher of hot tajiz and a plate of egg pastry for her breakfast. Smiling shyly in greeting at the two women, she placed the pitcher near Rejat's cup and sat down next to her aunt.

"Good morning, Morgana. Did you sleep well?" Elas picked up a round yellowenn fruit and started peeling it. She noted her niece's clothes looked rumpled from her pack, but her face appeared refreshed from her dreamless night, her loose dark blond hair still damp from a recent washing.

"She slept perfectly well, can't you tell by her face?" Rejat smiled and offered Morgana a cup of tajiz.

She took the cup. "Thank you. Yes, I slept very well, Aunt Elas." She lowered her gaze to her plate.

"Eat, Morgana. I know how long it's been. Last night doesn't count." Elas glanced distractedly at her sister.

"My name is Rejat, Morgana. You can call me that," she said, returning Elas' glare. "Well, you didn't formally introduce us yesterday."

"Formally? Sorry, I'm surprised you noticed. Shall I correct the mistake now? Very well." Elas rose from the table and looked at her niece.

"Morgana, may I offer to present my beloved half-sister, Rejat Tala-Lael, Aza Har Travelaar Mirii, of the Lasah Hawk Hold." She turned to her sister. "Rejat, may I offer to present my beloved niece, Morgana, daughter of Brea and Tillan, Master of the Brejjard LandsHold, of the Kesh River Valley."

Rejat raised her cup. "I welcome you, Morgana."

Morgana's eyes met hers. "I welcome you, Rejat, lady of my vision."

The red-haired Mirii regarded her with slight irritation in her gaze. "So, you remember my visit?"

Morgana pulled out the red tassel and cloth strip from her skirt pocket, holding them in her open palm before her. "Are these yours?"

Rejat's face went blank, then she plucked the items from Morgana's hand. "Yes, but how did you get them?"

"The tassel was on my tree."

Rejat held the tassel up and looked at Elas. "Can you tell me how a *forced visioning* can leave physical remains?"

She shook her head, the surprise also in her eyes. "Maybe you are better at it than you know."

Rejat snorted. "In the condition Stil was in? I'm good, but not that good!" She dropped the tassel on the table. "Where did you find this?" She waived the strip of cloth.

"On the fisher's island, near the middle in a large thicket. I was hiding from some men and I sort of stumbled across it."

"What men?" Elas and Rejat said at once, their words almost matched.

"Foresters, I think. On horses. They were riding the south bank trail, looking for something," she looked at Rejat, her eyes widening. "You! They were looking for you!"

The Mirii leaned across the table towards her. "Show me!" she hissed, then glared at Elas. "I'm sorry, but this is too important!"

Morgana pushed her meal aside. "Tell me what to do," she said and swallowed nervously.

"Close your eyes, Child, I won't hurt you." Rejat leaned closer and placed her hand on the young woman's temple. "Show me what you saw." Her scan was swift as Morgana concentrated on replaying the images of the two men at the river. She released her and sat back, her eyes dark. "Those are not Foresters. They're part of the group who've been trailing us." She leaned her elbows on the table and began twisting a lock of her hair, staring off into the garden.

Morgana blinked. She had felt only the briefest of contact with the Mirii woman. She turned to her aunt. "Can you see who they are?"

Elas leaned close and placed her hand on Morgana's brow. Again the scan was swift. "No, I've never seen these men. They do wear the garb of Foresters, though."

"Well, they're not. They handle weapons too well for Foresters," Rejat replied, picking up her cup again.

"When did they start following you?"

"In the Varan, near the old Trader's Pass. I nearly fell across them," she said, her scowl deepening. "I wasn't paying attention, I was scanning back for any followers; you know what that pass is like, I didn't see them until too late."

Morgana slowly resumed her meal as she listened. She had never met anyone who had crossed the Varan on the old trail before and had a growing feeling that she needed to pay close attention to the Mirii's words.

Elas stared at the fruit she had just peeled. "Do you have any idea who these men really are?"

Rejat closed her eyes. "No. It could've been just a coincidence, they may have just been marauders. The greeting we gave them could have caused them to pursue us." She leaned back and crossed her arms in front of her, a sour look playing across her face. "They won't forget us for quite some time; I had to take out two of them."

Elas stared at her. "Aza Har, you killed two?" she whispered, her face stricken.

Rejat's gaze met hers. "I had no choice, they would have killed us."

"And they followed you?"

"Yes," she sighed. "and were fortunately unsuccessful, though not from lack of trying. Stil was hurt. "

"You were hurt also."

"But not as bad. We had to fight, but with Stil hurt, we had to run. And they were carrying Keethra blades." She stared angrily at the table. "Lost my long blade in the process."

Morgana looked up from her plate. "Keethra? What is that?"

Rejat flicked a glance at her innocent question and began absently rubbing her left shoulder. "It is steel, coated with a sulfurous mixture of herbs, minerals and oils." With a cutting motion she dropped her hand to the table. "On a dagger or sword it permits the weapon to penetrate our shields. And some carry it as a protection against the Azerii."

Elas shook her head. "Enough of that for now. Since Morgana saw them we are at least forewarned. We shall keep a broad scan out in the future." She turned to her niece as she finished her plate. "We have other matters to discuss. Have you had enough breakfast, Morgana? Rejat?" At their nods she continued. "Good, why don't we go sit in some shade in the garden. I think it's going to be another warm day." She rose from the table carrying her cup and taking the pitcher of tajiz and began walking to her garden. Rejat and Morgana followed, Rejat grabbing her cup and the plate of still warm bread. Elas led them to a pair of benches under a large spreading tree in the center of the garden, the benches angled to view the main house and the rolling mountains beyond.

"I still say you should have been an Earth-Singer, Elas," Rejat said as she placed her cup and the plate on one of the benches, her gaze covering the glorious landscape.

Her sister smiled. "Yes, well, it's not my true talent, but I do love this place." She looked out over the garden, feeling her pride in its splendor. The garden centered around a large willowarr tree. A spiral path of pebbles flowed out around it, with four stone walks matching the four directions reaching out from the tree at the garden's heart. The herbs, flowers and stones radiated with her essence, the air and soil felt sacred and powerful.

Rejat laid a hand on the gnarled trunk of the tree. "Was this here?"

Elas nodded. "Yes, he's an Ancient One. I think Tagar's father had the EarthKeeper talent. He preferred this hold over his own, in his last years."

Morgana set her cup down on the bench next to Rejat's and reached out to place her hands on the cool brown bark of the tree. She abruptly pulled back, then touched the tree again. "He laughed!" she said, a joyous look on her face.

"Yes, he does that sometimes." Elas placed the pitcher beside the other cups, then moved to the other bench. She sat down and patted the stone surface beside her. Morgana impulsively hugged the old tree then walked over to sit beside her.

Rejat strolled to the other bench and sat beside

their cups. "He's a grand one, Elaa. Sometimes, I salute your choices."

"Do you mean the tree, or Tagar?" she grinned.

She crossed her arms, a grin of resignation plying her face. "All right, both. Are you satisfied?"

Elas laughed. "Someday I'll tell you about some of my other choices."

They bantered on a little while longer until Elas noted Stara was through clearing the garden table. Sipping at her tajiz, she took her niece's hand to mind speak. *Morgana?*

The young woman shivered at the voice in her head and stared at her aunt. "Aunt Elas?" she whispered. "How did you do that?"

Elas lowered her cup and turned to her. *Morgana, it is called Mind Speech. My thoughts touching yours to communicate. You can do this also,* her aunt sent, her eyes never leaving her niece's face.

"I can—mind speak?" she said in wonder.

"Yes. We shall teach you," Elas replied aloud. "But right now I want you to listen carefully. You have a great choice ahead of you. A very wonderful choice, but also a difficult one. You must listen with both your head and heart." She released her hand.

"I will try." Morgana's face was full of awe for her aunt's abilities.

"Morgana, tell me of your visions. Your dreams you've had lately."

"My dreams?" she hesitated, remembering the blackness.

"Yes, I know you've had them. Please don't ask me how I know, I'll tell you later. Please, we need to know." She glanced briefly at her sister.

"You may have prophecy talent, Morgana," Rejat said with more compassion than her usual tone.

"Prophecy? But they're just dreams, or nightmares..." her voice trailed off.

Elas took her hand again. "Show us the nightmare. We can help you so it won't frighten you so much in the remembering." Her aunt nodded to her sister and Rejat rose to sit on the ground in front of Morgana, taking her other hand.

Morgana looked down at the red-haired Mirii. Rejat's copper eyes shown like fire, but a cold one, she thought, remembering Stara's words.

*She doesn't understand me, Morgana.* Rejat's cool thoughts flowed over her. *I am here to help you.*

Morgana turned back to her aunt. "What do I do?"

"Just like before, only relax," Elas' words lifted her apprehensions. "Remember the night of your dream. Remember where you were. Let the dream begin slowly."

She took a deep breath, closing her eyes and releasing her mind to flow into the memory of the dream. She was faintly aware of the presence of other minds and felt strangely detached as the dream began. Her empty home and the voices, the enveloping darkness, her family standing outside like death, the Others calling her, warning her and the plume of Blackness claiming her as its own, then truth like a fiery sword shattering the vision like glass.

Morgana's eyes popped open, the sudden brightness of the garden forcing her to shut them just as quickly. Her companions exchanged glances that echoed the fear they held inside.

Rejat dropped Morgana's hand and stood,

stepping away to face the distant mountains. "She has the talent, Lady of Mists, *does she have the talent!*" she swore and rubbed her fists across her eyes.

Elas still held Morgana's hand, scanning for anything she may have missed. Her niece opened her eyes again, squinting at the sunlight. With her free hand she placed her cup in Morgana's hand. "Here, it's cold, but drink it anyway." She glanced at her sister's rigid back, then rose somewhat shakily and moved to her side.

Rejat's hand shot out to grab her wrist. *It's Dayana's Vision! It's the same as she showed me!* her mind voice shouted roughly. *That's why I knew it was her! Only Dayana saw you in the Vision too!*

*The Awakening is at hand.* Elas sent coldly.

Rejat turned and stared at her. *Do you feel it too?*

*Yes.*

*But how can this be? The Covenant promised us it would hold forever!*

"The Covenant is wrong, Rejat," Elas said abruptly, breaking their mind link and turning back to her niece who watched them with questioning eyes. "I'm sorry, Morgana. We didn't mean to desert you. Your vision was very strong."

Rejat swore again, then sat on the other bench, staring off moodily over the garden.

Morgana took a deep breath. "What does it mean?"

"It means you have the talent." Elas sat next to her. "It means that your choices are even more difficult."

"What are my choices?"

Elas stared at the trees beyond the garden. "To

come with us to Communion, to learn of your other talents. To join the Mirii."

"Or?" her voice lowered softly.

Elas turned to study Morgana's eyes. "To stay here, in the valley and be what your society wants. To deny who you are."

Morgana shifted her gaze to the ground in front of her. "I can't stay in the valley. My father will make me marry a man I don't want."

"Your father can't make you do anything, Morgana." Rejat's voice was fuming with irritation. "Right now he doesn't even know where you are."

"But if I stay here," she glanced at her aunt, "he'll find out, and—"

"I have to go to Communion, Morgana. I can't protect you from your father." Elas clasped her hand again. "Do you really want to run from him all your life?"

Morgana sighed, then gazed up at Rejat. She would know what to do, she thought. "I think I've been running from him for so long that I didn't know what else to do. I may as well start over by going with you and finding out where I belong. I certainly never fit in here."

Rejat's smile was hard. "I knew there was some fire in her."

Elas suppressed her elation for a moment longer. "Communion is a long way from here. It will not be an easy journey."

"Where is it?"

"Communion is held on the Sumarkh Plateau, well beyond the Varan Mountains."

Morgana's eyes went wide. "Where the Vondarii live? With the Lii horses?"

"Yes, they roam the plateau. You've heard of

them?" Elas smiled thoughtfully at her niece's sudden interest. If she knew something of their destination, it might make their journey easier.

Morgana nodded, her excitement childlike in its simplicity. "I met someone once, who told me about the Vondarii and their horses. He was very—well—he knew a lot about them," she hedged off, looking slightly embarrassed.

"Well, Morgana, so you have…"

"Rejat!" Elas said sharply, catching her niece's reddened face. "I remember the boy, Morgana. You mentioned him to me a long time ago." She watched her sister's smirk out of the corner of her eye. "Anyway, it is a long journey and we must be there by the Autumn Equinox."

"I'll go, Elas. When do we leave?"

"We'll need a few days here to prepare, then we must move quickly," she replied, glancing again at her sister.

"We have much to teach you," Rejat added, her voice sounding distant as she watched the younger woman.

"I think I have much to learn," Morgana answered her, turning her gaze to the Varan Mountains behind her aunt's home.

# Chapter 11

Tagar rolled to his back and slowly opened his eyes toward the light slipping in through the window's shutters. The sunlit angles told him it was well past his usual time of arising. Probably past noon, he thought as he rubbed his hand over his eyes. He glanced over at Elas' side of the bed and brushed his hand under the light blanket. The coolness told him of her long absence. He sighed and glanced up at the ceiling. Near the window a soft shimmer of light hovered, playing above the window frame.

"Morning, Brealyth," he said to the shimmer. For a moment it stopped, then skittered around the room, at last coming to rest at the door, as if waiting for someone to open it. He sat up, grinning at the Azerii's antics. "Tell Elas I'm finally getting up," he said as he pulled a bed robe around his broad shoulders, running his hand through his hair.

The Azerii shimmered briefly into a small girl-child form in front of the door. She threw him a reproachful look, then silently laughed at his returning false scowl. Before his oft flung boot hit the door she was gone.

He smiled at her playful game. Remembering her mistress' impending departure soon brushed his

132

smile away, as he stood and walked to the window. Too soon, he thought as he opened the shutters, she will have to go and for such a long time. Almost a year, she had told him. The journey was long and sometimes difficult. Dangerous for a woman, even more for a Mirii Healer. "I will not be alone," she had reminded him. There were others she would join once out of the valleys. "I will not be with you," he had replied, sadness filling his voice. *You are always with me,* she returned with her gentle mind voice. *Wherever I am, you are always with me.* Her strong yet gentle touch had awakened his fire even though they were both exhausted from the strenuous journey behind them. She echoed his passion, her mind voice bringing their souls even closer as their physical bodies embraced.

Tagar gazed out over the garden of the hold as he warmly reflected upon their evening's pleasures. The muted voices of Elas, Rejat and Morgana brought him out of his contemplation, just as Stara's sharp knock and entrance with hot water and towels brought his attention back into the room. From the window he greeted his house steward, ignoring her intrusive movements but listening to her impish chatter as she fussed about Brealyth's morning activities. Stara and Brealyth also played the game; the Azerii amazing the elder woman with light displays of varying intensity, then appearing in odd locations as she held hu'man form, usually of a girl with wild gray eyes and silvery-blond hair, or of a woman resembling Elas. Stara had rid herself of any fears of the Azerii a long time go through the loving playfulness of Brealyth's actions.

"Yer breakfast is past waiting fer yer sleepfulness. Would ye prefer some 'ta else fer lunch?"

"Just some hot tajiz will help for now, Stara,"
he replied, gazing back at her from the window ledge.
"Move yerself down and it'll be waiting fer ye,"
she replied, and shot him a quick grin as she turned
and left the room.

✳

Morgana sat beneath the ancient tree gazing at
the mountains while Elas and Rejat discussed their
journey. Her thoughts fell away from their conversation as she traced the distant heights. The emerald
slopes seemed to beckon her forward and she suddenly wondered what it would be like to fly above
them. She began to imagine herself as a great bird
soaring effortlessly over the abundant forests, past
cliff and meadow, catching mirrored glints of deep
forest pools and crashing white-water falls. She saw a
brilliant jewel of a lake, nestled at the foot of an immense crescent-shaped cliff whose silvered walls arch-
ed upwards around blue-green depths. She was glid-
ing down for a closer look when a piercing screech
wrenched her awareness back to her surroundings.

Morgana shook her head. She felt strangely
remote, as if part of her were still circling above the
beautiful lake. Her eyes unfocused, she blinked several
times before her vision cleared enough for her to gaze
up at a very angry Rejat and a troubled Elas standing
over her.

"What is it? What was that noise?" Her eyes
darted from one to the other.

"It was me!" Rejat snapped. "It is forbidden for
any but Mirii to gaze at the Eye of the Lady!" she
hissed.

Morgana frowned, puzzled. "I was just day

dreaming, like when I'm at my tr—the river." She turned to her aunt. "I don't understand, what happened?"

Elas shook her head. "I'm not sure I understand either, but apparently you were scanning the Eye, though how you got that far without an Azerii is beyond me."

Rejat swore under her breath, still glaring at Morgana, then spoke briskly, "How did you find it? How did you scan at all?"

"Scanning? What do you mean?" Morgana shook her head again. "I was just imagining myself as a bird, flying over the mountains, when I saw the lake; the Eye?" She glanced at her aunt for support. "Was that wrong? How did I find it? Why is it so important?"

Elas stepped back from her at the sound of footsteps coming toward them, forcing herself to relax. "We will have to discuss it later, Morgana. Just don't do that again without warning us first." She turned just as Tagar entered the circle, and smiled in response to his presence. Rejat turned away abruptly and moved a pace away to control her own emotions.

Morgana stood, greeting her uncle with a smile, while trying to calm her still-pounding heart. Rejat's screech continued to echo in her ears, though she suspected no one but herself and Elas had heard it. She decided she would have to wait sometime before she could get anymore answers to her questions, but the first one she was going to ask was why did she upset Rejat so much? And was this a prelude to the journey before them? She did not relish the idea of always being the focus of Rejat's anger on what looked to be a long and difficult trip.

135

✳

"Of all the wrecking!" Rejat spouted, her hands locked firmly at her slim waist as she paced before the old tree.

Elas frowned at her rigid movements. "Rejat, sit down. You're avoiding the issue. Your anger is totally misplaced. Morgana did not scan the Eye just to annoy you. She wasn't even aware she could do it!"

The red-clad Mirii suddenly stopped to turn and face her sister. "Then can you tell me how she found the Eye if she didn't know how to scan?"

"That's not the point. The scan could have led her anywhere if she truly thought she was imagining it. Maybe it wasn't really a scan." Elas looked troubled again. "Maybe it was her Visioning."

"Don't you think I know the difference between a scan and a vision?" Rejat snarled.

Elas' eyes flashed her anger back at her Mirii sister. "Of course, and I know the difference too, but this time it was different somehow. Morgana wouldn't lie about this; why are you so upset?"

The red-haired woman crossed her arms and half turned from her sister to gaze out over the hold. Moments before, Tagar, sensing the tension between them, had offered to take Morgana around the hold since it had been a few years since her last visit. Both women had almost audibly sighed in relief when she had gone, and launched into a renewed discussion of Morgana's flowering abilities.

"Why do you think it was not a scan?" Rejat still glared at the mountains as if they were responsible for the young woman's waywardness.

"I don't know, it just felt different, almost like she was being led rather than searching. But I didn't sense any other presence," she added hastily at her sister's quick look. "Besides, how could she scan, let alone even that far, without an Azerii?"

"But you don't think it was a vision either?"

"No, it wasn't the same as any I've ever had, or anyone else's that I've been witness to."

Rejat sighed, stubbornly slipping off her anger. She dropped her hands and walked over to the pitcher of tajiz, pouring herself another cup, then sitting beside Elas. "If she is showing her talents this soon and this strong, how are we ever going to get her to Communion in time? She will have every wild Azerii batting at her 'til she can't see straight, and we'll be going crazy trying to keep her from meld."

Elas picked up her cup and stared into it. "Then we have to teach her to shield herself, or," she glanced up at Rejat's expectant look, "we'll shield her with the Protection Ceremony."

"We'll teach her to shield," Rejat said flatly.

*

The rest of the day went smoothly for Morgana as her uncle took her around his LandsHold. She soon moved the brief discussion of her awkward new talent to the hindmost corner of her thoughts. She enjoyed visiting the various scenes of her uncle's home; though similar to her father's hold, there seemed a wider variance to the people who lived on these lands. Her father demanded respect from his holders. Tagar simply received it. His hold people were at ease with their HoldMaster. She had always felt the distance between her father and his people.

"Why do you and Elas have a House Steward?" she suddenly asked him as they were walking back to the main house late in the afternoon.

Tagar smiled, "And your father doesn't."

Morgana frowned slightly, "My mother says she has no need of a House Steward, she prefers to run her own home. She does seem to enjoy most of her work, especially cooking, but sometimes I think she could have more help. I never asked Father about it. My sister and I always help."

"That's probably why you never had a House Steward," he replied, waiving at two young hold boys playing in the long grass along the path before them. The boys waived back, then scurried on ahead, following a large dog running up and down the path chasing imaginary sticks they pretended to throw.

She thought about his response. Her father did have a hold steward. Rican lived in a small house with his family not far from the main house, and though her father worked regularly with his steward, she did not recall his ever setting foot in the main house. She wondered why. If her father did not trust him why did he bother to employ him at all?

Tagar interrupted her thoughts. "Elas was raised in the Mirii holds; she has never been like any of the women of the valleys. I'm not sure she worked long in the kitchens of their holds." He smiled again at his niece's bemused look.

"So that's why she's always complaining about my mother spending so much time on her hold duties? Who works in the kitchens of the Mirii holds? Or don't they have any kitchens?"

Tagar laughed at her words. "From what she has told me, I know they certainly do have kitchens. But their holds are managed differently than ours. You will have to ask her or Rejat about how they're run."

She glanced away at his mention of the red-haired Mirii. She scooped up a small stone and tossed it into the trees. He noticed her change of mood. "Don't let Rejat frighten you. She just feels out of place here. She's been given a task she didn't want and she's never been patient with anyone who is not Mirii."

His niece stopped abruptly in the middle of the path. Tagar turned to face her, watching her eyes for the troubling emotion that she held inside. "Why is she so angry with me?" she said softly, turning her face away from his piercing gaze.

"I don't think she's angry with you. I think she's worried about this journey to Communion. And her own visions." He stepped closer and placed his hand on her shoulder.

She looked up at him. "Her visions? Not mine?"

He squeezed her shoulder. "You aren't the only one with the frightening visions. Elas told me Rejat had a distressing vision also, the morning after we picked her up at the fisher's dam. We were at the Brenan LandsHold, the day after your sister's betrothal feast."

Morgana's eyes seemed to look through him. "And I didn't come when she asked for my help." Her voice carried a vein of guilt.

Tagar pulled her close to embrace her. "Stop right there, Morgana. Rejat is fine, here and now, that is all that matters. You gave Elas the message and she understood where you did not. There is no need to blame yourself. Rejat did not know we would be coming to your father's hold. She simply reached out for you first because you were closest at the time." He stepped back and tilted her chin up to look her in the eyes. She did not look away.

"Thank you, Uncle Tagar," she said quietly and brushed his hand with her own as they resumed their walk back to the main house.

✳

The evening meal at her uncle's hold proved to be very different from the same meal at her father's. Where Tillan had required customary solemnity at the day's end, this supper was a repeat of their previous late night excursion into the kitchen. They were provided with plenty of good fare and the conversation flowed across the table. Morgana listened in delight as she watched and shyly participated in the meal's thriving discourse, which focused mostly around Brient pulling odd bits of information from Tagar and Elas about their trip and his answers to his father about the hold management in their absence. At the close of the meal Stara shooed everyone out of the kitchen, the women stepping out to the garden table to enjoy the early evening and further discuss their plans, while Brient dragged his father off to the gathering room to talk more of hold affairs.

"Brient certainly is enthusiastic about his hold-crafting," Rejat said. She stood at the far side of the table, gazing back at the house and yard, her arms folded loosely across her chest as she cradled her cup of tajiz in one hand.

"He would like to see Tagar begin trading more with other holds outside of the northern valleys. I think Brient wants our hold to become as well known as some of the larger holds in the Southlands." Elas sat down with her back to the house and looked over her garden past her sister. She began watching

140

her niece who stood beside her, focusing on the fading sunlit mountains.

*Morgana, tell me what you see,* she pushed her mind voice, brushing her niece's awareness.

Morgana started and turned to her. "I'm sorry, I was just looking at the mountains," she said and pulled a chair back from the table to sit beside her aunt.

Elas smiled and sipped her hot tajiz. "Look at the mountains again. Focus on the highest ridge, the one with the cliffs. Tell me what you see."

Morgana took a deep breath and stared at the golden cliffs. She started to feel as if she were withdrawing from her surroundings, like being pulled into a funnel and the funnel's narrow end was the cliff face beyond. Suddenly her view exploded out before the sun drenched wall. Panic shot through her as she found herself aloft above a great abyss of rock and dark forest at a terrifying height. An unsounded scream echoed through her mind as she grasped at empty air around her, until just as abruptly she was yanked back from the floating void to find she was clutching the table edge with Rejat and Elas standing next to her, their hands on her head and shoulders.

She stared at her hands, her knuckles white as she gripped the table linen. A sob burst through her, releasing the anger and pain of the past few days, mixed with the confusion of her new-found abilities which she was now beginning to see with more trepidation than excitement. The two women let her tears run freely, and linked with her thoughts, they soothed the frightened young woman, *Release the anger, Morgana,* Rejat's mind brushed across her pain. *Release your fears,* her aunt echoed with her gentle mind touch, each sharing to lift the burdens that she had placed upon herself. When her sobs finally stopped, she raised her eyes to them. Both Mirii wore their Azerii auras, glowing gently silver in the fading light, their faces full of compassion.

"What ha-happened to m-me?" she stuttered, her gaze once more locked on her aunt.

"You threw your awareness out over the cliffs," Elas said gently. "I'm not sure how, but it was much more than a scan this time."

She turned to Rejat. "Can you do this also?"

Rejat smiled, her surprise evident in her eyes. "No, not like that I can't," then shook her head as if something had tickled her ear. "Well, almost, but not with that much distance or accuracy. And not without assistance."

"Like what happened this afternoon?" she asked hesitantly.

"Well, yes. Sorry I yelled at you, you just surprised me. You did a scan of sorts. I just didn't expect it."

"How? How did I see—what do you call it, scan? No one taught me." Morgana leaned back in her chair, wrapping her arms about her tightly, her gaze shifting from one to the other.

Elas released her Azerii first, sighing as the silver light dimmed around her. "We don't know for certain. Your talents are manifesting very rapidly, faster than we expected. We don't know what all of your abilities will be. We are just as amazed as you are." She rose from the table to light a wall lamp beside the kitchen door.

Rejat sat at her right and placed her hand on Morgana's shoulder again. "We need to know what your talents are as soon as possible, or this journey is going to become very difficult." She placed her other hand on the table. As her Azerii light faded, she cupped her hand above the table cloth and a soft light started glowing between her fingers. When she moved her hand away a small ball of light remained, casting a soft glow that illuminated their faces.

Morgana stared at the curious light. "How did you do that?" she whispered. At Rejat's shrug she turned to her aunt who sat beside her again.

"Why are my—talents—appearing so fast? I was not aware I even had any abilities like this."

Elas' expression shifted in consideration. "I suspect it's because you've accepted your new choices."

"What? I don't understand."

"Sometimes, when you accept something new into your life, the Lady gives you more than you ever dreamed of."

"Certainly more than we're prepared for," Rejat added, a bemused grin flitting across her face.

Morgana stared at the glowing sphere on the table. "But, if my talents are going to cause problems for everyone, then how am I going to be able to go with you to Communion? Won't the mist ponies," she hesitated as she searched for the right words, "I mean the Azerii, be following me?" Her concern stood plainly in her face.

Rejat nodded, "Yes, we have discussed that problem. The wild Azerii, or mist ponies as you call them, can be such pests at times. Playful, but still pests." She folded her hands on the table before her, then leaning forward she added, "We shall teach you to shield yourself. It's not difficult, but it requires practice and an awareness of your surroundings. It will keep most of them at bay, though some will still try to distract you."

"How?"

"The wild Azerii see us as playmates, Morgana. They see a shielded Hu'man as a challenge. They will try to provoke a response, and when you are shielding, you aren't as likely to return the response they want."

"What's the response?"

"It's exactly what you did the night you left your father's hold. To follow them. If any are not ready to meld, they will lead you to one who is, away from any interference by other Hu'mans or Mirii and their Meld Azerii. It's a game to them."

"Ready to meld? What do you mean?" A shiver slipped through Morgana.

Rejat's eyes locked on hers. "Meld—merging your awareness with an Unnamed Azerii, and if you are not prepared," she paused, her eyes never leaving Morgana's face, "the Azerii could force their awareness on you."

"Then they were leading me upriver to..." she trailed off as she thought about what could have happened.

"Yes, we believe they were leading you to one ready to meld, though we don't know why they stopped, unless the Kir-Latt was another distraction?" Rejat turned and gazed thoughtfully at her sister.

"Yes, the Kir-Latt," Elas echoed, "why would one allow itself to be used that way?"

Rejat shifted uneasily in her seat. "It must have been the Azerii in my vision. It tried to control the Kir-Latt and it broke contact long enough to drive Morgana toward us."

"Your vision, Rejat, how is it connected with mine?" Morgana asked with some uneasiness.

The Mirii leaned her forehead on her upraised

hands. She took a deep breath, her own apprehensions evident in her posture. "I believe we saw the same Dark Azerii in our visions, a very powerful Unnamed One."

"Where is this Azerii now?"

"With all the others. They are all from the same source, Morgana. Until they are joined in meld with a Hu'man, they are all part of the Unnamed, the whole." Rejat turned her gaze toward her sister again. "I sincerely hope this one is still held by the power that holds all of them. At least that's what the Covenant tells us."

Elas snapped her head up. "The Covenant, what did they say about it?"

"Something about their breaking free," Rejat replied distantly.

"The wild Azerii? But aren't they already free?" Morgana's glance flicked between the two women.

"The mist ponies, as most Hu'mans call them, are like children," Rejat leaned back and placed her hands flat on the table. "They are what we call wild; unruly, fractious and uncontrollable. Free beings who come and go as they please. They are totally savage as far as the Hu'mans are concerned."

"And the Azerii ready to meld?"

"Are of the same energy." She raised her hand. Another glowing sphere quickly took shape upon her open palm, identical to the first. "They are indistinguishable. The time of meld is so swift that even after all the generations the Mirii have been in existence, we still can't separate those Azerii ready for meld."

"Then, why haven't I—'melded' before now?" Morgana said, confused by Rejat's words.

Elas spoke softly, "Because of the Covenant

and the power that holds the Azerii from forcing meld." She held up her hand that wore the garnet ring. "Each year the Azerii who are ready for meld, wait at certain places for the Mirii to bring the Chosen Talents who have been prepared. This ring, called the Barii Ring, represents the joining of all the Mirii with the power of the Covenant."

"And the Eye of the Lady?"

"The Eye is one of the places where the melding ceremony is held. You must not speak of it with any who are not Mirii." Rejat's voice carried a tone of commanding reverence.

"And Communion?"

"Is the time." Elas took a sip from her cup, her eyes still on her ring. "That is why we must leave soon and travel quickly. We must join the other Mirii before Communion."

Rejat closed her hand, extinguishing the second sphere. "We may not have time, Elas. Morgana may be ready now."

"What do I have to know to be ready for meld?"

"It's not just a matter of lessons or rules, Morgana." Elas clasped her niece's hand in her own. "The Azerii meld with a Hu'man because of what we are— physical beings. We experience sensations that they can imagine, but not feel. They cannot touch the earth, they can only know it is there. They cannot feel love, pain, joy, all that life here offers. So they desire it through the meld with a Hu'man."

"You must be able to choose your Azerii," Rejat held up her left hand, a garnet ring almost identical to her sister's glowing brightly on her third finger. "You must know your Azerii and not allow yourself to be taken by one who would rule your body. You are

146

the life giver, Morgana, not the Azerii. Through meld you will give physical form to your Azerii, and it will give of its abilities to you."

"Enough of this for now," Elas said suddenly. "We must teach you to shield. It's getting late and we have much to do tomorrow." She rose and pulled Morgana to her feet.

# Chapter 12

"Concentrate, Morgana. You must hold the shield around you like a wall, a wall of blue fire that neutralizes all energy that is thrust upon you." Elas sat on one of the benches under the willowarr tree in her garden. A glowing sphere beside her cast eerie shadows around her and the young woman facing her. Rejat sat on the other bench, monitoring Morgana's first shielding attempt.

*She is doing well, Elas,* Rejat's thought slipped through her concentration, *as if she has done this all her life.*

*On some level she has,* Elas returned, then refocused on her niece. She suspected Morgana had been shielding around her father for a very long time. *Tillan doesn't allow much freedom in his hold,* she thought to herself as she watched the silent woman before her.

Morgana stood rigid, her eyes tightly closed as she struggled to see the blue wall she had been told to visualize. Flaring images seemed to bounce around behind her eyelids, mocking her efforts.

"Breathe, Morgana, don't hold your breath." Elas watched her straining body gasp for the absent breath, and a slight relaxing of her shoulders came with the release. "Build your shield slowly, don't force the image. If you can't see it in your mind, just know that it is there. Believe in your intent, that is all that is required now."

Elas stood and slowly began to walk around her niece. She could feel and see her shield now. Rejat was right, it was as if Morgana had been doing this for years. The shield wavered above her head, the blue wall not quite forming the proper seal over her crown. She raised her arms and softened it into completion.

Morgana suddenly gasped. In her mind she saw her shield! With her aunt's assistance the image had finally formed behind her eyes. A cool shimmering wall of bright blue fire surrounded her body from the ground to over her head, extending a short distance around her. She opened her eyes as she reached out her hand to tentatively touch her shield, but with her eyes open it was not discernible. Closing her eyes once more, she sensed that her shield extended out beyond her reaching hand.

Elas stepped in front of her as she opened her eyes again, a shy smile on her face as her aunt nodded her approval.

"Did you look beneath your feet?"

Rejat's features were amused at Morgana's swift doubtful glance from her aunt to her and then to the ground. She closed her eyes once more. Looking inward, she saw her shield firmly in place in the earth beneath her feet. She breathed a sigh of relief as she opened her eyes to smile at Rejat, "I believe my shield is complete," then looked at Elas' affirming expression.

Her aunt laughed softly. "Now that you have your shield, you must know how to hold it and release it." She sat down once more facing Morgana. "Holding a shield against the wild Azerii can be a challenge to any Mirii, but especially to an untrained Talent. They will pester you unmercifully to get you to respond in any way." She motioned for her to sit beside her. Morgana started to move, then stopped to see if her shield went with her.

The two Mirii laughed. "I'm sorry, but you must realize it is your shield, so of course it moves when you do," Rejat laughed, "Don't be upset, Morgana, Elas and I both wondered the same thing when we learned to shield for the first time."

Elas took Morgana's hand and pulled her beside her. "I just wanted you to experience your shield standing up first. Now I want you to lower your shield, then raise it again next to me. I'm going to raise mine, so be aware when our shields touch, of what it feels like." She let go of her hand.

Morgana closed her eyes, seeing her shield around her. How do I lower my shield? With her thought the blue fire around her slowly dimmed and faded from her inner sight. Startled at the ease of releasing it she almost didn't notice Elas raising her shield until an icy tingle formed beside her, blocking out the warmth of her aunt's presence. Morgana hastily built her own wall around herself once again, this time the shield appearing completely and she felt a prickly sensation on her left as their shields met.

Another presence began tingling her shield on her right. She opened her eyes to look and saw a man sitting beside her, Rejat behind him, smiling over his shoulder. She jumped to her feet, startled by the stranger's appearance.

Elas turned to Rejat and said smoothly, "Will you kindly ask Stillyth to behave himself? Either that or introduce him to Morgana."

The red-haired Mirii laughed and hugged the man's shoulders. "Morgana, this is my Azerii, Stillyth. He was just curious to know if you could feel his presence. I'd say you did, wouldn't you?" She winked at her sister.

Morgana took a step toward him. "You didn't tell me the Azerii could look like people, Elas." She studied him closely, and he returned her gaze with equal interest. Dark curly brown hair framing his lean face, he had the same penetrating dark copper eyes as Rejat and was clothed in a dark red tunic, trousers and boots similar to his Mirii.

"Get any closer and your shield will push him over, Morgana," Rejat said, watching her move within an arm's length of her Azerii.

"The Azerii can take any form they choose," Elas spoke up as her Azerii appeared behind her in full light body. "This is Brealyth."

Morgana turned to face her aunt's Azerii who shifted from her starlight form to that of a small wild-eyed girl, then an adult woman closely resembling Elas, dressed in a long scarlet gown. She stood calmly, a slight smile caressing her features.

Morgana glanced back at Rejat and Stillyth. "Can I touch them? I couldn't touch the mist—wild Azerii, my hand passed right through them." She looked at her aunt for permission.

Elas nodded, "Only when they or their Mirii permit it. In physical appearing forms, the Meld Azerii are as solid as you and I." She looked at her Azerii who still smiled gently at her niece, then Brealyth walked forward and held out her hands.

Morgana took the Azerii's hands in her own. They felt as real and as comforting as her aunt's. She turned back to Rejat. Stillyth laughed soundlessly at his Mirii's inner words, then rose to offer his hands as well. Again, the feeling of solid warmth flowed from the Azerii's touch. Morgana released his hands and he stepped back to stand beside Rejat.

"You dropped your shield," Rejat said flatly, an ironic glint in her eyes.

"What? I—oh, how did I drop my shield?" Her cheeks suddenly reddened. She closed her eyes and looked, Rejat was right.

"That is one of the ways the wild Azerii get their response, Morgana. You must be aware of the games they can play." Elas stood, releasing her shield and put her arm around her niece's shoulders. "Enough for now, we have more work to do tomorrow."

✳

Morgana sat on the edge of her bed, a candle flickering beside her. The house was very quiet. Through the partly open shutters she could hear the calling of a night bird in the moonlit forest. She had been practicing shielding, each time the blue wall appearing and disappearing faster than before. She could feel a change in the air around her, her skin tingling slightly when her shield was up. She tried to remember what it felt like when she was sitting next to Rejat's Azerii. His presence was different than her aunt's, but she had jumped so fast when she saw him that she couldn't remember in what way. She thought of the wild Azerii at the river and the one whose name she had asked. What did their energy feel like? And their glimmering lights, how did they create their light?

Glancing at the fluttering candle, she thought of the glowing spheres Rejat had produced. Stretching her right hand out before her, she stared at her palm and imagined a glowing ball of light centered in her hand. Nothing happened. She laughed suddenly as the thought came to her that if she created the glowing sphere she would probably drop it in surprise. She lowered her hand, then raised it again as another idea came to her. Closing her eyes, she imagined the sphere sitting on her palm. A warm tickle slowly began to fill her hand. Concentrating on her inner vision, she hushed a growing excitement as a feeling of warmth touched her hand. Finally she peeked, half expecting to see a ball of light sitting on her palm. Instead, shadows were all that crossed her hand.

She lowered her arm, now tired from the rigid position and gazed at her hand. It was warm, warmer than her left hand. She repeated her efforts with her other hand. This time the warmth was even less noticeable. She tried her right again with the same results as before. She decided to try again after she talked more with Elas and Rejat; maybe one had to have an Azerii to create such things.

A long yawn escaped from her lips. Turning, she blew out the candle and slipped under the blankets. Imagining her shield around her firmly as her aunt had guided her to do, she calmly fell asleep.

The next day came as bright and clear as the previous one. She was roused again by Stara and quickly dressed and joined her aunt in the garden for breakfast.

"We have much to accomplish today, Morgana." Elas gazed out past the garden where Tagar and Brient stood talking with some of the holders in the outer yard. "We have to find you suitable clothing for this journey. What you brought won't be warm enough for the mountains."

Morgana took a sip of tajiz. "I left all of my winter clothes. I didn't know where I was going..." she let her voice trail off.

"I know. I think I have some clothes that will fit you. We are pretty close in size." Elas lowered her sight to her hands.

"Why can't Tagar come with us?" Morgana had caught her aunt's long gaze on her mate.

Elas looked up at her, a note of surprise in her face. "Because he is not a Talent, or a Mirii. He has no choice," she replied softly.

"Why? You are his wife, why can't he go as your companion?"

"The Mirii are very private people, Morgana. Unless he was a Talent, he can't go with us," she answered irritably, her hand twisting her Barii ring.

"But the Kir-Latt spoke to him, and he heard it. Doesn't that count as a talent?" Morgana persisted, feeling somehow the importance of this knowledge.

"Not to the Mirii. Some hear the Kir-Latt, but not the Azerii."

"But he sees your Azerii."

"All can see the Meld Azerii when they are in physical form. I don't think he has ever seen the wild Azerii." She turned her gaze to her husband again.

"Have you asked him?"

"What?"

"Have you ever asked him if he has seen the mist ponies?"

"Morgana, why are you asking me these questions? I can't let Tagar come with us. We've already discussed this." Elas struggled to control her anger. She felt so much pain at leaving him anyway, why was her niece doing this? She stared at her in frustration.

A shimmer over Morgana's head broke her anger. She slowly rose to her feet, her face still. "Morgana, raise your shield."

"Why?" The young woman's eyes flickered concern at her aunt's sudden change of tone.

"Do it now."

Morgana closed her eyes briefly, then opened them again. "What is wrong?" The shimmer above her moved higher, out of her shield's reach.

"Brealyth, Become!" Elas called her Azerii softly, her niece watching in silence as her Azerii's aura appeared brightly around her. She raised her hand. "Come over here, slowly."

Morgana rose from the far side of the table. As Elas watched, the shimmer rose also, then remained in place as she moved around the table to her aunt's side.

"Elas, what's wrong—oh!" she gasped in surprise when she turned to see what her aunt was looking at. A shimmering figure of light stood behind the chair that she had just vacated.

"What do you see?" Elas still held a raised hand over the table.

"A light, shaped—like a man, but very transparent. Like the wild Azerii."

Elas stared at the intruder, and through Brealyth she requested the figure's intentions.

"It doesn't know what you mean, Elas," Morgana said, her surprise evident in her hushed voice.

She glanced sharply to her niece. "You can hear this one?" It was not communicating to Brealyth; her Azerii remained silent.

"Yes, but not very well. It's like an echo,"

155

she paused to listen. "It says it wants to help."

"Help? Help who?"

"You." Morgana turned to her aunt. "It wants to help you."

Elas drew a sharp breath, then silently called her sister. "Ask it its name."

Morgana returned to the figure. "It doesn't have a name," she said, throwing a confused glance to her aunt. "It says you must do the naming."

Thudding footsteps were suddenly enhanced by Rejat's swearing as she careened through the doorway behind them. She stopped, whispering her Azerii's name as she took in their situation and stepping next to her sister.

The intruder spoke to Morgana once more as she stared at the shimmering being. "It says it will not stay in anger's presence; it will come again when you have the need." She could feel its energy tingling against her shield. Why had she not noticed its presence with her shield down? Then as quietly as the being had appeared, it was silently gone.

Elas lowered her hand. Rejat pulled at her unruly hair and glanced sideways at Morgana before she turned to face her pale sister. "What was that all about?" she said, still breathless from her flight.

Her sister released her Azerii to follow the strange visitor and sat down shakily. "I don't know, I believe it was a wild Azerii, but I've never experienced any of them acting like that before." She glanced at her niece, "Did it say anything else?"

"Wait a wrecking—Morgana heard it?" Rejat looked skeptically at both of them. At Elas' hidden words she stopped her questions.

"No, Elas, or not that I could understand. It seemed, or felt, sad. I think it knew you were upset."

She sat next to her. "Are you all right?"

Elas brushed her hands through her hair. "Yes, I'm fine. You didn't feel its presence, did you?"

"No, not until after I raised my shield, after I saw it. Then I could feel it a little."

Rejat straightened her tunic and sat across from them where Morgana had been sitting. "Dayana's gonna love this one. What did it say it wanted?" Her eyes locked on her sister.

Elas looked up at her. Stillyth's aura was still joined around her form. With a nod Rejat sent him off to search with Brealyth. "It said it wanted to help me." She poured herself of cup of tajiz and took a long sip.

"Help you? How?"

"I don't know. Morgana and I were talking about Tagar when it appeared." She glanced back at her niece. "Why all the questions about Tagar?"

"I don't know," she replied uneasily. "It just seemed, well—important, I guess. I'm sorry if I upset you."

Elas shook her head. "No, it's just an issue we have already talked over." She took another sip, then continued, "I will certainly miss him though."

Rejat snorted. Morgana looked from her to Elas as the two Mirii exchanged glances. A thought crossed her mind; why is Elas' Azerii female, and Rejat's male? More questions bubbled up, but she was suddenly nudged by her aunt.

"Come on, let's go find you some clothes."

Her questions continued to churn around in her mind throughout the rest of the day but the opportunity to voice them never seemed to rise. By the evening meal she had pushed them to the recesses of her concerns, feeling the time for answers would be on the journey before her.

✳

In the hours before dawn a rider came noisily to the hold. Morgana heard the dogs announce the arrival and felt sure the rider had been sent by her father to look for her. She hazarded a peek through the shutters, but the view from her window faced the garden, not the road into the holdyard. The darkness below offered no answer to her questing sight, so she slipped back into her bed. Tense voices filtered through the house, but nothing she could understand reached her ears. She closed her eyes and willed her fears away.

As she tried to relax, the acute memory of her brief scanning attempt flowed back into her awareness. She sat up, her mind racing as to the possibility of repeating that 'accident'. She began to imagine the rooms below, sending her mind wandering to find the gathering room where she suspected her uncle would most likely meet with this visitor. Suddenly, her imagined journey was interrupted as a strong pair of hands shook her back into her awareness of the room she occupied.

Morgana snapped open her eyes. With his aura glowing around him like a fire, Stillyth towered over her, his hands firmly grasping her shoulders. A look of stern reproach was in his eyes, but he released her before she could say anything and raised his hand to touch her lips.

*Rejat says NO! You will reveal yourself!*

She sat up straighter. "I can hear you!" she loudly whispered, startled by this new revelation.

He seemed unimpressed. *Some have the talent,* he replied. *Use your mind talk, not voice, too loud.* He grimaced at her outburst.

Morgana chewed her lip in concentration. *Tell Rejat I'm sorry, but I think that rider is from my father's hold!*

The Azerii sat down cross-legged on the floor beside her bed. His eyes took on a faraway look for a moment, then his gaze returned to her. *Rejat is very angry, I will not tell you what she says. Very unpleasant thoughts.*

She suddenly pictured the strange being who had appeared in the garden. Angry, Rejat's anger, that's why it left. It was because of her anger, she thought and glanced back at Stillyth.

He looked uncomfortable. He touched her hand, *Yes, I hear. Some Azerii are fearful of anger. Strong emotions, draws many, repels many,* he sent.

*And at Communion?* Morgana asked, her own thoughts beginning to form an answer.

*Emotions. Strong emotions bring strong Azerii. Fear draws anger, acceptance draws love. You will know, Morgana Elissii.*

"What are you, Stillyth?" she whispered softly, staring into his gentle copper eyes.

He smiled in reply, *In my naming, I am love.* His expression shifted, *Do not be in judgment of my Mirii, for in judgment you will fail.* Then, with another smile, his aura brightened and he was gone.

Morgana sat in the darkness of the room, thinking about his words and what was happening elsewhere in the hold. She could still hear bits of conversation from below, but the words were still unrecognizable. She finally gave up and lay back to drift once more to sleep.

She woke to find a stern-faced Rejat standing

in front of her window, the morning sun streaming through the slits in the shutters behind her making her copper hair appear on fire. She was wearing a plain gray tunic and trousers instead of her usual Mirii attire.

"I know, I know, I'm sorry, Rejat. I just wanted to know who had arrived. I felt sure my father had sent him." She quickly rose and started to reach for her clothes.

Rejat said nothing. She walked over to her and stopped her with a touch. *Listen to me. You do not know how much talent you have. You must think very carefully before you attempt anything you do not fully understand. You could have given all of us away. The man who came was from your father's hold. A very superstitious man, from what Elas told me. He was wearing Keethra Ironstone.* She dropped her hand to her side.

Morgana stared at the Mirii as the image of the rider appeared in her mind. "You mean it was Toryon?" She thought of her father's hold steward, Rican, and his younger brother, Toryon. A simple man, she had always thought of him as quite harmless. "What happened?"

The Mirii crossed her arms and glanced at Morgana's clothes. "It appears your father is trying to rouse the whole valley to look for you. One would think someone had stolen his prize stallion, or his favorite—well, anyway, this man was sent to check here and we're not going to give him any opportunity to find you here."

"What did he say?"

"Ask Tagar for the specifics. I only got an overall view from Elas. She told me this man was one to spread tales though, so you'll have to keep out of sight 'til he leaves. Here, put this on." She handed her a brown tunic and skirt from the pile of clothing Elas had found for her the day before. "Not a great color, but you'll not be as noticeable in it. You'd better cover your hair too."

She pulled on the offered clothes, then found a tan scarf in the pile. As she tied it around her head she glanced in the small mirror on the side table and grimaced at her reflection. "I'm not sure Toryon would miss me in this. My father thought brown was an appropriate color for women to wear. He always approved when I wore it."

"Your father certainly has a lot to learn about women. Your poor mother." Rejat turned away and walked back to the window. She glanced through the shutters. "We have to get you out of the house without being seen by this Toryon. Tagar has put him in with his hold steward's family. Elas told me their cot is on the west side of the hold, so we can take you out the east through the garden. Are you ready yet?" She impatiently turned from the window.

"Yes." Morgana took a last look in the mirror, tucking her hair under the scarf.

Rejat glanced a final time through the shutters. "Come on. Quiet." She moved to the door. Placing her palm on its smooth surface, she paused briefly as if listening to the hallway beyond. She nodded to Morgana and opened the door softly.

The two stepped carefully into the hall, Morgana closing the door just as quietly as Rejat had opened it. The long hall had stairs leading to the main floor off to their right and towards the front of the house, but Rejat turned left and pulled Morgana after her. They walked to the end of the hall where a window gazed out over the southern fields behind the house. Sheer fabric clothed the window, the shutters open wide to the summer sun. Rejat glanced quickly outside, then placed her hand on the wood panel at her right on the west wall near the ceiling. She muttered a few words and a small door appeared which she silently opened, revealing the landing of a darkened staircase. Producing another of her glowing spheres, she led her companion down the narrow stairs, the door closing softly behind them.

At the bottom of the stairs, she stopped before another small door. Again she listened for a moment, then releasing the sphere, she opened the door and stepped through, pulling Morgana with her. They were in the storage room behind the kitchen. Rejat sent, *Wait here,* then slipped through the door. Morgana stood alone in the dark. After a few minutes the Mirii returned carrying two covered baskets and handed one to her. *This way,* she sent, then led her through a door that opened out to the southern edge of the kitchen garden.

Rejat walked casually through the rows of vegetables, Morgana following close behind and trying to look as calm as the other appeared. They went through a gate in the border fence and along a trail through a field of bramble berries and into the forest beyond. The path twisted and divided through the wood until she felt certain they were lost in the tall thickets and skyward trees, then abruptly opened into a circle of light. They faced a small meadow, a ring of trees enclosing a wildflower strewn floor. A circle of blackened stones and earth marked a firepit in the center, surrounded by five old wooden benches, moss covering their upright sides and supports, the grass between them growing low from past use. Morgana felt awed in the presence of the circle, as though she stood within a sacred place.

Rejat finally spoke. "This is an old meeting place," she said and walked to the nearest bench, placing her basket down and motioning Morgana to do the same. She took the cover off of her basket and pulled out a large piece of fruit bread, handing it to Morgana. "Ah, Stara does feed us well," she quipped as she sat down beside the basket and pulled out a piece for herself. "What's in yours?"

Still awed by her surroundings, she set her basket next to Rejat, nibbling on the bread she had received and gazing up at the trees enclosing the circle. She turned completely around and then sat down beside her basket. Rejat had already plucked off the cover and was lifting out a warm jug of tajiz and two small pottery cups.

"What kind of meeting place?"

"Hmm?" Rejat filled a cup and handed it to Morgana. "What kind? Mirii, of course. Elas and I used to meet here when things were difficult at Tagar's hold. When his first wife was still alive. And his father, your grandfather. I couldn't get near the hold without him raising a ruckus. He tolerated the Mirii only as long as they stayed out of his sight."

"My Grandfather?" Morgana sipped at the tajiz. "But I thought he hated the Mirii. He used to tell us some stories."

"Yes, I'll bet he did. Where do you think your father got his ideas? Your father has probably never even met a Mirii either."

"Except Elas."

"Elas doesn't count. She never wore Mirii red in the valleys. Your Grandfather only knew her as a 'Mediciner'. He wouldn't call her a Healer, that might mean Mirii." Rejat took a gulp of tajiz. "He looked the other way when Elas came by. She said he avoided her, but wouldn't stop her from coming to the hold. Especially since Tagar's wife was ill a lot." She pulled another piece of bread from her basket. "Others use this place sometimes."

"Others? You mean the wild Azerii?"

Rejat smiled, her mouth full of bread.

*Why would Azerii need a place such as this to meet?* Stillyth's amused thought brushed Morgana's mind. She laughed at the absurdity of her question, then stopped at Rejat's startled expression.

The red-haired Mirii lowered her cup, staring at Morgana, then turned as her Azerii appeared in hu'man form, sitting on the bench next to her. *She can hear you?* she sent to him briskly.

*Yes, Laa, she has the talent.* He winked at Morgana who had fallen silently uncomfortable.

"Of all the Wrecking! Stars, Child! Why didn't you tell me?" Rejat shouted at Morgana, mixed emotions flitting across her face.

"I just found out last night, I didn't know it was that important." She looked from Rejat to Stillyth and back.

*Be calm, Laa, Elas is coming.* Stillyth sent his warm calming thoughts to his Mirii. *I will watch the man, Brealyth says we leave at tomorrow's first light.* His aura flared and he disappeared from the circle.

Elas' eyes were full of her anger when she arrived in the grove a few moments later. She took one glance at their expressions and asked, "Well? What's wrong?"

Rejat flashed a wry grin. "Nothing that can't wait for your news. Have some tajiz." She held out her cup.

"Thanks, I will." Elas took the offered cup and sat on the bench next to her.

"Well?" Rejat pushed.

"Toryon's on his way back to Tillan's hold, thank the Lady. I scanned him for any suspicions about Morgana, but he honestly doesn't think she came here." She glanced at her niece. "He thinks you went to the west, to Corgin's Landing. He seems to think you've a man somewhere in that city to run to."

Morgana laughed, "Toryon never could understand me either. Corgin's Landing? I've never even been there. I wonder where he ever got that idea?"

"Must have been all those trips to the river," Rejat quipped, then at Morgana's fallen expression added, "Sorry, Morgana."

She smiled gamely. "I'm all right. You're probably right, though. I usually avoided the men around the hold by going to the river. I'm sure stories were told about me, but my father wouldn't stand for gossip, so they would have to keep their tales pretty quiet."

"It doesn't matter anyway, Morgana," Elas handed Rejat her cup, her expression calmer, "as long as you know who you are."

Rejat pushed again. "What else is going on?"

"Mia's back. Jeven and his family are fine. Tillan sent someone to their hold too. She was almost smug about how well she told the man she hadn't seen Morgana since she came with us to Brenan's LandsHold. Told him she saw her ride back alone too."

"She may overcome her shyness yet," Rejat said, a smile of approval in her eyes.

"She had two of Brenan's holders with her and she was leading the way. They're already heading back too."

"Did they ride all night?"

"No, they camped out north of Tillan's hold last night, then left before dawn." She smiled at her niece. "They didn't have any side trips like we did."

"No Kir-Latts, huh?" Rejat tossed a yellowenn fruit to Morgana.

"No, no Kir-Latts." Elas stretched her legs towards the firepit. "All right, what happened?"

Rejat shook her head. "Nothing as serious as your intrusive neighbors. Morgana can hear Stillyth." She waited for her sister's reaction.

She didn't have long to wait. "Morgana can— wait, why didn't you tell us? Wait—" Elas stood, her face the same mixture of emotions as her sister's had been earlier. "Brealyth, Become."

As her Azerii flowed around her, she placed her hands over her heart. Her Azerii quickly appeared beside her in the small girl form, gazing up impishly at her Mirii's face. *Brealyth, speak to Morgana.*

The Azerii/girl glanced at the young woman, then back to Elas. *What would you have me say?* she sent.

*Just ask her if she can hear you.* Elas laid her hand on Brealyth's shoulder.

Brealyth turned to Morgana. *Stillyth says you can hear Meld Azerii; is he correct?*

She smiled at the Azerii. "I guess he's right. I can hear you very well, when you direct your thoughts to me."

Brealyth raised her hands to her face and laughed silently, then straightened to face Elas, the playful grin still on her face. *Yes, Elaa, she hears me very well!* She silently laughed again, then at her Mirii's nod disappeared in a sparkling mist.

Elas sat down again. "Well, Morgana. I certainly never expected this from you." She leaned forward, a smile on her lips. "I congratulate you on your talents." At her niece's relaxed smile she went on. "But, I must ask you, if Rejat did not," she glanced at her sister who returned her gaze with a nod, "never, never attempt to scan or throw your sight, or anything else that you do not fully know how to do. It could create the most terrifying effects, to yourself, or someone else, such as your excursion over the cliffs." When Morgana's face went pale at that memory, she continued. "You have so much talent that you do not understand, Morgana. You were creating a Shadow of yourself in the house until Stillyth stopped you."

Morgana's eyes went wide. "A Shadow?"

"Yes, not complete, but enough that I called Rejat to stop you. Brealyth was busy with me, so Rejat sent Stillyth. If Toryon had seen that Shadow, he would have gone running back to Tillan yelling about Mirii ghosts and Azerii demons and we are not ready for the whole valley to discover us yet."

"I'm sorry, Elas. I won't try that again," she said quietly, her eyes on the fruit in her hand.

"Oh, yes you will, but under our guidance," Rejat spoke up before Elas could resume. "But not until we leave the valleys and are sure of our journey through the Varan."

"And speaking of our journey," Elas fixed her sister a stern glance, then looked again at Morgana, "we leave before dawn. I want to be an hour on our way by first light. Brealyth says our brief guests are well out of the way, so we can go back to the hold and start packing."

167

✳

The early morning sky was still black, the shining stars casting the only light when Stara roused Morgana from her bed. She had slept lightly through most of the night, the imaginings of her journey flitting amongst her dreams, pushing her to wakefulness until through utter exhaustion she finally slept.

Once awake enough to think, she quickly washed and dressed in the gray tunic, trousers and chza hide boots her aunt had given her to wear, tying her hair behind her head with a silver cord. As she placed a wide gray belt with a silver buckle around her waist and glanced in the mirror she was suddenly struck by the familiarity of her clothing. Then she remembered Elas had worn similar clothes when she had traveled in the past. There is something evasive about this color, she thought, as if one could pass by unseen. She remembered her mother remarking about Elas' subtle travels, as if no one were really sure if they had seen her or not. Brea had always said how easily Elas could appear when needed and then just as effortlessly vanish.

Rejat's voice calling her from downstairs sent her scrambling for the door. She yelled, "Coming!" and then turned and grabbed her almost completed packing, stuffing her few remaining belongings inside and tying it closed. She picked up her pack and the heavy wool cloak her aunt had given her and headed for the door.

At the bottom of the stairs she deposited her pack and cloak next to the others already waiting, and hurried to the kitchen where she could hear Rejat, Brient and Stara talking. Stara had prepared a light breakfast for their journey, "Just enough to get them bodies awake," she said, as she handed Morgana a plate of food. Elas and Tagar joined them a few moments later. Morgana watched Rejat talk easily with Brient, her cool demeanor to him left behind in the past two days. Mia slipped in quietly and gave Elas a long embrace, her face showing the same sadness of their imminent parting that Morgana saw in her aunt and uncle's faces. She thought again of the strange Azerii's appearance, and her unanswered questions. I'll find out eventually, she thought. Elas and Rejat also wore the same gray clothing as hers, except both still had their hair free and the wide belts each wore had elaborate silver threads stitched in swirling patterns. She wondered about the significance, deciding she would find out about that later, too.

Abruptly Rejat stood and placed her cup on the table. "It's time," she said and turned for the door. All followed except Elas and Tagar, picking up their cloaks, packs and supplies, and went outside to the holdyard where the two Azerii, in horse form, along with the gray filly the Brenan's had given, waited with the HorseKeeper. In the flickering torchlight Rejat tied her gear on her Azerii's harness behind her saddle, Brient helping Morgana with hers, while Stara and Mia stood watching in the doorway of the house.

Rejat, her eagerness to be off evident in her movements, finished loading her Azerii. As she tied and covered her hair with a gray scarf, she silently called her sister. *I'm sorry, Elaa, but it's time,* she sent gently. A moment later Tagar led Elas out of the house, carrying her pack and gear. He approached her Azerii and waited until Brealyth nodded her permission, then placed the supplies on the harness while Elas said her final good-byes to Mia and Stara, and then Brient when he finished with Morgana's horse.

Morgana was toying with her horse's reins when she found her uncle beside her. He placed his arms around her and enfolded her in a big hug. "My heart goes with all of you, Morgana," he said softly, "Take care of Elas and Rejat. I know you have more talents than either of them suspect. Follow them, learn from them what they can teach you, then listen to your own heart. Trust your dreams, Morgana. Find your own truth." Then he kissed her forehead and released her as she numbly spoke her goodbye, her words lost on her lips. He smiled down at her face, then turned from her and walked over to Rejat, surprising her also with a warm embrace and soft hidden words.

The rest of their farewells were sad and brief, each in their own way murmuring the words in their hearts to those who would be sorely missed. But as the sky began to glimmer in the light of a new day, Morgana climbed onto her horse and followed Rejat and Elas out of Tagar's LandsHold, to begin her journey to Communion and to her new life.

# Chapter 13

The Rayanii forest was tall and wild in high summer, the warm air full with scents and sounds, the earth seeming to overflow in its green mantle of towering pines and rustling thickets. Wildflowers waved abundantly from every open pocket of ground like bright stars in the tall grasses, their many colored petals fluttering with the slightest breeze.

The forest invited the riders into its depths with open arching branches on a little remembered but very old path. For three days they followed this path, deeper and higher into the foothills of the Varan and away from the ordered society of the Northern Valley Holdings. They crossed the Kesh river twice, fording high northern and southern branches to avoid any of the LandsHolds that rimmed the river's path. They rode silently and quickly, three gray-clad figures who seemed like shadows flowing through the emerald dreamscape of another world. Their mounts traveled through the forest as if the ground wore a carpet of deepest moss. No one saw them.

On the dawn of the fourth day, Morgana was checking her horse's harness for the third time while she waited with her aunt for Rejat. They were almost to the old Trader's Pass, another hour or so, the Mirii had said. She had gone ahead to scan for other travelers, such as those she had crossed before. She would contact Elas when she knew the way before them was clear.

Morgana pulled herself up onto her horse and absently patted the gray's neck. The past few days were like a dream to her. A waking dream, she mused. She felt as if she were coming out of a long sleep, her body tired from the unaccustomed riding and sleeping on hard ground, but her mind seeming clearer than ever, her awareness of the energies flowing around her sending her thoughts to questing. Elas and Rejat had insisted on her tight control of her shield and the silence of their ride gave her time to study her surroundings. She felt the inner strength of the forest all around her. She had always known of its beauty, but now she recognized the power of the forest and understood some of what her mother had tried to tell her. My mother only felt fear here, she thought sadly, as she gazed at the mountains above them.

*Your mother was taught to fear the world, Morgana.* Her aunt's gentle mind voice intruded in her thoughts. *You're not closing enough, try again.* Elas had turned to her, and she faced the trail once again.

She pushed her mind shield higher as her aunt had taught her, "to guard your thoughts from those you do not wish to hear," Elas had told her on their second day: "There will be times you will not wish your deepest thoughts to be known, by Mirii or Azerii. Better to learn now than let something slip later."

Morgana considered her aunt's words again. Their conversations on this journey had been kept to almost total mind voice. She was learning quickly how to hear her companions, but she still had difficulty closing her inner talk from intruding on them, both Mirii and Azerii. Brealyth ignored most of her musings, but Stillyth delighted in interjecting his own comments, to her embarrassment and Rejat's irritation.

*It's time,* Elas' mind suddenly brushed hers, *Rejat says all clear. We can go.* Her aunt climbed onto her Azerii and they started up the path once more.

Most of the old trail wandered through the Varan on fairly even ground, the towering cliffs of her scanning experience farther to the north than the pass. But as they began their last climb, the trail became more narrow and rugged, the slopes around them steeper. Morgana suddenly became very aware again of just how clumsy the horse she rode appeared on this rocky ground. She glanced up at Elas' controlled posture on her mount's smooth pace and wondered about the sure-footed Azerii. She tried to see the trail ahead of her aunt, but the trees crowded close blocking any further examination.

They had ridden for close to an hour when Elas stopped and motioned her niece to her side. She pointed ahead. *This is the tricky part of the trail.*

They gazed out over a broad expanse revealed before them. The trail wound along a break in a cliff, open to the gathering winds that blew through the pass. Trees clung sparsely and tenaciously above and below the trail, loose shale and rock pooling below several narrow patches. It did not look welcoming.

*Where is Rejat?* Morgana sent hesitantly.

*On the other side of the Pass, around that last bend.* Elas patted her hand. *Just follow me, Rejat says the trail is still good. If you'd feel better walking rather than riding, go ahead.* She smiled reassuringly.

Morgana looked at the pass. Far below, the cliff face ended in a wide expanse of loose rock, a curving green wall of forest at its base. She took a deep breath, then slid off her horse. *I'll walk.*

Elas smiled, then slipped to the ground also. *I will too. Rejat will laugh, but I need the exercise more than Brealyth.* She patted her Azerii's shoulder.

As Brealyth started across the narrow expanse of open trail, Elas stepped back beside her niece as she fidgeted with her horse's reins, unsure the gray mare would stay clear of the loose edge of the trail.

*I'll take her.* Elas held out her hand. *I can guide her across.*

Morgana cast a puzzled look at her aunt, then handed her the reins. She watched as Elas held them securely in one hand and placed her other hand on the mare's forehead. Her aunt nodded for her to follow Brealyth, then started after her Azerii with the calm gray.

Morgana's eyes warily examined the open trail. As she started across, she discovered it was not as narrow as it appeared from a distance. Hugging the rising side there was room enough for two horses, but the steep slopes above and below and the brisk winds around reminded her again of her scanning venture. She pushed the memory away and focused on her aunt and the gray horse before her.

As they rounded the last curve of the cliff face, she looked up past Brealyth. With relief she saw Rejat on her Azerii at the end of the narrow path, the enclosing trees behind her seeming to welcome them. The Mirii was grinning broadly at their chosen method of travel. Morgana shyly returned her smile as she joined her, then sent a grand thanks to her aunt as she returned her horse.

Rejat laughed aloud and slid to the ground. *I think that walking a bit is a very good idea, I could use a stretch too,* she sent to both. *The way is clear before us, but we should keep moving quickly if we are to be out of the upper Varan by moonrise.* She turned, and with Stillyth at her heels, began walking away from the old Trader's Pass and into the enclosing forest beyond.

✳

The clear bountiful days of summer continued as they traveled east through the Varan. The farther they rode from the pass, the more Rejat and Elas seemed to relax. They still kept up their brisk pace, both Mirii concerned that they reach the place of Communion before the approaching Autumn Equinox.

As the days passed, the two women began to talk more openly of their past, using the mind talk only when they scanned for the presence of other forest travelers. After the third day from the pass, Morgana started asking Rejat about her life. At first she sensed the other's irritation at her questions, but with Elas' encouragement, Rejat relented in telling some of her story.

"I became Mirii when I was twenty-one," she began the next morning after they resumed their journey.

"At the Eye of the Lady," Elas added, ignoring her sister's frown, "where I also joined my Azerii."

Rejat turned in her saddle to glare at Elas. "Who's telling this, you or me?"

Elas laughed, "We were both there, that's

when we met." She smiled at Rejat and caught Morgana's puzzled glance.

"I thought you said you were sisters," she said.

"Half. Our father is an Aza Tor Travelaar." Rejat faced the trail once more. "He's now Elder Aza Tor at Zerren's Gate Hold. He's been there for about five years now. Said he'd had enough of roaming about in this lifetime. Dayana keeps trying to get him to come to Lasah as Elder, but he thinks she just wants him to journey for her again."

"Will he be at Communion?" Elas asked her.

"I think he will, but he'll avoid Dayana, I'm sure," Rejat replied, laughing at the memory of her father's words. "He still cares for her, but he says it's too hard to live with a woman who sees so much before you do."

Elas sighed, "Yes, she can be difficult to be around. Her sight is so clear."

"Who is Dayana?" Morgana asked her aunt, "You've mentioned her name before."

Elas nudged her Azerii closer to Morgana's horse. "Dayana is Elder Visioner of Lasah Hawk Hold, the largest of the holds. She is also my mother." She shook her head, a sad smile on her face. "Most Visioners choose not to have children, but Dayana's Visions guided her to Morant, Rejat's father, and thus to me." She smiled brighter as Rejat turned to glance at her again. "Having a mother who is an extremely strong Visioner is very difficult for a child. I resented my mother's guidance when I was growing up. She saw so much of who I was to become, that I felt I had no choices. As soon as I became Mirii I left and went with Rejat to Zerren's Gate for a year before I started my journeying. Dayana wanted me to be a Visioner after her. But she knew I had choices that she could not interfere with—to be a Healer."

"She keeps reminding me of that too," Rejat said, glancing back at her. "Of how she almost took away your choices, Elas. She has grown calmer over the years."

"I'll see her at Communion," she replied, "and then hear what she says. It's been five years since we spoke last. If she starts again on those old issues, I can remind her that you are a stronger Visioner than I am, Rejat."

Rejat spoke over her shoulder, "Please, Elaa, I get enough reminders from her, living in the same hold. She knows exactly what my feelings are about visioning!"

"Why?" Morgana interjected, "Do you dislike having the Visions?"

"You ask me that after the Vision you had?" Rejat nearly stopped her Azerii to glare at her.

"Morgana, remember the fear you felt in your dream?" Elas moved closer and sent a warning look to Rejat, who turned with a scowl and urged Stillyth forward again.

"Yes, but it was only a dream, not real. I've had bad dreams before, but I woke up and it was over."

"Well, when the Mirii dream, or Vision, they fully experience what happens in the Vision; including the fear and the pain in the difficult ones. They can't tell the difference from the vision or the waking world until the vision has run its course. They feel the emotions and can't move out of them until it's over. It can be very frightening at times, leaving the Mirii defenseless to what is happening around them. And the Visions don't just happen in sleep, they can happen at any time, in any place. Most Visioners rarely leave their holds because of this."

"My Visions, thank the Lady, are few," Rejat said, her back held stiff upon her Azerii.

They rode on for a while in silence, Morgana thinking about her aunt's words. Then Rejat resumed her story as if the subject had never been mentioned.

"I grew up at Zerren's Gate. My mother was Aza Har from Sekkett Hold. She was with us until I was six, then she returned to journeying for her hold. As I said, I became Mirii when I was twenty-one. After that I spent one season at my hold, then began my journeying. I spent the first three years on my own, traveling all around, learning my path. Then I went to Lasah because I had a vision," she paused and shrugged her shoulders, "that I couldn't read. So I went to see Dayana. And stayed for a year. Then they put me to journeying for the hold."

Morgana thought to ask what her vision was, but at Elas' expression she withheld her question, deciding that Rejat would tell her if she wanted.

"Elas and I journeyed together several times. We seemed to cross paths almost seasonally, but particularly when I came through the northern and southern valleys of the Varan's west side. She seemed to develop a fondness for the region I could never understand."

"It was all that green, Rejat. The Coumar forests and eastern plains of the Sumarkh are so dry in summer and fall." Elas winked at her niece. "Though I will admit I found the western Varan and its people challenging to my journeys." She laughed as Rejat turned to look back at her, a silly grin creasing her face.

"Why do you call yourself Aza Har Travelaar?" Morgana asked Rejat, "What do the words mean?"

"Travelaar is what we are. Journeys are what we do," she replied. "To be Travelaar is to answer our vision to travel, to journey from place to place, using our talents as needed. We journey amongst the holds, passing information from each, keeping the contacts open and sometimes finding other Talents along the way. Aza Har, is something else again. Hard to put into words." She shook her head. "The Warrior Within." She became silent.

"The warrior within?" Morgana repeated her words, then looked at Elas. Her aunt shook her head, *Rejat must tell you,* she sent.

Once more the three grew quiet, as the trail narrowed before them across a rocky slope, forcing them to ride in single file. They continued in silence until the sun reached its zenith, then halted for a brief meal and rest.

"Aza Har and Aza Tor," Rejat began again as she sat next to Morgana to share a yellowenn fruit, "female and male respectively, are those Mirii whose talents include strength and skill in movement, of both physical and energy movements; well, Stars! Of weapons and what you would call sorcery. We are old warriors who have not been able to shed our past."

"They were warriors, mercenaries in their pasts, Morgana." Elas sat beside her sister and placed a comforting hand on her shoulder.

"Warriors? Like the PeaceKeepers in the cities?"

"Stars—No!" Rejat's words held a bitter edge. "Hu'manSlayers, paid assassins, child."

"When?"

"Past lives, not this lifetime—though there have been moments," Rejat smiled grimly, "like with those wrecking Foresters we ran across on the way to your valley." At Morgana's puzzled look she paused, struggling to find the words that the younger woman could understand.

"In the early times—before the Mirii holds fully came to be. When a meld was formed with a soldier; unless that Hu'man had great aversion to taking life— which, if he or she did they probably would not have been a soldier—the taste for killing would have been enhanced by the Azerii. As well as the ability, through weapons or energy manipulation. What your elders would call spells or witchcraft. There was much violence done to others, as well as to themselves. Anger and fear play greatly amongst the warriors. Anger at their own fears. They see themselves as victims to their emotions and try to manipulate others to ease their own pain. Doesn't work, of course, but they don't know that."

She took a deep breath. "I choose to be Aza because of my old anger. But I am a warrior of the heart, the Warrior Within. When the Mirii holds were formed, they drew all the meld soldiers to them and created the Aza. It means 'chaos' in the ancient tongue. They became what you call the 'PeaceKeepers', helping to defend the hu'mans from the Dark Azerii who would force meld. Then, after the people became our enemies, the Aza defended the Mirii holds and wards and helped to erase these places from the people's memory. The Aza only kill in self-defense. We prefer to use our talents to sustain life, not take it. But we have old angers to release, and this is the way for us."

She leaned back, clasping her knees for balance and watched Morgana's face, which had gone from confusion to intense concentration as she listened to the Mirii.

Elas squeezed Rejat's shoulder and stood. "We can talk more later. We need to keep moving."

Morgana found her questions seemed to be multiplying rather than abating, as she and Rejat followed Elas' lead and picked up their food packs, preparing to resume their journey. They stopped again before dusk, Rejat keeping them moving past a rough open part of the trail in case they were spotted, then leading them to a well-hidden ravine to rest for the night.

They spoke little during their meal, Morgana still trying to understand Rejat's words. She felt the older woman said much that was full of double meanings and left more unsaid. Aza Har, Warrior in her past, not this life? What did she mean? A past life? Another old memory slipped through her mind, of her grandfather talking about those who believed in such nonsense and his unpleasant remarks about those people. Yet both Mirii seemed to accept this concept as a simple fact. Why were her people so disturbed by these beliefs? She briefly wondered what her past lives were like and started to ask Elas when Rejat suddenly hushed them with a silent frown.

The red-haired Mirii stood slowly, her Azerii quietly flowing around her. Elas stood also, her eyes intent on her sister's face. *Silence, Morgana. Shield,* the inner words darted from her aunt. Elas abruptly turned and walked to Morgana's horse.

Morgana raised her shield and watched her companions. Rejat's awareness seemed miles away, her eyes gazing into the darkness beyond the small circle of light of a single sphere she had placed by their packs. Elas held the mare's head, much as she had when they crossed the pass, the horse relaxing and trying to playfully nudge her aunt's shoulder. She began to wonder where their Azerii were when she heard the Others, the wild Azerii. Their voices started low, sliding and building around her, just like the night in her mother's garden. Calling her, beckoning her, *Morgana Elissii, come and play, come and play with us! Come and be one with us! Morgana Elissii, Morgana, Morannon, Morgu, Morgana!* their voices becoming trilling notes of impossible variations as they called her to run and join them.

Morgana held her breath, concentrating on her shield. In her inner-sight she could see them, their pony forms dancing around her, careening above her head, their sparkling lights cascading as they played. She opened her eyes and saw their glistening bodies almost touching her, daring her to move away. She held her ground, struggling to remember Elas' words, "Don't talk to them, don't respond."

Then Brealyth was among them. Like a scolding mother, Elas' Azerii flowed in full light form into their midst. The wild Azerii responded by clinging to her light, and as she gathered them she expanded her aura until the last one was absorbed, then slowly moved out of the clearing, taking them with her.

Morgana turned to her companions. Rejat was still linked in scan with her Azerii, her eyes unfocused on their surroundings. Elas gave the gray a final nudge that left the horse asleep on its feet, then rejoined her sister. *It's not over yet,* she sent, then began scanning her Azerii's progress.

Rejat raised her arms and uttered unheard words. Her Azerii aura glowed brighter, then faded from her body as Stillyth left her, her awareness slowly returning to her surroundings. "We're about to have company," she said flatly. She raised her open hands again, a second sphere hovering in the air as she released it, lighting the clearing and her tired face. "We have company," she repeated, then turned and sat on the log beside their packs.

"Who?" Elas shifted her scan back at her sister's words.

"Another Mirii, named Drek'h," Rejat replied, her hands now clasped before her. "Stil is helping him. He's south of us, a short distance."

"Who did you pick up first? Drek'h or the wild Azerii?"

"Neither. Foresters were first. They're about an hour, maybe two, south of us, on one of the side trails."

"Elas jumped at her words, "Foresters? How close?"

"Far enough to miss this," she returned irritably and waved a hand at the sphere overhead. "I suspect the wild Azerii had a hand in this."

"Why? They don't usually play complicated games." Elas stole a quick glance at her niece. "To get to Morgana?"

"I think so. They wanted you and me to be busy, so, well, it's possible. We'll see what Drek'h says. He should be here shortly." She looked up at Morgana, her eyes dark. "Are you all right?"

Morgana hesitated, then nodded. "Yes, but I see why you warned be about the mist—I mean wild Azerii. Their presence was much stronger this time. I felt as if they were going to push me over."

"That's because you know how to shield now," Elas said, "They didn't have to try very hard when you left your home. You were already going the direction they wanted anyway." She stepped over to embrace her. "You did very well."

Morgana smiled, then turned to Rejat. "Who is

Drek'h?"

Rejat snorted. "Good question. Drek'h is Aza Tor Travelaar. A real journey-taker. He claims no hold or ward as home. A real loner." She reached down and extinguished the first sphere beside her pack.

Morgana shook her head; something was buzzing in her ears. "Kitteryth says you don't like him," she said, then looked surprised at her words. "Who's Kitteryth?"

"Kitteryth is Drek'h's Azerii. She doesn't like me either," Rejat grimaced. "Watch her, Morgana, she plays more games than some wild Azerii," she said, then gazed at the dark around them, sending her scan out again.

Elas watched Rejat for a moment then turned back to her niece. "Drek'h is young, a few years older than you. He wasn't raised in the Mirii holds. He was abandoned by the Vondarii when his Lii horse died. I met him a few years ago. He journeys through the valleys sometimes. He's a good Healer, but doubts his abilities. He doesn't feel comfortable in the holds, that's all."

"He avoids Lasah," Rejat added, her gaze returning with her scan along with her scowl, "even when he's called." She stood up. "He's here."

A slight rustle through the trees, followed by a loud snapping of a branch and a young man appeared in the sphere's light. Drek'h was tall and thin, with sandy blond hair that flowed in waves to his shoulders around his golden tanned face. He wore the dark red coat, trousers and tall boots of the Mirii with a dark gray cloak pushed back from his shoulders. A mixed expression of fatigue and relief crossed his long face as he greeted the Mirii before him, "My thanks, Rejat, Elas, for your company." His voice carried a trace of another realm. He held out his hands, palms forward, a soft glow emanating from them.

Rejat stepped forward to return the gesture. "Greetings, Drek'h." She touched her hands to his, then moved back as Elas approached, a scowl lingering on her face.

"Welcome, Drek'h," she said and touched his hands, her gaze intensified as their palms met. "May I present my niece, Morgana, of the Brejjard LandsHold in the northern valleys. Morgana, this is Drek'h, Aza Tor Travelaar Healer." She withdrew slowly, her eyes still locked on their visitor.

"Welcome, Drek'h," Morgana said, sudden shyness making her voice low. She raised her hands to him in like gesture but did not step forward.

"My thanks to you also, Morgana," he nodded, noting her wariness, his bright blue eyes intent on her face. "Kit tells me you hear all Azerii. Is that true?" He pulled his hands back and cradled his left arm protectively.

Morgana felt a soft tingle on her forehead. Something told her she had just been scanned. She pushed out with her mind talk, *You don't believe your Azerii?* her face remaining neutral.

He smiled, his face suddenly reddening. *Yes,* he sent back, *I'm sorry, my curiosity sometimes gets the better of my judgment. Especially around your People.*

*The better? Or worse?* She found herself smiling at his easy manner.

Drek'h laughed aloud, then clutched his elbow in earnest. "You're right, Morgana, my apologies," he said roughly.

Rejat huffed her impatience. "Are you two through?" She glared at Drek'h. "Tell me what you

185

were doing on the south trail, and when did you pick up those Foresters?" She crossed her arms and sat again, her angry gaze lifted to his suddenly pale face.

Elas intervened, stepping toward him, "What's wrong with your arm?"

He looked uncomfortable in her scrutiny. "Nothing, I—we..." he trailed off as she approached and took his left wrist in her hand, wincing as she pushed his sleeve back.

"Drop your shield, will you? I can't see what's wrong," she demanded, then hissed at what she found.

Morgana edged closer. The sphere's light was too dim to see well; she wanted to know what her aunt was doing.

"Come over here, Drek'h." Elas pulled him by his right hand to the log Rejat was sitting on. "Sit," she commanded, releasing him long enough for him to do so, then nodding to her sister as she slid over. "Could you add another light?"

Rejat's face became impassive as she produced another sphere above Elas and Drek'h. "What'd you do? Argue with that tree we heard you fall over?" she said, the disdain clear in her voice.

Drek'h winced again as Elas pushed his coat sleeve farther back. "No, Rejat, I only wish it had been the tree."

A bloody slash crossed through his tunic sleeve just above his elbow. Elas sucked in her breath again at the sight of a deep gash in his upper arm. "This was a from a Keethra blade, wasn't it?" she said as she knelt and placed both hands over the wound. "Morgana, would you bring me one of the waterskins. Rejat, will you stop harassing him and assist me please?"

Morgana brought her waterskin and handed it

to Rejat, then stood aside to watch.

"We need to get your coat off, Drek'h," Elas said, still holding his arm. "It's a wonder you haven't lost more blood from the looks of this. Morgana, Rejat, can you release his cloak and help him get his arm free of his coat?"

As Morgana fumbled with his cloak, Rejat reached around and released the wide belt that held his coat around his waist. Drek'h sat still, his face pale under his tan, his eyes closed. As soon as Morgana removed his cloak, Rejat looked at Elas and in one swift movement Elas released his arm and Rejat pulled his coat clear of his left side and arm. The lower sleeve of his tunic was soaked in blood. As Elas held his arm once more, Rejat pulled a small dagger from her boot top and cut the sleeve from wrist to shoulder, then setting the dagger aside, she picked up the waterskin. At Elas' direction she poured the water into the wound until Elas said "Enough."

"Drek'h, where is your Azerii?"

"Kit? She's with Stillyth," he replied, his eyes still closed, pain seeping into his face.

"Call her back. Brealyth is too busy for me to call her. You have to heal yourself, Drek'h. You must call her back."

He opened his eyes. "I can't heal myself," he whispered, his eyes reflecting the sorrow of his belief.

"Yes you can, Drek'h. I'll guide you. Call her back."

He closed his eyes again. With a deep sigh, he called Kitteryth back. A moment later she appeared in light form behind him.

"Call her to you," Elas ordered.

Drek'h took another deep breath. "Kitteryth, Become!" His Azerii flowed to him, enclosing him in her brilliant aura.

Elas closed her eyes and joined him in a tight mind link. *Form the Circle,* she told him.

*I can't, Elas, it doesn't work for me. I've tried it before, I just can't do it.* His mind was edged with fear.

*Yes you can. Just do as I say. Now, Drek'h, do it!*

A feeling of anguish flowed from him, but he did as she commanded. In his mind a spot of light appeared; he expanded it into a line, curving away, then around to join its beginning.

*Complete it. Make it whole.*

He struggled with the image, but finally the circle became full and sealed.

*Now, the Triad.*

Again his mind twisted before completing the pyramid within the circle.

*Good, now place them on your crown.*

With a sigh of relief, he envisioned the combined symbol on the top of his head. Suddenly the symbol sent a wave of energy down from his crown, through his spine and out each of his limbs. At his injured arm, the wave hesitated before moving to his hand.

Elas took his right hand and placed it over the wound. *Now, direct the symbol. Direct the energy, Drek'h.* She released his arm, standing to move back a step.

Drek'h took another deep breath, his Azerii aura still glowing around him. He moved the symbol down from his crown, through his head, throat, right shoulder and down his arm to his right hand. Then he pushed white light through the symbol from his hand and into the wound.

As Morgana watched, his Azerii aura faded from around his body to glow forcefully from his right hand. His shoulders became tense with the effort of directing the healing energy to his arm, sweat beading on his face. He suddenly jerked his head up and snapped his eyes open. "Kitteryth, Be Thanks!" he exclaimed, then cautiously moved his right hand away from his arm. In the quickly receding light from his outstretched hand, she saw that a finger long scar was all that remained of the wound.

Drek'h looked at Elas as his Azerii slipped from his body to stand behind him as a small dark-haired woman. Kitteryth's face glowed happily as she hugged her Mirii's shoulders. "Thank you, Elas," he said numbly, his face now revealing his awe as well as fatigue.

Rejat handed him the waterskin. "Well done, Drek'h. Now remember this."

The young man nodded his head, taking a long swallow from the skin, then handing it back to her. She retrieved her dagger and washed it, then tossed the waterskin to Morgana.

"All right, Drek'h, now tell us what happened," she said as she dried her blade on her coat.

Drek'h sent his Azerii off to join Stillyth who was making sure the Foresters did not find them. "I was coming up the east ridge trail to connect with this one, to get to the Sumarkh. I just came through the Lefurn Pass a few days ago, from the southern valleys, when we spotted a group of Foresters. They tried to stop us, but we managed to slip through. I thought we had lost them when we turned north, but they followed," He paused, a look of frustration on his face. "I thought we had lost them again yesterday. We spent the night in a small ravine, half day's ride south of here." He stopped again, looking from Elas to Rejat, then lowered his eyes. "I was caught by a vision. Started right at daybreak, I couldn't stop it. It took me right out of this world." He started visibly shaking at the memory. "Kit couldn't do anything; she saw the Foresters coming and tried to distract them, but they were carrying Keethra blades. She grabbed me just before one of them could run me through, but he still caught me on the arm. Brought me back real fast." He swallowed audibly.

Rejat sat down next to him. "Can you show me what these men look like?" she asked, her tone unusually gentle.

"I can show you the ones at the pass, but I did not see the one who almost killed me."

"That's all right, I just want to know if these men are from the same group who tried to take me and Stil." She placed her hand on his temple for a brief moment while he relayed the images to her.

"Well?" Elas asked, her concern over his news creeping into her voice.

"They're not Foresters either." Rejat leaned forward on her knees. "I don't recognize any of them, but I'd bet they're from the same group."

"Why would these men be watching the passes?" Morgana felt a growing unease from their words.

"Unless we catch one and ask him, I'm not sure we'll find out. We'll just have to watch all the trails." Rejat glanced at Drek'h again then slipped her dagger into its sheath. "Care to share your Vision?"

Elas stepped forward to place a hand on Drek'h's shoulder when his face paled again at Rejat's words. "I think we should let him rest. We need to keep a scan out for those men, and the wild Azerii," she added as Brealyth returned within the clearing.

✳

After finishing their interrupted meal, which they shared with their new companion, Elas insisted Drek'h get some sleep; then saw to it that he would stay put with a little 'push' to calm his restlessness. Stillyth and Kitteryth returned with news that the Foresters were hopelessly lost and should not trouble them for the night. Both Azerii were buzzing with playful energy; Rejat finally calling Stillyth in irritation, Kitteryth settling herself in protective aura around her sleeping Mirii. Brealyth went out to keep first watch on the area. She told Elas and Morgana what she had done with the wild Azerii that left them smiling in surprise at her audacity.

"She took them to Callendae?" Morgana said, her eyes wide with silent laughter.

"You heard her. What do you think will happen there?" Elas replied smugly.

"I would say there's going to be a lot of happy children and angry frightened parents."

"Well, maybe we'll find some new Talents in Callendae. We haven't found many in the cities in a long time."

"But won't their parents just punish them for talking about what they have seen?" Morgana suddenly felt some sadness at the lost memory from her own childhood.

"Yes, but maybe some of the older ones will see them too and remember." Elas smiled at her own memories. "Like you."

"I just hope those older ones have someone they can talk to, to tell them what they've seen. Someone like you, Elas."

"Or like Tagar," she smiled again. "Someone

191

who'll believe."

"Tagar. Elas, I think—"

"Morgana, not now." Her aunt abruptly stood. She looked for her sister who seemed to have slipped away with her Azerii. "You must get some sleep. I'll tell Rejat to have Stillyth take the second watch. Then we must all get some sleep. I don't think those Foresters will give up that easily. We leave at first light."

# Chapter 14

At the first hint of dawn on the horizon Elas gently shook Morgana awake. Unwinding herself from her blanket and cloak, she pushed her hair from her face. After more than a week of sleeping on cold ground she still felt stiff upon arising.

Rejat handed her a cup of hot tajiz. She still marveled at the Mirii's ability to change the liquid from ice cold to steaming hot without a fire. Rejat simply smiled the 'you'll-find-out-soon-enough' smile when she had asked about this and the light spheres a few days earlier.

Drek'h was already on his feet, his cloak pulled close around his slim frame. His face had lost the pallor from the night and now seemed to glow from within his healthy tan. He held a cup in his left hand and nodded his greeting to Morgana.

"Why am I always the last to wake up?" she complained to herself as she stood, careful not to spill the tajiz.

*Must be all those comfortable beds in your past,* Kitteryth's thought tickled in her head.

She glanced at Drek'h. He returned her gaze with a shrug. *You're the one with the exceptional talent,* he sent. *You talk to her, she won't listen to me.*

Morgana rolled her eyes skyward. First Stillyth, now Kitteryth, she thought, careful to keep her mind shield up. At least Brealyth doesn't rub it in.

As if called, Elas' Azerii suddenly appeared in light body in the center of the clearing. Elas stopped her packing and looked up at her Azerii. *They're moving again, Elaa,* Brealyth informed her Mirii. *We must move quickly.*

"All right, Brealyth," Elas said aloud. "Rejat, we're going to have company soon. We'd better leave now and eat on the road."

Rejat tossed the contents of her cup and started repacking their food supply, Stillyth appearing in horse form beside her.

Morgana quickly followed suit, rolling up her blanket and giving Rejat her cup. She grabbed her pack and headed for her horse, Drek'h stepping beside her and picking up her bridle and saddle. He smiled. "It's been awhile, but I think I remember how use these." She stopped to watch him as he stood before the mare, presenting the harness to her out-thrust nose, then placed the saddle on the ground and pulled the bridle over her willing head. As he readied her mount, she felt a sense of old sadness in his movements, but only returned her thanks for his assistance.

As she handed him her blanket and pack to tie into place, Elas called to them to hurry, "Let's go, it's almost light." A last tug on the mare's harness and she swung up into the saddle.

Drek'h's Azerii was right behind him. In horse form, Kitteryth took the appearance of a tall midnight black mare, a strange contrast to her rider's blond hair, Morgana thought, considering Elas' Azerii's silver coat and Rejat's Azerii's copper one.

They left the ravine in silence as the sun brightened the morning sky, Rejat leading the way again, followed by Elas, Morgana and Drek'h. When they rejoined the main trail, Rejat stopped them. *We'd better Veil, Elas. Those Foresters are too close,* she sent.

Elas nodded and motioned Morgana and Drek'h between them. As one, the two Mirii woman repeated the Veil over their companions. Then, urging total silence, they returned to the trail heading east and out of the high Varan.

They rode all morning under the Veil. Few words were exchanged except between Mirii and Azerii. Morgana kept her mind shield up, closing her own thoughts from the others, for fear the Foresters might somehow hear. Her horse remained quiet also; she wondered if one of the others were possibly suppressing the mare's occasional whinnies.

When the sun was at its peak Rejat stopped them again. They had traveled far from the ravine. She sent her scan out for their followers. For several minutes she sat rigid on her Azerii, her awareness far behind, searching for the Foresters. At last she relaxed, turning to the others.

"It's safe, we've lost them, at least temporarily." She nodded to Elas and the two raised their arms and released the Veil.

Morgana leaned forward on her horse and patted the gray's neck. The mare in return suddenly let out a brief whinny, as if she had held back all morning just for her.

Drek'h sighed explosively, rubbing his Azerii's shoulder. "They were the same ones, weren't they?" he said to Rejat.

"Did you expect anyone else?" She seemed puzzled by his words.

"I don't know, my Vision—" he abruptly broke off and looked away.

"What? What about your Vision?" Rejat edged her Azerii towards him. He looked at Morgana and Elas, then to her; his fear at the memory of his vision was evident in his face.

"Show me, Drek'h," she insisted, "Show me what you saw."

He lowered his eyes, then slowly held out his right hand. Rejat nudged Stillyth right alongside Kitteryth. She placed her hand in Drek'h's and closed her eyes. Mixed images flooded her mind, of great cities in ruin, open lands laid to waste, and the Madness! The raging Madness of the Dark Azerii inhabiting the People, and their destruction of themselves and their lands, their homes, everything in total blindness. And the soldiers, the warriors, marching in blindness to their master's orders of death to the Light Ones, the Darkness consuming all the Light, and some of the warriors wearing the brown and green of the Foresters!

She snatched her hand away, nearly losing her balance on her Azerii. Drek'h too, wrenched away his hand, as if passing on the vision had seared his palm.

Elas brought Brealyth next to her sister's Azerii. "What was it? Rejat, are you all right?"

Rejat shook her head. "No, but I will be. Drek'h, I'm sorry, but I had to know. I had a Vision not too long ago. It was equally unpleasant, no, I take that back. Yours was worse." She shook her head again as if to clear the memory of their exchange.

Elas touched her shoulder. "We should eat and rest now, and you can tell me about it later."

They ate their meal quickly in a small clearing not far from the trail. Kitteryth took watch with Stillyth, the Mirii deciding it was safer to keep track of the Foresters for as long as they continued to follow them. When Elas asked her sister about Drek'h's vision, he uneasily decided to show her himself instead of letting Rejat relay it for him. Again the response was the same, Elas pulling away from him as if she'd been burned. She then briefly told Morgana what she had seen.

Morgana felt her heart contract with her aunt's words of the vision. It was different from her dream, but she knew it was part of the same warning. The Darkness consuming the Light. She shivered in response to those words.

Something else puzzled her. "The Light Ones, Elas. I don't understand. Who are the Light Ones?" she asked as they prepared to ride again.

Elas stopped packing and turned to face her niece. "We are the Light Ones. So are the people who live in harmony with the land, their neighbors, the animals, plants, fish, the Azerii 'mist ponies', all who seek the Light of their own Truth. All who live by that Truth. Even your father, who struggles with his own truth. He believes he has that truth. He doesn't know that is what he is. We may see him differently but only he can change himself. All those who recognize their choices and take full responsibility for those choices."

"And these Foresters?"

"These men are being given a false truth, a belief in no choice. They are old warriors as well as the Aza. They simply do not see their past or their choices." She turned back to her packing.

Morgana pulled herself up onto her horse, Elas' words rattling around her head. Choices again.

197

The Light Ones, Darkness, and the path before her. All this reminded her of the night the wild Azerii had tried to lead her upriver. Had they really been leading her to an Azerii to meld? Or had they actually just led her in the direction she was now going? Away from the valleys and towards the pass she had already crossed?

*When you seek your Truth, all choices are the same. They will all lead you to your Light, Morgana Elissii,* the words whispered in her head and she nearly turned her horse around; she had heard the voice again! But glancing at her companions told her that no one else had sent or heard those words and they quickly left the clearing to return once more to the road to Communion.

Four more days they continued, resting briefly during the daylight hours to eat their cold meals while the nights were kept short. They stopped at dusk only when they found a safe grove or thicket and left by dawn with the three Azerii taking turns watching for intruders. The Foresters continued to follow them, their persistence worrying the Mirii and pushing them faster than Elas and Rejat would have liked. Morgana seemed to hold up, but her horse was getting tired. Drek'h kept a close eye on the mare, frequently riding before her and watching the ground for any loose stones or tree roots that the mare might trip over and become lame.

As the fifth day drew to a close Drek'h sent Kitteryth out to look for their followers while he also scanned the area. They had located a large cave a half mile from the trail, one that Rejat had used in past travels. The hills they crossed were rugged, the trees thinning out as they approached the plateau. Great cliffs and narrow canyons with pockets of long needle trees ranged along the trail, offering less cover from prying eyes than the dense forests of the western Varan, so the cave was a welcome respite to the companions.

As Elas and Rejat prepared their camp for the night, while Morgana rubbed down her horse, Drek'h returned from his scan with news from Kitteryth, "They've gone back!" he shouted, his words echoing through the cave before him as he stood at its entrance.

"What? Are you sure?" Rejat came leaping out and nearly ran into him. "Are you sure?" she repeated.

"Kit says she saw them turn back; they're nearly a full day behind us. She says they were arguing amongst themselves. She couldn't tell about what, only that there was much anger," he replied.

"Could be they're splitting up. Still!" she said as she strode out of the cave past him.

"Doesn't she trust Kit?" he said to Elas as she joined him.

"She doesn't trust the Foresters, Drek'h. Although she has made a few comments about your Kitteryth." She smiled at his bemused look.

"Well, I trust her," he said, then he and Elas walked out to stand beside Rejat as Morgana came up.

"What's going on? Did you say the Foresters have gone back?" she asked Drek'h.

"Yes, that's what Kit says." He looked at Rejat who was now in scan with her Azerii. "She doesn't believe Kit," he added, shaking his head.

Rejat's tense body slowly relaxed as she returned from her scan. She glanced at her three companions around her.

199

"Well?" Elas asked her first, a slight smile on her face.

"Well?" echoed Drek'h and Morgana almost at the same time.

The red-haired Mirii dropped her gaze to the ground, then back at Drek'h, a frown of irritation on her face. "All right, tell Kit I apologize. Stil says she's right, they've all turned back."

"I will tell her, Aza Har." He smiled at her as she scowled once more at the ground. "Hard to lose the warrior sometimes, isn't it?"

She returned his gaze. "Yes, Drek'h, sometimes it's very hard."

He reached out and clasped her shoulder. She suddenly laughed and swung her arm over his. "Let's eat!" she said and the two walked back into the cave with Elas and Morgana following.

They spent the night in the cave, building a small fire near the entrance, their Azerii still watching over them as the three Mirii discussed whether they should spend the next day resting at the cave. Rejat was eager to keep moving, but Elas knew her niece was getting overly tired as well as her horse. Even she was feeling the strain; she had not journeyed this far for some years. They finally decided to wait till morning and scan again for their followers and then decide.

✳

Morgana woke early. Something troubled her sleep that she could not put a name to. She felt a presence but could not identify it, a feeling that she was missing something. She rose, careful not to wake the others and slipped out of the cave.

Brealyth greeted her as she stood before the

cave entrance, gazing up at the myriad stars overhead. She returned her greeting.

*What troubles you?* the Azerii asked in a tone quite like her aunt's.

*Nothing, everything,* Morgana sent back. *Feelings I can't describe, of being here and not here. Of someone else, watching and waiting. Of having the answers when I don't even know the questions.* She wrapped her cloak tighter around herself, her unsettled thoughts sending a chill through her body.

*What is it you seek?*

She stared at the blackness of the trees, her mind in silence. *I seek myself,* she finally sent.

*Then you will surely find yourself,* the Azerii returned, a tone of certainty in her thought.

Morgana sighed, rubbing her arms for warmth. "I certainly hope so," she said aloud to the night.

When Elas rose at dawn she found her niece asleep, wrapped in her cloak beside the entrance to the cave. She decided to let her drowse for a while longer. At least until she heard what her Azerii had to say. *Brealyth, Laa, where are our persistent friends?* she sent from the clearing before the cave.

*Friends, Laa? I did not know these were friends we were hiding from,* her Azerii's reply sounding almost sincere.

*All right, pardon my words. Where are the Foresters?*

*Very far away, Elaa; they still head back to the mountain passes. Away from us.*

*Good, we need the rest. I'll tell Rejat.* She started to turn back to the cave, her thoughts on the extended rest she desired.

*Elas, Morgana is troubled.*

She stopped and looked skyward for her invisible Azerii. *What do you mean?*

*She is troubled by the words, in her mind. We think it is the One.*

Elas nearly jumped. *The One from her Vision? The One who forced the Kir-Latt?*

*Yes, We believe it is the One yet to be named.* Brealyth materialized beside her in the girl child form, her gray eyes held her mirrored concerns.

Elas knelt before her and took her hand. *Has this one contacted her directly?*

*Not directly. We sense it is near, it is trying to reach her through her dreams. But she has learned to shield well.*

Elas released her hand. *How close is it? Did it send the wild Azerii?*

The Azerii/child's eyes became distant, then returned to her face. *We do not know, it avoids us. I did not feel its energy with the others, but it could have sent them.*

Elas started to stand again when Brealyth grasped her hand. *Elas, it could have sent the men.*

"What?" she said aloud. "Brealyth, get Stillyth and Kitteryth." She stood quickly and yelled to Rejat and Drek'h.

Morgana jumped awake as her aunt called the other two Mirii. She was surprised to find that she had fallen asleep in front of the cave watching the stars. She stood up stiffly and walked to her aunt just as Rejat and Drek'h appeared.

"Elas, what's wrong? Stil says you called him too." Rejat twisted her hair away from her face.

"Yes, Kit says the same. Do we have the Foresters back on our trail?" Drek'h added, running his
hands over his sleep filled face.

"Brealyth, I want you to link with Stil and Kit
and tell all of us what you told me."

*Yes, Elas.* The Azerii closed her eyes. Her
aura began dancing brightly around her small frame as
she mind-linked with the other two Azerii. *We think
the one who was in Morgana's and Rejat's Visions, and forced the Kir-Latt, may have sent
these men after you. We do not know how, yet,
but there was much darkness around one of the
men.*

As one, Morgana and the Mirii exchanged
glances, then turned back to Brealyth. Rejat asked her,
"Can you show us this one?"

The Azerii looked confused. *No, it has not
been named. There is no identity.*

"No, the man, can you show us the man?"

She looked at Drek'h. *Kitteryth can show
you.*

Drek'h's Azerii flowed into her hu'man form
next to Brealyth. She took her hand and turned first to
Rejat, then to her Mirii.

"Show us, Kit," he said.

Kitteryth frowned. *His energy was dark,* she
pouted. *He tried to kill you.*

*I know, Kit. But Rejat wants to see him.*

She grimaced, then sent them the image
through the other two Azerii. A tall man with dark
hair, beard and eyes, wearing the Foresters' clothing,
but his movements were that of a hunter.

Rejat's eyes narrowed as she received the image from Stillyth. Aza Tor, she thought. A Warrior.

Drek'h shuddered, Kit's image stopped just as

203

the man pulled out a large dark blade to strike.

Elas noticed more. "His energy is like the Kir-Latt," she said to Kitteryth, Brealyth showing her the one they had healed. Its energy aura had been damaged by the forcing meld of an Azerii. She sensed from Kit's image the same damage.

Kitteryth nodded. *Yes, it felt like that. Much darkness around the man.*

Rejat swore softly and looked at her sister. "Well? What do we do about this now?"

Elas sighed and crossed her arms. "Thank you, Brealyth, Kitteryth, you too, Stillyth." The two Azerii who held form disappeared. "What we've already been doing. We take this knowledge to Communion, and keep a sharp scan out. Rejat, do you think we need to do a Protection Ceremony on Morgana?"

"A Protection Ceremony?" Morgana's eyes met Rejat's briefly before turning to her aunt.

"No," the Aza Har replied. "I think she's shielding well enough. Besides, with two Aza and a Healer around her all the time, who says she needs any more protection?" She smiled cheerfully at the younger woman. "Now, did Brealyth say where those Foresters are?"

"She said they're still on their way back to the passes." Elas looked relieved. "So I think we should stay here a day. We could all use the rest, especially Morgana and her horse."

Her niece lowered her eyes, "Please, Elas," she looked back up to her aunt, "I'm all right, the mare's a bit tired, but don't let us slow you down."

"Morgana, you are not slowing us down. We've come much farther and faster than I expected, thanks to our followers." She flashed a wry smile. "Besides, I'm tired too. So is Drek'h."

He looked surprised and began to protest, "Wait, I'm not—"

"Shush, you didn't have a proper rest after healing your arm. Less than a night's sleep is not enough. Well, Rejat?" She turned to her sister's thoughtful gaze.

Rejat's reply was a loud yawn. "Fine, as long as those men are out of scan. I could use a day off. So could Stil."

"Good. Then we leave tomorrow morning. Now, let's take advantage of this day, shall we?" Elas said and turned toward the restorative darkness of the cave.

✳

Morgana was restless. After so many days of riding, she felt awkward not doing anything. She spent the morning exploring the area around the cave while her companions slept inside, their Azerii still keeping watch outside. By noon she decided to check on her horse. She found the gray was not alone when she got there.

Drek'h heard her approach. "Hello, Morgana," he said without turning. He was stroking the mare's head and feeding her some sweet grass. The mare nuzzled his hand when he turned to look at her.

"How did you know it was me?"

He smiled and pointed to the front of the cave. A shimmering haze hung softly above the entrance. "Kit."

"Oh." She stepped to the mare's side. "She likes you."

Drek'h smile saddened. His melancholy flowed over her. She heard his Azerii send, *Don't,* then fall

205

silent.

"What do you call her?" he said, his sorrow ringing in his voice.

"The Brenans gave her to Elas and Tagar. Her name is Kahja," she said, keeping her voice neutral.

"Have you ever seen the Lii horses?" he asked her, a far off look in his eyes.

"No, I've never been out of the northern valleys till now." She began stroking the mare's shoulder. "I met someone once, he had seen them. He told me a little about them, and the Vondarii."

Drek'h seemed to draw inward at her mention of the name. He leaned his head on the mare's. "I was Vondarii," he said heavily. "Did you know they don't own the Lii?"

"Yes, my friend told me. He said the Lii choose their riders." Morgana watched him. She could almost see his pain. She remembered what Elas had said about his abandonment by the Vondarii when his horse died. "Drek'h, you don't have to tell me," she said softly, studying his face.

He straightened up, his blue eyes shifting from her to the mare. "I know," he whispered.

His sorrow was so powerful, she found herself wanting to comfort him, but she had been told too many times by her father to avoid others' pain, and her own. She held her place.

Drek'h stroked the mare's head again, staring into the gray's eyes. When he started speaking again, his words were carefully deliberate. "He was the same color...a bit darker on his legs, with a black mane and tail...nose too...bigger, of course, than she is.... He chose me when I was seventeen...before then, I rode different horses, their choice, always. It was at the Midsummer Naming Ceremony...he just walked right up to me, out of sixteen others.... I was the first that day...he told me his name was Rakker...and that I would be his forever. "

He paused, his eyes brightly edged. "We were together three years. I saw his first foal born...and the second.... The mare was silver, like Brealyth.... The mist ponies play with the Lii, did you know?" he said as he looked up at Morgana briefly, then lowered his gaze once more.

"It was fall...we were hunting for my clan...on the western edge of the plateau, amongst the ravines. I had spotted a chza buck, an elder, with a good set of horns...I knew my clan would be pleased if I brought him in—" He hesitated again, the memory still close.

"We ran the chza right into the path of a Kir-Latt—Rakker was running full out, he saw the Kir-Latt before I did and twisted to avoid running it down...he fell, on the rocks...I was thrown clear.... When I went back to him...he was dying." He clutched the mare's head, struggling to hold his emotions in check. Morgana heard Kitteryth somewhere in the back of her head.

"I stayed with him the rest of that day...and all the night. He died at sunset....the Kir-Latt watched too—I know they are a part of the Tribe of Elders." He paused again, his eyes tightly closed. "I walked back to my clan the next day. I took a lock of Rakker's mane with me,...placed it before the First Stallion. He accepted my words, but my—the Vondarii did not. When I told my words to the clan elders, they said I was careless...they said I was no longer...Vondarii.... My father...drew my name off the Records.... I was cast out."

Abruptly he sat down in front of the mare. His tears flowed freely, he did not seem to care if she was there or not. He clutched his hands together before his chin. "If I'd been...Mirii then," he whispered through clenched teeth, "I—could have saved him." He lowered his head into his hands.

Kitteryth again buzzed in Morgana's ears. She shook her head, then asked her, *What is it?*

*Tell him, Morgana,* Kit sang in her ear, *tell him, "You are mine forever."*

Morgana looked up at the glowing mist that was Kitteryth. *What do you mean?* She felt an unexplained emotion fill her heart.

*Just tell him.*

She lowered herself beside the mare's front legs. "Drek'h?" He did not answer or look up.

"Kitteryth wants me to tell you something."

He glanced at her, his clenched hands covering his lower face, tears streaking his cheeks.

Morgana felt her heart expand. "Kit says, 'You are mine forever.'"

# Chapter 15

Morgana went back into the cave, her mind troubled by her inaction and her heart deeply saddened by Drek'h's words. She had felt unable to move towards him, and left him after giving him Kitteryth's words.

She slept, dreaming small dreams; of wild mist ponies playing with magnificent Lii horses, of the two becoming one, of the past becoming present, and spoken words on stone falling to dust. And of the Light joining all.

The smell of wood smoke and hot tajiz brought her awake. Rejat and Elas were preparing a meal over a small fire near the mouth of the cave.

"Drek'h's gone," the red-haired Mirii said as she joined them.

"He's gone? When did he leave?" Morgana suddenly felt a sense of guilt wash through her.

Rejat looked up at her. "Stil says a couple of hours ago. Said he was very sad. What did he tell you?"

She sat beside her aunt. "He told me about his Lii horse. Why he was cast out of the Vondarii. Kahja reminded him of his, I guess." She started fiddling with a small rock, then suddenly looked from one

Mirii to the other. "I didn't know what to do."

"Did you listen to him? Let him talk?" Elas said, still focused on preparing their meal.

"Yes. Kitteryth kept bothering me while he was talking, when I finally asked her what she wanted, she told me to tell him something."

"And did you?" Her aunt finally looked at her.

"Yes," she hesitated, "though I felt funny about saying it, but when I repeated what she told me, I felt, well, better."

"Then you did right." Her aunt went back to her preparations. "The best thing a Healer can do is listen. To feel the sadness, and not try to stop it or deny someone their experience. Sometimes simply expressing the words can help to release the past."

"You did well, Morgana," Rejat added, "That's why you felt better when you gave him Kit's words. He probably would not have heard them any other way." She handed her a cup of tajiz. "Welcome, sister, to the Healer's way."

They talked again later of their absent companion, Morgana finding her thoughts drawn to his intriguing background, while they sat beside the fire and watched the stars come out through the wisping smoke.

"When did you first meet Drek'h?" she asked Rejat, her concern still edging her voice.

"I ran into him one winter at Tasken Hold, several years ago. He was journeying through; he never stayed in any hold for very long. He'd gone 'round the southern edge of the plateau from Mahdii Hold. That's where he became Mirii. Callent, Aza Tor of Mahdii, picked him up off the plateau after the Vondarii left him. Did he tell you that he was hurt when his horse died? Broken shoulder. The wild Azerii told Callent's Mirryth where he was." She paused to take a long sip of her tajiz. "Almost all the Vondarii children have talent, but their Elders don't want to lose any of their people to the Mirii, so they have a code they teach them, it's really shielding, to keep them from melding with the Azerii."

"Drek'h says the mist ponies play with the Lii horses," Morgana said, then remembered her dream and Kit's words.

"I wouldn't be surprised. From what I've heard, their Naming Ceremony is similar to ours, only the Lii choose their companions." Rejat's face took on a thoughtful look.

"The Lii have something in common with the wild Azerii, but I'm not sure what it is," Elas said, her eyes on the distant stars.

"When did Drek'h become Mirii?" Morgana asked, part of her thoughts still on Kitteryth's words.

"About two years after Callent found him." Rejat stared at her cup. "He was really a mess, from what Callent told me. Could hardly walk, been out on the hills for a week. Callent thinks the wild Azerii pestered him to keep moving west, towards the Varan. If he'd stayed on the plateau, he'd have probably died."

Morgana suddenly found she missed his company. "Do you think we will we see him again?"

"Oh, I think he'll turn up. After he's done some more healing." Rejat tossed another branch on the fire and moved closer for the warmth.

*He will return, Morgana Elissii,* the voice whispered in her ear.

✳

Early the next morning, Elas and Rejat each produced a drab gray bundle from their packs. When they opened them, Morgana saw they contained a set of clothing, all in the shades of the forbidden Mirii red. Rejat's set she had already seen; the coat now mended from the shoulder injury she had received on her flight to the valley. But her aunt's was new to her. Similar to Rejat's, the coat was a mixture of materials and printed fabrics, all containing shades of red, wine and scarlet. Where Rejat's coat was of the darker reds, Elas' contained the brighter tones. Both coats were embellished with small metal disks and blackened gold braiding. The coats were loose fitting, with half sleeves held on by ties so they could be slipped off when the weather permitted. They reached below mid-thigh in length and were held in at the waist by a wide leather belt. The coat was worn over a simple long-sleeved shirt and narrow chza hide trousers also in red. Rejat's knee-high cuffed boots matched her coat, while Elas still wore her gray ones. "I left my boots on my last journey, at Mahdii," she said, as she adjusted the cuff of her left boot, "I knew I had to pack light to go through the valleys and they took up too much space."

"When was that?" Morgana watched her aunt stand to adjust her belt over her coat.

"About seven years ago. When I brought Mia home." She gave a final tug on her coat and held out her arms. "Well? What do you think?"

Morgana smiled. "I think it's beautiful. I know what my father would think."

Rejat snorted. "We all know what your father would think. And most of the valley with him. I'm still surprised Brenan and Siva never said anything." She gave her coat a vigorous shake, then put it on.

"Kaill owes the Mirii his life. When he was much younger, an Aza Tor Travelaar saved his life in the foothills of the southern Varan. He spent a few weeks journeying with him." Elas pulled at her boot cuff again.

"Anyone I know?" Rejat said as she placed her belt around her narrow waist.

"Yes. Our father."

She looked up, the surprise evident in her tanned face. "You're kidding? Morant? I thought he didn't like the valleys."

"Oh, he's come though them a time or two."

"Well, he never told me much about it. Course I haven't really talked with him about his journeys in a long time." Rejat started packing up her earlier traveling clothes.

"Why are you putting on your Mirii clothes now?" Morgana asked as she twisted her gray scarf in her hands.

"In another day or so we'll be on the plateau. We have left our hunters far behind and we will probably run into the Vondarii at the edge of the forests. I'd rather they knew who we are. Travelers don't enter the Sumarkh without some risk. The Vondarii watch the plateau for all intruders. They do not interfere with the Mirii because they know we respect the land and her creatures. They also respect the abilities of the Aza." Elas handed her a red sash. "Tie this around your waist, then they will know you are a Talent and they'll leave you alone."

Morgana took the sash and studied its fine weave for a moment. The color was so vibrant, fiery red, brighter than her first vision of Rejat in the river's mists. *Mirii Red, I'm wearing Mirii Red,* she thought to herself as she slipped the sash around her waist over her gray belt.

*You'll be wearing all red very soon, Morgana Elissii,* the voice whispered in her mind again. She looked around for the source. Both Mirii were busy packing up. She called to their Azerii, Stillyth answering her first.

*What is it, Morgana?* he sent, slight impatience in his mind voice.

*Did you hear the other?* She repeated what the voice had said.

He seemed perplexed. *No. I will ask Brealyth.* A breath later he returned, *She did not hear this one either. Tell Rejat next time you hear this one. It is not here now.*

Morgana turned to finish her packing, then stepped outside. Kahja whinnied softly as she approached. "I know, I miss him too." She patted the mare's shoulder and started saddling her.

The sun had been up an hour when they left the cave. Stillyth and Brealyth had scanned the trail before and behind them and reported no other travelers in their vicinity, so, with much rested and lighter hearts, the three rode out and rejoined the old trail east to the Sumarkh.

They rode easier that day, the two Mirii still sending an occasional scan out but not pushing themselves to the previous speed of their journey. Elas and Rejat felt they had gained a few days from their quickened flight through the eastern Varan and the day's rest had not delayed them.

As they traveled east, Morgana watched the land change around them. The western forests of the Varan were thick with tall firs, cedarjinn and needle trees, the underbrush almost choking the old path in some places with its bushy and rampant growth. On the eastern side the forests opened to more needle trees, the ground covered with tough, low growing brush and berries creating thickets between the larger trees, with more grassland appearing as they traveled through the lowering eastern foothills.

By evening's camp they had come within sight of the Sumarkh Plateau. Golden hills with pockets of needle trees shimmered in the late summer's heat making the air quiver in front of their eyes. The hills above the plateau became hotter as they traveled east; the two Mirii both removed the sleeves from their coats by noon, their travel cloaks long since rolled and tied onto their mount's harnesses with the mid-morning light.

They camped in a thicket of small trees and berries, high and deep enough for them to be hidden from the trail and retired early, planning to rise before dawn to escape some of the heat on the trail before them.

The next day's advance took them through rocky bluffs where needle trees and berries clung tenaciously to the crevasses in the rugged walls. Winding springs, many dry in the late season, scattered at their feet. All around the yellow grasses and sharp thorny brush began to take the place of the varied green foliage of the western and upper eastern Varan mountains. Rejat began watching the springs closely, looking for the one that would lead them to the Timmar River and on to the place of Communion at the large lake in the middle of the plateau. "The trail starts getting spread out here," she told Morgana. "Many travelers—not Mirii, of course—attempt to avoid the Vondarii, so they try different paths through the Sumarkh. Easier to just follow the Timmar though." At every running spring they checked their waterskins, Rejat also starting to look for small game to add to their lessening provisions.

By the next morning, as Elas had said, they were on the edge of the Sumarkh. Morgana marveled at the immense rolling hills of yellow grasses and dusty-green brush. She had envisioned a land flat and featureless, not the subtle shadings of the low hills in the varying light of a summer's day. Soft golden hues mixed with pale greens, blues and browns of the various plants and earth that marked the plateau. A variety of animals existed here; hawks and ravens, many smaller birds, some familiar, some not, the large chza that Drek'h had mentioned, wild goats and rockland sheep, more varieties of small furred creatures, and the Lii horses.

They saw one of the Lii as they made camp that evening in a small valley near one of the many dry creeks that emptied onto the plateau. The Lii was riderless but not alone. Elas saw the wild Azerii following the large golden stallion as he watched them and then turn away to the darkening hills.

"Did you see them? There must have been a dozen with him," she said, then took a drink from her waterskin.

"No, Elas," Rejat replied, "I was scanning past the Lii for the Vondarii. I'm sure by morning they'll know we're here."

Morgana found herself holding her breath. The stallion was so beautiful! Better than any of the finest valley horses, she thought.

*Of course they are,* Brealyth slid her thought in her ear. *They are free and they know it.*

*Free and proud,* she sent back, then went to

216

check on her horse once again. Halfway there she stopped and turned to Rejat. "Are there any wild horses on the Sumarkh?"

"You mean not Lii? Like in the southern valleys?" Rejat sat down, her pack beside her.

"There might be, but they'd probably stay with the Lii rather than alone, without a herd or stallion to follow."

"There are wild horses on the Telandra plains, small herds." Elas grabbed her pack and started looking for something inside it. "I've seen the herds."

"So have I, but on the Sumarkh only the Lii roam the hills. I don't know what the Vondarii would do with an ordinary horse," Rejat replied, looking in her pack. "Probably nothing. If the horse isn't Lii, they might figure it has to take care of itself." She pulled out a packet and held it up. "Tajiz."

Elas sighed audibly. "I thought I'd lost it."

Morgana continued over to her horse. The gray was pulling at the grass at her feet. She grabbed a handful and began rubbing the mare's legs. She suddenly thought of Drek'h. Was he trying to avoid the Vondarii? That might be why he had left. Facing them again might be too painful, or would they remember him and somehow forbid him from crossing the Sumarkh?

She finished preparing the mare for the night and rejoined Elas and Rejat. "Will the Vondarii prevent Drek'h from entering the Sumarkh?" she asked them as they finished preparing their evening meal.

Elas handed Morgana a plate of food. "I don't think so. He's Mirii now. They respect Aza abilities too well." She handed Rejat her plate and filled her own. "He might not meet his clan anyway. There are many family clans on the Sumarkh. He may meet a

217

clan that doesn't know or remember him. It's been, how long, Rejat?"

Her sister thought while chewing. "Hmm," she mumbled, then swallowed, "about eight or nine years, I think."

Morgana nibbled at her food. "Why would his clan cast him out? It wasn't his fault his horse died."

Rejat shook her head. "Try and tell them that. They think the Lii are divine beings, the Lady's favorite children." She rolled her eyes skyward.

"But he said the First Stallion accepted him and the Elders didn't," she persisted, her thoughts confused.

"He did?" Elas said and exchanged glances with her sister

"Yes, he said the Elders didn't believe him. They said he was careless."

Elas stared at her niece, then shook her head. "It sounds to me like he was cast out for another reason then."

"Maybe he was used?" Rejat took a deep breath. "For what reason? I've never known the clans to be deceptive."

"Maybe we'll ask him when he rejoins us," Elas said, glancing at the dark hills behind them.

✳

The sun rose hot and heavy in the east, lighting the hills in fire-rimmed gold. Morgana had just finished saddling her horse and was waiting with her aunt while Rejat sat cross-legged on the ground, doing a full body scan of the area with the assistance of her Azerii. It was similar to her accidental scanning experience, as Elas briefly tried to explain, only with her

Azerii she could scan much farther than alone.

For several minutes they waited quietly before the red-haired Mirii relaxed her shoulders and leaned her head over her knees. She slowly straightened up. "We're almost on the spring. If we go north, three hills, we should be right in line to head east with the spring to the Timmar." She called her Azerii to form and slowly stood.

They rode as she directed until they found the spring, then turned and followed its easterly course through the rolling hills.

It was almost noon when Morgana heard the many voices of the wild Azerii. They were heading towards her, flowing over and around the hills with several Lii horses running in their midst. Rejat spotted the horses first, then swore at the sight of so many wild Azerii amongst them. "Shield!" she shouted at Morgana, who had already done so. She and Elas slid to the ground, their Azerii swiftly changing to their light forms beside them.

"They're driving the Lii!" Elas exclaimed, pointing at the approaching herd.

"How can they? The Lii have full awareness!" Rejat shouted back, then directed her Azerii, "Stil, can you and Brealyth grab the wild Azerii and tell the Lii where they're going?"

*We shall try, but there may be too many to gather,* her Azerii sent in reply; then he and Brealyth were off towards the Lii to warn them of their dangerous charge.

"Elas, watch Morgana's horse," Rejat said, then stepped in front of the mare.

Morgana struggled to hold her shield and the nervous mare. She could feel the gray quiver in fear at the oncoming Lii herd. Elas stepped to her left and placed a calming hand on the horse's shoulder. "Be calm, Morgana. Hold your shield."

Rejat raised her arms to the sun. In her hands, light echoed forth and crystallized into a shimmering wall before her, reflecting even more of the sun's rays at the onrushing Lii. The horses suddenly veered off, splitting at her shield wall to circle around them. Their companion wild Azerii stopped before the reflecting wall, glittering and buzzing before its mirror-like surface.

Brealyth and Stillyth swiftly flowed into the momentarily distracted wild Azerii, drawing them into themselves as before. Then, when all had been gathered, they lifted their expanded glowing forms and departed for the mountains behind them.

Rejat dropped the sun shield as soon as the Azerii were out of sight. Wearily, she turned to her companions. "Well," she breathed heavily, "now we only have the Lii."

Elas glanced at the surrounding horses. There were about thirty moving uneasily around them, keeping out of reach but not leaving. "We could talk to them."

"Only if they'll talk to us," her sister replied and glanced at Morgana, still sitting rigidly enclosed in her shield on her horse, her eyes clenched shut in concentration. "Morgana, are you all right?"

"Morgana?" Elas laid her hand on her niece's knee, then jumped back as if shocked. "Rejat, she's fighting the One! The Dark Azerii!"

"What?" Rejat shouted, then tried to touch the young woman also. She snatched her hand back, cursing as she met Morgana's heightened shield with pain.

It had come swiftly, unnoticed amongst the

wild Azerii, her shield again brushing them off, their voices ringing around her but out of reach. But while the others were being gathered by the two Meld Azerii, it had silently passed Rejat's shield and enveloped Morgana. She felt an overwhelming darkness surround her, the bright sunlight lost in the black cloud of the Dark Azerii's energy. She pushed her shield out, but met a resistance too powerful to break. In sudden comprehension she realized what was happening— this Azerii was seeking to force meld upon her! *Morgana Elissii!* the voice rang in her mind, *Morgana Elissii! Morannon.... Morghu.... Mordlyth! Mordlyth!* it screamed at her, crashing against her shield. She held onto the inner vision of her shield like a bright blue wall of fire to light her way against the One who would consume her and drive her mad. Fear pulsed through her body, raging at her own resistance, the shield becoming painful to behold as it flared brighter and brighter. *Truth!* the word suddenly pounded in her head, drowning out the Other, *I am the Truth!* she screamed at the Dark Azerii. *I am the Truth!*

Her eyes flew open as the Dark Azerii suddenly left her. She looked down at Rejat and Elas, their faces filled with their concern. Her horse snorted and shivered beneath her as if also released from the Other.

"Morgana, are you all right?" Elas reached out a tentative hand to her knee, quickly drawing it back.

"Ye-yes, Elas." Morgana closed her eyes briefly and took a shaky deep breath. "I—think so."

"Drop your shield a little, will you?" Rejat held the nervous mare's head. "Let Elas check you out, Child. We saw what was happening."

"I'm fine, Rejat." She lowered the intensity of

her shield to allow her aunt to scan her, then began to slide off her horse. "I'm just tired," she said, blinking rapidly in the bright light. As she slipped out of the saddle, Elas had to catch her to keep her from falling.

"Yes, Morgana, but let me look at you." Her aunt helped her sit as Rejat steadied the mare, glancing at the Lii still circling around them.

Elas' scan was swift. Noting the Azerii had not been able to push through Morgana's shield, her exhaustion from the intense effort to hold and throw off the Dark Azerii was normal. She returned her scan and smiled at her niece's bemused expression. "You did well. That one is very powerful, and very sly. We shall have to find a way to watch for this one." She gave her a warm embrace.

Morgana suddenly felt her tears well up. "I was so scared, Elas," she whispered and lowered her head. "It was so strong." She looked back up at her aunt.

"But you succeeded in throwing it off." Elas gently smoothed her hair from her face. "You are learning not to run from your fears. That's why you were able to push it away."

"Do not hold onto your fears, Morgana," Rejat spoke up over her sister's shoulder. "Your fear will draw to you exactly what you do not wish to face. You have acknowledged your fear, now put it aside or it will come back even stronger."

Morgana wiped at her eyes and looked past her aunt to the surrounding Lii. "Why are they still here?" she said softly.

Rejat handed Elas the mare's reins. "Good question. Maybe we should ask them." She stepped away from them and looked around. Most of the Lii were young mares with a few colts and fillies amongst them. No stallions, she thought, then in a strong mind voice sent, *Graceful Lii, we have need of your wisdom.*

＊

Rejat and Elas sat in the tall grass, with Morgana asleep, her head in her aunt's lap. She was exhausted from the psychic battering the Dark Azerii had given her. Her horse Kahja grazed quietly nearby under Rejat's firm mind control. They had waited an hour in the hot sun, the Lii preventing them from moving from the rise. Both Mirii had tried to communicate with the horses to no avail. They would not move on or mind speak with them. So they silently waited for their Azerii to return.

The two Mirii spoke few words, both at a loss for the Lii's actions. Rejat was frustrated, she had never heard of the Lii preventing anyone from crossing the plateau unless the Vondarii were with them or an intruder had attempted to catch one of their number. She had spoken with the Lii on her journeys across the Sumarkh in the past, and always receiving some answer to her mind voice. But this time they remained strangely silent.

Elas looked skyward. A lone fayr hawk appeared, soaring lazily on the air currents above them. She nudged her sister from her scowling at the Lii. *We have company.*

Rejat raised her sight and caught the bird as it called out, its cry sending shivers down her spine, then abruptly vanishing from the sky.

*Who do you think is was?* Elas sent, smoothing her niece's hair from her face.

"I have an idea, but I wish he'd shown up

sooner," Rejat said crossly, then stood and brushed the grass from her legs.

"Why are Stil and Brealyth taking so long?" Elas' gaze slipped to the mountains behind them.

"They gathered a lot of wild Azerii, Elas. They'll have to travel some distance to lose them, I imagine. And if they ran into that Dark Azerii..." she trailed off as she began to scan, "Wait, they're coming, I hear Stil."

"Yes," Elas tried to carefully move Morgana's head from her lap so she could stand. "I hear Brealyth."

At her aunt's movement, Morgana started awake. A flash of dream slipped through her, something about her horse. "Kahja?" she said as she groggily sat up.

"She's right over there, Morgana," Rejat said absently, her eyes still on the western horizon.

"No, I think—" she broke off, rubbing her eyes and glancing at the surrounding Lii.

"What is it?" Elas reached out and began rubbing Morgana's back, pushing her energy to help her regain her awareness.

"I had, a dream? About Kahja," she said, looking from her horse to the Lii. "I think they want us to release her."

Rejat held out her arms as Stillyth appeared before her in hu'man form. She warmly embraced her Azerii, then turned to Morgana as Brealyth shimmered around Elas. "What do you mean, release her?"

Elas looked up at her sister. "She could be right, why else would they still be here? There are no Vondarii around or we would have seen them by now."

Rejat leaned back against Stillyth. "Well, I've never traveled across the Sumarkh with a horse." She glanced up at her Azerii's face. *Who was the fayr hawk?*

*He will be here soon, Laa,* he sent back, a secretive smile on his lean face.

"I thought so," Rejat replied smugly. "Well, let's wait a bit and see what he says. He knows the Lii better than we do."

"Drek'h?" Elas stood, her Azerii slipping into the child form beside her.

"Yes." Rejat took a waterskin that Stillyth gave her and drank deeply, then handed it to her sister. "They probably called him." She glanced again at the Lii.

"I don't think he'd hear them, Rejat," Elas said, then took a drink before handing the skin to her niece.

"Drek'h's coming?" Morgana said, trying to hold back a yawn.

"Yes, we are to be blessed with his company once again," Rejat said. Stillyth hugged her playfully at her sarcasm. She grimaced, then a smile crossed her face as she exchanged words privately with her Azerii.

Brealyth plucked at Morgana's shoulder. *You are well?* she sent, her small serious face gazing into Morgana's. *We were concerned; Elas told us of the Dark One.*

*Yes, Brealyth, I am well.* She flashed the Azerii a smile. *But I would rather not have to do that again.*

The child smiled. *We shall watch over you more closely, Morgana.* She looked up at Stillyth; he was gazing down at them over his Mirii's shoulder.

*Won't we?*

*Yes,* he sent, then at Rejat's query, told her of their journey.

"Stil says they took the others to Mahdii."

"Why Mahdii?" Elas' face shifted in puzzlement.

*There were too many for us to hold long.* Brealyth took her Mirii's hand. *We needed help from the Meld. It was the closest.*

"That explains the time." Rejat looked towards the hills behind them. "Here comes Drek'h," she said as his Azerii's hoofbeats became audible.

Morgana stood to watch. Just over the last rise they had traversed, a blond, red-clad rider on a black horse came galloping across the golden hills. Drek'h's face came into view as his Azerii slowed to walk the last few lengths to the standing Lii horses. He slipped off Kitteryth and walked towards them. A pale gold mare barred his path briefly, then moved aside to let him through their circle.

Drek'h's face was flushed with emotion. His eyes greeted Morgana first, he sent, *You are well?* then without waiting for an answer spoke aloud, "I'm sorry, we came as fast as we could." He glanced back at Kitteryth as she suddenly vanished. She fluttered into the white and silver fayr hawk form and settled onto his shoulder, startling him. "Kit!" he blurted, then at Rejat and Elas' smiles he tried to relax.

"Well? Why won't the Lii let us pass?" Rejat's irritation flared in her voice.

He took a deep breath before answering, gazing first at her, then at Morgana. "Because you hold one of their own." He looked back at Rejat.

Elas spoke up first. "One of their own? But the mare's not Lii." She looked at her niece; Morgana's face held little surprise at his news.

"They call the mare their own. If you want to move on, you must release her." His eyes returned to Morgana.

Rejat swore, fixing her hands on her hips. "Then how do we travel? Morgana isn't going to walk to Communion and our Azerii can't carry two riders for that distance. We'll never make it in time if one of us has to walk!"

Drek'h remained silent for a long moment, staring at Morgana. "The Lii will tell you," he finally said, his voice low, his gaze still on her.

She nodded her head, then turned and walked to her horse. Kahja stood quiet, her nostrils quivering as if in anticipation. She began removing the saddle and pack harness, then slipped off the bridle. "You are free, Kahja," she said softly to the gray, a twinge of sadness washing through her as she patted the mare on the shoulder. *Be free, Kahja,* she sent, not knowing if the horse could hear her thought. She stepped back.

Kahja lifted her head high and let a ringing whinny pierce the air. Shaking her head, she suddenly turned to face Morgana. The mare thrust her nose into her face, blowing softly, then swung away and quickly trotted off to join the Lii.

Morgana watched as the Lii welcomed the gray into their midst, surrounding her and moving away from the hu'mans behind her. She was aware of Drek'h's presence before he spoke. "You could not hold onto her, the Lii had claimed her."

"I know. I had a dream." She felt a new sadness within her. Was it her own or from Drek'h?

"Wait for the Lii to tell you," he said roughly and walked away.

As she watched the herd move away, a bronze filly began to move toward her, its head held high as it approached to stop a few feet from her saddle and pack. She glanced back at her companions. The three Mirii stood silent; she sensed Drek'h had told Rejat and Elas not to interfere.

She turned to the filly. What do I do now?

The Lii snorted and pawed the ground. *I am Starrynn. I will carry you on your journey.* The filly raised her head again and walked up to Morgana and blew into her face.

An overwhelming joy swept through her heart. She reached out and touched the velvet nose before her. *Thank you, Starrynn. I am Morgana.*

# Chapter 16

Morgana turned and gazed back at her companions, a brilliant smile on her face. On the rise behind her stood the three Mirii, a mixture of emotions on their faces.

Rejat nodded impatiently to her, then turned to Drek'h. "You'd better tell her how to saddle that filly, she doesn't know the Lii."

Elas enjoined him also. "Yes, she still needs your assistance."

Drek'h's face registered his discomfort at the scene before him. With a heavy sigh he walked toward Morgana and the Lii.

The filly swung her head and huffed a greeting to him and his Azerii, still perched on his shoulder. *This one carries much sadness, but he knows us,* she sent to Morgana.

Kitteryth chirped loudly and vanished as Drek'h stopped beside Morgana. "I'll help you saddle her. The Lii don't need bridles though, you can pack it away." He picked up her saddle and turned to the filly, holding it out for the Lii to see and speaking hushed words that held no meaning to Morgana. Starrynn raised her head, nodding her consent. He placed the saddle on the filly's back.

*Have you carried a Hu'man before?* he sent, as he adjusted the girth.

*I have carried another's Light before now. I choose to carry this one,* she replied, her mind voice sounding almost indignant at his question.

Morgana watched Drek'h saddle and harness the bronze filly, who held still as if she were accustomed to the procedure. Much was the same; it was the manner in which he placed the gear on the filly with great reverence for this creature who chose to carry the rider. She held the discarded bridle in her hands, then slipped it into her pack when he stepped back.

"What do I need to know about the Lii?" she said, glancing from the bronze.

Drek'h looked at the ground, then at the hills around them. "You must always ask the Lii's permission, and respect their words. They are always in command of their form, unlike the horses of the Outerlands." His eyes returned to her, the shadow of his past still evident. "That is all you need to know." He turned and walked back to Rejat and Elas.

Morgana turned again to Starrynn. The filly regarded her with patient eyes. *Your companions are restless. I suggest we join them,* she sent, nuzzling her nearest hand.

"Yes, all right," Morgana said aloud, then sent, *May I ride you?* her mind voice uncertain of the proper words.

*I have already said I would carry you,* Starrynn replied, a hint of amusement at her discomfort. She shifted her body closer to Morgana, who quickly pulled herself up onto the filly's back.

Morgana felt at a loss to guide the Lii horse she now rode without the reins in her hands, but Starrynn, sensing when her rider was securely in the saddle, turned and gently walked over to the waiting Mirii. The three were once again mounted as they watched her approach. Morgana smiled at them and held up her hands.

"Don't worry, Morgana, she knows where you're going," Drek'h said, then started off towards the east, his face still trying to mask his emotions.

Rejat and Elas smiled in return. "Are you ready, Child?" Rejat said. "We've still got a long way to go, so just hang on." She nudged her Azerii after Drek'h; Elas and Brealyth sidling next to Morgana. The Azerii and the Lii touched noses and exchanged greetings silently.

"How do you feel now?" her aunt said, her smile radiating across her face.

"I feel wonderful!" Morgana said, breathless excitement filling her words. "But what do the Vondarii do with their hands?" She laughed and held her arms out wide.

*They hold on!* Starrynn sent, picking up speed, her mind voice laughing with her new rider's excitement.

Morgana grabbed the filly's mane, laughing again at her situation and the Lii's quick sense of humor. Elas and Brealyth kept pace with them and they quickly rejoined their companions.

They rode eastward all afternoon, keeping a steady pace as the land allowed, slowing occasionally to cross narrow stretches of broken ground that the spring flowed through on its way to the Timmar River. By dusk they made camp on the east side of a low bluff overlooking the spring. Drek'h began building a low fire while Elas and Rejat prepared their meal and Morgana unsaddled the Lii.

The filly had mind spoken little through the afternoon's journey; now Starrynn nuzzled Morgana's shoulder as she removed the saddle and pack harness. *Morgannah, be not concerned for the man. He will soon find his own truth and free himself from his pain.*

"How did you know?" she whispered, her surprise evident in her voice. She had kept her thoughts about Drek'h shielded, and the Lii's words went right through her.

Starrynn pulled at the grass at her feet and looked back at her. *All Lii are one, we can see within. This man has gained much from your healing, but he has more to heal. And to forgive. He will.* The filly dropped her head to graze once again.

Morgana grabbed a handful of the grass, thinking of the Lii's words and began to rub the filly down, which delighted Starrynn immensely. She whickered softly and sent, *You have much Healer's Light in your hands!*

She whispered her thanks and continued, her thoughts spinning about Starrynn's knowledge as she finished caring for the Lii. She would have spoken more, but Rejat called her to join them, their evening meal almost ready. She started to ask Starrynn about the next morning's ride when the Lii sent, *I shall be with you as long as I am needed;* then the filly returned to her grazing.

The evening's talk around their supper was subdued; the three women tired from the day's encounters and Drek'h's emotions still churning within him, keeping him silent. Rejat and Elas continued trying to comprehend how the Dark Azerii had slipped past the Mirii's sun shield and why the Lii had claimed Morgana's horse. At the mention of Kahja, Drek'h spoke up, his face full of shadows. "The Lii claim all horses who enter the plateau. They see no difference between themselves and the Outerland horses."

Morgana turned from watching the Lii at the edge of the firelight. "Why is that?"

He glanced at her, then lowered his chin to his embraced knees as he sat before the fire across from her. "The Lii honor all choices. They do not interfere when another makes a choice that they would not."

His voice still carries the old pain, Morgana thought, but a new understanding seemed to flow within him. She thought of his absence and pondered again over the meaning of his Azerii's words.

Starrynn whickered softly, then trotted out of sight. Another Lii answered her from the darkness above them, the call deep and resonant. She watched her go, a moment's concern flickering through her, then recalled the filly's words. And Drek'h's. Choices again, even horses made their own choices. Do all creatures? Even the ones we kill for food? And what of my tree? She tried to remember the song of the cedarjinn, the words that held no meaning to her mind but spoke to her heart. Was the tree telling me to move on, to follow the Mirii? Did my tree choose its own destruction? Her thoughts jumped about in her mind, bringing slivers of a new awareness within her.

Rejat spoke up, trying to mask her irritation. "Why didn't you tell us the Lii would claim Morgana's horse?"

Drek'h turned his gaze toward her. "You did not ask," then shook his head before she could speak again. "I did not know you had never taken a horse through the Sumarkh, nor that Kahja had made the choice to join the Lii. When you held her through your mind, the Lii remained until they could reach Morgana."

"Through my dream," she said softly, remembering the fragments as she had slept beside the two Mirii.

"But why wouldn't they speak to us?" Rejat demanded, her temper flaring into the night.

"Because you held Kahja. And Elas was too concerned over Morgana and the Azerii to hear them. So they reached Morgana through her dream, it was the only other way."

"Past her shield? How?" Elas said.

He shook his head again. "I don't know how, but I know they can. Maybe it was Starrynn, she might have chosen to join Morgana long ago. I only know because," he hesitated as he stared into the fire, "they reached me through my shield."

"Drek'h, when did you hear the Lii again?" Morgana heard the quiet intensity of her words ring within her as she watched him. She was vaguely aware of Kitteryth's presence nearby.

Drek'h looked up at her, taking a deep breath. "It was two days after I left. At the edge of the Sumarkh. I heard the First Stallion call me." His eyes glimmered in the firelight. "I haven't heard them since the day I was cast out. I haven't allowed myself." His gaze returned to the fire as he dropped his chin to his knees once more.

Morgana suddenly rose and walked over to sit beside him. She tentatively reached out and placed a hand on his shoulder. "I'm glad you came back, Drek'h," she said softly, hearing the double meaning in her words. He turned his head to stare at her, then moved his hand to hers. She reached out and embraced him, he quietly returning her gesture. They held each other close, the heart-healing silence filling the circle of firelight around them. When he released her there were new tears in his eyes as he gazed back at her face.

"Welcome home, Drek'h," Elas said from his other side, her healing energy carried aloft in her words. "You have been lost long enough. We welcome you back to your own Light."

"Yes, Drek'h," Rejat echoed her sister's words. "welcome home."

The evening's silence was abruptly shattered by the ringing voices of many Lii surrounding them, echoing the Mirii's words and welcoming Drek'h back to the Sumarkh. Then they quietly vanished back into the darkness, leaving the companions to their rest in the star-filled night.

*

Morgana woke with Starrynn blowing in her ear. The dawn's light was already edging into the sky, tingeing the hills around them with silver. She sat up, looking for her companions as she patted the filly's nose. *I'm awake, I'm awake,* she sent to the Lii. Drek'h was still asleep off to her right, Kitteryth's aura lights glimmering over him like suspended raindrops. Rejat was up, stirring the fire to life for their breakfast, Elas still asleep behind her. Stillyth appeared with an armful of wood which he carefully placed beside his Mirii, then with a flashing grin and *Good morning* to her, he was gone in the brief flaring of his aura.

Rejat started making the tajiz she was so fond

of after the fire reawakened before her. *Morning, Morgana, did you sleep well?* she sent, smiling at the Lii who was still pushing her nose into the young woman's ear.

*Yes, Rejat, better than I have in some time,* she sent in reply, then yawned and stretched. She scratched Starrynn's nose, which seemed to be what the silent filly wanted, then unrolled herself from her bedding and stood slowly, leaning on the horse beside her. *Do you need more water?*

Rejat nodded and held out a hide bucket. Morgana pulled on her boots, then grabbed the bucket and walked to the nearby spring, the Lii almost on her heels. She carefully filled the bucket, then returned to the fire and handed it back to Rejat. She started to turn and found Starrynn again beside her. *What are you doing?* she sent, feeling crowded by the Lii.

*I wish to know more of your Light,* the filly replied. *You are not like the others.*

*What others?* she sent, staring into the liquid brown eyes of the Lii.

*Our companions, the ones you call Vondarii. You have much more brightness around you.* The Lii nuzzled her face. *Why is that so?*

Morgana wrapped her arms around the filly's neck. *I don't know, Starrynn,* she sent, *I'm still learning about my light,* she sighed into the Lii's ear.

Starrynn shook her head gently. *Then I shall learn too, as long as we are together.*

They broke camp an hour later and headed east along the spring toward the welcoming sunrise. Rejat still led the way. As the strongest scanner, she

could alert the others first of any contact with the inhabitants of the plateau. Drek'h rode last; he too was
a strong scanner and kept his sight out for the wild
Azerii, while Elas rode next to her niece, her watchful
eye on her shield for any disturbances that slipped
past the other two Mirii.

They traveled for several hours, occasionally
accompanied by a few Lii who roamed continuously
on the plateau. The Lii seemed curious about the
travelers, especially Drek'h and Morgana. Drek'h had
told them of the Lii's habit of greeting visitors on the
plateau, so they were unconcerned with their new
companions who sometimes trotted alongside their
mounts, touching noses and mind talking in shielded
whispers.

Morgana quickly became accustomed to the
reinless habit of riding the Lii and began watching the
Mirii around her. All three Azerii had bridles with
reins that their riders held loosely. The bridles were
without a bit, only a headstall with reins which were
only for appearances, Elas had told her when she
questioned about this. "We have to journey through
many lands where the people do not know us. Our
Azerii put on the illusion of being merely 'horses', but
we do not control them. Because of the Meld, we
work as one, like the Lii you now ride."

They stopped briefly at noon to rest and share
a meal near a wide shallow turn of the spring. Morgana pulled off her boots and stockings and hiked up
her trouser legs to wade into the water, trying to cool
down in the midday heat. Before long Drek'h and
Rejat were copying her; the two Mirii then began
playing in the water, laughing loudly as they splashed
each other and then Morgana as she quickly joined in.
Elas stood well back, leaning against her Azerii, her

mind elsewhere on scan. Stillyth, Kitteryth and Starrynn watched their antics, then all three trotted into the spring to stand next to their riders, to cool their feet as well.

Morgana leaned against Starrynn as the filly dropped her head to drink. She gazed across at the two Mirii, feeling somehow content in their presence. Drek'h and Rejat had long since taken their rich Mirii coats off in the day's heat and now stood in shirt and trousers, dripping wet, laughter embracing their faces as they turned to their mounts.

"How do the Vondarii survive in the heat, Drek'h?" Rejat said as she cupped water into her hands and promptly dumped it on her head.

He knelt beside his Azerii and brought a handful of water to his face. "They don't travel in the high heat of the day, as do the foolish Mirii on their way to Communion." His voice still held an edge of loss at the mention of his people. Rejat looked up and stared at him, her eyes mirroring the regret of her words.

They returned to their journey as the sun began slipping westward, stopping in late afternoon when Rejat and Drek'h both scanned wild Azerii amongst a large group of Lii a short distance to the north of them. But the Lii apparently were keeping the Azerii engaged, so the companions resumed their eastward pace.

By evening's camp they noticed heavy clouds moving northeast from the mountains and a brisk wind had replaced the gentle breezes of the day. Rejat pulled out her cloak and wrapped it around her, muttering about the unpredictable weather that sometimes occurred on the Sumarkh. While Drek'h stood and watched the incoming storm, Morgana wondered if he would know what the change would bring to their surroundings. As a precaution they made camp on high ground rather than in the protected ravines near the spring, both Rejat and Drek'h speaking of the chance of flash flooding from rain in the mountains, rushing down into the water courses of the plateau. Neither wished for a surprise dunking, so the companions huddled in their cloaks against the chill winds that crashed down from the high reaches and across the Sumarkh.

With the morning light the rains had reached them, bringing a cold and misty drizzle. The Lii seemed to enjoy the change, Starrynn huffing noisily as she waited for Morgana to finish saddling her. The Azerii also appeared pleased by the change, but Rejat tugged at her damp cloak and scowled at the wet scenery around them. Drek'h and Elas ignored her and the weather, and Morgana sat quietly shivering in her cloak when she finally pulled herself up onto the Lii's back.

They followed the spring which turned northeast and by mid-morning Rejat pointed out the Timmar River in the distance, a shimmering band of silver that wound south-eastwards through the rolling hills towards the heart of the Sumarkh. As the morning progressed the clouds began to lift and by noon the sun broke through, lighting the Timmar with gold, its banks bright green and yellow with the tall grasses that followed its course. The winds also began to rise, sending the companions' hair and cloaks twisting in the breeze, their Azerii and the Lii's long manes and tails whipping around their bodies.

A few hours later they reached the banks of the river, normally a wide shallow flow, but now filled with the previous night's run-off from the mountain storm. Rejat and Elas sighed audibly when they stopped briefly, both still concerned over reaching their destination in time. Elas told Morgana they still had a long way to go, the Sumarkh being very wide across its northern half. It could take another ten or more days to reach the lake, but by following the river their course would be more accurate than if they had tried to find the lake without it. There were few landmarks on the plateau, only the rolling hills that appeared endless if one became lost in their midst.

They rode along the southern bank after crossing the spring they had followed the past few days. Drek'h grew withdrawn again, his feelings of his reluctance to meet the Vondarii apparent to all. Elas sent to Morgana, *I don't think he has been across the plateau since he became Mirii,* her mind voice edged with Healer's concern for their friend.

Morgana turned to gaze back at him. Drek'h's eyes carried the far-away look of scan, he had returned to watching for the wild Azerii. She turned back to her aunt. *What will he do when we meet them?*

Kitteryth's mind voice edged in between them. *I will take care of him.*

Elas, receiving her words through Brealyth, glanced back at Drek'h's Azerii. "Yes, I think you do very well, Kitteryth," she said to both Morgana and the Azerii.

Their evening camp was made in a shallow ravine above the Timmar, out of the wind that still rushed across the hills. The few Lii who had followed them during the day slowly disappeared as the sky grew dark, and as soon as Morgana had unsaddled Starrynn, the filly was off on their trail. After their meal, Drek'h and Kitteryth also slipped away, leaving the three women to talk around a welcome fire, the

240

two Azerii out on scan.

"What are the Vondarii like, Rejat?" Morgana asked over her cup of tajiz, her cloak wrapped against the evening's chill.

"Colorful," she said easily, a secret smile edging the shadow of her lips. "They roam the plateau, after the Lii, camping along the springs and rivers that feed into the Te'rakk Lake in the center of the Sumarkh. They hold their Naming Ceremony at midsummer. It's their biggest festival of the year. Most of the clans gather at the southern end of the lake and wait for the Lii to claim their new companions." She took a long sip from her cup. "I was a guest of theirs once, several years ago. I was honored to witness the Naming Ceremony. They don't let many travelers into their midst, but I had a close...friendship," she hesitated and glanced at her sister, "with one of their hunters."

Elas looked up from the fire. "Rejat, will you stop acting like Morgana will be offended by your ways. She will learn of them anyway, so stop hesitating every time you talk about one of your 'friends'."

Morgana laughed as she suddenly grasped her aunt's reference to Rejat's intimate relationships. "Yes, Rejat, tell me more about your 'friends'." She glanced at Elas' wry smile, then back at the other Mirii as she scowled at the fire.

"Just habit," she said, her expression dancing in the firelight. "Most Outerland women have this strange idea about men." She shrugged. "The Mirii don't have their training, thank the Lady," she sighed loudly, her smile replaying upon her features.

"So tell us about the man," Elas said, her voice touched with impatience.

Rejat's gaze became distant for a moment,

241

then returned to the fire. "The Vondarii are very colorful people, did I say? They live in clan or family groups of about thirty or more." She glanced at her sister. "I'm getting there. I was journeying for Lasah to Varan's Reach one summer when I came across a Vondarii hunter who'd had a run-in with a salkinn. It had injured his Lii, clawed the left shoulder and foreleg badly. He had managed to kill the cat, but his Lii couldn't travel. He had put his clan flag out for help, but was too far from camp for spotters to find him soon, so Stil and I healed the Lii and Kevass invited us to his clan. They're very honor-bound people; sometimes that's their trouble. Anyway, it was a few days before the festival and all the clans were at the lake. Kevass took me in to meet the Vondarii Elders and told them what we did. So they invited me to join them for as long as I could. I think they were as curious about Mirii as I was about them. Kevass spoke our language well enough that we could communicate, so, well," she hedged again, "we enjoyed each other's company for about a week before I had to return to my journey." She pulled out a small pouch from a pocket in her coat. "He gave me this." She held up a string of dark round beads mixed with slim white pieces, handing it to Elas, who looked it over carefully then passed it over to Morgana. "It's made of garnet beads with the salkinn's teeth."

Morgana turned the necklace over in her hands to study the long, dagger-like teeth. "What's a salkinn?"

"A very large plateau cat," Rejat said. "Not as big as the Kir-Latt, but just as dangerous. They live mostly on the southern part of the Sumarkh, though they have been known to travel north. Kevass said they don't usually bother the Lii, but he was tracking a chza buck when it came at him."

Morgana handed the necklace back to Rejat, shivering as the Mirii passed her the image at her touch; a large straw-colored animal with dark legs and tail, lying on the ground, blood from a dagger thrust in its neck just above the shoulder, and a man with gold hair and dark blue eyes, his face weary from concern for his injured horse. The image faded as she withdrew her hand.

Rejat toyed with the necklace for a moment, then replaced it in its pouch and back into her coat's hidden pocket. "The Vondarii don't have the same rules as the Outerland peoples, about marriage and such nonsense." She glanced again at her sister who remained silent. "So their customs may seem strange to you, Morgana. Just keep that red sash visible and the men will honor your choice to be Mirii and leave you alone." She refilled her cup from the small clay tajiz pot at the edge of the fire.

"You said this man, Kevass, spoke our language?" Morgana said, her puzzlement rising at this new information. Her past friend had not mentioned this difference, nor had she met anyone else who spoke of the Vondarii with such knowledge. "They have their own?" She looked at her aunt as she returned her gaze with a nod.

"Yes, the Vondarii have their own language, but some know the Outerland tongue as well, enough to speak to travelers. They retain their culture even when the Outerlands lose their own, or build another." Elas stood and stretched. "I think it's time we got some sleep. Drek'h will be fine," she added at her niece's concerned face.

"I'll watch for him," Rejat said, looking out at the blackness of the nearby river. "Kit will have him back soon. I don't think she wants him to encounter the Vondarii without us."

An hour later Drek'h rode his Azerii back into camp. He saw Rejat sitting by the fire, her eyes closed in scan, her hands held loosely in her lap with her Azerii glowing faintly around her. He slid quietly off Kit so not to disturb her or Elas and Morgana, wrapped in their blankets and cloaks, asleep beside the fire.

Pulling his cloak tighter against the chill, he sat before the fire, across from Rejat and next to Morgana, his pack behind him. He eyed the distant Mirii, knowing better than to interrupt her when in scan, then saw the cups and tajiz pot sitting on the stones edging the fire. He picked up the pot, finding they had left him some and it was still warm. Gratefully he poured the tajiz into a cup and took a long sip, staring moodily into the flames. Kitteryth nuzzled the back of his head, then sent, *I shall assist Brealyth and Stillyth in scan. Please be not so sad. The Lii have honored you, why not the others?* Then she blew on the top of his head and was gone.

He did not reply. He couldn't help feeling lost, returning to the Sumarkh. He had avoided the plateau for so long, if only his vision had not called him to Communion. It had been easy to avoid the plateau, even if it took him farther out of his way to journey around the immense plain and its inhabitants.

The Vondarii, his people once, how would they greet him now? He was still Vondarii even when dressed in Mirii red; his heart told him so a thousand times over. But he had been cast out, his mind said, as one dead to his clan. He still knew the old tongue, even after not using it all these years. His mind brought up images of his family, his friends, and his

Lii, Rakker.

He knew the truth now. He would not hear it from Kitteryth, so she had pushed Morgana to say her words, *'You are mine forever'.* Rakker, now Kitteryth, the name did not matter, their spirit was the same. He had wanted to die after Rakker was gone, but the wild Azerii wouldn't let him. They had pushed him and led the Aza Tor Callent to the bereaved Vondarii, who took him to Mahdii Hold to join the Mirii. He remembered his day of the meld. He had tried so hard to deny the Unnamed Azerii who came pleading for his naming, rejecting them with his shield and mind, determined not to be Mirii. Then one had appeared to him with such total love and compassion that he couldn't deny, and with his comprehension of her name, their meld was formed. Their bond was complete. He would never be alone again.

Drek'h took another sip, watching Rejat, deciding she was probably full body scanning with her Azerii over the plateau, looking for either the Vondarii or other Mirii on their journeys. He thought about joining Kit to find out, when Morgana stirred from her sleep.

*You're back,* she sent sleepily, smiling up at him. *Are you all right?*

He nodded wearily. *I'm well enough,* he sent. He took another sip, then glanced back at her.

*You are worried about meeting with your people again?*

His face remained impassive. *I am no longer Vondarii as far as they are concerned.* He turned his eyes to the fire, then looked down at her again. *What about you? Why are you here?*

Morgana looked up at the star-filled dark. *I never seemed to fit in, in the valleys.* She glanced back at him. *Is that what you mean?*

*No husband? No family?*

*Family, yes, husband, no. I never met anyone I cared to marry. My father would that I had. If I had stayed—he would have forced me to marry.* She felt a twinge of pain at the memory of her father's words. She looked back at Drek'h, his eyes meeting her gaze. *Did you? Were you married?*

He leaned back against his pack. *No, the Vondarii don't marry in the way the Outerland people do. But I didn't have any Chosen then. Or now.* He gazed at the fire again, seeking to withdraw from his memories.

*I'm sorry, Drek'h, I don't wish to hurt you.* Morgana sat up and gazed out into the surrounding darkness.

"It's not you, Morgana," he said softly, his face turned towards her. "I just don't know how to face my past. I've avoided it for so long," he continued, trying to keep his voice low. He glanced at Rejat, but she was oblivious to their hushed conversation.

Morgana turned back to him. "We'll help you, Drek'h. I think that's why we're together. To help each other find our way." She reached out and touched his knee.

Drek'h took her hand, feeling her own great sadness inside and wondering what it was. He put down his cup. "Thank you, Morgana, for your caring. You truly have a talent, the Healer's talent, with words." He smiled at her quick wordless denial, then released her hand and pulled his bedroll from his pack, placing it next to her, then rolling himself under his cloak and blanket. He reached out for her hand again, gazing at her as she turned to face him.

"I wish I had your talent with words. My healing talent seems to bewilder me sometimes. My words get lost in my emotions. I don't think you will have that problem. I think you will be a good Healer, Morgana. I hope you will be happy as Mirii." He stared at her darkened face.

*I hope so, Drek'h, I really hope so,* she sent in reply, more to herself.

✳

*Morgana! Wake up!*

Rejat's mind voice barked in her head. She groggily opened her eyes. "What is it?" she said aloud, closing them again at the morning's brightness.

"Look, across the river." Elas' voice was edged with excitement.

Morgana slowly turned and sat up. Across the Timmar River on a low rise stood six Lii horses, with riders. Each rider wore golden tunics and leggings with elaborate designs on the shoulders and sleeves and held a tall lance with a narrow multicolored flag just below the bright metallic tip. Their hair was long and free, varying from palest blond to light brown, their skin deeply tanned. They sat upon their Lii, radiating fearlessness and strength, watching the Sumarkh's visitors. Their Lii stood patient and interested, with ears thrust forward in rapt attention.

She glanced around her. Elas sat beside her, preparing their breakfast. Drek'h and Rejat stood on the other side of the fire, their Azerii glowing brightly around each as they watched the Vondarii hunters.

A clatter of hooves brought her attention back to the river. From behind the Vondarii Starrynn appeared, stopping briefly to nuzzle the nose of the nearest Lii, then trotting down the rise and splashing her way noisily across the river. Once on their side, she walked up to Morgana, then turned to face their visitors and let out a shrill whinny that echoed across the river.

"I think we have just been announced," Rejat said dryly.

The Lii across the river returned the filly's call, accompanied by their riders mimicking the sound and raising their lances high, before turning and riding away into the northeastern hills.

Morgana lowered her gaze to watch Drek'h, Rejat beside him with her hand on his shoulder. Both Mirii held themselves rigid as in light scan. She turned to Elas as she resumed her preparations. "What will the Vondarii do now, Elas?"

Her aunt looked up. "Why don't you ask the Lii? I'm sure she spoke to them." She smiled easily and added, "Don't worry, they know who we are. They have no quarrel with us."

"Starrynn," Morgana turned and found the bronze had moved back to the river. She reached for her boots and sent, *Starrynn, can you tell us what the Vondarii were doing?* then rose and started towards the Lii.

The filly huffed at her. *Why? Do you fear them?* She swung her head to gaze at her rider.

Her answer stopped Morgana. *No—I don't think so,* she sent, then stepped to her mount's shoulder. *I was just curious. I've never met any of the Vondarii before.* She reached out and stroked the smooth neck. *Except Drek'h.*

The Lii raised her head to blow softly into her face. *Then let your curiosity be as a light before you, to brighten your path.* She nuzzled Morgana's cheek, then turned to the river again. *You will be pleased,* she sent, then dropped her head to drink.

Sensing Starrynn had said all that she was going to about the Vondarii, Morgana turned back to her aunt to help with their meal. Rejat and Drek'h were talking quietly, their words lost by the river's murmur. When the two returned to their waiting breakfast, Drek'h was struggling to hide his unease while Rejat complained to herself of her too-long night's scanning, though she had found both the Vondarii and another group of Mirii on that scan, plus a large pack of Kir-Latt to the north of them.

"Kir-Latt? How big a pack?" Elas found interest in their appearance. The Kir-Latt generally roamed only the mountains and perimeters of the plateau.

"About a dozen or so," Rejat said between bites. "They seem to be heading southeast, towards the river." She shook her head. "It's got me interested too, but I couldn't reach the leader to find out why they're here. I can try again tonight."

"What about the other Mirii?" Where are they?" Elas handed Rejat a cup of tajiz.

"They're from Varan's Reach. They're about five days ahead of us, three Aza, six Travelaar Healers, and one Visioner. Daskan."

"Daskan?" Her expression filled with disbelief, then concern. "I thought he would never journey. I wonder if he's had the dark Visions. That would be the only reason he would leave the ward." She glanced at Drek'h, who sat beside Morgana, staring into his cup. She turned back to Rejat. "Which Healers? Any I know?"

"Berranta srii Kadryth? She was the only one I think you know, and Aza Tor Makett srii Collyth, he was leading. Met him last summer. Good scanner, that one, he met me first last night. Said they'd just missed a few Foresters through the north-eastern arm of the Varan themselves. They just left a large Vondarii clan a day ago; we should run across them in about two days, unless they move. Makett said they can't wait for us, Daskan isn't having an easy time of it, so they're pushing on to the lake." She drained her cup. "We'd better get moving, it's getting late." She rose to start packing her gear.

"Yes," Elas said absently, her mind still on the strange appearances of the Kir-Latt and the Visioner of Varan's Reach. "Come on, Morgana, Drek'h." She nudged her niece as she stared over her shoulder at the filly by the river. "Rejat's right, we still have some distance to cover." She quickly began her packing to resume their journey to Communion and hopefully gain the answers to the dark visions behind them.

# Chapter 17

Drek'h stood silent upon the rise, staring over the gold-rimmed hills to the east. Behind him in horse form, Kitteryth nuzzled the back of his neck, her soft breath wisping through his long hair. He still felt lost. His emotions churned within, his fear washing through him at the memory of the morning's appearance of the six Vondarii riders. What would they do if they remembered him? What would he do? His thoughts slipped and twisted within his mind until he couldn't think anymore.

It was dusk. They had journeyed all day along the Timmar without further contact with the Vondarii. Rejat had tried to get Drek'h to lead for reasons she would not give, but Elas had thankfully interceded. They made camp early when the returning summer heat forced them to stop along the river at a deep ravine, offering some shade in the few scrub trees filling its rough sides. The river formed a deep pool near the ravine, deep enough for a swim which the three women had quickly taken after camp was set up, while Drek'h and Kit had climbed to the ravine's crest to scan. Within his Azerii's awareness they searched to the west, away from their destination and the Vondarii, soaring over the Varan and south towards Mah-

251

dii, returning to his body only when Rejat sent Stillyth to call them back to join their company for the evening meal. Afterwards, he returned to the rise over-looking their camp and to his solitary thoughts.

He abruptly sat down, facing the darkening eastern sky. He softly called his Azerii to him and began to full body scan. Kitteryth, with Drek'h's total awareness merged within her, shimmered from his body to the form of the fayr hawk and lifted above the rise on the evening air, pushing her form higher into the oncoming night and towards the starlit horizon.

Morgana sat before the campfire, combing out her still damp hair. Their swim had been exquisite after so many days of long riding in the heat. All three women had washed their clothing and put on fresh garments while drying out their previous wear on the few trees in the ravine. As she untangled her hair she glanced up at the overlooking rise to Drek'h's lonely form. He was sitting in the last remnants of light, facing the east. She saw the pale hawk shimmer above him and lift towards the night, soaring over their camp and the river beyond.

Rejat and Elas also saw the hawk. In the bright firelight, the two Mirii sat and watched, then turned their attention to the flames before them. Rejat tossed a branch of deadwood on the fire sending sparks sky-ward. *He concerns me, Elas. He's still avoiding his past.*

*It's not his past anymore, it's become his present. He can't keep running much longer.* Elas poked at the fire with a long stick.

*Then why didn't you urge him to lead to-day?* her sister sent impatiently. *It would have been a perfect opportunity for him to face his fears and get over them.*

Elas shook her head. *No, Rejat, I don't think so. We can't force him. He has to find his own way, in his own time. We can't push him anymore than we already are. It has to be his choice. Better to wait and let him work out his own path.* She glanced across at her niece gazing out at the river, her thoughts apparently lost to the surrounding darkness. She turned again to her sister. "Do you want to try scanning for the Kir-Latt again?"

Rejat sighed. "All right, but just them. I was out too long last night, I didn't get enough sleep after that." She shifted to a more comfortable position and quietly called Stillyth to her.

As Rejat sent her awareness out on scan with her Azerii, Morgana returned her attention to the two Mirii. "How does she scan, Elas?" she said quietly, watching the other woman. "What does she see?"

Her aunt glanced at Rejat, then rose to sit beside Morgana. "She becomes one with her Azerii's thoughts, his mind. She sees what he sees, in the form of energy, like a cluster of stars, or rainbows in the mists. They can go a great distance from her body to search the area for other people, the Azerii, and sometimes the Kir- Latt," she said in a low voice, watching her sister again. "They won't always communicate, like the Lii, but I think we should try to find out why they're here."

"Is that what Drek'h is doing?" Morgana said, glancing up at the dark hill above them.

"Yes, but he is full body scanning, his Azerii has taken a physical form to carry his awareness, his mind, out of his body. It's different than Rejat's scan. She is using less energy and can return much more quickly from a meld scan. His Vision through Kitteryth is closer to what he would normally see, through his own eyes." She glanced up at the young man. "I wish he wouldn't do that up there," she said, turning her eyes to the darkness beyond him. "When one does a full body scan, all awareness is with the Azerii." She stood, her unease filtering through her movements. "There have been salkinn this far north; I think I'll go check on him. Rejat should be back soon. Wait here." She produced a glowing sphere to light her way and headed up the rise.

Morgana watched her aunt climb the hill and stop beside Drek'h, her sphere casting a dim light around them. She turned back to Rejat and thought about her scanning episode. She had not attempted the exercise again. A brief shiver slipped through her; she would not try again until she fully knew how.

A few minutes later Elas returned. "He's well, but I'll keep an eye on him. I set my guards around him."

"Guards? What are they?" Morgana looked around then back at Elas.

"Energy rings, we call them guards." She held up a thin glowing ring the size of her palm. "They only alert the owner to physical intrusions, such as Hu'mans, or large animals." She flicked her fingers and the ring vanished. "I don't know why he didn't put any out up there," she shook her head, "unless he just didn't think about it," she said sadly.

"Will he be all right, Elas?" Morgana glanced back at the hill.

"You really care about him, don't you?" she said, touching her niece's arm.

Morgana lowered her eyes to the fire. "Well, yes, I guess I do. He holds such gentleness, and such pain." She looked again at her aunt. "I wish we could help him more."

Elas returned her gaze. "We do the best we can, Morgana, but he has to help himself first. We can't know why he chose this path." She smiled softly. "But he is a gentle soul. I think he will become whole again, once we meet the Vondarii."

Rejat stirred from the other side of the fire, dropping her head forward as her Azerii left her. She exhaled roughly, then looked up at her companions. "Sorry, Elaa, can't find them. They're not where I expected them to be, or they're shielding or gone underground." She ran her hands through her hair. "I'm too tired to push anymore. Can you and Brealyth take over?" She stood slowly and stretched.

"Yes, Rejat, go to bed. Brealyth's already on scan and I'll watch Drek'h." Elas looked at her niece. "You should go to bed too. I think things will be more interesting tomorrow."

✳

Elas woke with a start. Something had triggered her guards around Drek'h. She rose quickly and gazed up at the rise. *Brealyth? What was that?* she sent, pulling on her boots. She began to climb the hill, a small sphere in her hand to light her path.

*It was the Lii, Elas. Starrynn is next to Drek'h. He has not returned,* her Azerii replied, her concern evident in her thoughts for the other Mirii.

*Not yet? How long has he been out?* She approached the top of the rise and saw the filly at the west guard's edge behind the unmoving man. She quickly released the rings and stepped next to Drek'h, bringing the sphere up to light his face. His body was rigid, his eyes tightly shut, his face pale under his tan as his breath came short and ragged. His hands were clenched into fists in his lap as he sat cross-legged in the grass.

*They have been gone about five hours, Elas,* Brealyth sent, shimmering into form beside her. The near mirror face of her adult hu'man form reflected her Mirii's worry.

*Can you call Stillyth without waking Rejat?* Elas knelt beside Drek'h. She couldn't safely touch him until she knew where his Azerii was.

Stillyth appeared swiftly in hu'man form at Brealyth's call. His face was also full of apprehension as he knelt beside her.

"Stillyth, can you find Kitteryth? I need to know where they are."

The Azerii nodded and vanished. Starrynn nuzzled the back of Elas' shoulder. *Why is this one so dark?*

She glanced up at the Lii. It was the first time the filly had mind spoken with her. *He has sent his awareness out of body with his Azerii. They have been gone too long.*

Starrynn huffed noisily. *I will call the Light One, Morgannah.* She turned her head away and whickered softly towards the river.

Morgana jumped awake as Starrynn's mind voice called loudly in her head. She sat up and looked around. *Starrynn? Where are you?* she sent. The fire's coals glowed dimly behind her. She looked up and saw the glow on the rise and the forms of the filly and three hu'mans.

*Morgannah, the man has need of you,* the filly sent, trotting down the rise to stop beside her feet. *Please come now.*

She pulled on her boots and climbed on the Lii's back. Starrynn quickly turned and took her up the hill. She slipped to the ground beside her aunt and Brealyth. "Elas, what's wrong?" she said as she knelt at Drek'h's right, noting his pale features in the sphere's light. "What's wrong with Drek'h?"

Elas produced a second sphere and placed it in front of Morgana. Her expression was grim. "He's been out on scan too long. Stillyth is trying to find Kitteryth." She glanced at the Lii behind her niece, unsure why the filly had brought her.

Morgana looked at Drek'h, then back at her aunt. "What will happen if he doesn't come back soon?" she said, alarm edging her words.

"He could die." Elas glanced at her hands. "I can't help him if he doesn't want to come back. He's let his fears push him to this." She looked again at the Lii, a thought slipping through her awareness. Light One, the filly had called her, remembering their earlier words. They have a connection, maybe that's why the Lii brought her.

Morgana stared at Drek'h's icy features. She swallowed audibly, her confused emotions crowding through her for this man who had become a friend. Her compassion surged within her and stirred something else. A memory; of pain, a loss, *Please, not another!* whispered through her head. She turned to her aunt, "What can I do?"

Elas shook her head. "Nothing yet. I have to wait for Stillyth to find Kit. If we touch him, it can break the link between his body and his mind. We have to wait." She twisted the garnet Barii ring on her hand anxiously, angry at her inability to act.

Morgana sat back on her heels. Starrynn abruptly thrust her nose over her shoulder, making her jump. "Wait, can the Lii help find them?" she said, the words rushing from her lips.

257

Elas looked up at the filly. *Can you help us? We need to find Kitteryth quickly.*

Starrynn vigorously nodded her head over Morgana's shoulder. *We shall try. But the Light One should also call,* she sent, then turned and trotted a short distance away. In the blackness of the night her ringing voice called out over the darkened hills of the Sumarkh. Moments later, answering Lii voices echoed back, then silence filled the night again.

Morgana stared at the western horizon. In the starlight she could barely make out the darker edge of the Varan Mountains. She turned back to Elas. "Starrynn said I should call too. How?" she asked nervously, afraid of repeating her scanning experience.

Her aunt sat unmoving, her face holding a moment of doubt before she reached for Morgana's hands. "Relax," she said, her encouragement returning, "I'll guide you." She turned to face her. "Sit comfortably; cross-legged is better. Good, now close your eyes."

Morgana did as she was told, still feeling trepidation at this venture.

"Take a deep breath, and feel yourself centered, calm. Build your shield and make it whole." Elas raised her shield as well, noting the sparkle of energy as their shields met at their hands. *Now, see yourself rising up gently, over your body, in the shape of a bird,* she sent, keeping her own awareness grounded in her body, *just imagine yourself as the fayr hawk, rising into the evening air, over the hills, soaring effortlessly in the night. All the plateau is open to your inner-sight. You can see forever,* her mind voice echoed, calm and serene.

Morgana felt as if she had become split. She

felt the warm earth beneath her body, the cool air around her on the rise, and seemed also to feel the colder air rushing through her arms—wings? The snap of the clear wind in her face—feathers? She soared higher and floated above the midnight dark hills.

*Now, Morgana, call Drek'h. Send out your voice, seek out Drek'h and Kitteryth.* Elas' mind voice seemed distant, echoing from some far away place. She opened her mouth and hesitated. Call him? How? How does the fayr hawk call?

*Call Drek'h and Kitteryth,* her aunt's mind voice whispered and another echoed within, *Open your heart and call.*

She remembered the fayr hawk call; high pitched, long and filled with starlight echoes. She took a deep breath and mimicked the cry. In her soaring awareness the call carried Drek'h's and Kitteryth's names. She called again, then waited. Silence answered her. Then a voice, filled with sorrow, returned her call. Far away to the north she turned her hawk awareness and repeated her call, pushing her heart's emotions through her voice.

With a flash of light, Stillyth's aura rushed past her like a falling star, following the answering call that carried her name. She hesitated, then tried to follow but found herself blocked by the strong call of her aunt's mind voice, *No, Morgana, come back now. Let Stillyth get them. Return to your body now.*

Morgana felt her hawk form struggle briefly, then swiftly turn back to return to her body. With a slight falling sensation, she brought her inner-sight back, opening her eyes to a stern-faced Elas, Brealyth's aura glowing brightly around her. Rejat was standing on her other side gazing off over Drek'h, her eyes reflecting her scan link with her Azerii.

"Where is he?" Morgana said, her voice harsh sounding in her throat.

"Stil has them," Rejat said absently, her eyes still distant. "He's coming." She knelt beside Elas, her movements tense.

Morgana looked up just as Stillyth appeared beside Rejat, his hu'man form blazing with his aura as he gently held the still form of a large fayr hawk. He held the bird out and gave it to the two Mirii, then flowed his being around Rejat.

The two women placed the hawk against the young man's chest. An anguished mental cry escaped from him as the form of the hawk dissolved into him, merging within his body and pushing out a surrounding black fog. Morgana gasped in shock, her fear returning as she recognized a fragment of her vision. The darkness of her dream enveloped him and the two Mirii's hands still pressed to his chest. She started to rise, then felt Starrynn's nose push her from behind. *Call him, Morgannah, call him again,* the filly sent and shoved her deliberately towards Drek'h.

She reached out and clasped his shoulder to keep from falling forward by the filly's push. She felt her shield flare around her hands as she touched him, the energy of the darkness feeling thick and cold. *Drek'h! Kitteryth!* she sent, closing her eyes against her fears, "Drek'h! Come back! Please come back!" she heard herself shouting, her heart filling her voice. "Please come back, Drek'h!"

An inhuman cry filled the night as the Darkness abruptly left him. She heard Kitteryth's voice crying in her mind as Drek'h suddenly went limp, held up only by her grasp. As one, Rejat and Elas seemed to breathe again, Rejat grabbing his left shoulder and with Morgana's now wide-eyed help, eased him back to lie on the ground, Elas' hands still on his chest. Drek'h's awareness weakly returned. He opened his eyes and looked around until he found Morgana, then reached out to her, clasping her hands to his chest and clenching his eyes shut as if in pain. She eased closer as her aunt continued to scan him.

Stillyth flowed back into hu'man form next to Rejat and handed her a waterskin. She brushed Drek'h's hair from his face and sent, *Well? Is he back?* her face masking her emotions.

Elas leaned back, keeping one hand on his chest. She looked at Morgana as she watched Drek'h, tears running down her cheeks. *She called him back,* she sent, glancing at Rejat, *He wouldn't answer anyone else, not even Kit. Did you know that?*

*Yes, Stil told me,* she nodded grimly. *So, what do we do with him now? What condition is he in?*

Elas sighed, watching Drek'h's face. He was holding Morgana's hands possessively, his eyes still tightly closed, his breathing easing somewhat. She sent her scan out to Kitteryth, who was still merged within his aura. The Azerii was exhausted and would need to rest for a few days. "As for Drek'h," she turned back to her sister, "he's worn out. Physically, and psychically. He needs rest, both of them do. We'll have to ask the Lii for their assistance. Kitteryth can't carry him, and we can't wait here. We're running out of time."

Rejat held out the waterskin for Morgana. "Here, see if you can get him to drink some of this." As Morgana untangled her hands from his grasp he seemed to tense again. Elas sent her healer's energy to calm him. Morgana raised his head to help him drink from the waterskin, then returned it to Rejat as Drek'h reclaimed her hands.

Rejat stood stiffly, "Well, we'd better get him down to the fire; it's too cold to leave him up here." She leaned back wearily into her Azerii's embrace.

Elas pulled back her scan. "Yes, but I think Morgana should stay close to him. He seems to need your touch." She raised her hand to her niece's shoulder.

Morgana looked up, her eyes still bright. "He won't answer me, Elas. Why won't he mind speak?"

Her aunt stroked her shoulder. "He's worn out, Morgana. Give him time. Come, let's get him to the fire. Stillyth, can you carry him?" She rose and pulled her niece to her feet, Drek'h still clinging to her hand as Stillyth and Rejat picked him up. Elas grabbed the two spheres and with Starrynn at their heels, they carried the stricken Aza Tor back to their darkened camp.

✳

Dawn came all too quickly for Rejat. She woke first as the sun broke over the eastern hills of the Sumarkh and washed the sky with gold. She stared at the limitless blue above and listened to the plateau as Stillyth's aura caressed her body. *Morning, Stil,* she sent, stretching under her warm blanket and cloak.

*Good morning, Laa. I know you don't wish to rise, but we still have much distance to travel. Would you like me to gather some wood for the fire?* he sent, his aura sweeping gently through her hair.

*What I'd really like,* she smiled coyly, *we*

*can't do in present company.* She sent her Azerii
the image of her quarters at Lasah, and the fond
memories of their private times there.

*Then we should resume our journey so we
can return to your beloved home,* he returned, his
mind voice filled with amusement at his Mirii's choice
of memories.

*Yes, well,* she sat up stiffly, *you know me,
Stil, always one for Pleasures.* She ran her hands
through her hair and looked around the campsite.
Next to her Elas stirred then rolled over to gaze sleepily up at her.

*You're awake? Why?* she sent, closing her
eyes against the oncoming day's brightness. *I thought
we were going to sleep an hour later.*

*We have, Elaa,* Rejat sent, looking at the
eastern skyline. *I wish we had more time; I'm still
tired from my scanning the other night. Now this,*
she nodded her head towards Drek'h, *what shall we
do with the fool? Drug him and carry him to
Communion?* Her temper flared at the thought of
their reluctant companion.

Elas sat up and looked over at her niece and
their friend, asleep on the other side of the fire. They
were lying close, Drek'h on his back with Morgana's
hand still clamped to his chest while her niece was on
her side facing him. She sent her scan to Drek'h; his
mind was tightly shielded, Kitteryth's aura met her
scan gently, her presence still locked around her Mirii.
She returned her scan and turned to her sister as she
pulled on her boots. *He's all right, but he's got his
mind shield up tight. Kit's still there too. We're
going to have to see if another Lii can help if
we're going anywhere today. Starrynn is too*

small to carry both of them.

Rejat knelt by the cold firepit. *It would be very handy if one of those big Lii stallions would just happen to drop by, wouldn't it?* She leaned over and began rebuilding the fire. *Then he could carry them both.* She snapped her hand over the wood and a small flame caught hold of the tinder.

Elas pulled on her boots. *Yes, that would be very fortunate, especially the way Drek'h is hanging onto Morgana. I wonder...* She got up and stepped over to kneel beside her niece. Holding her hand over Morgana's sleeping form she began to scan once more.

Rejat looked across at her sister just as Stillyth reappeared with a small bundle of wood. He placed it next to her and glanced at Elas. Rejat turned to him and sent, *Do you think you could find that large gold stallion we saw a few days ago and ask him if he can help us?*

Stillyth nodded. *I shall try, Laa, but what if you need me? This could take some time,* his mind voice echoed concern. *The Others are not far away, the one last night returned to them.*

*Wild Azerii? How close? Are they with the Lii again?*

*They are with the same Lii we saw a few days ago. They are moving southeast also, almost as we do,* he sent, touching her shoulder.

*Was the one on Drek'h the same one who tried to force meld on Morgana?*

*There can be no way of knowing, Laa, their energy is the same. You know of this,* he chided gently.

Rejat nodded. *I know, I know. Just once I*

*wish they'd choose an identity first, then we could separate them.* She leaned her head against his shoulder. *Never mind, I'll be fine, but we need the Lii's help.* She hugged him fiercely. *Hurry back, Laa.*

Stillyth returned her embrace, then smiled and vanished from her side. She added the wood he had brought to the fire and began to make a pot of tajiz. Elas finished her scanning and crossed back to sit beside her. *Well? What did you find?* Rejat sent without looking up.

*I'm not sure how, but it appears Morgana is sending him a form of healing energy,* Elas replied, clasping her hands in her lap. *She has linked with him on a heart level, through her mind voice and her hands. I think that's why he answered her and no one else. I'd have to ask a Visioner about their past connections to know more.* She shook her head. *This could complicate things, Rejat.*

*Anymore than this?* Her mind voice sounded doubtful. *I don't know how, unless they became lovers.* She dumped a portion of the tajiz into the pot and began stirring it briskly.

Elas stared at her sister. *A relationship based on mutual pain is the worst kind, you know that. Morgana must know she can't save him from himself.*

Rejat frowned at her words. *She isn't Mirii raised, Elas, she doesn't know the difference. Besides, she just feels sorry for him.*

*Don't assume that, I think they share a past somewhere. She has been concerned for him ever since they met.*

265

*Drek'h's been lost too long, Elas. He affects everyone that way. All loners do.* Rejat glanced sideways at her sister.

*You're a loner too, Aza Har,* Elas sent sharply, reminding her sister of her own past.

*Yes, but I don't carry my pain in my aura the way he does. I've also worked through a lot of my past. He hasn't.* She leaned back and glared at the fire. *Besides, I choose to be a loner.*

*We all choose.* Elas returned, her thoughts beginning to calm.

*So what do we do? How can we keep them apart? Seems Drek'h needs her healing.* Rejat raised her gaze to meet her sister.

*We wait for the Lii, and hope Morgana remembers her choices.*

✳

Morgana stirred slowly, grasping at the dream that slipped from her. Images; of a man walking with horses, leading him to a city of gold with tall multi-colored banners snapping in the summer wind, while she was at the front riding a tall golden stallion who took her through the city and beyond, leaving the man and the horses within its boundaries. And the song of the city's people, whispering to her heart, calling her name like an embrace and reclaiming the man she left behind. As she turned to recapture the image of the city, Drek'h's face appeared before her, smiling, his eyes filled with an inner peace that she had never seen.

*Morgana, wake up.* Elas' gentle mind voice dissolved her dream. She opened her eyes and gazed at the sleeping form beside her. Drek'h's hands still claimed her right hand to his chest. She gingerly slipped out of his grasp and quietly sat up. He stirred slightly, his face registering some discomfort at her release. She turned to look across the fire at her aunt as she began preparing their breakfast.

Elas rose and brought her a cup of hot tajiz. *How do you feel?*

*Very tired, Elas. I had an interesting dream though, just before you called.* She sent her the images she could remember.

Her aunt's face held a thoughtful expression. She glanced at Drek'h then turned back to her niece. *This dream could have been a Vision, but we'll have to wait and find out later. Can you talk to Starrynn and see if she will call another Lii to carry Drek'h? Kitteryth won't be able to for a few days, at least until Drek'h is back to himself, and we can't wait here.*

Morgana reached for her boots. *I'll try.* She stood shakily and looked around. The filly was not in sight. *Where is she?* she sent to the two Mirii.

Elas glanced up at the hill behind them. *Brealyth, where is Starrynn?*

*She is with the other Lii. To the north of you,* Elas' Azerii sent, her light shimmering above the hilltop.

Morgana climbed the rise to gaze out over the northward hills across the river and sent her mind voice to the distant Lii. *Starrynn, please come, I have a request of you and your companions.*

A distant whinny echoed across to her, *I shall come when you have the need,* the filly sent in reply, her mind voice brisk, shutting out any further contact.

Morgana stood briefly, puzzling over the Lii's words. I have need of you now, she thought as she returned to their camp.

"Well? What did the Lii say?" Rejat asked, her voice low. She handed Morgana her breakfast.

"She said she will come when I have need of her." She sat next to her aunt as she scanned Drek'h again. "I don't understand, we need her now, why won't she come?" She began nibbling at her food.

Elas released her scan. "What was it Drek'h said, when you released Kahja?"

"To wait for the Lii."

"Well, then I guess that's what we'll have to do." Her aunt picked up her cup and took a long sip. "We'll have to wait. She glanced at her sister. "Any word from Stillyth?"

Rejat shook her head. "Not yet. He was worried about leaving us. Seems the wild Azerii are still with that Lii herd to the north of us. That's where that Unnamed Azerii returned to last night."

Morgana stared at Rejat. "That was an Unnamed Azerii?"

She nodded, "Yes, but we don't know if it was the same one who tried to force meld on you."

"But Drek'h has Kitteryth, why would another," her confusion rang in her words, "why would another try to force meld on him?" She glanced at the sleeping man, then back to Rejat.

Elas spoke up. "Because his awareness wasn't there, and neither was Kitteryth. All the Azerii saw was a Hu'man body, there was no mind to stop it or show it otherwise, so the Azerii tried to meld with him. It failed because Drek'h wasn't there to name it. When we assisted Kitteryth and Drek'h to reclaim his body, the Unnamed Azerii had to leave. The energy of a Meld Azerii and Hu'man is greater than the wild or Unnamed Azerii."

Morgana shook her head. "Why is the name so important?" she asked, looking from one Mirii to the other.

Rejat sighed. "Because, when you name your Azerii, you give it its identity." She stared at the fire. "When the two become as one, the Triad shall flow into Being..." she said absently.

Morgana stared at Rejat as the Mirii's eyes suddenly held a distant cast. "Rejat?" she said, then glanced at her aunt.

"No—leave her—watch Drek'h." Elas' words cut sharply as she quickly rose to her sister's side. Catching Rejat's cup just as she dropped it, Elas grabbed her as the vision overwhelmed her awareness.

Morgana went to Drek'h, hearing Kitteryth's soft buzzing in her ears. She placed her hand on his as he stirred fretfully beside her, her presence immediately calming him. She turned to watch Elas and Rejat.

The red-haired Mirii's face was contorted in fear, her body clenched tightly on her knees before the fire. Elas held her shoulders, her face a mask of concern as she supported her through the vision. *"The fire!...fighting!....Varan—Varan's Reach—they're gone!....They're gone!"* The words burst through Rejat's clenched teeth, her eyes clamped shut against her inner sight as Elas struggled to hold onto the stricken Aza Har. *"They're gone!"* she sobbed explosively, then suddenly her eyes flew open as the vision left her as abruptly as it had come. She shuddered forcefully and clenched her fists to her eyes, leaning back against her sister.

Stillyth flowed into the camp. In hu'man form he went straight to Rejat. Like a child she reached for him and he held her to his heart, his unheard words sent to calm his vision-struck Mirii, while Elas, her face troubled by the memory she had shared, added her healer's energy to calm her sister.

Morgana sat across from them, her heart edged with fear at their emotions. At her side, Drek'h stirred, his eyes still distant. Once more he clung to her hand, in her mind his voice spoke weakly, *Morgana, call the Lii.*

She dropped her gaze to stare at his face. "How? How do I call the Lii?"

He closed his eyes, his expression strained as he sent her what she wanted. *Stand at the river. Say to the Lii, "Graceful Lii, we have need of your wisdom." Then wait.* He opened his eyes briefly, his exhaustion still evident. "Go," he said, his voice barely a whisper and released her hand.

She stood slowly, watching him until he closed his eyes, then turned and glanced at the others. Elas and Stillyth were still focused on Rejat, who shivered violently in their grasp, her face still pressed to her Azerii's chest. She turned away and walked to the river, Staring out over its expanse she sent Drek'h's words, *Graceful Lii, we have need of your wisdom.*

*Shield, Morgana!* a voice shouted in her head. She raised her shield quickly, then turned to look for the owner. None of her companions met her gaze, so she raised her sight to the ridge above. Brealyth's lights were no longer visible.

*Brealyth? Was that you?*

*You have called the Lii, the wild Azerii are with them,* Elas' Azerii sent briskly.

Morgana felt her face go pale. Had she called danger to herself by calling the Lii? She closed her eyes and poured more of her energy into her shield. *I will not allow any to reach me,* she sent fiercely. She opened her eyes again and found Brealyth beside her in the child form, one small arm stretched out, pointing over the river. She followed her direction and saw the answer to her call.

The Lii were coming. A dust cloud rose in the morning air as they galloped over the hills towards the river. When they came into view a few minutes later, she saw their companions, the wild Azerii, their glimmering pony forms and lights playfully shifting amid the Lii. The herd was large, more than double the size of the first they had encountered which had claimed Kahja and brought Starrynn. They neared the Timmar and stopped, gazing out expectantly at the travelers across the river.

Morgana watched anxiously as the Lii stretched out along the opposite bank, She could hear the wild Azerii calling her, but they were apparently content to remain within the herd. As she waited, two horses began moving from the center of the herd, and as the Lii moved aside to let them pass, Starrynn finally appeared with a large golden stallion beside her. At the river's edge they paused briefly, then splashed their way into the wide expanse, their heads held high above the deep wash of the pool she had enjoyed only yesterday.

Morgana and Brealyth stepped back a few paces as the two horses approached them, their glistening bodies shedding water in rivulets. Starrynn walked to her and blew softly into her face. *I have come, Light One, to bring you another for your need.* She swung her head towards her companion.

271

*This is the First Stallion.*

She stroked the filly's shoulder and gazed at the other Lii. The First Stallion was much taller and heavier than Starrynn, his broad back a full three hand-spans higher. He lowered his nose to her face and huffed his greeting, *I am the First of the Lii. My name is kept hidden by the Elders of my People. You may call me Skyrynnar.* He blew gently into her face. *I shall assist you and your companions for as long as you have the need.*

Morgana sent her thanks, *I am Morgana. I, and my companions, thank you greatly, Skyrynnar.*

# Chapter 18

Elas pulled her scan back from her sister. At the edge of her awareness she had felt the approach of the Lii herd, but had remained watchful of Rejat's condition until she knew the vision had ended. She looked past their camp to the river's edge where Morgana and Brealyth spoke with two of the Lii. She rose somewhat unsteadily to her feet and carefully stepped past Drek'h. He lay on his side, his body as closed as his eyes and mind as she lightly scanned him. Her Azerii turned at her approach and met her with an embrace as a daughter would her mother, sending the words Morgana had shared with the Lii. *Starrynn has brought the First Stallion to aid our journey,* Brealyth sent, a calm excitement riding her thoughts.

Elas nodded her reply, relief washing over her. She met her niece with a smile, then raised her hand to block the brightness of Morgana's heightened shield from her inner-sight.

"Ah, we have help from the Lii, Elas." Morgana's words rang with her uncertainty. "Is Rejat all right?"

"She will be. Her Vision was traumatic, but thankfully short." She glanced back at her sister, still

273

in her Azerii's arms, her body now calming. She turned again to Morgana. "You hold your shield high, can you lower it a little? No one can approach you," she said, squinting at her bright aura. *I'll tell you later about her Vision.*

Her niece complied. "The wild Azerii are with the Lii," she said, pointing behind her. "I didn't want to draw any to me while you were busy."

"It's all right now, they have gone."

"They have?" Morgana turned to look. Behind her the two Lii waited patiently. Across the river the herd had moved back into the hills, seemingly without making a sound beyond the water's murmur. "How did—they were just there!" she tumbled her words as she faced her aunt again. "I didn't hear them leave."

Elas smiled briefly, "The Lii sometimes act like the wild Azerii, don't they?" she said, turning back to their camp.

As Morgana followed Elas and her Azerii, she saw Drek'h struggle to pull himself upright, Kitteryth's lights glittering around him. He propped himself up on his elbows, then raised his gaze to their approach, his eyes finally meeting Morgana. She knelt beside him, her eyes flickering from him to Rejat.

Elas returned to the fire and began to raise it once more to finish cooking their breakfast. "Drek'h, how do you feel? Can you eat something?" she asked, glancing at the man whose back was to the fire.

He didn't answer. He watched Morgana, then slowly reached out for her hand once more, his face expressionless.

Morgana heard Kitteryth buzzing. "Kit says he will, whether he wants to or not." She smiled at his Azerii's insistence. She watched him as he lowered his eyes, then turned his head towards Elas.

"Yes," he finally replied, his voice a rasping whisper. He turned back to Morgana.

Rejat stirred from Stillyth's embrace. She sat up stiffly, rubbing her face and looking around, avoiding their eyes until she found her cup of tajiz. Her hands still trembled as she held the lukewarm cup and stared into its contents.

"Morgana, could you get some more water?" Elas handed the bucket to her, then handed Drek'h a travel cake. He slowly began to eat, his Azerii prodding him while his darkly circled eyes followed Morgana. Elas watched him as he finished, then returned once again to his curled position. She was tempted to scan again, but turned back to the fire. She caught her Azerii's child-like gaze slipping from one distressed Mirii to the other. *Brealyth, can you look for the Vondarii? I think we're going to need their assistance for a few days.*

*Yes,* she quickly replied. *We saw a gathering not far south, on another branch of the river.* She disappeared from the camp to search.

Morgana returned and handed the water bucket to her aunt. She glanced at Drek'h, then sat next to him again, accepting her breakfast from Elas. She picked at the travel cake. *Elas, why does he keep watching me? Is he going to be all right?*

Her aunt began preparing another pot of tajiz. *I believe he keeps hanging onto you because of your energy, and maybe because of your past. I can't explain it now, but it appears you have connected with him on a heart level, and you're sending him a form of healing through your hands,* she sent, looking up from her task.

*Healing? Me? How?* Morgana's eyes shifted

275

from Drek'h to her aunt. *And what past? I never met him before this journey.*

*Not this life, a past one, one that you shared with him. As for your healing energy, all beings have the ability, it's just not recognized by your society. I think his spirit and physical body recognize your healing talent even if his mind doesn't.* She handed her another cake. *I think you can help him in the next few days, but you must remember—you always have your choices,* she sent, her mind voice suddenly hesitant.

Morgana stared at her aunt. *Choices? What do you mean?*

Elas sighed, stirring the now hot tajiz. She reached over and took Rejat's cup from the Mirii's absent grasp, refilling it and handing it back to her. *Choices. I mean, your choice to be Mirii.* She glanced at Drek'h's silent form beside her niece, sensing a bond growing between them. *Morgana, what does he mean to you?*

*I don't understand, what do you mean?*

Elas gritted her jaw. *Do you care for him?* she sent briskly, her gaze once more on her niece. *Do you love him?*

Morgana's eyes went wide. *Love?* She glanced at Drek'h, his tired eyes were still locked on her. She turned back to her aunt. *I—don't know.*

*Morgana, what I'm asking is if he asked you to be his consort—I think that's the term the Vondarii use—would you? Remember, it's your choice.*

*Consort? You mean like you and Tagar?* She turned her gaze to the fire. *I don't know, Elas. He's never even asked me to—well—he's never said anything like that.* She looked at her aunt again. *But, I think I do care for him in some way. I just don't know how. Why do you ask?*

Elas poured herself some tajiz and took a sip. *Because of last night, when Drek'h answered your call. Not Stillyth, not Brealyth, not the Lii. He answered only you. I don't even think if Kitteryth had been able he would have answered her either. You called him through your inner-voice and he answered.* She paused briefly and then sent, *I think that he is in love with you.*

Her niece stared numbly at her, then dropped her gaze to Drek'h. His eyes were closed in sleep.

*Morgana, understand me. There is nothing wrong with your feelings for him, or his for you. But remember your choices; if you want to become Mirii, you must come with us to Communion and then on to one of the holds to become a Talent. If you love this man, be clear with yourself, and with him.* Elas emptied her cup as her Azerii appeared beside her. "Now ask the First Stallion if he will carry you and Drek'h." She began cleaning up their cooking gear.

Morgana looked up at the Lii, still waiting at the river. "Carry us both? Why?" she asked as she handed over their cups and plates.

"Because Drek'h can't ride alone right now. He'd fall off in a very short time in the state he's in. You're going to have to help him." She turned to her sister. "Are you ready to travel?"

Rejat nodded. "Yes," she said, her voice strained. She still leaned against Stillyth, his copper eyes hooded with his concern. "I'm as well as expected after my usual...Visioning. We may have to keep it a

277

short day though. Between Drek'h and I, we aren't in the best shape for journeying."

"Well then, we Healers will have to take care of things today, won't we, Morgana?" Elas nudged her niece's shoulder. "Go, talk to the Lii; we need to get moving."

Morgana rose and approached the Lii. *Sky-rynnar, can you—will you,* she corrected herself, *carry the man and myself on our journey? Until the man is able to ride his Azerii?* she added, watching the First Stallion for his response.

The gold nodded and huffed his answer. *I shall carry you both, as you need me,* he sent, nudging her shoulder. *Do not fear me, Light One. I am as the others.*

She flashed a surprised look at the stallion. *I'm sorry, I don't understand.*

The Lii snorted at her feet. *I am the equal of the other Lii. I am simply chosen to be the First. We are all part of the whole.* He swung his head away, ending the conversation.

She turned back to the camp and began to pack, the words of the Lii merging with her aunt's. More to think about, she said to herself, then started gathering up Drek'h's pack as Elas roused him from his sleep.

An hour later they returned to their journey, Morgana having placed her pack with Drek'h's on Starrynn. Her saddle rested firmly on the big stallion upon which she now sat, behind Drek'h, with her arms around his waist clasping the gold's thick mane to hand on. A haggard-faced Rejat sat stiffly on her Azerii, letting Elas and Brealyth take the day's lead. As the company left the ravine and resumed following the Timmar southeast, Morgana turned and glanced behind them at the rise overlooking their camp. In the late morning air a faintly shimmering hu'man form stood on the ridge, watching them leave. She thought of asking Kitteryth who the being was, when the light form disappeared, leaving her with a feeling of missed remembrance. She turned forward again and inwardly checked her shield.

\*

They rode slowly at first, taking short breaks along the way throughout the morning. At noon they rested again for an hour as the women's Azerii scanned for the Vondarii to the south. When they returned Stillyth informed his Mirii that the clan they had spotted earlier was moving farther to the southwest, away from their previous camp.

Rejat shook her head. "We have to keep moving east, Elas, we can't detour after them. We'll have to push ourselves and hope we can make up time tomorrow, after a decent night's rest." She glanced at Drek'h, as he slept beside Morgana, her hand on his shoulder as she stared off at the river, her eyes distant and troubled. Kitteryth had chosen to rest elsewhere for a while, her Azerii lights were no longer visible around her Mirii. Rejat turned back to her sister and sent, *You spoke to her about Drek'h?*

Elas took a sip from her waterskin and nodded, glancing briefly at Morgana. *Yes, she knows about her choices, I think she will honor them, and him.*

*Have you told her my Vision?* Rejat sent, her eyes filled with the terrible memory of her Sight.

*Not yet, she has enough to worry about. I'll tell her later, unless you want to.* She watched her

279

sister's face.

*No. You're better at interpreting than I. Besides, it's too easy for me to get caught up in the emotions again, and I'm too tired to hold on right now.* She turned away and glanced over the eastern hills. A few Lii still paralleled their course on the other side of the river. She looked back at the golden stallion waiting patiently behind Morgana, Starrynn at his side. *How did she do that?* she sent to Elas.

*What, call the stallion?* Elas smiled. *I imagine she has no idea. I'm sure the filly had something to do with that. You too; you did ask for the large gold stallion we first saw on the edge of the plateau, didn't you?*

Rejat snorted. *Stil told Brealyth?*

*Yes. He also told her he didn't find the stallion.* She paused, breaking off her thought. *He just looked in the wrong direction,* she continued, then slowly stood as Brealyth flowed into horse form beside her. "We'd better get moving again. Are you up to leading for a while?"

Rejat sighed loudly. "Yes, but I'm not up to scanning very far. Did Brealyth spot any other clans to the east?" She stood shakily and leaned against her Azerii.

"No, but we'll keep checking. Don't worry about scanning. I just want to keep an eye on Drek'h," *and Morgana,* she added. She turned to her niece who was trying to wake the man beside her. Elas sent a mental 'push' to Drek'h, and he groaned as he opened his eyes. He was still shielding from all of them. "Come on, Drek'h, we've got to go," she said and helped Morgana pull him to his feet.

They journeyed the rest of the afternoon with

one short break. Stillyth scanned ahead, then returned after several minutes to relay through Rejat that
the way before them was still clear. No Vondarii appeared camped on the Timmar within his sight, he
told her, his mind voice heavy with concern for their
progress, adding to his Mirii his willingness to search
again.

*Later, Laa, much later,* Rejat replied with a
warm yet weary sigh.

On a smooth stretch of ground near the base
of a low cliff they made their night's stop, Elas helping Morgana with the two Lii horses as Rejat set up
camp. Drek'h watched them silently, his Azerii once
again joined with him, her aura sparkling softly
around him. After their meal they retired early, Stillyth and Brealyth again scanning their surroundings
for any of the plateau's inhabitants.

Morgana woke in the middle of the night and
turned her eyes to the stars. The silver moon had
made its way back into the sky once again, reminding
her of her past escape from her father's hold. A silent
brightness flowed from her eyes at the memory of
what she had left behind; her family, her home and
friends; all the life she had ever known, and the safety
in that knowing. And now the great risk she was taking on this journey into the unfamiliar. My future,
where does it lie? Am I truly to become Mirii? Or is
this journey a mistake, a wishful escape from the pain
of my life, unfulfilled in the society to which I am accustomed? Her doubts floated around her troubled
mind.

Drek'h stirred beside her. On her other side
Elas slept peacefully, her calm presence comforting
Morgana's restlessness. As the man shifted in his
sleep her thoughts turned to consider him, and her

aunt's words. Do I love him? She had felt drawn to him, that much she admitted to herself, right from the start. But love? Well, maybe there was some love in her fondness and concern for the Aza Tor. She had never met anyone like Drek'h. He was a few years older than her, yet he appeared to be more mature than any man his age she had met. Until they reached the Sumarkh he had seemed strong in an unassuming way, skilled at the demands of their journey, quiet and yet open in his manner with her and the other two Mirii. He seemed so confident after the healing of his arm until they neared the Sumarkh, and then his fears had nearly destroyed him. Why was he so afraid of his past?

She remembered her dream. The golden Lii she rode had to be the First Stallion, and she was leading Drek'h back to a golden city with banners flying in the Sumarkh's breezes. She wondered what the Vondarii camps were like. Did they have golden tents with banners rippling in the winds?

Drek'h stirred again beside her. *Morgana?* his low mind voice echoed in her head. She turned to face him; in the moonlight she could see his face, his eyes gazing upon her.

*Drek'h? Are you all right?* she sent.

*Morgana,* he sent again, then reached for her hand. She returned the gesture, clasping his hand in hers.

*Are you well?* she sent again, but found his mind shielded once more. He closed his eyes, his hand securely in her own. After a few moments his breathing returned to the slow restful pace of sleep. She turned her eyes skyward again and allowed herself to do the same, his presence now seeming to comfort her as well.

The summer night ended swiftly, bringing a morning bright and clear in sharp contrast to the weariness of the travelers. On the ridge above their camp Rejat stood and gazed at their surroundings, trying to get a firm picture of where they were on the Sumarkh. With Stillyth scanning and relaying images to her, she glumly decided that they had lost more time than she had anticipated. She dropped her sight to her companions. Elas was just preparing their morning meal with her niece's help, as Drek'h somewhat unsteadily returned from washing up at the river, his Azerii trotting at his heels in the form of a small black cat.

*Stil, any sign of the Vondarii?* she sent as she stared at the river once again.

*No, Laa, but there are more wild Azerii joining the Lii to the north.* Stillyth flowed into hu'man form next to her. *We shall have to watch them. The One may return again.* He clasped his Mirii to him.

Rejat relaxed in his embrace. "Just what we need, more wild Azerii," she said sourly, then leaned her head against his shoulder. *What about Makett and the others? Any sign of them?*

*No, they are too far ahead. I can reach them, if you need me to, but,* Stillyth glanced back at Morgana, *do you really want me to? I do not think it would be wise right now.* He looked down at his Mirii's upraised face.

She sighed heavily. *No, you're right, with the wild Azerii so close, we can't take the risk. Let's hope the Lii keep them busy.* She turned from his arms and they walked back to join their companions.

Elas looked up as Rejat knelt beside her at the fire. "Well? Did Stillyth find them? Brealyth says she had no contact last night." She handed her a cup of tajiz.

"No Vondarii, but more wild Azerii, with the Lii." Rejat took a sip, then leaned back against Stillyth as he sat behind her. *How's Drek'h?*

"Ask him yourself." Elas looked up at the young man sitting on the other side of the fire next to Morgana, with Kitteryth curled up in his lap.

Rejat turned to Drek'h. "Well? How are you?" she asked, watching his eyes as they slid from Morgana to herself.

"I—am tired, just very tired, Rejat," he said, his voice still hoarse and barely above a whisper. "I'm sorry for all the trouble I've caused you." His eyes dropped to the fire.

Rejat bit back the words she wished to say and simply shook her head. "Forget it. We've all had our bad times. Just don't full scan for a while. We're too tired to haul you and Kit back a second time."

He nodded silently, his eyes still lowered, then looked up at Morgana as she nudged his elbow and handed him a plate. Rejat watched the soundless energy that swept between the two young people from the simple exchange. *I think Elas is right about those two,* she sent tightly to her Azerii, *and things could get even more interesting very soon.*

They returned to their journey, picking up their pace from the previous day's ride, the two Azerii now rested and able to match the Lii who accompanied them. Rejat again took lead, scanning occasionally for other travelers while Elas kept close to Drek'h and Morgana. The day started clear, but by mid-afternoon a sharp wind slid across from the Varan, bringing broken clouds and sporadic bursts of rain that cooled the day's heat but dampened their spirits. The Timmar began to alternate between muddy rushes and clear flows as small springs irregularly appeared along its banks. As they made their evening camp at dusk, the wind was roaring across the plateau, the sky nearly blanketed in darkening clouds with the half moon spilling its light through fleeting breaks. There were no trees for shelter from the wind, so they struggled against the sudden and frequent gusts in the enclosing curve of a low east-facing bluff, their cloaks wrapped against the chill. The two Lii left them as soon as they were unsaddled, Starrynn not even waiting for the rubdown she so enjoyed from Morgana's hands. They ate their meal cold, worried that a fire could get out of control in the wind with the grass being so dry in late summer.

Morgana huddled between Drek'h and Elas with a hot cup of tajiz that Rejat had heated with her Mirii skills, warming her hands. The Aza Har sat on her sister's other side, her eyes distant as she scanned with her Azerii for the elusive Vondarii. She had placed two light spheres at their feet while they shared their food, then left them there to cast their light against the stormy dark of the night. Their evening conversation was brief; they were running out of time. As Elas and Rejat began watching the sky their silent exchange brought a strange uneasiness to Morgana of the coming gathering. She tried to question her aunt about Communion, but her answers were evasive, saying she must wait until they joined the other Mirii.

Several hours later Morgana found herself unable to sleep. She stared at the storm-tossed sky, her companions on either side drowsing heavily while their Azerii watched over them. The spheres cast their gentle light over the rock and grass nearby, and beyond the wind she could hear the steady murmur of the river. All day she had watched her companions and thought about their journey. As she rode behind Drek'h on the big Lii she had tried to talk to him, but for his own reasons he remained withdrawn, his mind shield still high. His Azerii could offer no help, she clung to Drek'h in whatever form pleased her, telling Morgana to wait, be patient with him. Then Kitteryth too became silent.

She suddenly rose and gingerly picking up one of the spheres, walked down to the river clutching her blanket around and over her cloak. She found a sandy ledge to sit upon and placed the sphere beside her. The wind crashed around her fiercely, tossing her hair into her face. She wrapped her hands around her hair and twisted it into a single mass, then held it to one side as she stared out over the blackness of the river. *Why am I here?* she wondered gloomily. *Why did I leave everything behind? Wasn't there something worth staying for?*

*No one...no one...*the voice whispered behind her eyes, seeping into her heart, spreading her doubts through her mind. *No one...*the words echoed again, and she felt her tears rise.

*Why?* she demanded of the voice within, *Why wasn't there a place for me? Why was I there if there wasn't anyone for me?*

*You are there only for yourself,* the voice murmured behind her eyes. *You must remember, you came for you, no one else. No one...no one...*

Morgana shivered and pulled her wrappings closer. *I came for no one? All my life I was told there'd be someone for me. Why?*

*You are the One, the only One for you. There is only you and no other. No one, no one.*

*Only you.* A warmth began to slide from the words in her mind. *You came of your own accord, to create all that your spirit desires. Alone, but never alone. When the two become as One, the Triad will flow into Being.*

"But I don't understand," she whispered to the river, her tears flowing freely now. A sob escaped her heart and she lowered her face to her knees to release her confusion into the night.

A small furry creature brushed her ankles as a pair of hands gently grasped her shoulders. She quickly looked up, her hands darting to hide her tear-struck face, and was startled to see Drek'h in his dark Mirii coat kneeling beside her. His eyes were full of concern behind the fatigue he still carried. He moved her hands away from her face and brushed her cheek softly. "It's all right, Morgana," he whispered, his voice still broken. He wrapped his arm around her shoulders and gently pulled her towards him. "It's going to be all right." She felt her tears rise anew as he held her and her sorrow became unveiled in his comforting presence.

They sat together for a time, Drek'h holding her in the dark, watching the river and sky until the moon broke through the darkness of the early morning hours. Her tears spent, she leaned her head against his warm chest, listening to his breathing. They had not spoken, he had simply let her cry, holding her in support of releasing her tears. *Do I love him?* she thought and felt a surge of warm hope slip within her heart. *Yes....* She raised her head to look at his face. In the pale moonlight his gaze met hers. He lowered his head and gently kissed her brow.

She sat up slowly to face him, watching his

eyes. "Drek'h, I..." her voice trailed away, her mind unable to place her emotions into words.

He smiled sadly down at her. "You called me back. I couldn't hear anyone but you." He lowered his eyes. *Morgana, I—love you,* he sent and dropped his mind shield completely.

Like a frightened child hoping to be soothed, his heart emotions washed over her, flooding her with fear and joy. She felt herself adrift and shook her head, then looked up at him again. His face was filled with his inner turmoil. He started to call back his mind shield.

"No—stop, Drek'h!" She hugged him closer and kissed him on the lips. She felt his shield waver and her heart expand as she dropped her own shield. *I love you,* she sent as their kiss lingered. She felt her tears return as they parted, and she reached up to touch his cheek. It was tear-crossed as well.

He gazed into her face. "I have been alone for so long. I was afraid you would not feel for me—" his voice broke again and he lowered his eyes. *I would not keep you from your path, Morgana, but I had to tell you. You have been a light for me since I met you,* he sent, his voice strained from his fatigue.

Morgana felt her eyes flood again. Why did this man affect her this way? She pulled him closer and kissed him again.

They spent the rest of the darkness holding each other, exchanging few words and soft lingering kisses. By first light, they were asleep in each other's arms with Kitteryth watching over them through the softening night.

✳

Elas woke first and sat up, rubbing her eyes and blinking in the bright morning light. She glanced to her right, Morgana and Drek'h were gone, their bed rolls still beside her. She looked over at Rejat who still slept, her blanket pulled over her head. *Brealyth, where are Morgana and Drek'h?* she sent to her Azerii as she began to unwind herself from her blanket and cloak, searching for her boots.

*They are at the river, Elaa.* Brealyth flowed into her child form in front of her. *They were talking. Kitteryth is with them.* She held up her Mirii's boots then placed them in front of Elas.

*Talking? About what? Oh, never mind.* Elas shook her head. *As long as they're still here, and safe. Maybe she finally got through to him; that stubbornness of his will be his failing.* She pulled on her boots and stood to stretch for a moment, then grabbing the bucket, began walking down from the bluff to the river.

She gazed at the sky as she walked. The storm had passed over during the night and taken the harsh winds with it. Small scattered clouds lingered above the plateau, thinning out towards the eastern horizon. She lowered her sight as she approached the river and saw two dark blanketed forms lying together on the sandy ground a few feet from the water's edge. Drek'h was awake, his head upraised on his hand with Morgana enfolded to his chest. The top of her head was all that was visible. Kitteryth, in a much larger cat form, lounged behind her.

A flash of concern crossed Drek'h's face as he saw Elas approach. He tried to mask the fatigue in his eyes as he greeted her in silence.

*So, have you claimed her?* Elas sent, stepping past them to fill the bucket. She felt her concern for her niece echo in the briskness of her thoughts.

*I have not claimed her, Elas. She has her own path, I will not interfere,* he sent, a tone of defense in his mind voice.

Elas turned to stare at the couple. Morgana was sound asleep; Drek'h's face shouted for the rest he still needed. *You will not claim her as your consort? What if she chooses to stay with you?*

He lowered his eyes, an old sadness flowing through him. *I have been Mirii long enough to know when another has true talents. I will not claim her. If she claims me, then I will go with her, to Lasah, or wherever she is called.*

*And what if she doesn't claim you?* she sent roughly, then suddenly felt dismay at the anger escaping in her words. She dropped her gaze in regret.

Drek'h looked up at her again, his pain clear in his eyes. *I will abide by her choice, whatever that is.*

*And you'll let her go?* she pushed as she met his gaze once more, needing to know he would truly not interfere with her niece's decisions. It would be difficult enough for both of them now.

His eyes briefly flashed anger. *I am Mirii. I have been well lessoned in the laws of our People.* His gaze fell to Morgana. *I will not interfere with her choices,* he repeated, then looked up again. *Will you?*

Elas was taken aback. *I simply presented her with her choices,* she snapped. *I've—we—take her to Communion, to recognize her talents before* the Elders. *She always had the choice to refuse.* She caught herself; Drek'h had a point. Were they both interfering with Morgana's future choices? Leading her on to what each perceived as the right direction?

She nodded her head slowly. *I see, you maybe right. We shall each strive to allow Morgana to make her own decisions.* She pulled up the overflowing bucket and turned back to their camp, then stopped to gaze back at him. *I can't help but hope she chooses to go on,* she sent, her sympathy gentling her mind voice. *She has so much talent, so many gifts to share with an Azerii, and the Mirii.* She resumed her steps up the rise.

*I know, Elas.* He watched her go, then lowered his gaze to Morgana again. *I know,* he said to himself, as his sadness pressed against his heart once more.

Morgana stirred slowly, wrapped in Drek'h's aura and physical embrace. She raised her head to look at his face, his eyes again meeting hers. In the morning's light he smiled down at her but his face held a sorrow behind his eyes. *What's wrong?* she sent, raising her hand to his cheek.

*Elas has seen us. She knows.* He kissed her hand softly.

"Oh. Well, it'll be all right, Drek'h. I'm sure she understands." She pushed herself to a sitting position beside him. She touched his cheek again, then brushed his hair from his forehead. She found herself unable to speak, her words seeming impossible in the moment. She studied his face, as if seeing him for the first time. She saw his fear and love mixed together in his eyes, and his fatigue. The full scanning had drained him more than any of them knew. She still didn't understand why he had lost himself that way.

She brushed her hand through his long hair. "Why did you go so far on your scan?" she asked, her words edged with her own fears.

Drek'h's eyes dropped to her knee. His mind shield flared briefly, then he forcefully lowered it. "I'm not sure I can put it into words. I guess I just wanted to run away. From everyone and everything. I've been running for so long," he paused, his eyes bright. ""Even after I heard the Lii again. I couldn't stop feeling afraid, to come here again after all this time. My whole world was the Sumarkh, I never imagined leaving it." He sat up beside her. Kitteryth rose to lean against his back, her large black frame nearly as high as his shoulder. She purred loudly, pushing him towards Morgana's embrace. He smiled at his Azerii's antics, then his sadness returned. *I nearly lost Kit too,* he sent, burying his face in her hair at her shoulder. "I wouldn't listen to her, and she kept going, even though she knew what could happen. I just didn't want to feel anymore."

He leaned back to look at Morgana's face. "Scanning can be dangerous," he whispered. "You can get lost in it. You can't feel anything when you do full body scanning. You leave your emotions behind. That's why the wild Azerii want so desperately to meld with a Hu'man. Because they can't feel anything. They don't know the joy, or the pain, of being alive." He kissed her again, them lowered his head to her shoulder.

She wrapped her arms around him once more. "I'll help you, Drek'h," she whispered, holding him close. *You don't have to be afraid anymore, you're going home.* The words whispered in her head with the fleeting image of the golden city from her dream.

*You're going home.*

✳

From her bedroll at the bluff face, Rejat eyed Morgana and Drek'h as they talked by the river. She glanced at her sister, gathering stones for a small firepit for their breakfast, now that the winds had left them. "Well, I guess you were right. Did he claim her?" She reached for her boots after kicking off her blanket and cloak.

Elas leaned back on her heels. "No, not yet. He says he won't, but this still worries me. I think he's been shielding from us because of his feelings for her. I'm afraid he looks at Morgana as his healer, as if she can save him from his past. Her compassion for him is very strong." She placed the stones in a small circle then added some pieces of wood and brush to the center. "We'll just have to wait and see what occurs after Communion." She flicked her hands over the pile and sparked the fire to life.

"Maybe I should talk to her," Rejat said, rolling up her bedroll, "before things get too far out of control. The last thing the Visioners will want is a pregnant Talent."

Elas turned to stare at her sister. "I think it would be better if I talk to her about such things. After all, I'm familiar with the valley women. You, my dear, have no sense of diplomacy about these matters." She smiled, then handed her the tajiz pouch.

The red-haired Mirii laughed. "Yes, well, I do get to the point much faster though. But I suppose you're right. She is your niece." She began filling the small clay pot with water. "How is Drek'h otherwise? Can he ride alone?"

Elas looked at the couple by the river. "He may say yes, Kit may say yes, but I say no. They'd better ride together another day or two. He's still worn out; I don't think he or Morgana, for that matter, slept much last night. He still looks dead tired." She went back to her preparations.

Stillyth flowed into form next to Rejat. *There is a Vondarii clan to the northeast, on the other side of the river, near the north branch,* he sent, his curiosity filling his thoughts.

She turned to look up at him. *Can you show me how far?* As her Azerii relayed her the image her expression fell.

"Well? What does Stillyth say?" Elas stopped to watch their exchange.

"They're a bit far. Probably two days northeast. It would take us off this fork of the Timmar and up the north branch to reach them." She shook her head. "I don't think we've got time. The moon will be full in about seven more days." She grasped her Azerii's shoulder, silently thanking him for his efforts.

Elas sighed. "Where were those riders from— the ones we saw? North or south clans?"

Rejat glanced at Stillyth. "He says he thinks they were from this clan; their banner markings were the same." She looked back at Elas.

"Would they come after us?"

"Not unless we really needed help, and we didn't appear to when they spotted us." Rejat glanced back at Drek'h. "He could call them, through the Lii."

Elas frowned. "But he won't. His pride; he is Vondarii, remember? You said it yourself, they let their pride get in the way."

Rejat nodded. "Well, they won't come for Mirii, and we aren't that bad off. We'll just have to travel faster." She stood as Morgana, Drek'h and Kitteryth approached. "Morning," she said, debating whether to comment on their new situation, then decided against it. She saw the exhaustion in Drek'h's eyes and realized Elas was right; the Aza Tor probably would still have trouble staying in the saddle through a hard ride.

Drek'h and Morgana both looked uncomfortable, Morgana moving to assist her aunt, while Drek'h knelt at the other side of the fire, his Azerii next to him. He glanced up at Rejat, and she nodded to him impassively.

*Remember and honor her path, Drek'h,* she sent to the young man. *She does not know Mirii ways. You can teach her.*

*I know. Elas and I have spoken on this,* he sent, then raised his mind shield again.

Morgana glanced up at Rejat. *You don't approve of this?* she sent, her mind voice troubled.

*Me? Approve?* She smiled and stretched luxuriously. *You need no one's approval, Morgana. Do as you will, celebrate your Pleasure with this man, it is a great gift.* She glanced back at her Azerii standing behind her, his face reflecting her smile. *We shall talk later, Child,* she sent, amusement filling her thoughts.

# Chapter 19

They left the bluff an hour later, the two Lii arriving as needed, to help them continue their journey. Morgana rode before Drek'h on the stallion, after he protested that he could hang onto her for a change. Before he mounted; the First Stallion huffed and sent his greeting, giving Drek'h the name he had already given to Morgana.

*Skyrynnar says he approves,* he sent to her once they were moving again.

*About what?* she replied, enjoying the feel of his arms about her waist. *Do we need his approval?* she laughed.

Drek'h held her tight. *No, but my family— the Vondarii—always thought they needed the approval of the Lii. Especially the First Stallion.* A tone of bitterness edged his words at the memory of his last day with his clan.

She leaned back into his chest, feeling his sorrow. She placed her hands over his. *Please, don't be sad.*

He leaned his head over her shoulder. *Hang on,* he sent, pushing his emotions aside, *or Skyrynnar will slow down. He knows we're in a hurry.*

He kissed her cheek as she grabbed the gold's mane firmly.

She watched the plateau sweep by. In the past few days the Sumarkh's hills had dropped lower to resemble the rolling grasslands she had heard of from the few travelers who had crossed the vast terrain. Tall grasses covered the ground more than the scrubby trees and brush of the western rim. The Lii accompanying them became more frequent; throughout the day a dozen or more roamed on either side, and now and then a young stallion would appear calling his greeting to the First Stallion.

Rejat called a rest stop as the sun reached midafternoon. They had ridden hard through most of the day, the easier hills allowing them to move swiftly. They stood upon a long rise and stared off at the slowly moving Timmar, its waters shimmering an invitation to the hot weary travelers. She slipped from the saddle and walked a few steps away. "I'm going to scan; I think we've covered more ground than I thought we could." She sat down in the tall grass, her Azerii moving up behind her, then disappearing into her aura.

Elas slipped off Brealyth and looked around. A cloud of dust was moving in the north, its origins lost in the low hills beyond the river. Probably more Lii, she thought, then turned to Morgana and Drek'h.

Her niece was wiping the dust from her face. Drek'h sat behind her with his head down, his fatigue still with him. Kitteryth was nowhere in sight.

"Morgana, how's your water?" she asked, and slipped her waterskin off her saddle. *Drek'h needs some,* she sent, then took a sip from her own.

Her niece nodded, pulling the waterskin free of the saddle lacing and handing it to Drek'h. He looked up and absently took the skin.

"Drink it, Drek'h," Elas ordered, stepping towards them. She didn't like the way he looked. He nodded and took a long drink.

Starrynn whinnied from behind Brealyth. *The Others are coming,* she sent, shaking her head toward the northern hills.

Elas followed her gaze. The cloud was closer, moving southeast and paralleling their path along the Timmar. She glanced at the filly. Starrynn's ears were thrust forward in intense interest. *What others, Starrynn?* she sent, moving to her Azerii's shoulder. Uneasiness began to slip through her. *Brealyth, what does she mean?*

A bellowing scream from Skyrynnar split the air as a large dark shape fell over them. *"Shield, Morgana!"* Elas shrieked as she turned and called Brealyth to her. She yelled at Rejat, but she was deep in scan, then turned to the stallion again. Skyrynnar had recoiled at the sudden appearance of the Dark Azerii in a giant adjii raven form, nearly throwing both riders from his back. He now stood rigid, his eyes wild in rage with the effort to break free of an unknown control that held him motionless. On his back Morgana clung to his neck as if frozen while Drek'h held her in his grasp, his face wracked with pain at the contact with her bright shield. Kitteryth suddenly appeared in the fayr hawk form over his head, her aura pulsing white above him. She screamed in frustration, unable to join her Mirii by Morgana's shield. The Dark Azerii ignored her as it hammered at Morgana's shield. In the image of the large black raven, its aura churned with a dark fog that swept around it with each thrust of its illusionary wings.

"Rejat!" Elas yelled again and the other Mirii

started to respond, her Azerii's lights dancing around her body as she finally returned from her scan. "Rejat! It's the Dark Azerii!" she shouted over Kitteryth's shrieks and the Lii's harsh cries. She heard Starrynn's mind call and turned to see what the filly was clamoring about.

The Lii, the same herd with whom the First Stallion had appeared, had swelled in number and the wild Azerii were again in their midst. The sound of pounding hooves began to merge with the confusion of noise around Elas as the Lii rushed towards them, flowing across the hills and through the river to reach their captive leader.

Starrynn threw herself before the stallion and shrieked her anger at the Dark Azerii. She reared up, snapping hopelessly at the attacker, then dropped to her feet to begin a high pitched tone that surged from her throat at the combatants. Behind her, Rejat lurched to her feet, her Azerii flaming beyond her aura. She stepped beside the filly and faced the stallion. Raising her hands, a line of blue energy spread before her in the earth and lifted into a wall arching towards the embattled Lii. The Dark Azerii shrieked in defiance when it met the blue wall, but continued to plague Morgana.

The Lii and the wild Azerii crowded closer, the horses blowing and calling in nervous anger. The wild Azerii circled the companions, the influx of emotions drawing and repelling them around the Dark Azerii.

"Elas! Come here!" Rejat shouted. Her sister moved quickly beside her. "Put your hands on my back, heart level. This One has become bolder, I need your strength!" she yelled, her voice straining above the din.

A fleeting thought skipped through Elas—but

I'm not Aza—then did as asked, opening her healing energy to be directed by her Mirii sister.

With her sister's energy, Rejat pushed the blue wall higher to cut the Dark Azerii from its prey. The wall slowly climbed up and over the stallion and his riders, Kitteryth shrieking in dismay as she found herself outside the shield wall. She turned quickly, flaring her aura wide to gather all the wild Azerii she could. Her aura created a great cloud of light, pulling them away from the Dark Azerii and calling more after her.

Starrynn abruptly turned to face the ring of Lii, raising her head and calling into their midst. One by one they answered, facing the top of the rise, their heads held high as they matched her voice. The sustained tones reverberated through the air, straight at the Dark Azerii still pounding against the Mirii shield. With a sudden flash of crimson it turned and fled, breaking the image of the raven and scattering the remaining wild Azerii in its wake.

Elas looked skyward. "They're gone, Rejat!" she yelled over the voices of the Lii. She gazed anxiously over her sister's shoulder. The blue shield still firmly enclosed the stallion and his riders. *Rejat! they're gone!* she sent inward.

Her sister nodded curtly, whispering words and drawing the wall back. *Call Morgana, she's still shielding high.*

Elas withdrew her hands and energy and stepped to Rejat's side. *Morgana! Hear me! Lower your shield!*

Starrynn and the other Lii fell silent, watching as the Mirii's shield receded from the stallion. Skyrynnar still stood rigid, his body trembling. As the blue wall faded into the grass at his feet, he abruptly screamed again and launched himself into the air.

Rejat and Elas jumped aside as the stallion pounded the earth before them, their Azerii taking form to haul them away from his sharp hooves. Morgana appeared oblivious; with her shield still high she clung to the stallion's neck as if tied on, but Drek'h hit the ground hard behind the raging Lii.

"Drek'h!" Elas shouted, running towards him, her Azerii beside her in horse form, pushing her away from the stallion.

"Morgana! Drop your shield!" Rejat yelled as Stillyth pulled her to her feet.

A pool of velvet darkness surrounded Morgana. Deep, dark and safe, she clung to its depths, not feeling anything. Voices echoed from above, shimmering with the energy of each word, sliding over and around her as she watched them, out of reach, out of time, immobile and alone.

*Morgana.* A voice called her name. It was filled with compassion, its energy warm and soft.

*Morgana, you can't stay here.* An overwhelming sense of peace reached her from the voice.

*Why?*

*Because you do not belong here.*

*But I want to be with you,* she cried. A nameless fear slipped through her mind.

*You are always with me. I am always with you.*

*Where? Why can't I see you? Or feel you? Who are you?* she whined, her fear pushing her away from the comforting voice.

*I am all around you. I am within you. You will know me when you are ready. You will see me when you have learned to open your eyes and your heart.* The voice soothed her, pushing her fears back to the hidden recesses of her mind. *You*

*must go now, you have much to learn, and to
teach. Go now.*

*Who are you?* she cried once more as she
began to rise from the darkness.

*In my naming I am Love.* Whispered echoes
of the voice receded from her as she felt herself rise
back into the surrounding chaos of her body.

*Pain!* Intense, blinding pain, but not her own,
shook through her and she found herself locked on
the back of the plunging stallion. She drew her shield
back, the brightness of her intensity dazzling her inner
eye. The stallion stopped almost immediately, his
head lowered to the grass at his feet, his sides heaving.

Starrynn thrust her nose into her face. *Light
One! Get down!* the filly sent harshly. Morgana's
limbs were cramped and unresponsive; she tried to
move and fell into Stillyth's arms. The Azerii lifted her
off the Lii, depositing her a short distance away, while
Rejat began stripping the saddle from the stallion's
back. She felt dazed as she watched the red-haired
Mirii drop her saddle next to her, turning to the stallion again.

A mirror image slipped from the First Stallion
to stand beside him. It shifted to a brightly glowing
hu'man form. Rejat stiffened, her gaze locked on the
being. "Elas, can you come here a moment?" she said
evenly.

"What?" Elas turned from scanning Drek'h as
he lay unconscious. "What is it?" She looked back
then rose and moved cautiously toward her sister. *Is it
the same one?* she sent tightly.

*I don't know,* Rejat replied, her eyes steady.
*Why are you here?* she sent through her Azerii.

"It says it was called," Morgana said absently.

Rejat and Elas glanced quickly at her, then back to the glowing form.

"Who called it, Morgana?" Rejat asked.

"It says Drek'h." She felt the being's gaze directed at her.

"Why?" Elas said.

"To hold the Lii. To keep Skyrynnar from running. To protect me." She clutched her arms around her knees as she suddenly felt her emotions return in a crashing wave. The frightening memory returned of the Dark Azerii's attack and Drek'h's forceful hold as he shoved her forward on the stallion. She had slammed her shield against it with such intensity that she had fallen into oblivion. "Where's Drek'h?" She struggled to stand, turning her awareness away from the others. Stillyth caught her again.

"Morgana, wait," her aunt turned to her, "ask it it's name."

She felt her tears rise unbidden as she asked the being Elas' question. "It says it is not time for the naming. It says you know that." She leaned against Stillyth. "Please, where is Drek'h?"

Elas turned again to face the light form. It took a step toward her, then faded from the Lii's side.

"Come on," she said, turning back to her niece. "Let's go see Drek'h."

✳

"Drek'h?"

The name had a familiarity to it, but the sound of it was all wrong.

"Drek'h? Can you hear me?"

What was it? What did I do this time? Something was all wrong here, must find out what happened.

"Drek'h! Wake up!"

I'm not asleep, why did she say that? Who was she? Why did she say my name all wrong? Must think, must remember.

Pain, right shoulder, hip and head; why do I always hurt? What happened to me? He opened his eyes to the faces around him. Elas on his right, her hands on his chest. Rejat, Stillyth and Morgana were on his left. Morgana had been crying, her tears had run trails down her dusty cheeks. He started to reach for her, then flinched when he moved his arms, pain lancing down both limbs.

"Hold still, Drek'h. You've taken quiet a pounding from Morgana's shield." Elas moved her right hand to his forehead. "You've got a mild concussion, plus deep bruises from the Lii tossing you. Nothing broken though." She placed her hand back on his chest.

"Morgana, are you all right?" he asked, his voice still ragged. His head was beginning to pound;

"Yes, Drek'h," she replied, her voice faltering also. "I'm sorry about my shield hurting you." She rubbed her hands across her face, brushing her tears aside.

He closed his eyes and tried to relax under Elas' healing. *Stars, I hurt! Why did I fall off the Lii? What happened? How did I get here?* he sent to her, trying to open his own inner healing centers.

"Just let me take care of you this time," Elas said reassuringly. "You're too tired to do your own healing right now. I'll let Rejat tell you how you ended up flat on your back."

The red-haired Mirii huffed, "First, I want to know how you called an Unnamed Azerii to hold the

Lii from bolting."

He squinted his eyes open enough to look up at her. "What? Call an Unnamed Azerii? Are you serious?" he croaked, shutting his eyes again. *How could I do that? I was trying to keep both of us from falling off!* his mind voice nearly shouted at her. His head started to swim. *I remember pushing Morgana forward, then, brightness, and pain; her shield? Then nothing, and now I'm here.* Elas' energy was making him feel light, it was hard to concentrate.

"Well it appears, from when I rejoined you, that the Dark Azerii was trying to beat its way through Morgana's shield while you were hanging onto her, and something was controlling the stallion, to keep him from running or tossing both of you into the dust." She shook her head, then filled him in on the rest of what he had missed, adding her surprise at the Lii herd's cry that drove off the Dark Azerii and the appearance of the Other, claiming to have been called by him.

Drek'h was having difficulty keeping his attention focused. *Other Azerii?* he sent, his mind voice sounding lost.

"Yes, Drek'h. It said you called it to hold the Lii." Rejat glanced at Morgana. "To keep him in one place."

*Kitteryth?* "Where's Kit? I can't hear her." He opened his eyes and tried to rise, then groaned with the effort, closing his eyes once more.

"She's getting rid of the wild Azerii she picked up." Rejat stood up. "Relax, Drek'h, she'll be back soon. Let Elas take care of you. I'm going to check on the stallion." She glanced at Morgana again. *Tell him to rest, he can't do much else right now,* she sent, then turned away.

Stillyth stood beside Skyrynnar. The stallion raised his head as Rejat approached. *The Light One and the returning Healer, are they unharmed?* the gold sent to her, his breathing still full of effort.

*I was just going to ask if you are well,* she replied. *We were concerned for you. My companions will be fine, the man has a few bruises. Morgana, I'm sure, regrets causing you pain from her shielding.* She stepped beside her Azerii, wrapping her arm around his waist.

Skyrynnar huffed at her and raised his head. *I am aware of the Dark One's intent, and the Light One who held us. I am unharmed.*

Starrynn whickered softly. *We know the Light One did not intend to harm.*

Rejat nodded. *She's got a strong shield, our Morgana. I'm sure Drek'h will think twice about holding onto her when she's shielding in the future.* She leaned against Stillyth and gazed over the Lii herd to the river below. *Let's go get some water, Stil. I'm sure we could all use a drink.*

A low cloud of dust in the northeast hills caught her eye as she and Stillyth wound their way through the standing Lii. "Now what?" she said as she paused to look. "Stil, what is that? More Lii?" She pointed at the distant haze.

Stillyth vanished from her side, soaring quickly to the hills north of the river. A few moments later he returned, settling to the earth beside her in hu'man form once more. *Laa, it is the Vondarii. They are heading south; we should see them very soon,* he sent, his mind voice edged with anticipation.

Rejat grasped his arm. "The clan you saw

this morning?"

*Yes, the same. They appear to have just picked up and moved suddenly. It is the hunters who move towards the river.* He smiled at her. *They follow the Lii, another herd precedes them.*

"They're coming to the First Stallion—of course! Because of the wild Azerii? No—wait—they have to have been traveling for hours, they were too far away for us to meet them." She looked past Stillyth to the Lii at the top of the hill. The gold stallion turned to gaze at her, then he and Starrynn began moving towards them.

"Why do I think the First Stallion had a voice in the Vondarii's movements?" she said absently. "How far are we from the Timmar's north fork?"

Stillyth glanced at the river. *About a half day's journey, Laa.*

"Then we did travel farther than I expected." She turned to the river again. "Tell Brealyth about this. I'm going down to the river. We still need that water." She resumed her steps down the rise.

At the bank of the Timmar she was quickly joined once more by her Azerii. *Elas says we should ask the Vondarii for their assistance. Drek'h needs more rest.* He held out two more waterskins from Elas and Morgana.

Rejat filled her two as Stillyth stepped beside her to fill the others. "I knew she was going to say that. Well, she's probably right. Drek'h's certainly having a hard journey this trip." She rose, capping the skins and turning as Skyrynnar and Starrynn arrived.

The two Lii moved into the shallows, taking long drinks before raising their eyes to Rejat and Stillyth. *You have need of our brothers,* the gold stallion sent to Rejat.

*When did you call them?* She stared at the stallion, wishing the Lii were not so evasive in their words. "Just like the Kir-Latt," she muttered to herself.

*Time is of no importance. We saw the need, our brothers will help you and your companions.*

*The Vondarii don't usually assist the Mirii.*

Skyrynnar raised his nose from the water. *You have the need. The Lii and the Vondarii answer all who have the need. Do not the Mirii?*

Rejat shrugged. *Yes, we try. Not all know how or when to ask though.*

*The Lii do not have to wait to be asked. We know.* The stallion turned to his companion. Silent words were exchanged between them. Starrynn huffed and moved out of the water and up the rise. The gold raised his head and called out to the herd above. They answered by slowly moving down to the river.

*The brothers are coming. They shall assist you,* he sent and stepped from the river's shallows toward the hill.

Rejat watched the First Stallion return to her companions on the top of the rise. "Stil, I think I need my coat."

\*

Morgana watched her aunt care for Drek'h. Under Elas' gentle control, he lay silent, his eyes closed while dull pain flowed from him in subtle waves. His hands and forearms were ruddy from holding Morgana through her intense shield. "Shield burns," Elas told her. "They'll go away in a day or two." She was more concerned about his head injury; she scanned him frequently as she sent her healing strength through him.

Unable to assist, Morgana let her mind wander over their situation. She glanced after Rejat as the Mirii moved towards the river, her thoughts turning to the Azerii who had held the stallion. Drek'h claimed not to have called it, yet it had come to hold the stallion and keep him from running or throwing her and Drek'h to the ground. What would have happened if the Azerii hadn't been successful? Would she have been unable to keep her shield high and prevent the Dark Azerii from forcing meld on her? She glanced at her aunt, wondering again about the Azerii in her garden. Was this the same one?

Elas sighed and sat back, withdrawing her scan as she removed one hand from Drek'h's chest. She glanced up as Brealyth slid into the child form next to her. *Stillyth says the Vondarii are coming towards the river. Shall we intercept them?*

She looked back at Drek'h, then caught her niece's fatigued expression. *Yes, tell him we need their help. Drek'h needs a day of solid rest. I'm sure Kit will need it also when she returns.* She glanced up as the two Lii started down to the river.

Brealyth nodded, *It will be good to have a rest. You are getting too tired, Laa,* she sent as she slipped back into her light form.

Elas looked up, smiling at her Azerii's comment. She's right, I am tired. She turned back to her niece. "We're going to have company again; Stillyth says the Vondarii are headed this way."

Morgana raised her tired face. "Are they coming to help us?"

"I don't know." Elas' eyes became distant for

a moment. "Brealyth says she thinks the Lii might have called them. Apparently their whole camp is moving, not just a few hunters. We'll see." She refocused on her niece. "Why don't you get some rest while we wait, while I watch Drek'h."

"I'm all right," he said softly, opening his eyes. He glanced at Morgana, shading his gaze with one reddened hand. *I'm just a little woozy,* he sent, smiling crookedly up at her.

"Yes, Drek'h, I know." Morgana gently placed her hand on his shoulder. He reached over and clasped her hand in his, ignoring the pain.

He looked back at Elas. "The Vondarii? The same clan as the riders we saw?"

"Seems to be. Stillyth said the banner markings were the same. Did you recognize them?" She pushed her energy higher to dull his pain.

He closed his eyes once more. After a long pause he answered. "Yes, they are from the fifth clan, the Storm-Rynnok'h, Keepers of the Northern Waters."

"Do you know if they will help us?"

He glanced back at her. "If they were called by the First Stallion, they will. Otherwise they'll pass by. Tell Rejat," he tried to rise but gave up quickly as the movement caused him more pain. *Tell Rejat to ask for Water Rite,* he sent, frowning at his injuries.

"Water Right?" Elas repeated. "What is that?"

He glanced again at her, then quickly closed his eyes. "Water is sacred to the Vondarii. The Water Rite is a ceremony of honoring the Lady, and asking for assistance," he said, his voice returning to its huskiness.

Elas nodded, realizing the difficulty he had in giving her this information. "I will tell her. Thank

310

you." She pushed her energy higher again. "Now, I want you to go to sleep. You won't help yourself by moving around yet." She gave him another 'push' before he could block her and soon his breathing eased into that of a sleeper.

"Morgana, stay with him. Get some rest too, or do I have to 'push' you also?" She smiled as her niece shook her head and lay down beside Drek'h.

*What are you going to do?* she sent, her eyes still on her aunt.

*Talk to Rejat, and get my coat.*

# Chapter 20

Sarduk'h rose in his stirrups, working the stiffness out of his legs from the hard ride. His Lii, Tarnn, slowed his pace, feeling his rider's change of weight. *What troubles you?* the bronze stallion sent, his steps easing across the long grass.

*I'm getting too old for this,* his rider grumbled. *Why are we moving this time?* he sent as he settled back down in his saddle.

*When the First calls, we answer,* Tarnn replied, his mind voice confident of his direction.

*Why the urgency?* Sarduk'h rubbed his right knee. *Have the others become lost?*

*The First does not say, he only says come.* The stallion brought his pace up to join the other riders and their Lii once more. *We shall soon know.*

Sarduk'h gazed past the forward riders to the grass-stroked hills beyond, the rest of the unclaimed Lii moving quickly ahead, calling their companions onward. A few wild Azerii ran in their midst. Bothersome creatures, he thought, watching their illusions mix with the horses. I wonder why they tolerate them.

*Your children like them,* Tarnn responded to his rider's roaming mind.

*The children like their games. They will learn.* He took a firmer grasp on Tarnn's mane as the stallion began climbing another hill. Halfway, up the Hunt Leader Keran signaled for them to stop. The unclaimed Lii had paused at the top. Sarduk'h and Tarnn pulled up next to Keran.

"The river is over this rise. The Lii say we should approach slowly." The Hunt Leader gazed over the heads of his companions as a soft breeze lifted their following dust high above them.

"Does the First say why we are called?" Madeh spoke up, wiping a hand across his sweat creased face.

Keran shook his head. "It is not for us to question," his stern gaze making the younger man regret his words.

"Sarduk'h, Tren, Colkenn, we shall go with the Lii." His eyes roamed the other hunters. "You shall wait here, until the Lii call." He raised his lance high as his mount turned quickly, leading the three to the top of the rise.

As they rounded the hilltop he paused once more, the others spreading out beside him. Viewing the Timmar River below, a large herd of Lii waited along its banks as their unclaimed joined them in the shallow waters.

Sarduk'h whistled softly. At the crest of the opposite hill, the First Stallion stood with another Lii and four hu'mans. Three of the figures wore the red of the Mirii. The fourth wore gray; at the waist Sarduk'h could just make out a narrow strip of the Mirii color. "Is this why he called the clan?" He almost wanted to laugh. The Elders would not be pleased.

Keran glared at him. "The First would not have called us without good cause." His Lii started forward.

"You shall have to use your Outerland words again, Sarduk'h. Be correct in your tongue," he said over his shoulder.

Sarduk'h and the other two hunters followed, Tren throwing him a crooked grin. "The clan will not be pleased," the younger man muttered lowly.

Across from them the First Stallion and two of the Mirii began descending the hill, stopping amongst the Lii at the far bank of the Timmar. Keran held his lance high as they reached the near bank.

The First Stallion called out to them, his deep voice resonating across the flow. *Be welcome, my brothers, I have called you for a need,* he sent to the four Vondarii hunters.

*Graceful Lii, we honor your wisdom,* they returned as their mounts began to cross the waters. Once on the far bank Sarduk'h started as he took a closer look at the First's companions. Two Mirii women; their Azerii flashing around them, one tall with long fiery copper hair wearing a coat of dark reds, the other slightly shorter, her dark blond hair flowing over the shoulders of her bright red coat. Both wore close fitting trousers and tall boots, a dagger hilt protruding from the boot cuff of the red-haired Mirii. *Aza,* flashed through his mind, noting the easy stance that belied the quick reflexes of the Mirii warrior. He had met a few Mirii Aza in his years, but did not remember a woman among them.

Rejat crossed her arms before her. *Calmly, Elaa, they know who we are,* she sent to her sister whose nervous energy flowed from her.

Elas nodded to the Vondarii. *Well? Don't just stand there, talk to them,* she sent, her irritation growing at her sister's easy manner.

*I will, I will, don't rush me. The Lii has to*

*start things moving, since he obviously called them.*

Skyrynnar turned his head to the two Mirii. *I have called for your need. The companions will assist you,* he huffed at them, then turned back to the hill.

Rejat stepped forward. The four Vondarii remained upon their mounts, turning impassive faces toward her. She gazed over them, nodding to each man as she looked for the Hunt Leader. Her eyes came to rest upon the eldest. A man of late middle years, his dark blond hair graying at the temples, he sat calmly upon his bronze Lii stallion. He sat with the ease of a seasoned hunter, his lance held casually in his left hand. Their eyes met; he glanced quickly to his right, indicating her choice was wrong. She lowered her eyes briefly and tried again. The next man, close in age, with pale blond hair tied back from his deeply tanned face, sternly regarded her with mixed emotions in his light blue eyes.

In a halting Vondarii tongue she began, "I am Rejat, Mirii Aza Har Travelaar of Lasah Hawk Hold. This is Elas, Mirii Travelaar Healer of Zerren's Gate Hold." She indicated her sister with an outstretched hand. "We are headed for our Communion, at the great lake of the Lady." She paused, glancing at the elder hunter; he held a faint smile on his face. She looked at the other riders; two wore the same expression, only the Hunt Leader seemed unmoved by her flawed speech. "We, and our other two companions," she pointed up the hill behind them, "ask for Water Rite."

The Hunt Leader stiffened. His elder companion shifted beside him, his expression one of complete surprise. Rapid words were exchanged between the four hunters, then the leader turned to the eldest and spoke briskly.

The older man nodded and turned to Rejat. "We greet and honor you and your companions." His Outerland words carried a heavy accent but clear meaning. "We are from the Storm-Rynnok'h clan. I am Sarduk'h, this is Keran, Hunt Leader," he indicated the stern-faced man on his right. "My hunt brothers are Tren and Colkenn," he nodded towards the other two riders to the leader's right. "They know very little of your tongue. I am better." He smiled at her. "You have asked for Water Rite. How can we assist you?" He slipped down from his horse, speaking to the others briefly in their tongue, then turning to face her again.

"One of my companions was thrown by the Lii," Rejat said, noting the hunter's startled look at the thought of a Mirii riding a Lii. "He was already ill; we were being assisted by the First Stallion and another Lii, the filly." She pointed at the hill again. She began walking up the rise with Elas and Sarduk'h beside her, the older Vondarii motioning for his companions to follow as she continued telling him of their predicament.

With the mention of the Dark Azerii, Sarduk'h's expression shifted to one of worry. "Your other companion, is a Talent?" he asked as they approached Morgana and Drek'h.

"Yes," Rejat replied as Elas stepped past her to kneel beside Drek'h. She placed a hand on his forehead, gently waking him from his forced sleep. Across from him, Morgana lifted her face, her reticence filling each movement. Starrynn thrust her nose over Morgana's shoulder and huffed her greeting to the Vondarii.

316

Sarduk'h looked carefully at the other two companions as Rejat introduced them. The young woman wore the red sash of a Talent around her waist. She appeared to be several years younger than the two Mirii women. The man, still groggy from the Healer's skills, wore the Mirii red. At the sound of Drek'h's name, Sarduk'h moved to take a closer look, the other hunters remaining behind beside their mounts. "Another Travelaar, Aza?" he asked Rejat, noting the man's blond hair, blue eyes and golden tanned skin.

"Drek'h is Aza Tor, Travelaar Healer, from— Mahdii Hold," she replied, adding the hold even though Drek'h did not claim it. She watched the hunter's expression. *He has to know Drek'h is Vondarii,* she sent to Elas.

Drek'h struggled to sit up, Elas and Morgana quickly assisting him. He looked up at the Vondarii, his eyes straining to focus through his pain. A call from overhead sent them all looking skyward. Kitteryth, in the fayr hawk form, came crashing down to stop abruptly above her Mirii, then disappeared into his aura. His face shifted for a moment as he welcomed her, then he glanced up at the hunter.

"I am Drek'h, Mirii Aza Tor Travelaar. I welcome your assistance," he said in Vondarii, his words slow and clear though his voice was still hoarse.

Sarduk'h knelt before him. "You have been injured by riding the First Stallion?" he said, studying the younger man's face.

Drek'h grimaced as he pulled his knees up. "I was injured by being thrown by the First Stallion." He returned the hunter's gaze, gingerly leaning his arms on his knees.

"You are Vondarii?" the hunter pressed.

317

Drek'h dropped his eyes briefly, then looked up again. "Yes." His voice rasped with exhaustion.

The older man's face became thoughtful. He glanced across to Morgana, his smile returned. "I am Sarduk'h. My People welcome and assist you." He clasped his hands together as he rose and turned to his leader, speaking rapidly and mentioning Drek'h's name to the others. He turned back to Rejat.

"We shall honor Water Rite as soon as we take you to our clan."

Rejat's face filled with worry. "How far is your clan? We must be at our meeting place before full moonrise."

Sarduk'h turned to his leader and spoke in Vondarii, "Have our clan made camp?"

Keran stood with his arms folded to his chest. He looked at the First Stallion, his eyes becoming distant, then as the gold returned his gaze he said absently, "The First says we shall assist them forward. The clan is at the joining of the rivers." He turned his gaze back to the older man. "They have traveled quickly for this meeting. Tell them," he said, nodding towards the Mirii.

Sarduk'h turned back to Rejat, relaying the other man's words, then added to Drek'h, "Can you ride?"

He was about to speak when Elas lay a hand on his shoulder. "He will need assistance," she said briskly, "he has been unconscious." She glanced down at Drek'h, his gaze meeting her with a spark of anger in his blue eyes. *You cannot ride unaided,* she sent firmly, her thoughts closed for discussion.

Drek'h glanced up at Sarduk'h. The older man simply shrugged and stated in Vondarii, "Who can argue with a Healer?" then stepped forward and held out his hand.

The Aza Tor took the offered hand and rose shakily to his feet with help from Morgana. Elas stepped back to retrieve their waterskins. Drek'h spoke his thanks to Sarduk'h, then leaned against Morgana, his head swimming with his movements.

"Is your chosen strong enough to help you stay on your horse?" the hunter said in Vondarii, watching the young woman standing somewhat unsteadily herself.

"She's not—she can manage," Drek'h said, his eyes shifting from the two beside him. "Can you ride alone, Morgana?" he turned to her, his words in Outerland.

She stared at him. *I can help you,* she sent, gingerly holding his arm. She glanced over her shoulder at the First Stallion. *Maybe he'll carry us both again? Shall I ask?*

"Morgana, maybe you'd better ride with one of the others," Rejat stepped in, watching her face. Elas nodded beside her.

"You took a rough time also. If you two ride together you may both fall off." Elas handed Morgana her waterskin. "Can two of your riders carry another?" she said to Sarduk'h, ignoring her niece's fallen expression.

"Elas, I'm not that tired." Morgana glanced from her aunt to Rejat. "I can ride alone," she said stubbornly, "if you don't think I can help Drek'h." She glanced back at him.

Drek'h carefully took her hand. *Ask Skyrynnar.*

She turned back to the First Stallion. The gold stood beside her abandoned saddle, his head raised high. *I shall assist you, Light One. Let one of the brothers assist the returning Healer.*

Morgana faced the Mirii and the Vondarii. "The First says he will carry me. Will one of you assist Drek'h?" she said, suddenly aware of the honor the Lii gave her in the hunter's eyes. She lowered her gaze in thanks.

The elder man smiled and held out his hand to Drek'h once more. "I think my Tarnn would feel most honored."

A short time later they were riding again. Elas and Rejat upon their Azerii, Morgana on Skyrynnar, while Drek'h rode in front of Sarduk'h on his Lii, Starrynn following with the two packs. Keran led the way, two hunters on either side of him, as he moved down the rise through the milling Lii herd and across the Timmar to rejoin the rest of the hunters on the other side. Without a word they followed; behind them the Lii resumed their travels across the open Sumarkh.

✳

Under starlight and hushed winds they approached the Vondarii camp well past nightfall. With the Timmar to their right they had traveled the last few hours carefully, the riders trusting the eyes of their mounts and taking a slower pace to avoid injuries in the dark. The unclaimed herd of Lii led them over the rustling mounds of grasses towards their goal, the Storm-Rynnok'h clan camp, now on a broad flat rise overlooking the joining of the Timmar with its northern fork, the Koreth River, as the Vondarii called it.

Sarduk'h held the nearly unconscious Drek'h before him as he urged his Lii to quicken the pace.

Beyond him, his Hunt Leader called out upon sighting the watchfires of the clan. The two Mirii women on either side of him also hastened their mounts forward, Elas reaching out to clasp his arm as they traversed the last rise before the camp.

*Easy, Sarduk'h,* she sent, ignoring the Vondarii's startled gasp at her use of mind speech. *Drek'h has not been well, the days have been very hard on him.* Her Azerii moved closer to his Lii. *Let me see him.* She reached for the Aza Tor's shoulder.

Sarduk'h felt Tarnn slow to pace the Mirii's horse. "What happened to him to cause this?" he asked in Outerland, his eyes searching the darkness for Elas' face.

"You shall have to ask him," she said absently, her voice echoing the distance of her scan. "It has been a matter of his choices."

Rejat on Stillyth slowed to move beside Morgana, riding on the gold stallion behind Sarduk'h's Lii. *Morgana, are you awake?* she sent, watching the younger woman jump in her saddle.

*Yes, Rejat, just about,* she sent back her sleepy reply, looking up at the Mirii beside her. "Is that the Vondarii camp?" she said aloud, her eyes reflecting the dim glow of the watchfires on the hill above them.

Rejat turned to look. "Yes, we're almost there. I didn't think we'd see it 'til morning. They must have moved pretty fast to be here waiting for us."

"Do you think the Lii told them to move here?" She glanced down at the stallion she rode.

"Yes," Rejat said flatly. "Come on, keep awake, we're here." She turned as they crested the top of the rise, Stillyth moving up to Sarduk'h's left side, Elas on his right, remaining close to watch Drek'h.

Morgana felt Skyrynnar quicken his steps to meet the Vondarii who called to the Lii from their camp. They passed the watchfire on the ridge, two young men of the clan cheering their welcome to the returning hunters and the unclaimed Lii with them. She looked past her companions to the camp. Several large dark shapes rose out of the grassland, their painted sides and tall banner poles shifting from several fires and torches, set to light the camp site for the evening's return of the clan hunters. Many people moved in the flickering light, some carrying torches themselves, as they began moving toward the arrivals. The unclaimed Lii moved to either side of the camp, allowing a few of the people to greet them, then turning to the open grasses beyond the tents. Voices tumbled over each other, calling greetings to the hunters, pointing and talking excitedly about the newcomers amongst them. As the clan spotted Morgana on the back of the First Stallion their voices began to recede. In hushed tones they watched as the gold strode purposely in the midst of the hunters, his head raised high as if surveying the clan's reactions to his chosen rider.

They rode into the center of the camp, Keran leading with four hunters flanking him, then Rejat, Sarduk'h with Drek'h, then Elas and Morgana with the other hunters around and behind them. Keran stopped before a large central fire, slipping off his Lii to stand. On the other side of the fire a larger tent stood; at its entrance two tall banner poles fronted the doorway where several elder men and women waited. Keran walked solemnly around the fire to stand before the elders of his clan. He placed his lance into the central elder man's hands, bowing his head as he did so. Words were exchanged between them, then his lance was returned and he faced the Mirii, motioning them forward.

Sarduk'h turned to Elas. "The Elders will wish to speak to all of you, but I don't think your companion here is able." He eased Drek'h forward as Elas slipped from her mount to stand and assist the Aza Tor to the ground, the hunter Tren stepping forward to help. Drek'h moaned softly, unable to stay awake for long, he reached clumsily for support as Sarduk'h let him down. Elas raised her hands to his head while Tren held him up and pushed him to sleep. She glanced at the hunter for any reaction. Tren merely nodded and picked up the unconscious Mirii.

"Is there a place I can tend him? And Morgana, she is exhausted too," she said to Sarduk'h. "Rejat can speak for all of us." She glanced past the older hunter at her Mirii sister, who nodded in return.

Sarduk'h slid from his horse and walked to the elders, bowing and speaking briefly, then returned to Rejat and Elas. "A place is being prepared. We shall honor Water Rite with the Mirii Rejat as your representative." As Rejat slipped from her saddle to stand beside him, the other hunters began moving around the fire to honor their elders before leaving to care for their Lii and seeking their own tents for the night. The hunter Colkenn stepped up to the First Stallion and held out his hand towards Morgana. She glanced once at Rejat who sent briskly, *Get down, follow Elas,* then took the offered hand and climbed down tiredly from the gold's back. Colkenn started to remove her saddle.

A soft whicker from behind called her. "Starryn, I'm sorry, I almost forgot you!" She turned to the filly waiting patiently behind the other Lii, hugging her neck. Then, following Colkenn's actions she began removing the packs and harness. Once all the gear was removed she patted Starrynn on the neck. *Do you wish me to rub you down?* she sent, absently leaning against the filly's shoulder.

Starrynn snorted, turning to nibble her arm. *No, Light One, you have struggled enough this day. Rest yourself, and I will rest also.* Her soft nose brushed Morgana's face.

The First Stallion moved to her side. *You and your companions shall rest here. Our brothers will care for you.* He softly blew in her face, then with the filly alongside, moved out of the circle towards the surrounding grassland.

Morgana stood beside the packs and harness, aware once again of the voices around her and the stares the Vondarii gave them. She glanced back at her aunt as a woman of similar years tugged at her sleeve to follow, motioning to the hunter to bring Drek'h along.

"Come on Morgana," Elas said over her shoulder as she started after the woman. She picked up her pack and would have grabbed Drek'h's also when another hunter from their escort, a young man near her age, stepped up. He raised the pack and harness to his shoulder, smiling broadly and nodding his head towards Elas. She glanced at Colkenn as he turned and started after her aunt. A last glance at Rejat told her the Aza Har was busy with Sarduk'h and the elders, and would be for some time, so she turned and walked quickly with the other hunter after Elas.

They went past the large central tent to the ring of tents beyond, passing three and stopping at the fourth, its banner pole empty of any cloth save for narrow ribbons that trailed down in the soft evening breeze. Standing at the entrance were two young women who proudly held their torches like the hunters held their lances, throwing brief curious glances at their guests. Morgana slipped past them into the tent moments after her aunt and Tren, who was carrying Drek'h. The interior was well lit; small oil lamps hung from the supports casting a warm glow about the simply furnished enclosure. Soft hides covered the floor as well as a large woven carpet of a pattern she had never seen before. The tent was tall enough for all to stand except against its curving walls. A richly woven curtain hung across the middle, dividing the area into two rooms. The walls and roof of the tent appeared to be large chza hides sewn together in random sections, making the tent snug from outside elements.

The chattering voice of the Vondarii woman scolded the two hunters who stepped in behind Morgana, carrying the packs, harnesses and saddles. They hurriedly set the gear on the floor against the wall, then were nearly pushed out by the woman's words. The woman turned, and pulling wide the curtain in the center, motioned them to the other half of the tent. Once beyond, Morgana saw four bedrolls laid out, sleeping furs rolled at the head of each. The woman directed Tren to place Drek'h gently on the nearest and with Elas' guidance they stretched the sleeping man out.

Elas sat beside Drek'h, her hands on his chest and forehead. She glanced up at the Vondarii woman who spoke to the hunter as he left, and then knelt beside Elas to stare at Drek'h. Morgana moved to his other side and touched his shoulder. Her aunt looked up and smiled at her. "He'll be all right. I just didn't want any arguments from him tonight. He needs to rest, and so do you."

The Vondarii woman reached across and tapped Morgana's arm. She spoke rapidly and motioned for her to follow. Morgana looked at Elas. "What is she saying?"

Her aunt shrugged. "Just follow, I'm sure you'll be fine. Don't try to mind talk though, they consider it intrusive." She returned her gaze to Drek'h.

Morgana rose as the other woman beckoned her through the curtain opening. On the other side a low round table had been placed to one side, around it more furs had been piled as cushions. The woman guided her to the nearest fur and signed for her to sit. As she did, another woman entered the tent carrying a tray with a pitcher and four cups.

The first woman spoke again to Morgana as the second poured water into the cups. She watched and waited, shyly wondering what was being said. The second woman knelt before the table. At a nod from the other, sitting across from Morgana, she raised a cup before her and softly spoke over it. She handed the cup to the first woman, who repeated the gesture, then handed the cup to Morgana.

She took the offered cup, her eyes flitting from one woman to the other, then held the cup before her and struggled to repeat their words, adding, "Thank you, Lady, for our companions' assistance." The two women smiled, then the second took the cup from her and took a sip. She handed the cup to the other who did the same, then handed it again to their guest.

Morgana smiled and took a sip from the cup, then placed it before her on the table. The two women watched her, then the first motioned for her to drink all of the water. She smiled in understanding and drained the contents which pleased the two. They began speaking again, then the second rose and left the tent. Morgana picked up another cup and pointed to the curtain. The woman nodded and rose with her, opening the fabric so she could take the water to her aunt.

Elas raised her hand from Drek'h's chest to take the cup from her, repeating her own soft words over it before drinking all of its contents. *I think we've just been given Water Rite, Morgana, informally though,* she sent as she handed the cup back. *Now I hope they will feed us and then let us sleep.* She took another glance at Drek'h. Satisfied he would not move for some time, she rose and followed her niece to the front of the tent. She sat where Morgana had been, the Vondarii woman motioning for Morgana to take her place.

The second woman returned a moment later bearing a loaded tray of food. Flat breads, smoked meats, vegetables and fruits filled the wooden platter to overflowing. She quickly placed the tray beside the pitcher, speaking her unknown words, then turned from the tent once more. The other woman repeated her words and slipped outside after her.

The two guests exchanged glances then stared at the feast before them. After weeks of slim rations on their journey, the Vondarii had truly prepared an unexpected but welcome repast.

Elas picked up a piece of bread. "Well, Morgana, enjoy," she said, taking a bite, *and thank the Lady!*

Her niece smiled tiredly. "How long will they keep Rejat? There's enough here for all of us and more." She began to work on a strip of dried meat.

"Not long, I hope. I know she's tired. Hopefully Sarduk'h can do most of the talking for her. She's not at her best when she's exhausted. Brealyth's with her, we should know soon."

"Shouldn't Drek'h eat something?" Morgana eyed the tent's divider.

"He needs rest right now. I'll wake him long enough to get some water in him before we retire." She glanced at her niece, questioning herself about what she and the Aza Tor had spoken of before the day's shattering by the Dark Azerii. *Wait and watch,* the thought slipped through her head. She sighed and picked up a piece of meat. Smoked chza, well and good.

"How long do we stay here?" Morgana filled her cup again.

"Hmm, at least one full day; we won't be disturbed by the wild Azerii while we're here. The Vondarii have their own shielding methods."

"We have to reach Communion by the full moon?"

"Moonrise, yes." Elas chewed thoughtfully, trying to recall exactly how much time they had left.

"What if we don't make it? What then?"

"We'll make it," she said firmly. "We must."

Morgana gazed at the ornate rug as she ate. "What was Rejat's Vision?" she asked, not looking up.

Elas glanced unhappily at her. "More destruction. By men wearing Forester green, and the Dark Azerii. I'd rather not give the details right now." She stared at the wall behind her niece. A sudden image of Tagar flashed before her inner eye. Stars, I miss him! And it's going to be so long before we're together again. She shook her head, willing the brightness of her eyes to be gone.

Morgana looked up as voices beyond the tent filtered through. "Sounds like Rejat," she said as she rose to the door flap.

The tent closure was pulled aside briskly and Sarduk'h, the first woman and Rejat entered, the woman speaking rapidly to the other two as the Mirii dropped her pack to the floor. Rejat's face showed her strain as she tried to follow the other's words. She spoke slowly in return, then eyeing the laden tray, sat herself in front of the table and took the cup offered her by Elas. She repeated the Water Rite and tossed down the cup's contents. The woman suddenly stopped speaking and hurried out of the tent.

"Sarduk'h, my friend, sit," Rejat said, refilling her cup and handing it over to the hunter as he sat between the Aza Har and Elas. He too, repeated the rite and drained the cup in one motion, then glanced back at Rejat as Morgana returned to listen.

"Well?" Elas glanced from her sister to the hunter. "What was that all about?"

Rejat stared into her cup. "Stars! Why couldn't this be tajiz? Or your southern valley wine?" She plucked a large strip of meat from the tray, tearing into it heartily.

"Rejat, would you please explain what is going on?" Elas glanced at Sarduk'h who was trying not to laugh.

"Everything is fine, Elaa. We are most welcome here, though the Elders wish to speak to each of us." She raised an eyebrow at Morgana. "In the morning. Late, I hope." She chewed between her words. "That woman," she glanced at Sarduk'h.

"Talahs," he replied, picking up a piece of fruit.

"Yes, Ta-lahs. Well, she is Sarduk'h's cousin, and she doesn't think it proper for him to be here, 'specially since this is their Healer's tent, and no healthy men are allowed for more than a necessary moment." She gulped down a bite of fruit.

"I assume Sarduk'h is here for a necessary moment, then?" Elas eyed the hunter again.

"Where is their Healer?" Morgana asked quietly.

Sarduk'h glanced at her. "She is Seeking. She will know of her tent's use. She will allow." His face became solemn. "She has Visions."

"Visions?" Elas and Rejat grasped at his words. "What Visions?" Elas added, her expression marking her interest.

The hunter lowered his eyes. "I may not speak of them. When she returns she will talk with you," he said, looking up at her again.

"When will she be back?" Rejat asked crisply.

Sarduk'h eyed her change of tone. "Before you leave."

"How do you know, Sar-duk'h?" Morgana stumbled over the hunter's name.

He smiled gently at her. "We are clan. I know." He picked up a vegetable and began to chew slowly on it. "The Elders wish to speak to your companion, Drek'h. Do you think that will be possible?" He turned his gaze back to Elas.

"I believe he will be able, if they can let him rest until tomorrow afternoon."

Sarduk'h nodded, rising from his place. "Then I will leave you now. I will return to talk again in the morning. Late," he added, smiling down at Rejat. She returned his expression with a few words in his language. The elder man laughed, then strode from the tent.

After the doorflap closed, Brealyth and Stillyth flowed into hu'man forms in the center of the room.

Brealyth, in child form, slipped over to Elas' side as Stillyth knelt behind his Mirii. Both of their faces registered their nearing fatigue.

"So what did the Elders have to say?" Elas circled Brealyth's small shoulders. "Are we truly welcome here? I did not feel that from their Hunt Leader."

"The Elders want answers to some events that have come to their attention. Apparently we are not the only ones threatened by the Foresters." Rejat stuffed another piece of meat into her mouth and settled back against her Azerii. "The Foresters have been on the plateau up north." She looked away for a moment, then abruptly changed the subject. "Stil says we should wake Drek'h." She looked back at her Azerii. "Kit is upset?" He nodded and looked over his shoulder at the curtain.

"Morgana, can you hear Kitteryth?" Elas leaned forward. "Brealyth says she won't talk to her." She started to rise.

Morgana sat up straight. "I haven't heard her since this afternoon, before the Dark Azerii..." she trailed off and rose to follow her aunt into the other room where Drek'h still slept. *Kitteryth?* she sent as she gazed over the sleeping man, noting the absence of his Azerii's lights. *Kit, where are you?*

Elas knelt beside Drek'h and lay her hand on his forehead. She did not sense Kitteryth's presence near as she began to scan, then, released him from the sleep she had induced.

Morgana knelt beside him as he began to stir. "Why would Kit not speak to us?" she asked, then looking back at Stillyth. "Why?"

*I do not know. She left her Mirii after we came here. After Elas put him to sleep,* he sent, rising to stand at the curtain opening beside Rejat, her face awash with her exhaustion.

"Drek'h? How do you feel?" Elas still held her hand on his forehead. He gingerly opened his eyes and looked around, then reached for Morgana's hand.

"Sore, and tired," he yawned. "You pushed me out—twice today, didn't you?" he said, looking at Elas with a faint smile on his lips.

"You needed the rest." She removed her hand from his head. "Stillyth says Kitteryth is upset."

"Kit? She told me something, now I can't remember." He paused. "I can't hear her, where is she?" He started to sit, Elas and Morgana aiding him.

"We don't know. Stillyth says she left you right after     Elas put you to sleep when we got here," Morgana said, feeling a coldness rise within her.

Drek'h rubbed the back of his head and stared at the floor. "She said something, may have been a dream, something about the same one again." He looked up at Rejat. "The same Dark Azerii? Here?"

"Dark Azerii? Here?" she repeated, sitting down before him. "I didn't sense any of their energy here." She glanced at her sister. "Are you sure that's what she meant? Try calling her, Drek'h."

He closed his eyes. "Kitteryth, Become!" he said softly. A sudden wave of cold energy smashed through him, shocking his senses, then Kitteryth's presence surrounded and filled him, crying his name. He felt his own emotions overwhelmed by his Azerii. Opening his eyes, he was startled by the searching stare from Rejat. Withdrawing again, he sought to calm his Azerii and find out what was wrong.

"Drek'h," Rejat leaned forward, her movement echoed by Elas and Morgana. "Drek'h, what's happened to Kit?"

He shuddered briefly as Kit passed her words to him. "She was called—by another," he said, his eyes still shut. "It was the Madness; she heard a cry for help, from the—the Healer of this clan." He opened his eyes to their concerned faces. "She thought she could stop this one on her own."

Rejat and Elas leaned back from him, their faces filled with the knowing of the Dark Azerii's strength when forcing meld.

"It was, a child—" he choked on the images his Azerii gave him. "The Dark Azerii forced meld, and the Madness began again." He looked up at Rejat. "We've never come across—I, we've—been taught, but..." he trailed off, his gaze falling to his knees.

"I know, Drek'h. You've been fortunate." Rejat reached out and clasped the younger man's shoulder. "Stillyth and I have stopped it before, so has Elas. We both hope we never have to face it again." She rose and went to the table, returning with a cup of water. "Here, we've shared Water Rite. Drink." She handed him the cup.

Drek'h took the cup, repeating the Vondarii words, then drinking the contents. He looked up at Rejat again. "She says the child died, but the Azerii did not."

Rejat swore softly, dropping her head, then looking up again. "Where? How far away did this happen?"

He shook his head. "North, I can't tell how far from her images right now, she's too upset. Everything's dark." He looked briefly at Morgana. She sat rigid beside him, her head lowered. He reached out and touched her hand. She looked up, her eyes edged with tears.

"What about the Healer? Is she all right?" Elas

asked, placing a hand on his back.

Drek'h turned back to her. "Kit says she was unharmed, but shocked by the violence of the—the Madness." He looked at his hands, still red from his contact with Morgana's shield. "She is returning, the child was not of this clan. It was from another family, to the northeast. I can't get much else from her." He looked up at Elas again. His eyes were ringed with his sadness and that of his Azerii.

Elas nodded. "Well, we can't do anything now. If you can eat a bit you should, then we all need to get some rest," she said, then rose to retrieve the tray for him. As she placed it before him she sent, *I think Kitteryth would rest better in form, with you.*

He began picking absently at the food. *She won't agree, but I think you're right. I'll tell her.*

As the camp settled into midnight stillness, the companions slept easier than in several days past. Outside, two silver-winged fayr hawks perched on the crown of the Healer's tent, while within, close beside her Mirii, lay Kitteryth, again in the form of a small dark cat, her yellow eyes filled with starry tears.

# Chapter 21

The sounds of children's voices in muted tones washed over Morgana as she stirred slowly from her sleep. She opened her eyes to the warm darkness of the tent. Beside her Drek'h slept heavily, 'pushed' again she thought idly, by Elas' skills. She turned to sit and look around, sensing that the day was already well begun. In the small light filtering in from the doorway's gap, she could just make out her surroundings. Beyond Drek'h, the bed Elas had occupied was empty; so too was Rejat gone from her bed. Beside Drek'h she could sense rather than see the small black cat form of Kitteryth, pressed close to her Mirii's chest as he lay on his left side. She felt the sadness that flowed from the Azerii even in her sleep. The Madness she had tried to stop and the pain of witnessing a death had brought sorrow-filled emotions home to the Azerii. She remembered Drek'h's words about the Unnamed Azerii wanting to experience life, and the emotions that went with it; "even the pain," she whispered to herself.

A rustle and a burst of light brought her attention to the front of the tent. A soft glow began to fill the space beyond. She rose and slipped through the curtain. Elas stood alone, a small light sphere hover-

335

ing above her head.

"You're awake, good." She held a fresh pitcher of water. "Don't worry about Drek'h, he won't wake for some time yet." She placed the pitcher on the low table next to a new tray of food. "Rejat's been up for a couple of hours. She wanted to talk to Sarduk'h again. I got up an hour ago." She knelt beside the table and picked up a small brown fruit.

"I thought she wanted to sleep late." Morgana stretched, then joined her aunt at the table and poured water into two cups.

"She did. This is lunch." Elas smiled slyly. "I pushed you too."

She stared at her aunt. "You did? But I didn't notice anything."

"You were already asleep. I just made sure you stayed there a few hours longer. Is Kitteryth still with him?" She glanced over her niece's shoulder.

"Yes. She's so sad. I didn't want to disturb either of them." Morgana took a long sip of water, then picked up a piece of fruit. "The Madness; I know you said it occurs when an Azerii forces meld, but why couldn't Kit stop it alone?"

"She wasn't strong enough to break the forced meld. It takes a meld Azerii with her Mirii, working together, to free the Hu'man and negate the forced meld."

"Negate?"

Elas looked at her hands. "Destroy. If the Azerii forced meld once, it will try again until it is either transformed or finds its true meld with a Hu'man."

"You can destroy the forced meld, but not the Dark Azerii?" Morgana's face was rimmed with her confusion.

"The Azerii cannot be destroyed, but they can

be transformed through their own experience of forcing the meld. If they acknowledge the Madness they created, they will be transformed, and they will not seek the meld against another's will."

Morgana shivered. "Do you think this was the same Dark Azerii who tried—" she lowered her hands to the table, the fruit untasted.

"We have no way of knowing. Their energy is the same. Until they are meld, they are all part of the same source. No separation without the identity." She continued eating the fruit in her hand. "Try it, it's good."

Morgana took a bite of the strange fruit. Tart, yet sweet juice flowed from its dull appearance.

"When you've had enough, let's walk down to the river. Rejat will find us when the Elders want to talk."

Stepping out of the tent into the dazzling brightness of the day was almost a shock to Morgana's senses as she gazed at her surroundings. The Vondarii camp was alive with color and movement. Even in the warmth of the late summer air, the people and their possessions seemed to dance continuously. Brightly painted shapes covered the domed golden hide tents, their tall entrance banner poles with vibrant ribbons and flags caught every wisp of air. The people themselves wore equally bright clothing that moved playfully with ribbons, tassels and fringe.

A troupe of children caught sight of Morgana and Elas as they slipped from the tent. Laughing and talking excitedly they crowded close, touching Elas' bright coat and chattering their unknown words until the woman Talahs appeared and sternly sent them off. They slipped around Morgana, gently grasping her hands and then skipping away, bright smiles shining on her puzzlement.

Talahs approached, chattering to Elas again, who smiled but shook her head at the loss of her words. The woman smiled and pointed to her temple, then took Elas' hand. *It is not favored by our people to speak this way,* she sent haltingly, *but it is much simpler when one does not know the other's words.*

Elas smiled appreciatively. *Is it permitted then? We will not intrude where we are not welcomed.*

The Vondarii woman nodded. *I shall allow this, for your assistance.*

Elas sent the woman's words to her niece, *but only send when she has indicated her willingness.*

Morgana nodded her comprehension and looked at Talahs. "My thanks," she said aloud.

Talahs took her hand also. *Your words have no meaning, but the tone is pleasant.*

She smiled shyly. *My thanks for your sharing,* she sent.

Talahs' smile widened. *You are most welcome.*

"Morgana," she spoke her name carefully for her.

"Mor-gan-nahn." Talahs shifted her name in her words. "Ta-lahs." She placed her other hand over her heart.

"Ta-lahs." Morgana received another smile. "E-las." She pointed to her aunt. "Re-jat," she said, then pictured the red-haired Mirii.

Talahs laughed, speaking in Vondarii, then

halted to send, *She is fierce, like salkinn.*

Morgana smiled again. *She is Aza Har, warrior, like hunter?*

Talahs nodded, her face becoming solemn. *Yes, I understand.*

Elas touched Talahs shoulder. As the woman turned to her she sent, *We would like to go to the river, will you walk with us?*

Talahs smiled again. *Yes, I will show you the way.* She led them through the circle of tents to the eastern edge of the rise. At the crest of the small plain the Korith River tumbled a short walk below to join its larger branch, the Timmar as it headed south, the Korith cutting a deeper gash over time in the Sumarkh's hills. As they began to walk down the slope a few of the older children who had followed them called after Talahs. She turned and answered them, then continued ahead.

*They wish to follow. I told them to finish their duties,* she sent to Elas when they paused above the river bank. She glanced at Morgana. *They are very curious about you,* she sent, then turned again to the path.

*Me? Why?* she sent without waiting for Talahs to look at her again.

The Vondarii woman turned, a note of surprise on her face. She reached for Morgana's hand, then released it. *Because you wear the Mirii red, but are not Mirii, and you ride the First,* she sent, her eyes darting to the red sash at her waist.

Elas tapped Talahs shoulder. *We can send our thoughts where we direct them.* She cast a reproachful look at her niece. *If it displeases you—*

Talahs held up her hand. *No, I did not*

know, you can do this without the eyes? Or the touch?

*Yes, but we do not read the thoughts of another without their permission.*

The Vondarii's eyes widened. *It is not of our ways, but,* she glanced at Morgana, *it is much easier!* she sent and suddenly laughed.

Elas relaxed, pleased with the woman's openness. *Then let us continue to the water. I, for one, would like to bathe.*

*I know a place,* Talahs sent, grabbing Morgana's hand and motioning Elas after, *where we can swim.*

Rejat sat in the tall grass next to Sarduk'h, his bronze Lii standing nearby, cropping at the dense growth beside a small pool. They had ridden the short distance north of the camp to where the ground broke open abruptly into a narrow breach of rocky walls, the languid waters in its cooling depths fed by an underground spring. If the hunter had not known of its existence she never would have seen the rift, remembering the monotony of the plateau above in this region.

Sarduk'h tossed a pebble into the pool. Its splash and expanding ripples reminded Rejat of her visions, how they too seemed to be expanding, affecting more than just herself or the beings within her sight.

She turned her gaze to the sky. A silver glint of wing floated high overhead. *Stillyth? Any sign of the Healer?*

*No, Laa, not yet. Some of the Lii are mov-*

*ing northeast, towards the river's fording,* he replied, his tone floating lazily with the afternoon's quiet airs.

Rejat smiled. *You're certainly enjoying this day, aren't you?* she sent, an edge of playful sarcasm in her thoughts.

*I enjoy all the days with you, Laa,* he returned, *and the nights.* His image shimmered invitingly in her mind.

She blushed and ducked her head to laugh soundlessly. *Sarduk'h will not understand!*

*You can make him understand, Laa,* her Azerii teased, his thoughts smugly to the point.

She glanced up again at his effortless circles. *Stil, we shall have to spend some time alone, soon.* She smiled to herself. *On the wing would be nice for a change.* She caught Sarduk'h staring at her.

"Your Azerii?" he said, pointing at the fayr hawk above.

"Yes, he hasn't spotted your Healer yet. But he says some of the Lii are moving northeast, towards the Korith fording." She turned her eyes to her dusty boots.

Sarduk'h looked up at his Lii. The bronze turned his head towards him and huffed softly. "Tarnn says the others run to join our Healer. She will come soon, here. This place is special, sacred, to her." He rolled a knot of grass in his hands, staring out at the pool.

"Why did you bring me here?" She sensed the older hunter was not telling her something.

He glanced at her, his dark blue eyes revealing a glint of uncertainty, then took a deep breath. "I was told to look for a Mirii Aza, and for a Vondarii hunter who wore Mirii red, who was consort to a young woman from the other side of the Varan, Mirii, but not Mirii. And a Mirii Healer who no longer wishes to travel. Four people, and their companions; their Azerii and the Lii."

Rejat's eyes widened. "Who told you this?"

"Our clan Healer, Larann. She was given a Vision, that told her I was also a part of this. She also told me that the Aza would ask for Water Rite, which only the Vondarii share with their own." He shifted uneasily beside her. "She told me this several years ago. She said that I must go with them to their communion, and possibly beyond. That is why I was surprised when you asked for Water Rite. I had almost forgotten her words."

She nodded, remembering his reaction. And the Hunt Leader's. "Why is Keran wary of us? Has he some anger with the Mirii?"

Sarduk'h shrugged. "He is wary of all who are not Vondarii on the Sumarkh. He believes the Lady gave this place to us alone. He does not understand her law, that the land is for all, not the one."

"He holds much anger, Sarduk'h. Why is he Hunt Leader and not you?" she asked, knowing the boldness of her question.

He stared at her, his surprise plain in his face. He turned his gaze to the pool. "I—was not chosen." He watched his Lii drink from the waters. "I believe the First has other plans for me." He turned his gaze back to her. "You are right though, Keran is angry often."

A shrill cry from above brought their attention to the soaring Azerii. Rejat rose quickly as Sarduk'h's Lii swung around to his rider.

*What is it, Stil?* She shaded her eyes as she

342

looked for the fayr hawk.

*Several Lii are coming, riders too, from the river.*

Sarduk'h stared at his Lii, then turned to Rejat. "She is coming, something has happened. The Lii say she is very sad." He walked to Tarnn, climbing into the saddle. "Come, we will meet her on the plateau. She may want to be here alone."

Rejat pulled herself up behind the hunter and the Lii quickly trotted up and out of the canyon. On the rise above they stopped to wait. A dozen Lii appeared from the east, thundering across the grassland, four riders amongst them. She caught a gold flash to the south; turning, she saw the First Stallion approaching the rushing herd. He quickly joined the band, running smoothly alongside a tall white Lii who carried a woman rider. The herd closed upon the rocky ground that marked the beginnings of the canyon, then slowed to a trot, the white Lii and the gold keeping to the front until they stopped a dozen paces from Sarduk'h and Rejat.

The young woman on the white Lii was of slim build with white-blond hair flying about her shoulders, her face seemingly ageless. She was dressed in a pale gold tunic and leggings, her clan markings in white upon her shoulders and sleeves. Three other women in similar clothing rode amongst the Lii behind her, their mounts also white or pale colored. The women all stopped to stare at the hunter and his companion in silence.

Sarduk'h dismounted and walked the few paces to the young woman. Her face masked her emotions, until he held out his hands to assist her down from the tall Lii. She suddenly broke her silence and nearly fell into his arms, sobbing her pain outward.

The gold stallion nuzzled the hunter's shoulder, then turned and began walking back towards the Vondarii camp. The other three riders waited until the woman regained enough composure to turn and speak quietly to them, then they headed after the First Stallion.

Rejat sat uncomfortably on the bronze Lii, who seemed not to notice and began to nibble at the grass at his feet as he waited. Stillyth shimmered into horse form behind the Lii and, stepping beside the stallion, nudged his Mirii's knee. She reached over and tugged his mane.

When the woman stopped shaking she gazed up at Sarduk'h and listened as he spoke quietly to her, casting her sight to the Mirii behind him. He turned to Rejat, his glance calling her forward. She slipped off the Lii and stepped toward the two Vondarii.

In halting Outerland tongue the Healer spoke first, surprising Rejat. "I am Larann, First Healer to the Storm-Rynnok'h clan, and sister of Sarduk'h. You are most welcome here, Mirii sister."

Rejat felt a wave of unknown emotions slide through her. In stammering Vondarii she gave her name, "I—am Rejat, Mirii Aza Har, Travelaar Healer, of Lasah Hawk Hold. I—thank you." She glanced at Sarduk'h; his face had become reflective.

Larann wiped the tears from her face, then stepped forward to take Rejat's hand. *I am sorry for my outburst, but we had a terrible incident last night, and seeing my brother after this, well—it just came out,* she sent rapidly to the Mirii as she stared at her in stunned silence.

*I think we—I—know of your incident,* Rejat

sent in return, watching Larann's face. *I was told the Vondarii don't use mind talk. I am...* she trailed her thoughts off.

Larann smiled knowingly. *Tell me how you know of my sadness,* she sent, and gently pulling Rejat's hand, she began to walk to the canyon beyond, with Sarduk'h following while the Lii and Azerii remained on the grassland above.

✳

In the late afternoon shade casting from the ridge above, Elas, Morgana and Talahs sat undisturbed, breathing the coolness that rose from the waters they had recently enjoyed. They had dressed slowly, sending their thoughts and laughter freely over the river's rushing voice.

Talahs asked endless questions about the Mirii and their journey. She was impressed by the images her guests sent of their homes and of the rugged slopes and great forests of the western Varan. She told them little of herself, wishing instead to know of their lives. She did tell them she was consort with the hunter Colkenn, *a fine hunter and man,* she sent, smiling at both, and that she had a son of twelve years who was an excellent rider and would be a fine hunter and claimed by a great stallion at his naming. She smiled proudly at the thought of her son, and fondly of the boy's father, another hunter from a clan to the east of the Korith. She had spent five years with him after her naming by her Lii upon her seventeenth year, then returned to her family clan and had been with Colkenn for the past three years.

Morgana watched Talahs' lively expressions as she and Elas spoke of their lives. Consort, claiming, chosen? The woman's words left her feeling confused about Drek'h. As if the Vondarii read her thoughts, she suddenly asked about the Mirii Aza Tor.

*The other Mirii, your Chosen, will he be well?* she sent, her face expressing her concern.

Elas spoke up first. "Morgana, she thinks you and Drek'h have claimed each other."

She looked from her aunt to the Vondarii woman. *He's not—I don't...I believe he will be well,* she finally sent, her thoughts scattering quickly.

Talahs frowned at her broken words. *Is he not your Chosen?*

Morgana fell silent and looked across at her aunt. Elas decided to be direct.

*Morgana is unfamiliar with Vondarii ways, Talahs. She and Drek'h care greatly for each other, but they are not consorts.*

Talahs looked puzzled, then shrugged. *As long as it is well with you.* She suddenly smiled again and sent, *I did notice Tren and Madeh watching you, riding the First as you did!* She laughed softly. *It is a great honor, Morgannahn, to be named by the First.*

Morgana smiled modestly and lowered her eyes. *I consider all of us honored by the Lii, and the Vondarii.* She looked up again to Talahs' warm smile.

Brealyth suddenly shimmered into her child form beside Elas, startling the Vondarii into awed silence. She glanced at Talahs, then sent to her Mirii, *Rejat calls us, the Elders wish to speak with you and Morgana, and Stillyth says the Healer has returned.*

Elas quelled her reproach to her Azerii for her

abrupt appearance. *Has Rejat spoken with this Healer herself?*

Brealyth nodded. *Stillyth says she mind spoke with her for some time, and with the hunter Sarduk'h. Stillyth says she wishes to speak with Drek'h and Kitteryth.*

Elas started. *Rejat mind spoke with them?*

*Stillyth says the Healer mind talked with her first. The hunter she spoke aloud to.* Brealyth sounded surprised herself. *Hurry, Elas, Stillyth says she is impatient.*

Elas rose and shook out her coat in one motion. *Come, Talahs, Morgana, we need to get back quickly, Rejat says the Elders wish to speak with us.* She glanced at her niece. *Both of us, and the Healer is here.*

"What about Drek'h, Elas?" Morgana gave her tunic a brushing over then straightened her red sash around her waist.

"I'll check on him as soon as we get back. I think it's time to wake him. And Kit."

Many voices bustled around them as they returned to camp, Colkenn charging up to Talahs and speaking rapidly to her, his face shifting from worry to agitation at her delay. Elas nearly dragged Morgana into the Healer's tent when she hesitated in the crowd flocking around them. Inside were more visitors; Rejat stood talking with Sarduk'h and a pale-haired young women in a golden chza hide dress.

Elas straightened slowly. *We came as quickly as possible,* she sent to her sister. She had hoped she could rouse Drek'h without a gathering around him.

*I know, Elaa, but she wouldn't wait.* Rejat sighed heavily and stepped to her side and made introductions.

Larann stepped forward and grasped Elas' and Morgana's hands. "Welcome to my clan, E-lahs, Morgan-non," she said in Outerland, her bright blue eyes clear with warm intent. She turned her gaze to Elas. *I have spoken with your sister at length. I would like to speak to the young man who companies you, and his Azerii. Is that possible?*

As Elas returned the Healer's calm gaze, Brealyth shimmered into her child form beside her again and raised her serious eyes to the other woman. *She can hear all Azerii,* she sent to her Mirii.

Elas stared at Larann. *You hear them? Did you call Kitteryth last night?*

Larann lowered eyes that suddenly filled with tears. *I called out, to any that might hear and assist us. This one, you call Kitteryth?* *She answered and came, but she could not stop the Darkness from taking the child.* She tightened her shoulders and looked up again. *Rejat has told me that this Azerii is of meld with the man who is here, Drek'h?* She glanced at Morgana, who had shifted her gaze to the divider behind her. Larann gently squeezed her hand to reclaim her attention. *I just wish to talk to him and his Azerii. I will wait if he is unwell at this time.*

Elas glanced past her. *I would like to give him time to waken and refresh himself; he has had a difficult journey the past several days. Maybe you could talk to his Azerii first.* She shifted uneasily as Larann released her hand. *Let me wake them both.* She grabbed Morgana's hand and pulled her through the divider. *Call Kit for me, she might talk to you first,* she sent as she knelt beside Drek'h.

Morgana moved to his other side and watched her aunt place her hand on his temple. Drek'h was still on his left side, Kitteryth now behind him under his coat still in her cat form. The Azerii poked her head out and looked up with eyes still saddened by her experience.

Morgana knelt beside the small form. "Kitteryth?" A wave of sorrow showered over her as the Azerii closed her eyes and started to withdraw under the coat.

*Kitteryth, please talk to me,* she sent anxiously. On impulse, she raised Drek'h's coat and placed her hand on Kitteryth's back.

The Azerii suddenly vanished from under her hand. She reappeared kneeling beside her, as the small dark-haired woman, her eyes filled with the pain of her failure. She stared at Morgana silently, her thoughts clouded by her grief. Morgana reached forward and the Azerii swiftly wrapped her arms around her neck, her soundless cries shaking her slim frame.

Elas looked up, completely stunned by her niece's actions and the Azerii's behavior. She pushed Drek'h awake; he sighed and opened his eyes, then groggily looked up at her and started to roll to his back. The bump on the back of his head stopped him; he groaned, then looked around. "Kit?" he said hoarsely.

"She's here, Drek'h," Morgana replied, her voice uneven from Kitteryth's uncontrolled emotions which swept through her. He pushed himself upright with Elas' help and reached for her. His Azerii raised her tear-streaked face from Morgana's shoulder and shifted over to him, still keeping a hold on Morgana.

Elas sat back and placed a hand on Drek'h to push her healing energy. She glanced up as Rejat and Larann looked through the curtain opening. In the soft light Larann's face was filled with her compassion. *I will speak with them when you feel they are able,* she sent, then turned away.

Rejat stepped through and knelt before Drek'h, her gaze slipping to her sister. *I will tell the Elders it may be awhile yet.* She gently touched Drek'h's knee, then rose and turned away, taking Sarduk'h with her from the tent.

# Chapter 22

As dusk washed over the Sumarkh Plateau, Rejat sat alone before the Healer's tent, her Azerii again aloft in the fayr hawk form over the camp. Around her the Vondarii families were preparing their evening meal before their campfires, while the unclaimed adults walked through the camp to make certain all had what they required. From the small gatherings nearby, she could hear the murmur of talk in the deepening shadows. This was a special night; the whispered voices sang, their Healer had returned and they had guests to speak of. She watched silently as torches were raised to light the circles of the camp for the evening activities soon to begin.

She turned her eyes to the eastern sky and watched the widening moonlight caress the plateau. How many more days before full moonrise? Five? Three? Somewhere they had lost count, the hardships of this journey mounting as the days had progressed. She thought briefly of scanning for her fellow Mirii already at the lake, to tell them of their position. *We are coming, we will make it on time,* she told herself, then turned as the voices of her companions caught her attention.

Elas stepped from the tent, the metal disks on

her coat glinting in the dancing torchlight. She turned to her sister, her face crossed with fatigue. "Drek'h and Kitteryth can speak with Larann now. I think it best that they meet with her first, while we meet with the Elders," she said and stepped aside as Morgana slipped from the tent behind her.

Rejat nodded and stood. "I'll get Sarduk'h, he will know where Larann is." She glanced at Morgana's tear-rimmed face. Wordlessly she touched the younger woman's shoulder, then turned away.

Morgana wrapped her arms around herself and looked out over the camp. She watched the ribbons of the nearest banner pole shimmer in the soft breeze and wondered again about the journey she was on.

"Why did you touch Kitteryth when she did not respond to you?" Elas suddenly asked her.

She turned a questing gaze to her aunt. "Why? Is it wrong?"

Elas shook her head then looked away. "It is not done. The Azerii can be unpredictable."

Morgana glanced at the ground. "I didn't know, Elas. She was so sad. I just wanted to—hold her, I guess. To tell her it was not her fault." She felt her tears crest again. "Why did she leave him anyway?"

Her aunt stared past her. "I suppose that is my doing. I pushed him asleep so he would rest and not struggle to remain awake to deal with the Vondarii. She probably felt that he was well protected by myself and Brealyth, and you." She folded her arms before her and took a deep breath. "So when she heard Larann's call she just took off. I've heard of some Meld Azerii still acting like the wild, but I've never known any like that." She sat down in front of the tent. "I've never witnessed an Azerii react so strongly to an incident such as this."

"She was horrified, Elas," Morgana whispered
as she stared at the sky. "She shared some of the images with me. She was completely horrified that one
of her own kind would destroy a child to create the
meld," she sniffed, holding back her tears. "I think she
was in shock when she returned last night." She
glanced back at her aunt. "Why does the Healer want
to speak to Drek'h?"

Elas gazed at the moon. "Rejat spoke with her
at length. She did not have time to tell me. I think it
has to do with Kit's assisting her last night, and her
Visions that Sarduk'h spoke of." She stood as she
heard footsteps approach. *Dry your tears, we will
continue this later,* she sent, brushing at her coat.

Rejat, Sarduk'h, Larann and the Hunt Leader
Keran arrived, the three Vondarii dressed in their best
finery. Rejat stepped to Elas' side and asked her to
take Larann in to meet Drek'h and then return. She
nodded, slipping into the tent with the Healer behind
her. Morgana watched quietly, again pondering over
why the woman was so adamant about speaking with
the Aza Tor. Her musing broke off as Elas returned to
her side. Sarduk'h spoke to Rejat in Vondarii, then he
and Keran turned away.

"Come on, Elas, Morgana. We have words to
share with the Vondarii," Rejat said as she tugged at
her coat and turned to followed the two men.

They walked through the inner circle of tents
to the great central fire before the Elder's tent. Many
of the Vondarii had gathered around the fire; their
voices surging as their visitors appeared. Morgana
heard her name amongst their words, the sound of it
altered to flow in their tongue. "Morannon," they said,
pointing at her and uttering more that had no mean-

ing to her.

Beside the entrance of the Elder's tent two torch bearing hunters held positions at the banner poles, their faces impassive in the dancing light. The Hunt Leader stopped them and through Sarduk'h, told them to wait as Keran entered alone. Morgana glanced around at the people beyond the firelight. She spotted Talahs with Colkenn, the woman smiling encouragement as their eyes met. Amid the others she recognized the hunters Tren and Madeh and the other woman who had assisted them the evening before. Elas tugged on her hand as Keran returned, speaking to Sarduk'h, then leading them into the tent.

Inside the Elder's tent more of the people gathered, lining the sides and rear of the large single space. Larger than any of the other Vondarii dwellings, the central supports reached nearly twice a man's height. Small oil lamps were hung to light the interior and the floor and walls held brightly woven cloths and painted hides.

They followed Keran and Sarduk'h to the center where several cushions had been placed, facing a line of Elders; three men and three women, their faces and bearing reflecting their position in this society. All wore the pale gold chza hide clothing marked with clan and personal designs and each carried a staff or rod with various symbols and items along its length. They were invited to sit, Keran and Sarduk'h to the left of Rejat, Elas and Morgana. Words were exchanged by the Hunt Leader and the Elder man across from him, then they turned to Sarduk'h and Rejat and the questions began.

After introductions by Rejat, most of the conversation was about their journey and why they had called the Lii, as Sarduk'h translated. Elas answered each question clearly, directing her voice to the Elder who had spoken, her manner calm and open. As their words flowed past her, Morgana began to feel ignored so she turned her attention to studying the Elders. Before her gaze, their faces seemed to soften, their ancient aspects becoming lighter as they listened and spoke. An ageless grace began to appear around them that somehow lifted her sadness of the past few days from her heart and mind.

She found herself staring at the Elder across from her, a woman whose eyes held eternity and yet were filled with a beginning light. A silence fell around her and she felt the other woman's eyes search her face. She blinked once, suddenly aware that she was expected to answer, but did not remember hearing the question. She tried to look at her aunt, but found her eyes caught by the Elder's gaze.

A voice reached out and called her name. *Morgana, what is your intent?* Silver cords whispered around the voice of the Elder who matched her stare, eternal wisdom singing in her words.

"To find my truth, " she whispered.

*And?*

"To be Mirii."

*And what does being Mirii mean to you?* A trace of amusement rang through the cords.

"To honor my own truth as I find it. To be open to another's truth, and to follow my light to my heart. To be One." She felt her words float through her as if from a depth she had not known.

*Find your truth, Morgana Elissii. Be one with the Light of your Being.* The silver-edged voice shimmered around her, awakening her from the tenuous grasp of the woman before her. She blinked rapidly as her senses returned.

A hand reached hers. It was warm and compelling. She turned and found Drek'h's weary gaze meeting hers. He sat beside her, his Mirii clothing brushed free of their journey dust. Wordlessly he smiled and behind the shadow of his old pain she saw the image she remembered from her dream, the inner peace of his eyes. He was home.

She turned again as another voice caught her attention. Beside Keran, the Healer Larann stood and spoke before the Elders. She mentioned Drek'h and the Elders seemed to smile as if a shared remembrance was carried in his name. Then she spoke of Morgana, and they smiled again as the sound of her name somehow brought a light to their hearts. She watched the Healer speak, her very being radiant as she gave her words to her people. Even when she spoke of the Dark Azerii there was a compassion in her voice that filled the air around her.

As the Vondarii voices echoed about her, Morgana found eyes once more drawn to the Elder across from her. A sudden thought brushed her mind as she met the pale gaze. *You are my Teacher,* she sent softly to the other.

*Yes, Child, but not here. In another place, and time.* The eyes were filled with love and she felt an image slip through her of a young woman, tall and fair-haired, with golden skin and clear blue eyes. Sweet voices filled the air, mixing with the image until she felt her senses expand outward. She suddenly heard Drek'h and Elas call her name. She shook her head, the image lost but not the voices.

She looked up. Behind the Healer were six young women, joined with her in a song that filled the soft light of the tent. Around them the Vondarii faces were rapt with attentive joy.

Elas touched her hand. *Morgana, are you all right?* Beyond her Rejat cast a worrisome glance her way.

*I'm—not sure,* she sent as her inner-sight began to expand and overlapping images filled her gaze. The voices returned and she struggled to calm her breath. Closing her eyes, she willed her mind shield up until it blocked out the chaos that began to engulf her mind.

*Morgana, look at me.* A voice without fire rang in her head. She clenched her eyes shut, unwilling to answer.

*Morgana. Look at me.* A pale figure formed behind her eyes, its aura silver and white. She could not avoid it. It was in her mind.

Drek'h caught her as she fainted. He held her as Elas reached for her wrist to quickly scan. Rejat turned to the Elders, explaining of her exhaustion from their journey and asking for their understanding. With Sarduk'h's help, Drek'h carried her out of the Elder's tent and back to their quarters, Elas scanning her niece's shielded form along the way.

※

Silent shadows crept in ragged turns around the pale being within her mind, while pools of night lay beyond and surged towards her from the fringes of her sight. It filled her with a coldness as she watched. Her outer world was closed to her—she was trapped behind her own shield.

She tried to move but found her sight transfixed. The pale being shimmered closer, its aura spraying silver as it moved, sparkling around it like wings in a mist-filled day.

*Morgana, look at me. Hear the words that I say. Your time of Becoming is near. The strength of your Light will draw many to your Sphere. Be aware. The light that you follow will draw the Darkness to your shadow. Remember your Truth, for it is your sword in the darkness.*

She felt a thought float free. *Why are you here?*

The being swept closer and she felt the luminescence of its eyes flow through her mind. *I am a part of your Sphere, but you do not know me. You will remember me at your time of Becoming.* Her mirror image flashed before her in the pale eyes, then changed as a golden radiance filled her vision, reaching outward to drench the pale figure in aurora lights. The glistening being expanded into enfolding mists which spread until all that was visible was the brilliant radiance of its shining form. A wave of compassion suddenly filled her and she felt no more.

The distant music of many voices reached her ears as her awareness returned. She opened her eyes to several concerned faces. Elas' gentle smile returned as she placed her hand on Morgana's forehead. "Welcome back; you gave us a start back there."

"I'm sorry, I—didn't know—" her fatigue slipped between her words. "What happened?" She glanced around at the others beside her. Larann and Talahs sat on either side of her, the Healer's eyes were full of knowing. Drek'h sat at her shoulder, his Azerii once again glimmering around him. He smiled and stroked her hair.

"You tell us," Elas said. "It appeared to me that you were more exhausted than I suspected and fainted. Do you remember anything?" She placed her hand on her chest to scan.

"I was listening to you, and Sarduk'h, talk to the Elders, then, something happened—I'm not sure what. I think I spoke to the Elder across from me, and I remember your singing," she glanced at Larann, then turned her eyes to Drek'h, "and you took my hand. I don't remember your coming in though."

He looked surprised. "I came in with Larann and the other Healers. Sarduk'h introduced me to the Elders. You don't remember?"

"No. I remember, I know I shouldn't have, but I mind spoke with the Elder before me, but I don't remember what we said." She closed her eyes for a moment, then looked up at her aunt. "I guess I was too tired, the room seemed to shift and I felt like I was seeing two places at once. I raised my mind shield to block out the images, then I—I don't remember anything else." She glanced once again at the silent Healer.

Larann reached a hand to her wrist. *I wish to speak with you when you feel well,* she sent, her thoughts reassuring.

*Yes, I would like that,* she sent in reply, then looked back at her aunt again. "Well, what am I missing? I hear more singing." She tried to get up but was stopped by the lightness slipping through her head.

"I think you shall stay here for the rest of the night." Elas caught her and placed her hand on her temple as she lay down again. "You need to rest, we all need an early night, there has been enough talk to last us for some time. We shall tell you what you missed tomorrow," she added as Morgana's eyes darted from her to Drek'h.

A warm and comforting lethargy began to

wash over her as she calmly realized she was being 'pushed'. She closed her eyes to their caring faces and inwardly welcomed the solitude of sleep.

✳

The sun stretched languid over the Sumarkh, its heat shimmering the surrounding horizons of the Vondarii camp. In the midday brightness few moved excessively. Deep within the shadows of the rift canyon Rejat and Elas sat with the Healer Larann, their gaze turned to the liquid depths of the emerald pool in its heart.

*This is a sacred place,* Larann sent to the Mirii. *It was found by our forebears. The Lii have always known of it. When the rivers were low in times of drought, this pool was still here. When the rains come it will fill the basin of this canyon to empty out onto the plain at the eastern break. I have had many Visions here.* She turned her eyes to the two women beside her. *I had a Vision that you would come. Many years ago.* She returned her gaze to the pool.

Elas lifted her eyes to her. *What exactly did your Vision tell you?*

A shimmering softness seemed to outline the Healer's form. *Four will come. Three will wear Mirii red, the fourth will be marked by the color.* Larann's thoughts whispered from her mind into the canyon's silence. *The first will be a warrior and ask for Water Rite. The second will be a traveling Healer who no longer desires journeying. The third will be a Vondarii hunter who was disowned and is now Mirii and claims the fourth in*

360

*his mind. The fourth will be called 'Light One' by
the Lii and she will be as an innocent to her own
truth. She will also be as a sword to the minds of
the Mirii.*

Rejat's breath hissed from her lips as she turned her eyes to the Healer. *What do you mean?* she
sent, her thoughts shivering outwards.

Larann returned the Aza Har's gaze solemnly.
*You have the words of your own Visioner,* she
sent, glancing at Elas' equally stunned face. *You have
already witnessed the gathering of this Talent's
abilities. Do you not see the path of this woman?*

Elas turned disquieted eyes to her sister. "What
exactly did Dayana see?"

Rejat frowned at the waters. "You know Dayana. She didn't take me into her confidence. She only
gave me part of her Vision, the images of you and
Morgana, her family, and the Darkness." She twisted
a tuft of grass at her feet. "I am only Aza, sent to
bring you and Morgana back to Communion unharmed and in time." She glanced back at Elas. "Day-
yana's like all Visioners. She gives what she decides
is needed. She said I must bring Morgana, whether
you'd come or not. She did not think you would
come, Elaa," she added, her features easing.

Elas turned her eyes again to the pool. "Ever it
is we do not communicate. She has not changed."
She glanced sideways at her sister. "I almost didn't
come," she said as a ring of brightness filled her eyes.
"Would that I hadn't felt the call to Communion so
that I could have stayed with Tagar. His hold has become mine, not Zerren's Gate. My mother will not be
pleased." She wiped the tears from her eyes and
turned back to Larann. *Tell us what your Vision of
Morgana means,* she sent to the Healer who had

silently watched their exchange.

Larann's face filled with stern compassion. *She holds more talents than any of your chosen. Her strength of Light will draw the shadows to be cut away by her truth. I see her as a fire-rimmed sword, held aloft in the darkness by an unseen hand. I see that sword in the midst of Mirii red, cutting the red in two. She will be Mirii, and not Mirii.* She lowered her eyes to the shinning pool. *I see much change for all our peoples. My Visions have shown me how the Darkness grows in the hearts of many. The Dark Azerii long for release. I know of your Covenant. The Vondarii hear the voices of the wild Azerii. We have not listened for a long time.* She suddenly looked up at Elas. *I think it is time the Vondarii listened to the voices of the Others.*

*They have been crying for a very long time,* Elas sent absently. *We have been unable to assist them. The Mirii have not prospered quickly enough for them.* She blinked and turned to Rejat.

"We ride tomorrow, at first light. Straight through until we reach the lake. Communion is in three days."

*

It was well past midday when Elas woke Morgana and Drek'h from their pushed rest. She offered no apology as she explained part of her meeting with the Vondarii Healer. She purposely did not mention their discussion of her niece, knowing it would only confuse and trouble her to have such knowledge of her future.

362

After a leisurely evening meal, Morgana found herself walking through the camp towards the rim overlooking the darkening Korith River. A few older children strayed after her until she left the circle of tents, whispering the name they had given her then silently returning to their games beyond her awareness. She stood at the rim and gazed at the dark plain to the southeast. She could hear the river's voice below her rise and mix with the soft murmurs of the Vondarii and the gentle movements of a few Lii who lingered near this side of the camp.

A soft footstep approached her. She turned to greet the face of the gentle Larann. The Healer wore a simple woven tunic of pale yellow, her fair hair lifting slowly in the rising breeze from the river.

Larann smiled and spoke in Outerland, "I did not startle you? That is well." She reached out and took Morgana's hand. *May we walk and speak? Or would you rather be alone?* she sent, her eyes searching her face as she released her hand.

Morgana returned her smile. *I have spent more time alone in one place in the past several hours than I care to, due to my aunt's administrations. Yes, I will speak, and walk with you, as long as we have some light to see by.* She glanced at the darkening sky.

*We can circle the camp. When we need guidance, the Lii shall be our eyes.* Larann started walking slowly northwards along the river's rim. Morgana kept pace beside her, her eyes flowing from the Healer to the vast Sumarkh around them.

They walked for some minutes before beginning, Morgana abruptly flinging out the question she held unanswered. *Why did you have to speak with Drek'h, and his Azerii?*

Larann turned and flashed her a puzzled look. *I have spoken with all of your companions. As the clan's First Healer, it is my duty. Why does this trouble you?* The light of knowing suddenly returned to her eyes. *Drek'h, he is your chosen.*

*No—I—we—*her thoughts fell into pieces. She stopped and stared at the ground. *I—love him, but we have not claimed each other.*

Larann took her hand again and resumed their walk, gently pulling her forward. *I spoke to him of his Azerii, and why she came to my call.* A wave of sorrow swept from her, then was quickly gone. *I needed to understand why the Dark Azerii would do such a thing, and how to stop such a terrible event from happening again. And I needed to talk to his Azerii, Kitteryth, to give her my appreciation for her appearance.* She turned bright eyes to Morgana. *I needed her to understand she was not to blame for not saving the child.*

Morgana felt the memory of her last dream edge into her awareness. Larann silently nodded. *Yes, I shared your Vision. I too, saw the Lii bring him back to us, and to himself. And you. The First chose well. But I also saw more that I cannot share with you because it is personal to him. He will tell you when he is ready and fully understands.* She gently squeezed Morgana's hand. *He does love you, but he too has not claimed you as consort for fear of keeping you from your path. He honors you greatly.* She turned her gaze to the dark sky above. A filament of song slipped from her throat.

A low whicker reached them. Morgana turned as Starrynn and another Lii, a tall white mare, quietly stepped within reach. "Our eyes, for our talk," Larann said as she lifted herself to the mare's back.

Morgana hugged the filly, then pulled herself upon her back. The two Lii began walking beside each other.

*Do you remember the Elder who faced you?* Larann sent as they continued their circumference of the now fire-lit camp. *Or the words that you shared?*

She shook her head. *No. Last night, it all seems to be getting blurred. I'm not sure now that we did speak.*

*Know that you did.* Larann sent firmly. *She is First Mother, Mardeth, the Golden Light of the Vondarii. You will see her again when you remember her words. And the words of the Other behind your shield.*

Morgana stared at the light figure beside her. Larann's features were no longer discernible in the darkness. *What do you mean, Other?* She shivered as if a cold wind had been thrust upon her.

Larann reached out her hand to her. *Morgana Elissii, follow your Light and know that your Truth will be as a sword in the darkness. A fiery sword.*

Morgana sat in stunned silence as the Healer's words rang through her in otherworldly echoes. The Lii moved on, their rider's stillness enveloping the sound of their hooves in the plateau's night-cloaked grasses. She turned her eyes to the moon rising over the eastern horizon. It was nearly full.

# Chapter 23

The last run to Communion started early on the third morning, the Mirii's Azerii rousing them at the hour before dawn. They had prepared their packs the night before, the Vondarii supplying them with the additional foods they needed and filling their waterskins near to bursting.

After a quick breakfast they stepped outside to pack their gear on the waiting mounts. Drek'h again secured his pack on his Azerii, her countenance vibrant from her rest, hiding the sorrow of her recent experience. Drek'h himself seemed back to a renewed sense of spirit which Morgana had caught glimpses of only before they had neared the Sumarkh. As she watched her companions, she waited with her pack and saddle, wondering which Lii would offer her assistance for this final part of their journey. Her eyes searched their surroundings. Many of the Vondarii had gathered to see them off, a few of the hunters were seated upon their Lii amongst the crowd, but no riderless Lii approached her.

She turned to Drek'h. He stood beside Kitteryth, meeting Morgana's gaze, then stepping to her side and placing his arm around her shoulders. *Wait for the Lii,* he sent and gazed at their hosts, his smile warm upon his face.

A rustle of excited voices approached them from the direction of the Elder's tent. The companions turned their attention to the sound as four of the Elders, led by the Healer Larann, Sarduk'h, and the Hunt Leader Keran, parted the crowd and stopped before them. Keran raised his banner lance high and the whispering voices of the people subsided. He spoke briefly to Sarduk'h, who then stepped forward to Rejat.

The hunter nodded to the companions. "The Storm-Rynnok'h Clan wishes to give you farewell and safe journeys," he began, his voice raised to all. "You have honored us with your presence, we ask that you honor us again by accepting these gifts." He turned to Keran and nodded once more.

The Hunt Leader stepped to Rejat and held out a golden clan banner. With a reserved smile he handed it to the Aza Har and spoke lowly to her in Vondarii. Rejat smiled in acceptance, answering his words in turn. Keran nodded, then stepped back, his smile firmly broadened by her reply.

Larann approached Elas. She held a braided gold cord with a finger-sized crystal suspended from its length and placed the cord over Elas' head. "For clarity, and compassion in your path," she said as she centered the stone over Elas' heart. The two women embraced each other as Elas whispered her thanks.

As Larann parted from Elas, Talahs walked to Morgana. She held a folded bundle in her hands and opened it while speaking her words. The bundle became a red woven dress, with the clan markings embroidered in golden threads, the sleeves and skirt hems fringed in red and gold with small silver disks like those on Elas' coat. *For your time of choos-*

*ing,* the woman sent to her as she gently placed the garment in her hands.

Morgana felt her tears rise as she accepted the beautiful gift, speaking her thanks clearly aloud as well as sending her thoughts to the woman who had become a friend in their short time together. Talahs smiled and embraced her quickly, then moved back to stand beside Colkenn.

Drek'h looked up as the first Elder who had questioned them approached him. In his hands he held a lance, its height void of markings, and a red and gold bundle. He handed the bundle to Drek'h and spoke his words to the young man. Drek'h opened it to reveal another banner; its symbols carrying the clan markings in gold on a red background with the lower half empty. A wave of emotion flowed from him as he stared at the banner in his hands. He numbly replied to the Elder, who nodded and spoke again, placing the lance before him. The Aza Tor placed one hand above the Elder's on the lance, saying more words in Vondarii. The Elder nodded again, his face full of understanding as Drek'h released the lance. He carefully folded the banner as the Elder rejoined the others, their faces all carrying the acceptance of the Mirii's words.

As each turned to place their gifts within their packs, Elas choosing to wear hers, Sarduk'h stepped forward again, his voice raised once more in his tongue, then in Outerland. "We shall assist you in reaching your destination in time. The First Stallion has also called the Lii to your need."

Morgana glanced up as his words ended. From the western side of the camp she heard the approaching steps of horses. A golden head appeared above the crowd as Skyrynnar edged into the circle of

Vondarii. The stallion walked up to her and huffed his greeting. *I have come for your need,* he sent, blowing softly into her face.

"Thank you, Skyrynnar," she said aloud and patted the soft nose before her. Drek'h approached and greeted the First, offering to help her with her saddle and pack. The stallion huffed his acceptance to him as Drek'h and Morgana began placing her gear upon his wide back. The Vondarii watched, their voices again filled with awe at the First Stallion's assistance of this woman. Morgana heard her shifted name again slip amongst their words, as well as Drek'h's, and wondered what he had spoken of with the Elder and why he was so moved by the words.

Larann approached her as Drek'h finished with her saddle. The Healer embraced her and sent, *You will always be welcome here, on the Sumarkh. You have been given your third name, 'Morannon', which means 'from the Light' in our words. Remember this when you return to the Sumarkh.* She released her and began to move back. *We shall meet again, Morgana Elissii Morannon.*

Their final exchanges were swiftly done and when all were mounted, Rejat turned to see which of the Vondarii were to assist them in what could prove to be a hectic flight to the lake. Four hunters sat upon their Lii in a row; Sarduk'h, Tren, Colkenn and Madeh, their faces expressing their pride in this undertaking. Only Sarduk'h's face held an inner dismay, Rejat remembering his words to her of his involvement with the Mirii from Larann's vision. This journey could be longer for him than the others. She nodded her thanks to the four as Stillyth began to lead the company through the camp, toward the south-eastern rim above the river Korith as the sun cleared the Su-markh's eastern horizon.

\*

The summer days, which were growing per-ceptibly shorter as they headed east, seemed intermi-nably long in the hours spent traveling on their now quickened pace. They crossed the Korith River to fol-low the eastern side of the Timmar, its course now nearly due south. Their mounts kept to a fast trot, pounding through the Sumarkh's grasslands which sang of the coming autumn in their dry beds. The company took frequent short breaks to let their mounts rest, then resumed the tempo of their run southwards, always keeping the river in glimpsed view. Their conversations were few, the Mirii sending their thoughts only as needed, Rejat and Drek'h again scanning forward and behind for the wild Azerii who lingered with the unclaimed Lii herds. The Vondarii hunters also rode in silence, their Lii communicating for them when one needed a respite from the hard journey.

With nightfall they paused to eat and rest for an hour, then they were off again, their pace slower, trusting the eyes of their mounts to take them over the moonlit land safely. They paused to rest and sleep for a few hours when the moon had fallen for the night, then wearily moved onwards as dawn's first light brought them to their feet once again.

By mid-morning they were slowing again. Morgana felt she was becoming a part of her saddle and the Lii she rode, their movements flowing into one as the plateau swept past them. She watched Drek'h and the other Vondarii. They seemed totally absorbed in the hard ride; Drek'h had told her of the hunters' travels when they were in search of chza or other animals for food for their clans. The hunter and his Lii became as one, like the meld between the Mirii and their Azerii as they coursed the vast terrain of the Sumarkh, their senses straining to catch any sign of life within the immense waving stands of grasses.

When the sun reached late afternoon the Lii stopped, their sides heaving with their efforts. As one, the Vondarii slipped down beside them to walk for a time, Morgana and the Mirii doing the same. They walked for an hour, then stopped again to rest.

Starrynn and several other Lii slowly appeared as they rested beside the river. The filly approached Morgana as the First Stallion huffed in her ear, *We shall rest here. These others shall carry you the rest of your journey.* He nudged her shoulder.

She welcomed Starrynn, remembering she had not seen the filly when they left the Vondarii camp. She glanced around at the other hunters who were stripping their saddles off their Lii as another stood to take its place. Drek'h also was pulling his saddle and pack from Kitteryth as a silver-gray stallion waited behind him. Rejat and Elas watched for a moment, then, as they too were approached by two Lii mares, they began to do the same, their Azerii grateful for the rest.

Skyrynnar huffed at Morgana. She turned and began to remove her pack and saddle from his back, placing them on Starrynn. When she had secured the last strap she turned to the First Stallion.

Skyrynnar nuzzled her face. *Be of one heart, Light One. Follow your path with joy. You shall run with the Lii again upon the Sumarkh.*

She reached out and hugged the golden Lii's

neck. *I shall always remember you, Skyrynnar, and honor your assistance to me and my friends. Will I ever see you again?*

The stallion blew again at her face. *Know that all the Lii are one and you shall know the First again. Farewell, Light One.* The gold stepped away from her and slowly led the other Lii towards the river.

"Morgana," Drek'h said from the back of the silver Lii. "We must go."

She nodded silently, glancing around at her companions waiting upon their new mounts. She turned back to Starrynn and pulled herself onto the bronze filly's back.

✳

Their hard pace was resumed across the nearly featureless plateau. The middle lands of the Sumarkh had become as a great open span of endless grasses with few hills or ridges to break the brisk winds that now swept across it. The air was slightly cooler now that they had reached into the declining summer, the grasslands gold and bronze in the dry heat.

At dusk they stopped a short distance from the river to eat and rest again for a few hours. Morgana sat beside Drek'h as she watched Rejat talk with Sarduk'h, while Elas lay in the grass nearby, her Azerii sparkling over her. Madeh, Tren and Colkenn sat across from them, exchanging words as their fatigue allowed. The Lii stood around them loosely, grazing on the tall seed pods that waved enticingly in the evening's lessening wind.

A strange cry reached across from the river, bringing the hunters instantly to their feet, their lances in hand. The Lii around them huffed into the approaching night, stamping noisily as they faced the darkened fields towards the call.

Drek'h had also risen quickly, his Azerii flashing in his aura. Morgana stood beside him as Elas and Rejat approached, their Azerii glowing around them.

"What was it?" she whispered to her companions as they stared into the night towards the river.

"Salkinn," Sarduk'h said, his voice low and troubled. "They hunt on the Sumarkh. It must have killed near here, or have a den close by." In the failing light his face was edged with mixed emotions.

Rejat produced two glowing spheres and lifted them high, startling the Vondarii who were unaccustomed to Mirii talents. "Salkinn won't come near unnatural light," she said and cocked a brow at Sarduk'h's wary expression. "Stillyth, can you check out our visitor?"

*Yes, Laa, what would you like me to do with it?* her Azerii sent in reply as he shifted from her aura to his glittering light form.

Rejat laughed soundlessly. *Just look please, and tell me what you find.* She glanced at the hunters. They watched her Azerii's lights dance over the grasses to the river, an awed expression on their faces.

Stillyth's senses plied the terrain for the source of the cry. In light form he searched for the spirit of the creature, picking up smaller animal forms as he passed over the near side of the river, then moved over the rushing waters to look upon the other side.

Morgana felt something tickle the back of her head. A slip of a pale image shimmered behind her eyes as she turned. She looked down at the grass where her shadow from Rejat's lofted spheres lay solidly pointing to the east. A hidden remembrance surged through her, of shadows to be aware of. She raised her eyes along her shadow's path when a sudden movement caught her attention.

"Rejat, there's something—" she started, but never finished as the object burst forward shrieking amid the Lii. She took a step away from her companions and flung her shield up around her, falling to her knees before the creature that screeched continuously through its charge.

The Vondarii hunters snapped around as the salkinn leaped towards Morgana. Drek'h, with Kitteryth blazing in his aura, flung a protection shield over her head a breath before the cat struck at her. A burst of energy flared as the cat fell short of its prey, hitting his shield. Elas moved aside as Rejat called Stillyth back to add her energy to stop the salkinn.

"Rejat! It's the Dark Azerii! It's forced meld!" Drek'h's shout was filled with emotion as he watched the enraged cat, its eyes glowing brightly with the Madness. It crouched less than three paces from Morgana, who held herself motionless on her knees, eyes clamped shut in concentration as her shield roared brightly around her.

As the hunters readied their lances, Rejat suddenly ordered, "No! Don't kill it! You'll release the Azerii!"

The cat shrieked again, its eyes rolling in anger at the young woman out of its reach. Snarling at the companions, it gathered itself to jump again as the Vondarii circled uneasily, their lances poised.

The salkinn shrieked again and threw its body at the shielded woman. Bright flashes sprayed outwards as it met the doubled shields, falling back and turning quickly to strike again. Rejat raised her hands, sending a third force to block the salkinn. A ball of crimson energy began to encircle the cat. It screamed in panic as the Dark Azerii recognized the intent of the Mirii's sphere. It threw the salkinn body backwards, trying to desert the creature as it twisted violently away from the snare. A coalescing dark mist issued from the salkinn's body as it fell to the ground, the animal's life broken in its efforts. The Dark Azerii vanished into the night as a final breath left the salkinn's throat.

Drek'h and Rejat stepped forward to the cat, each dissipating the shields they had created. Elas and the Vondarii edged closer, the hunters still holding their lances at ready. Around them the Lii stomped angrily, huffing at the slain cat before their riders.

Elas stood behind her niece's shield and called. The young woman slowly opened her eyes and lowered her shield's intensity, staring at the great cat stretched out in the grass before her. She reached out and touched the nearest golden-brown paw, then burst into tears.

Drek'h reached over and clasped her hand. As she met his gaze she whispered "Why?"

He looked back at Rejat. She shrugged angrily. "The salkinn's mind and spirit were broken by the forced meld of the Azerii. It could not have survived." Her eyes glinted coldly. "We almost had it in the circle." She glanced back at Elas, holding her niece's shoulders, then to Sarduk'h.

The elder hunter's eyes were still on the cat. He reached a tentative hand to the still warm muzzle. The was the largest salkinn he had ever seen, a large male in its prime, its tawny body held few signs of age or combat. What a waste, he thought as he sat back on his heels. He looked at his companion hunters, their faces holding the same emotions as his.

"What do we do with it?" Morgana asked softly, her eyes tracing the ring of faces.

"The Lady will take him back to the Sumarkh," Sarduk'h replied evenly. He turned to Rejat. "Unless the Mirii?"

"I agree," she said quietly. "She can do best with her children." She knew the Vondarii would not take the hide of the salkinn or any creature that had been violated by the Dark Azerii. She glanced at Drek'h; he nodded silently to her gaze.

They moved the salkinn closer to the river, above the highest mark of the flood line, to lie in the golden grass of its home, and then built a rocky cover to keep the plateau's scavengers from its body. With the moon rising into the evening's embrace they returned to their journey. and Morgana gazed back at the stony rest of the salkinn, her tears wavering in her lashes.

*

They rode on for several hours, silently, their Lii treading carefully across the darkened grassland which shimmered under the moonlight and gentle night breezes. When the moon brushed the horizon they stopped once more to rest until first light, the three Azerii watching over them. As the morning sun began to warm their sleeping forms the Azerii and the accompanying Lii began to call their riders excitedly.

"What? What!" Rejat sat up abruptly as Stillyth took form beside her to tug on her arm.

*Rejat, look! Look Laa!* he sent, his face glowing as he pointed towards the southern plain. She rubbed her eyes to clear them of her cherished sleep and gazed off in the direction he indicated.

"Rejat, it's the lake!" Elas shouted as she stood next to Brealyth, her child form clutching her hand.

Morgana awoke to the voices of her companions as well as the mind voices of the Lii and the Azerii. She tried to ignore their pandemonium until Kitteryth pulled her blanket off, her dark eyes laughing at the stern look she received. *Rise, Morgana, rise! We have sighted the lake!* she sang, pulling at her elbow. The Azerii released her to pounce on her boots and wave them aloft, laughing silently.

Drek'h was tugging on his own boots a short distance away. He turned and admonished Kit to give Morgana her boots, then rose to pull her to her feet and point out the sight that had created such a disturbance so early in the morning.

A great shimmering ribbon lay along the southern horizon below a narrow line of dark rolling plain. The Te'rakh Lake reflected the morning sun like a silver-chased mirror, brightening the plateau around it with crystalline light, the very air above seeming jewel-like in its clarity. The lake of the Lady was immense, all the mountain rivers and streams reached the lake which rested nearly in the heart of the Sumarkh. Even now in late summer the lake was bright, the sands along its receding banks full of silver grains which continued the illusion of its vast appearance.

"How far away are we?" Morgana asked Drek'h as he held her close, his arms around her waist. She looked for the Mirii camps which the others had told her would be waiting but could see no marks upon the smooth plain bordering the lake.

"About a half day's ride I'd say," Rejat replied as she stood next to Stillyth. "We still have another river to cross; the camp is on the northeast side below the Kolsah River inlet."

Sarduk'h wiped a tear from his eye as he gazed at the lake. He turned as Colkenn spoke to him, his eyes also misted with reverence for the sight of their sacred lake.

"Colkenn wishes to ask Water Rite with the Mirii when we reach their camp," he said to Rejat.

She smiled warmly at the hunters and replied in Vondarii, "The Mirii will be honored to share Water Rite with the Storm-Rynnok'h hunters." She glanced at Sarduk'h, catching a glimpse of unease in the elder hunter's eyes behind his smile. "Let's eat quickly so we can complete our journey," she said in Outerland, watching his face as he nodded and turned away.

They consumed their breakfast as they packed, the three Mirii returning to their Azerii for mounts and thanking the Lii who had assisted them. Once again they followed the Timmar south, then turned east after a few hours to seek the Kolsah River and the ford.

Morgana felt her doubts rise again as she watched the Te'rakh Lake edge closer. Was she truly on her path? Would Communion be a time of great learning, or of missed opportunities because of her fears? She thought about her home far away to the west. Could she ever go back? After all she had experienced in the past weeks, the difficult moments included with the joyful? *No!* she heard, as a fierce joy rang through her heart. I would not go back even if I could. I have learned so much, I have so much more to learn. She watched the Mirii around her. Each rode their Azerii with total love in their hearts for the meld that they shared. Drek'h had tried to tell her of the meld, but had left much unsaid, his words failing to describe what she sensed was a very personal event which each experienced differently. She glanced at the Aza Tor behind her, his eyes meeting her. He smiled and she felt the warmth of his smile in her heart. And something else.

A bittersweet sadness slipped around her as she turned forward again and thought of Drek'h. Much had he undergone in the past weeks and she sensed that he had more still to work out. She was a part of it; Larann's words moved within her awareness. Neither of them had claimed each other, though they both acknowledged their feelings. There was a purpose in their love, a part of which seemed to be an acceptance of their different choices. Could they truly love each other and not hold the other from their path? She closed her eyes and pictured Drek'h in her mind. He was standing on the Sumarkh, dressed in Mirii red with Kitteryth shimmering around him and the Lii behind him as he held a golden tipped lance with the red and gold banner snapping in the wind. And Larann stood beside him, her pale hair wisping around her serene face. *I would not claim him from you, Morgana,* her thoughts softly echoed from her image. "He was never mine to hold," she whispered back as the image faded from her awareness. She shielded her mind from her companions as she brushed a tear from her cheek.

Her thoughts broke off as the Kolsah River flowed into view below a low ridge, the river wide and shallow around a lazy curve that reached northeast to southwest with a large sandbar near the center marking the river's ford. They waited for a few minutes for the Lii and the Azerii to catch their breaths before crossing.

A red-clad figure on horseback appeared on

the opposite rise above the river. As the companions watched, the figure stopped, the horse rearing while the rider called out in greeting.

Rejat suddenly stood in her stirrups cheering back, then turned her excited face to her sister. "It's Corry!" she yelled, then grabbed her Azerii's mane as he abruptly started forward. "Stil! Wait!" she shouted as he headed down the bank.

*I thought you wanted to see Corry,* he sent back smugly, his mind voice laughing. He stopped to wait at the water's edge, then turned to the river once again when their companions began to follow him.

The Mirii across from them waited as Rejat and Stillyth proceeded into the shallow ford, splashing noisily to the east bank, then climbing the narrow trail above. When they had reached the top, Rejat disregarded all formal greetings to jump from her Azerii and run to the other Mirii now standing beside his bay Azerii. She heartily embraced the man, laughing loudly as he returned her gesture. The rest of the company forded the river with more reserve than the Aza Har and proceeded up to join them. Elas moved forward to greet the newcomer when Rejat was finally through hugging him.

"Elas, this is Corry Anatt srii Hallyth, Aza Tor Travelaar for Lasah. My friend and companion on some of my illustrious journeys," she said, beaming at the taller man. "Corry, this is Elas srii Brealyth, Travelaar Healer for Zerren's Gate." Rejat pulled the man closer as she spoke, her face lighted with relief to finally be near the completion of their journey.

Elas returned her sister's grin and welcomed the Aza Tor, then introduced their companions while Rejat calmed her excitement. Corry nodded to each, his open face showing his pleasure at their arrival.

"You all look as if you've had a rough road of it," he said in a deep voice with a hint of accent from other lands. "You aren't the only ones. Come, the gathering is not far off." He squeezed Rejat's shoulder then returned to his Azerii.

Morgana studied him as he rode beside Rejat. Corry was near forty, a head taller than her, with dark mahogany hair and sage green eyes. His broad features were well tanned and freckled from the summer's rays, his dark red coat and trousers showing wear and dust from many long journeys. He talked easily with Rejat as they turned south again.

Two hours of brisk riding brought them to another rise and the broad inlet of the Kolsah into the lake. When they crested the ridge she caught her breath at the image that greeted her.

A broad plain which sloped gradually to the lake was filled with movement. Hundreds of pale colored pavilions and tents occupied the grassland, their pointed canopies reaching to the sky with gold and silver ribbons and banners fluttering in the wind. Amongst the tents were many people, more than Morgana had ever witnessed at any gathering in the northern valleys, their clothing dominated by the various shades of the Mirii red. A busyness permeated the scene as preparations were made for the evening's ceremony.

"Tonight, the gathering is complete," Elas said absently as she rode on Morgana's left. "We will have Communion tonight, when the moon rises in the east." She turned starry eyes to her niece. "We made it," she said to Morgana. "We made it!" she shouted to her sister, riding ahead of them between Corry and Sarduk'h.

"Yes, we certainly did!" Rejat exclaimed and

reached a hand to Sarduk'h on her right.

The hunter looked amazed. "This clan of Mirii is very large," he said to her in a voice slightly distant.

Rejat smiled at the Vondarii. "But not nearly big enough. We need more to be with us, we need more to assist the Unnamed Azerii—" she suddenly broke off, frowning at her words and turning her eyes forward again.

Sarduk'h grasped her hand firmly. As she glanced at him again, he smiled grimly and sent *The Vondarii will help, we will learn to listen. Larann says it is so.*

*Why did you really come?* she sent as she studied his face.

*To learn how to listen,* the hunter replied, then slowly released her hand.

More riders on their Azerii horses welcomed them as they entered the outskirts of the camp. They waved their greeting, some speaking in Vondarii to the hunters, which brought smiles to their weary faces. The two youngest, Tren and Madeh, spoke together eagerly as they spotted several young women amongst the Mirii, Sarduk'h commenting to Rejat that neither had claimed their chosen yet.

They rode on into the camp, Corry leading them to a large pavilion on the eastern side. They stopped as he dismounted and slipped inside. He returned a moment later. "You are expected amongst Lasah's camp. They have prepared a tent for you there. I'll take you over." He returned to his Azerii then turned left to the outer ring of the camp once more.

They followed the outer circle, winding through the various people who greeted them until they reached another large gold pavilion, a cross banner in white and silver hanging over its entrance.

Elas stopped Brealyth abruptly. In the doorway of the pavilion a tall pale-haired woman stood between two red-clad women. She was dressed in a robe of clearest white, with silver and red cords wrapped about her narrow waist. Her face was composed, her pale blue eyes devoid of emotions as she gazed over the weary travelers.

"Welcome, Rejat Tala-Lael, my Daughter," the woman said formally as the Aza Har slipped from her Azerii and approached. Her voice was low and clear. "I see you finally have completed your last journey for our hold." Her eyes flicked over Rejat's companions before resting on Elas. "Welcome, Elas, Daughter."

Elas dropped slowly from her saddle, moving as if she wished she were anywhere but here. "Thank you, Sha Dayana." She stepped before her Azerii. "May I present our companions," she turned to face the Vondarii first, "from the Storm-Rynnok'h clan; Sarduk'h, Colkenn, Tren, Madeh," each man nodding with their name, "Drek'h srii Kitteryth. Of Mahdii Hold," she added, noting his raised eyebrows as he left his saddle, "and my niece, Morgana, eldest daughter of the Brejjard LandsHolders, Tillan and Brea, of the Northern Varan Valleys." She nodded for her niece to dismount. "Morgana is a Talent of the first order," she said as she slipped down beside her mount.

"She must be to ride the Lii," the rich voice of one of the woman's companions spoke up. "I am Ridasah srii Sandryth, Elder Aza Har of Lasah." She stepped forward, extending her hands towards them. "My companions," she inclined her head to the pale-haired woman whose eyes flashed a moment's irritation, "Dayana srii Talyth, Elder Visioner of Lasah," then glanced to the smaller, rounder figure beside the taller woman, "and Carda srii Anryth, Elder Healer of Lasah. We welcome all of you and thank the Lady for your safe arrival." She stepped forward to the four hunters. "Welcome to our Communion gathering," she said in clear Vondarii.

Rejat stepped next to the dark-haired Elder. *They asked for Water Rite,* she sent when she turned to her.

Ridasah smiled, grasping her hand, *I know, the clans are always welcome to me.* She tugged on her hand and turned to Sarduk'h, "Come with me, I shall honor your Water Rite and give you rest for this night. Come." She began walking away with Rejat in tow and the four hunters and their Lii behind her.

Morgana turned as the Visioner spoke again. "Well, Drek'h, we have much to discuss, now that we finally meet. We shall talk after Communion. You have had Visions also?" She leveled her commanding gaze at the younger man.

Drek'h swallowed nervously. "Yes, Sha Dayana." He glanced at Elas. She was staring past her mother to the Elder Healer. "I have had a recent Vision—"

"Do not tire yourself by speaking of it now," Dayana interrupted him. "There will be time later." She turned to Corry. "Have their quarters been made ready?"

"Yes, Sha Dayana, they have been prepared. I was taking them there."

"Good. Then proceed. Elas, I wish to speak to you after you have rested. In two hours." The Elder Visioner turned swiftly as two young women appeared behind her, then stepped away into the Lasah pavilion.

384

Carda smiled quietly and stepped forward to take Elas' and Morgana's hands. *A terror, isn't she?* the Elder sent, then the three began to follow Corry. Drek'h and the Azerii and Lii followed behind them, the Aza Tor bewildered by their reception until Morgana slipped her hand to him and sent, *Dayana is Elas' mother.*

"Yes, she can be quite trying, but her Sight is still strong, so we put up with her," Carda rambled on, drawing a smile from Morgana and slipping her skills around Elas to calm her. "Of course, we don't let her know that; she means well, but she can be so abrupt." They followed Corry to a tent on the outer circle, a small banner with the Lasah markings in front. "Well, here we are. Now Elas, I know you are tired, but I want you to join me for supper before the ceremony begins, and bring Morgana and Drek'h," the round-faced Elder smiled at each in turn. "I promise I won't ask too many questions, and I want you to be amongst my Healers, Elas, unless you would rather join your Hold?"

Elas smiled tiredly. "No. Thank you, Sha Carda, I would like that. Will someone come for Morgana?" She clasped her niece's hand as momentary panic sparked in her eyes.

Carda smiled again. "Yes, I'll send one of my youngsters to prepare her." She turned to Drek'h. "The Aza Tor Callent has asked about you. Mahdii's tents are on the southern edge of the circle."

"Callent's here?" His face brightened at the mention of his mentor. "Shall I go to lodge in their camp, or," he glanced at Elas as Morgana squeezed his hand. "shall I stay here?"

"It is up to you, but I think you should stand with Callent for Communion," Carda replied, while

Elas nodded her agreement.

"Well, the tent's yours, so get some rest while you can." She smiled once again. "Corry, show me where Ridasah ran off with Elas' sister and the Vondarii, I'd like a word..." The voice of the Elder fell away as she and their escort left the companions standing before the tent.

"Elas," Morgana turned swiftly to her aunt, "what preparations? You still haven't told me about Communion," her unease ringing in her words.

"Morgana, it's nothing to be afraid of." Elas stepped to her Azerii and began to remove her pack. "Come on, let's get our gear inside and let our companions rest as well."

Morgana stubbornly chewed on her lip unmoving for a moment until Starrynn whickered her distress. Quickly she relented to begin removing her pack, saddle and harness from the filly while Drek'h did the same for Kitteryth, and Stillyth who had remained with them.

They dropped their gear inside the tent doorway, Morgana turning back to the filly. Starrynn blew softly in her face. *I wish to roll in the grass, you need to rest,* then she turned away to walk to the open plain. Brealyth, Stillyth and Kitteryth as one disappeared from their presence.

"I think we've been deserted," Elas said mockingly as she turned back to the tent. "Come on you two, Rejat will join us soon. We need sleep; this evening is going to be a long one." They followed her into the tent which was wide and shallow with three spaces divided within by simple drapes. The first and center room was furnished with a large floor cloth and a small table with several cushions round it near the back wall. The two rooms on either side were sleeping quarters, four mats were laid out in each. Elas and Morgana moved their packs to the right as Drek'h dropped himself beside the table, when a young voice asked to enter.

"Yes, come in." Elas turned to greet their visitor.

"I bring you greetings from Sha Morant srii Torryth, Elder Aza Tor of Zerren's Gate Hold." A dark-haired girl in a golden tan dress with a red belt entered, carrying a tray with a water pitcher and several cups. "He wishes to speak with Sha Elas," she said, glancing shyly at their tired features, "as soon as you are able. He said he will come here, if that is your wish."

Elas nodded, "Tell Sha Morant, I will speak with him here in one hour." She stepped forward to take the tray from the girl, Morgana interceding to place it on the table.

"What is your name?" Elas said gently, noting the shyness in her manner.

"Vael, Sha Elas. From Zerren's Gate." The topaz eyes lowered slightly.

"Well, Vael, how is my father? Is he well?" Elas took the cup Morgana handed her, offering it to the girl who quickly shook her head.

"Your father?" Her eyes widened. "He is well, but not pleased—oh!" she suddenly clasped her hand to her face.

"Never mind, Vael, I know my father. Sha Dayana of Lasah?" Elas smiled and nodded, then sipped from her cup.

"Yes, Sha Elas. I'm sorry, I should not speak of it." She swiftly straightened her shoulders. "May I go and give him your reply?"

"Yes, thank you." She renewed her smile for

387

the nervous girl.

"Then I shall bring him in one hour." Vael smiled and slipped from the tent.

"Morant is your father? I have met him, he is an impressive man." Drek'h sipped from his cup, his weariness returning to his face. "I was at Zerren's Gate three years ago. Spent a winter there. He did not mention Sha Dayana as I recall."

"He wouldn't, he's too kind for that. But she is a very difficult woman." Elas plopped down between Morgana and Drek'h. "He is impressive, I agree. I haven't seen him for, almost nine years, I think." She refilled her cup and took another sip. "Tajiz, I want some tajiz before I face my mother." She ran a weary hand through her hair.

"I want sleep." Drek'h finished his cup and placed it on the table. "Will you call me when Morant arrives? I would like to greet him, then go find Callent." He glanced at Morgana, *Would you like to come with me?* he sent to her privately.

*Yes,* she sent warmly in return, her eyes flashing despite her fatigue.

"Yes, Drek'h," Elas caught the silent exchange but ignored it. "I'm sure Morant will wish to speak to you too." She rose to her feet. "Well, I need some sleep before I face either of my beloved parents." She turned and left them for the comfort of the sleep her body desired.

Drek'h reached for Morgana. She rose to sit next to him and they held each other close, saying nothing, and everything.

# Chapter 24

*Elas, wake up.*

She lifted a hand to her face. *Brealyth?*

*Your father is coming, with the young woman.* Her Azerii glimmered over her as she opened her eyes. *I thought you would like to be awake before they arrive.*

*Thanks, Laa. How soon before they're here?* She rose and tugged at her hair.

*They are halfway across the camp. About five or ten minutes.* Brealyth shimmered into hu'-man form and handed Elas her coat, the sleeves already removed.

*Thanks, where are Drek'h and Morgana?* She slipped on the coat, wishing for a bath and a complete change of clothes instead.

Brealyth pointed to the central room. *They are where you left them. Asleep.* She tossed her Mirii an amused look.

Elas slipped her head through the divider. Drek'h was reclining on the cushions, his head propped in his hand. Morgana was curled against him with her head on his chest.

*They were tired,* Brealyth observed dryly.

*Aren't we all?* she sighed and turned to her

Azerii. *Have Kit wake them, I'm sure he won't appreciate my doing it. Or Morgana.* She turned back to rummage in her pack.

Kitteryth appeared in form next to Drek'h, a long blade of tufted grass in one hand. She waved it across Morgana's face. She woke with a start as the bristles tickled her nose, blinked a few times, then grinned at his Azerii. *You wake him,* she sent as she carefully sat up.

The Azerii flashed an impish grin and touched the grass to Drek'h's ear. He sighed and opened one eye. "Hi, Kit. Been playing with the Lii?"

She laughed soundlessly and stuck the grass between her teeth. *No, Laa, but that sounds like an invitation. Shall I go find Starrynn?*

"Where do you have the energy?" He sat up, wincing at still sore bones. He reached over to brush Morgana's hair from her shoulder, then paused as Elas entered the room. She was carrying the tajiz pot and bag.

"Morant is on his way. I thought you'd like fair warning." She placed the pot on the table and began filling it with the water from the pitcher.

Drek'h nodded. "Thanks, Elas." He started to stand, pulling Morgana up beside him. Kit whisked at his coat with the grass blade until he turned half irritated eyes to her, then she gleefully vanished from the tent. He turned and ran his hands through his long hair. "How much time do we have before moonrise?"

Elas stirred the crushed tajiz leaves into the pot. "About two hours after dusk. Morgana, you need to be back here in two hours, after I talk with Dayana." She rolled her tired eyes. "I can't say I look forward to seeing her again." She placed the cover on the pot, then held her hands on the sides of the container. A warm light began to spill from the palms of her hands.

Morgana knelt beside her. "Elas, you said to me—in your garden," Her aunt glanced up at her faltering words. "about Communion."

"Yes?" Elas felt her niece's apprehensions flow around her. Drek'h placed a comforting hand on Morgana's shoulder.

"Well, you said, Communion was the time of meld. Elas, is this my time?" Her eyes were suddenly full of her fears.

Her aunt quickly released the now hot tajiz pot and turned to her. "Communion is the time of meld, but not for all of the Talents. Only the Chosen, those Talents who have been prepared." She took her niece's hands in her own, holding her inner worries aside lest she give them away. "You are to become a Chosen, but not yet. There is much for you to learn at the holds. You will be prepared for your time of meld." She gave her a reassuring smile.

"But what if this is my time of meld?" Morgana said as she leveled her intense gaze at her aunt. "What if the Dark Azerii tries again?"

Elas suddenly felt a coldness wrap around her. "It cannot, not at Communion. The Covenant forbids it," she insisted. Sounds of movement beyond the tent walls broke her tension. "We have visitors." She rose and pulled her niece to her feet. "Don't worry, Morgana, you will be fine." She turned as Vael's voice called her attention.

"Never mind, Child," Morant boomed out before the girl could begin her introductions. "She knows who I am, or I'll remind her if she's forgotten." Elas watched her father step into the tent past the girl as she smiled timidly at his manner.

"Sha Morant, I see you're still charming the women of your hold."

Morant held his arms wide. "Elas, my girl! And I'm sure you'll still scold them for putting up with me, behind my back!" As she stepped into his embrace, his eyes were reflecting his humor at their words.

Elas leaned back from her father's embrace to look up at him. His bronze hair was streaked with gray at temples and beard while laughter etched his face around green eyes and a generous mouth and nose. Time had barely moved him in the years since they had spoken last, his broad frame still held the strength she remembered. *You have not changed,* she sent, her warmth enveloping her thoughts.

"And you, Elaa, you are as beautiful as I remember, what—it's been nine years? Where have you been keeping yourself?" His mellow voice flowed outward. He released her to turn his eyes to her companions, one arm around her shoulders.

"You know perfectly well where I've been." She tugged at his long hair at the nape of his neck. "Never mind. You remember Drek'h, of Mahdii." She nodded to the younger man standing next to Morgana, a discreet grin on his tanned face. "He joined us in the eastern Varan."

"Mahdii? Never!" Morant thrust his open right hand towards the Aza Tor. "Drek'h has no hold, or did some fair Aza Har persuade him otherwise?" He winked at Drek'h as they clasped hands. "How are you, my friend? You look as if you've seen the hard side of this summer's journey."

Drek'h returned the Elder's smile. "I am well enough, Sha Morant. I have a few bruises, but I was fortunate to have journeyed with Elas and Rejat," he dropped his gaze briefly, "and Morgana," he said, glancing up at her.

"My niece, Morgana, of the Northern Varan Valleys." Elas nodded to her niece as she met her blue-gray eyes.

"I have heard about you, Morgana." He reached for her hand. I've just spoken with Rejat and the Vondarii Sarduk'h; they have spoken well of you, and of your first journey." He smiled again and she felt his calm wash over her. "You will have to tell me of your journey when we have the time. It is always interesting to hear a Talent's impressions." As he released her hand his eyes darted from her to Drek'h and noted the energy between them.

"Thank you, Sha Morant, but—why are you interested in my impressions?"

Morant blinked, surprised at her response. "Because, Child, we all learn from each other's experiences. Each journey is valid, whether by Talent, Aza, Healer or Elder, or one who is closed to their spirit. Even the wild Azerii. All journeys are important." He flashed her his brilliant smile again. "And Rejat tells me you've already experienced some talents that only the Mirii have through meld." He abruptly lowered his smile. "Now, Morgana, Drek'h, I need to speak to my daughter in private for a while. Do you think you can explore the camp for a bit?"

Drek'h nodded swiftly. "Yes, Sha Morant. I wish to find Callent of Mahdii. Morgana is coming with me," he said as he reached for her hand.

"I'll send Brealyth after I've spoken with Dayana," Elas said as the two departed, "and get yourself a bite to eat! It's going to be a long day!"

✳

Morgana and Drek'h walked slowly between the various tents and pavilions of the huge Mirii camp, exchanging few open words along the way, but sharing hidden thoughts with hands embraced. She was amazed at the number of people wearing the various shades of reds and their variety of clothing; from the elaborate coats to tunics, trousers, dresses and the long flowing robes of the Elders. The Talents and Chosen wore golden cloth garments, with the wide red belt like the young woman Vael wore. Drek'h pointed out the Chosen as they wandered, each wearing an additional white cord around their waists. Their faces seemed somehow distant from the others, as if they had removed themselves in mind from their companions. She watched them until Drek'h abruptly pulled her towards a large pavilion from which wonderful smells of cooking emanated. They found themselves amongst tables of food and swiftly moving people. He grabbed two meat pastries from the nearest table, handing one to her and heading for the open air once more.

As they enjoyed their pilfered fare, he began to point out the banners in front of the tents, identifying each by hold name. "There are twelve holds and wards. Seven holds; Lasah Hawk, Tasken, Zerren's Gate, Adjii Raven, Sekkett, Southern Tekk, and Mahdii, it's the smallest, in the middle of the Varan range." He pointed at the nearest banner, a gold field with silver crescent moon and red triangle. "That's Tasken, they're in the middle of the Coumar Mountains, east of the Sarh canyon below the Sumarkh." He caught her wide gaze and smiled. "I've journeyed through most of the holds and some of the wards..."

He trailed off as a memory brushed by unwelcome.

"What are the wards?" she said as she finished her pastry and took his hand again.

"There are five." He looked up again. "Telann, Vesska, Dolphyn's Crest, Vadamii, and Varan's Reach." They passed another large pavilion and he stopped again, releasing her hand. Before them a small pavilion with a banner of green with gold stars fluttered from its standard. "That's Mahdii," he said, then began walking once more. "I haven't seen Callent for two years. He wasn't at the hold the last time I was there." He began nodding to some of the people around who greeted him, Morgana sensing his interest lay within the tent.

Two men in Mirii coats stepped from the entrance, one with his back to them, his long gray hair tied neatly at the nape of his neck. The other man nodded and the gray-haired man turned at their approach.

"I wondered if you'd turn up." A thin smile widened across the man's face.

"Callent!" Drek'h shouted the man's name and rushed forward. The two embraced each other roughly, the elder pounding Drek'h's shoulder.

Morgana paused to watch their warm exchange. Callent was near sixty, his height less than Drek'h's by half a hand. His dark eyes flashed his greeting to the Vondarii he had claimed from death on the Sumarkh. She heard his Azerii greet her as she stood several paces behind them. *Welcome, Light One. We thank you for bringing him back to the Sumarkh,* her gentle mind voice echoed through her.

She glanced around her. "How do you know?"

The Azerii quietly shimmered into form next to

her, appearing as a woman whose years matched her Mirii. *Your companion, Kitteryth, has shared with us. I am Mirryth, Azerii to Callent.* She wore a long dress in dark red, her dark gray hair cascading to her shoulders. She reached out and clasped Morgana's hand. *Come.*

Mirryth caught her Mirii's attention. Callent coughed softly and nodded as Drek'h turned, his face remiss for neglecting Morgana. He quickly introduced her to Callent and the other man, another Aza of Mahdii.

"Morgana is a Talent, niece of the Travelaar Healer Elas srii Brealyth of Zerren's Gate. She was assisted by the First Stallion of the Lii," he said proudly as he gazed at her.

"We were all assisted by the First," Morgana said and smiled at the three men. The Azerii beside her sent, *Well said,* and disappeared.

"Yes, well said indeed, Morgana," Callent nodded and glanced at Drek'h. "You certainly have impressed this young man. Come inside both of you, and tell me what else you've been doing on this journey of yours." Callent stepped back and drew the others after him into the cooling shadows of the Mahdii pavilion.

\*

"Tell me about Morgana." The Elder Visioner of Lasah leaned back in a low wooden chair beside a small softly draped table. She held a clear crystal glass in her hand, turning it idly as she watched her daughter's nervous face. They sat within her private tent near the outer cluster of Lasah's encampment, the sounds of the Mirii camp diminished without.

Elas raised her eyes to her mother. Dayana's pastel blond hair was more silver than she remembered. Her features had become more fragile looking with time, in direct contrast to her pale blue eyes which seemed to grow in strength even as the years were added to her body.

Holding the crystal that Larann had given her, Elas pushed its calming energy to her own use. "Morgana is twenty-three. She has never been married, nor traveled beyond the north-western Varan valleys. She knows little of the Azerii and the Mirii, only that which we have told her. She has learned to shield well, almost too well at times. She has given Drek'h shield burns once, blocked the Dark Azerii three times, thrown her awareness out of body and scanned the Eye." At Dayana's sudden glare, she paused briefly before continuing. "She has more talents appearing than I have encountered in any of the people of the Outerlands in a long time. She hears the Kir-Latt, the Lii, and all the Azerii, Meld and wild. She has some healing abilities, through her hands and heart, to Drek'h, she has—"

"Are they lovers?" Dayana interrupted coldly.

"Not yet, as far as I know. They have not claimed each other. I have spoken—"

"Has she had any Visions?" The older woman sat up straight, the cords in her hand visible as she tightened her fingers around her glass.

"Yes, one in her home, the last night she was there. It was the Dark Azerii." Elas stared at her mother. "Rejat and I have shared it; Rejat says it's the same as your Vision."

Dayana nodded impassively. "Yes, we have already spoken on this. Any other Visions?"

She sighed and dropped her eyes to the swirl-

ing floor cloth that brightened the austere surroundings.

"Yes, she saw the Lii claim her horse, and
Drek'h's return to the Vondarii. I think she has had
other dreams that hold the element of visioning."

"What else?"

She raised her eyes again to meet her
mother's. The cool intensity of her gaze invoked angry memories within her. She turned her glance aside.
"She has gained two of the several names called her
by her Vision. The first; 'Elissii', from a Kir-Latt of the
western Varan. The second, 'Morannon', by the Lii
and the Vondarii."

"Did she give you all of the names?"

"No, she mentioned the two, a few days back, I
don't remember when exactly." She suddenly turned
again to her mother. "Do you know of Larann, First
Healer of the Storm-Rynnok'h clan?" Dayana's face
remained unresponsive. "Larann is a true Visioner.
She saw our coming. She sees Morgana as," Elas
paused briefly, taking a deep breath, "as 'a fire rimmed sword, held aloft in the darkness by an unseen
hand'. Those are her words." Her eyes hardened.
"What did your Vision say of Morgana?"

Dayana returned her accusing gaze without reaction. "My Vision is as I have told Rejat. There is
more, but that is for the Council to be concerned
with. What a Vondarii Healer sees is of little matter."

Elas jumped to her feet, her face rigid with anger. "Morgana is of *my* concern! She has held off a
Dark Azerii who forced meld on a Kir-Latt and a
salkinn! Larann's Visions have the energy of truth
within them. I do not *idly* cast them out for your approval! Both Rejat and I, and Drek'h, have felt the
power of this Azerii, and I think it will break the

Covenant tonight to meld with her!" She stood before her mother, her fury rolling around her like a black cloud. "How can we protect her if we are all locked in Communion? She will be alone, did you think of the danger to her? Or the risk to all of us if Larann's Vision is true?"

Dayana rose slowly. "Calm yourself, Elas," she said, her voice sharp with her control. "Morgana will not meld with this one. She will be protected." She walked to the doorway, her white robe rustling softly with each step.

"How can you be so sure? What if you are wrong?" Elas demanded of her mother's callous stance.

"My Visions are *not* wrong!" The Elder Visioner snapped as she turned abruptly to face her daughter again. "You are overstepping yourself! You have claimed yourself as Healer, not Visioner. Do not attempt to interpret another's Visions when you have denied you own!"

"I will never be a Visioner if it means to manipulate others to suit my desires!" Elas hissed, struggling to keep her emotions and her voice in control.

Dayana drew back, her Azerii suddenly blazing in her aura. "Go back to your valley, Daughter! You have denied me for the last time!" Her words lashed out at Elas as her voice rose. With silent effort she resumed her untroubled pose. "You have brought Morgana as a Talent. We shall take her gladly into our hold. She shall be well guided into her time of meld. Then she shall be a dutiful member of our society. She shall be Mirii," she stated firmly.

"I will not leave yet. Morgana still has her choices and I intend she will have every possibility to be what she chooses. Not what the First Visioner of

Lasah guides," she taunted. "I trust my Visions—and
Larann's—enough to see that you choose to use Morgana to whatever suits you. Tell me, Mother, are you
trying to create your Vision of Morgana's future, or
destroy it?"

Dayana's face drained of color. "*Do not interfere!* The matter is out of your control! Morgana will
be trained to her best talents for her time of meld.
Now leave!" She raised her hands before her, her face
flooded with her ill-contained rage.

Elas locked her eyes with her mother's once
more. "I am Travelaar Healer of Zerren's Gate Hold. I
will leave when I am ready, and when I know Morgana is on her path, not yours." She flashed her angry
gaze and strode from the Visioner's tent.

✳

Supper with Carda, Elder Healer of Lasah,
proved to be the partial restorative that Elas needed.
She sat next to the older woman who radiated her
calming talents to those around her with warm smiles
and spoke comforting words to the companions who
gathered at her table. Elas had spent the hour before
alone, walking through the encampment to the lake
shore; once there she sat in silence and mulled over
her conversation with her mother. Rejat had been
wrong, Dayana had not changed, she still sought to
control everyone around her. The words of the Vondarii Healer echoed through her coldly; Morgana was
a danger to the Mirii society. Her mother knew it and
worked to use that knowledge to achieve what? An
end? Or a beginning? A sudden flash burst through
her; Larann had experienced all or part of the same
vision of Morgana that Dayana had, the fiery sword

400

held aloft by an unseen hand. Did her mother strive to be that hand? And by doing so prevent the rift between the Mirii?

A swift mental jab from Rejat brought her attention back to her surroundings. Carda was speaking with Sarduk'h as he sat on her other side. Across from him Morgana and Drek'h listened to the hunter's words of his past. The other hunters, Tren, Madeh and Colkenn sat at his left, politely listening to the Outerland words of which they understood little.

*Elas, where are you? Was Dayana that difficult?* Rejat sent while her eyes shifted from their hostess to her sister's troubled face.

She glanced at Carda, then replied, *Yes, more than ever. We must talk, soon and alone.* She turned again to the Elder and struggled to remain attentive to the unrelated conversation that flowed amongst her companions.

Carda suddenly turned to her. "I am remiss, there are things we must discuss before our grand event is to take place this eve." She swept guileless eyes around her guests. "Friend Sarduk'h, would you excuse us? One of my Talents will guide you and your company to the Elder Aza Tor Cadann, he is our able council member who will guide you through this evening's work if you and your hunters wish to participate." She smiled at Drek'h, "Could you and Morgana assist them? Then bring Morgana back here, say in half an hour?" Drek'h nodded and rose, as did the Vondarii, all echoing their thanks for the welcome food and talk.

Morgana hesitated, her eyes on her aunt. *Are you all right?*

*Yes, go, we shall talk before this night. Go, stay with Drek'h,* she nodded tiredly.

When they had left, Carda reached for Elas' and Rejat's hands. "Now, tell me what has occurred on your journey, especially about Morgana."

\*

Dusk fell heavily over the Mirii camp, drawing the warmth of the day from the earth and wisping it aloft on star-filled breezes. A deep felt expectancy began to permeate the air and every member upon the Sumarkh as each made ready for the Communion ceremony.

"Drek'h, have you ever experienced this? Communion?" Morgana wrapped her arms about her as a coolness began to spill from the lake nearby.

He placed his arm around her shoulders as they proceeded back to Carda's tent. "My time of meld was a type of Communion, but you mean here?" He turned his gaze to her face. "No, the last one, it was ten years ago. I was still a Talent at Mahdii. Callent was here though. He told me about some of it." He caught the expression that was held behind her eyes. "Why? What's wrong?"

She stopped and turned to gaze up at his worried face. *I'm afraid, I don't know what I'm doing here.* She dropped her eyes to the trampled grass at their feet.

He reached out, wrapping her in his arms and love. *You are here to become Mirii,* he sent, embracing her.

*And then what? Where—,* She leaned against him, her thoughts scattering. *What if the Dark Azerii tries again? I don't think I can hold it off another time. I could feel the salkinn, through my shield. I think it almost got to me, except for*

402

*your and Rejat's shields blocking it.* She shivered in his arms as her mind replayed the image of the dead salkinn.

Drek'h held her and gazed at the fading sky-line. *The Dark Azerii can't reach you here,* he sent calmly. *They cannot reach a Talent when they are within any large gathering of Meld Azerii.* He looked back at her upraised face. *The Meld Azerii protect the Talents. It's part of the Covenant.*

"But I feel," she whispered aloud, "something, I feel something will happen to me, that will be—" she stopped and turned her eyes away.

"I know, there was something I felt before the meld that I can't describe, it was a knowing, of a change in me." He brushed her cheek with his lips.

"No, this is different." She looked back at his gentle blue eyes. "Something happened at the Von-darii camp, when I fainted," she shook her head, "but I can't remember. I just know it. Something is wrong!"

Drek'h held her face and kissed her suddenly with a fierce but tender passion. *Nothing will go wrong! I will protect you!* his thoughts whipped through her as he held her tightly, his arms clasping around her once more.

She returned his kisses and through her bright tears a pale image shimmered once more behind her eyes.

*Nothing will go wrong, Morgana Elissii.*

# Chapter 25

They retraced their steps to stand outside the Lasah Healer's tent, where hushed voices carried from within. Morgana brushed her tears aside as she and Drek'h announced their presence.

"Enter," Carda answered them. Inside they found Elas, Rejat and Morant with her, seated along the long supper table which now held two oil lamps and an assortment of cups with the unmistakable aroma of tajiz. They exchanged greetings and Carda instructed them to sit, Morgana beside her while Rejat poured each a fresh cup.

Carda gently held Morgana's hand and gazed knowingly into her eyes. *No more tears, Laa, we have work to do,* she sent and pushed a calming wave through her. "I have been consulting with your Aunt and her dear sister on your behalf," she began and Morgana darted her eyes to the others. "They have informed me of your talents, exceptional that they are." She paused, her eyes meeting Morgana's once more.

"What are they?"

Carda leaned back, a hint of surprise flickering across her round features. "To start, you have healing, visioning and distance scanning abilities. Your mind voice is very strong, especially since you hear all the Azerii, plus the Kir-Latt and Lii." Her eyes seemed to reach through her for a moment before she continued. "Your shielding skills are extraordinary, as I'm sure Drek'h will attest to!" She raised her gaze to a point over her head, then returned to her face. "Hmm, I sense you will also be able to transmute your form."

"What is that?" Morgana glanced at Elas, sitting at Carda's right.

"Shapeshifting, you would be able to change your physical form," Rejat replied from behind Morant.

Morgana turned her eyes to the Aza Har. "To change my form? Like the Azerii?" her voice full of bewilderment.

Morant and Rejat nodded. "Yes, Morgana," he answered first. "Some of us have the ability."

"Do you?"

"Yes," he said simply. "So do my daughters."

Morgana raised her eyes to Rejat as she leaned on her father's shoulders. "It does come in handy at times," she said, and an odd smile slipped across her face.

She glanced at her aunt, Elas shrugged non-committally. "I have, on my younger journeys."

"Enough of that," Carda asserted, "we have been discussing more than just your talents. You need to be made aware of your choices within our society." She turned a stern gaze to each in her company.

Morgana felt her tension rise as she listened to the Elder. "Communion is a great gathering of our people, to reaffirm the Covenant with the Azerii, and the meld to take place amongst the Chosen. Elas has told me of your concerns of the Dark Azerii forcing

meld upon you at this time. She has also told you the
Covenant forbids this occurrence. She is correct. The
Dark Azerii cannot remain or move through the Meld
Azerii at Communion. Their life force energy is completely incompatible." Carda released her hand to
turn and sip from her cup before speaking again.
"During Communion you will join the Talents of all
the holds. You will be asked to follow their movements and words. If you feel you must shield during
the Chosen's time of meld, it is permitted, but not en-
couraged. You will be safe. All Talents are held in the
highest of concern." She patted her hand gently.
"Communion lasts from moonrise to moonset. The
energy will be highest at the apex of the moon; you
will see the Meld and the Unnamed Azerii, their lights
will brighten the plateau. You will hear them. They
may call you, but do not answer or follow them.
Again, if you feel endangered you may shield, but
mind shield only. There is more that occurs but you
will not be involved." Her eyes held a moment of for-
biddance, then she continued. "Afterward you may
stay with the Talents or return to the quarters Elas
and Rejat were given. On the morrow you will meet
with the High Council of the Holds and then you will
be asked to join a hold or ward for your training to
begin."

"My training?"

"To be Mirii is more than one path. Your talents will guide you, whether to become Healer, Visioner, Aza Har, Travelaar or EarthSinger. You have
already received some training by your journey; the
rest will take about one to three years, depending on
how quickly your talents fully manifest."

"That shouldn't be long," Rejat smirked over
her father's shoulder. Morant glared at her briefly,

then turned back to Carda.

"Then you will be ready for your time of meld," she continued and a radiance filled her face. "When your hold Elders know you to be ready, at the proper time you will be taken with the other Chosen to the place of meld nearest your hold."

"Like the Eye of the Lady?" Morgana asked, then held her breath.

"Yes, like the Eye." Carda's smile widened. "Now, have I allayed your fears?"

Morgana lifted her smile timidly. "Yes, Sha Carda."

"Good. Then we must proceed." She rose as a young girl entered the tent, dressed in the attire of a Talent. "Talji, please take Morgana to the other Talents and assist her." As Morgana stood and followed the girl from the tent, a cautious smile on her face to all, Carda turned again to address those remaining. "Now, beloved, we have an hour till moonrise. Let us make our preparations complete."

✳

The evening air was filled with autumn's breath upon the open plain east of the Te'rakh Lake as the Mirii assembled outside of their encampment. Each carrying a small glowing sphere, they filed out of the rings of tents and pavilions by their designation. Aza first; to create a ring of protection from the landscape's other inhabitants, then the Healers, plus the few EarthSingers and EarthKeepers who had answered this call to Communion. Then the Talents and Chosen entered the ring, the later moving to the side nearest the silent lake. Last came the Visioners of each hold, dressed in brilliant white, their silver and red corded belts reaching to their knees or lower. They were accompanied by two Elders of their holds, Aza and Healer as guide and support to the open energies that could flood the senses of the Visioners who were uncomfortable journeying out of the safety of their holds.

In nervous anticipation, Morgana stood next to Talji. She was now dressed similarly, with the red sash that Elas had given her around her waist. She had spoken few words with the girl whose shyness seemed to mirror her own, nor many with the other Talents from Lasah who regarded her in varying degrees, depending on which tale they had heard about her. They told her little of the ceremony that had begun, she suspected it was simply because they themselves did not fully know what was to take place. An air of secrecy had danced around the Mirii and she still felt apprehension at her involvement. Somehow, she still felt out of place.

The Elders and Visioners moved to the center of the circle, their glowing lights casting shadows erratically around them as if from the slightest breeze off the nearby waters. She watched each as they entered but found no friend in the glimmering darkness that surrounded them. A soft brushing touched her hair and she felt the familiar energies of Kitteryth, Brealyth and Stillyth wisp around her, as if to reassure her of their loving protection.

The moon began to ascend from the eastern rim of the Sumarkh over distant mountains that loomed black and mysterious in the night. The assembled Mirii placed their lights on the ground and turned as one to greet the glowing sphere. Raising their hands in momentary salutation, they watched the moon spill her light over the grassland and waited.

A breathless pause filled the night, then was released as countless Unnamed Azerii shimmered from the darkness into the star-scattered sky over the gathering. Exuberant cries filled the senses of the hu'-mans below as the Azerii greeted them. She heard other voices; the Visioners from the core of the circle began to speak in tones of calm welcoming, the convergence of their words ringing through the air creating an unrecognizable language to her ears. She glanced towards the Aza and the Healers who rimmed the Talents and Chosen. The lights of their Azerii began to blaze around each, brightening the outer perimeters of the conclave. The intensity of the mixed voices increased and she felt the return of overlapping images begin to flood her mind. Her panic flared as her memory of the meeting with the Vondarii Elders and the Pale Being waiting within pushed through her awareness. She struggled to hold her ground against the drowning of her senses as other frightening memories began to crowd her already overburdened mind. Images of the forms of the Dark Azerii began to revolve within her inner sight and the words it had demanded of her echoed in her head. *Morgana Elissii! Morgana, Morannon, Morgan, Morgu Elissii Varayni, Mordlyth! Mordlyth!* they screamed from the salkinn and the adjii raven, beating at her relentlessly from the unforgotten depths of her soul.

Morgana suddenly thrust her shield high, crying out in pain as her walls showered blue fire within her mind. She turned her gaze outward and was assaulted by the blazing images of the Azerii overlapping the hu'mans around her.

*We are One!* they whispered beneath their rackety cries.

"We are the Life," the hu'mans returned, their

eyes lifted to the moon above.

*We are all One Life!* the Azerii sang again and she sensed that the people around her were not listening anymore.

*We are all One Life, Morgana Elissii.* The voice slipped through her being and a pale shimmer seemed to emanate from around her. She raised her hands and gaped at the light that burst from her skin, as if she had suddenly become one of the glowing spheres that Rejat was so adept at producing.

"Who are you?" she whispered to her open hands.

*I am the Becoming.* A stillness filled her and she found her mind swiftly clear of the surrounding chaos. She turned her eyes aloft and felt the light from her body pulse outward, ringing and enclosing her in silver glimmering white light. *I am the Becoming,* the voice of the Pale Being whispered through her. *I am One.* She felt her mind join with the Other. *I am the Whole, the Heart and the Light. We are complete.* She glanced out towards the lake as an embracing compassion filled her body.

"Are you my Azerii?" she whispered as the pale image softly appeared before her.

*No.* Eyes of endless depth drew her forward. *We are One. We are the Anarii. We are the Whole, not the separation.* A shadowless hand swept towards the glowing forms beyond. *They perceive the separation. I am you. We are One. We are the Anarii.* The being slowly drew forward until she felt an expanding of her awareness as the Pale Other merged within her body, making her light shower outwards in aurora sparkles.

A golden wave of energy washed through her.

*We are all part of the Whole, complete and yet perceived as separate. We are All Life, both Mirii and Azerii, Hu'man and Starlight Beings. We hold both powers in One Light, Morgana Elissii.*

She began to walk from her place amongst the other Talents. "What do they see?" she asked softly as she passed her companions.

*They see their reflections and do not know it.* Her Light awareness guided her towards the Chosen. She gazed across to the still forms of the Mirii Talents who were prepared for meld. All looked unchanged to her physical eyes, her inner-sight perceiving them clothed in golden auras that swelled brightly, outshining the light spheres which had been abandoned by their feet. She looked past them to the Healers and Aza as she approached; all wore the same golden auras around their night-darkened physical forms, their faces enraptured by Communion.

*What do they feel?*

*What you feel now. Love,* the Other Within replied.

*What is Communion?* She was through the circle. Beyond was the sandy outline of the lake. She walked down the sloping bank and towards the distant waters that murmured in the moon-filled night. At the water's edge she knelt and placed her hands on its cool surface, filling its shallows with her light. She raised her drenched hands to her face, thrilling at the sharp cold that kissed her cheeks. She sat beside the water and gazed to the west.

*Communion is this.* Her awareness suddenly left her body, soaring aloft to the cloud of light that was the Azerii. A sense of total love and peace filled her as she joined the Unnamed Azerii whose voices had joined in a song full of beautiful magnitude. With-

411

out words, the song lifted and expanded her awareness outwards again as the earth fell away in a shower of light. She felt the minds of countless souls merge with hers, all separate yet complete and part of the Whole.

Her awareness shifted and she felt the earth beneath her once more. She was a comet of light blazing over the shifting surface to merge again with other Mirii and Azerii linked in Communion. She saw the holds; mountain fortresses buried in their rocky faces, and open wards, their towers ranging skyward in wide mountain valleys, their Mirii gathered in circles nearby with faces upturned to the moon and the bright Azerii above and amongst them. She soared over the hidden places of the Meld and saw the joy-struck Chosen as they merged with their Azerii. She shared in their rejoicing, experiencing the surge of pleasure that each felt as their minds touched their Azerii for the first time.

A dancing thought spilled through her. *Now I know what Drek'h felt when he named Kitteryth.* She laughed within and felt her being lift upwards again. Stillyth's words echoed from her memory, *In my naming, I am Love.* She saw the Sumarkh's broad fields return and felt the upper winds rush through her.

*Do I have another name?* she whispered to the lowering moon on the western horizon.

*Yes. You will find it in the stars, and it will be Love.*

*When will I know it?* The waters of the lake shimmered below.

*You already know it. You will hear it when you no longer need it.* A shimmer of light enveloped her once more as she opened her eyes to her physical surroundings. The moon touched the rolling hills beyond the wide lake's edge, its refection drawn out before her like pearls in the velvet of night, shifting with the ripples of the lake surface. She felt her radiance glisten outwards and dance on the sands of the shore. She laughed and raised her hands to the moon. She felt reborn, as if all the pain of her past had been released to the elements around her. She rose to her feet and walked along the beach toward the south, lost in the beauty of the night.

Two forms slowly joined her. Starrynn and Skyrynnar nuzzled the hands she extended, then the claimed Lii of the four hunters were beside them. In turn they approached her and gave her their names; Tarnn of Sarduk'h, Katesh of Colkenn, Vreen of Madeh, and Niika of Tren. They followed her along the lake shore and upon the grassland until a great weariness began to fill her body. She stopped and leaned against Starrynn and turned her eyes to the bright Mirii camp which now lay far in the distance.

*Sleep, Light One.* Starrynn brushed her velvet nose to her cheek. *We shall keep you warm.* The filly turned and carefully lay down at her feet.

Morgana gazed silently at the filly and the stallions around her. She lowered herself to the ground against the wide back and fell into a deep peaceful sleep full of marvelous images of racing Lii and reveling mist ponies.

✳

Morgana awoke to sunlight dancing on her cheeks, the tall grass around her waving in the soft morning airs. Before her sat four Azerii in hu'man form; Kitteryth, Brealyth, Callent's Azerii Mirryth, and another she did not recognize, while the Lii gathered around them in a loose circle. All in female form, their features were as varied as their Mirii and their expressions equally diverse.

Kitteryth's smile broadened fully as their eyes met. She reached forward to touch her hand. *Welcome, Laa, to the Forbidden.* Her eyes carried a knowledge far more ancient than her appearance.

Morgana sat up slowly to face her companions. "Kitteryth, I do not understand. What is the Forbidden?" she said aloud and felt a rush of pleasure at the sound of her voice. She raised a hand to her mouth, then gazed at her fingertips. A subtle golden light still emanated from her skin.

The Azerii smiled again and glanced at her sisters. Brealyth shook her head softly and sent, *You have crossed a barrier that our Mirii have created. They named it the Forbidden. We call it,* she glanced at the eldest woman/Azerii who Morgana did not know, *the Place of One. The Becoming.* A hint of sadness was held in her eyes. She turned to the elder whose face was etched in ageless serenity. Morgana followed her gaze to the other.

*I am Anryth, Azerii to Carda.* Gentle thoughts slipped from a slim face surrounded by silver white hair that fell in thick waves past her shoulders. She wore a loose silver robe that billowed around her narrow frame. Her features held no semblance to her Mirii, save for the warmth of her gray eyes. They sparkled lovingly to Morgana. *You have opened a door and entered a place that has not been here for all the ages of your people.* She smiled gently. *We welcome you to your new light, Morgana Elissii.*

Morgana returned a puzzled smile. "I still do

not understand you." She looked at Brealyth again. "Have I done something wrong?"

*To the Mirii, yes,* she nodded, her face a reflection of Elas'. *That is why they call it the Forbidden.*

*Understand us, Morgana,* Mirryth sent, her darkly grayed hair frothing about her face, *we are here to assist you. The Azerii welcome you to your new beginning. You are as a bright star in the darkness of the night to us.* She suddenly shifted her tone. *Look at your hands, what do you see?*

Morgana held her hands before her and saw the gentle glow. "I see my skin—I see my own Light!" She raised her eyes to Mirryth as the Other Within spoke through her as one.

Mirryth nodded. *They do not see their Light, except through us. They do not allow it. It is always there.*

*What do you feel?* Anryth sent, her face composed.

Morgana gazed down at her hands, then closed her eyes. A warmth filled and surrounded her. She felt at peace, sitting on the grass near the shining lake. "I feel," she opened her eyes again, "whole, more complete than I ever have." A thrilling energy began to radiate within her body. "I feel—free!" she suddenly burst out and threw her hands to the sun, laughing in delight.

*Hold onto that feeling,* Anryth's thoughts caught at her mind. *Never release it, never forget it. That is who and what you are.* As Morgana lowered her hands the Azerii reached forward and clasped them in her own. *They do not understand what you have become. They will try to hold onto you through your fears. Know that they cannot.*

Her smile suddenly collapsed. "What have I become?"

*The ancient ones were called Anarii. You are Anarii. You have come from the beginning and are now of the beginning. Full Circle.* A timeless light began to shine from Anryth's body. *We are the children of the Anarii.* She released her hands and stood slowly. *But we have lost the way to become Anarii.* Her radiance pushed outward as her body turned to light, pure and blinding. *Help us, Morgana Elissii, help your people, all the Hu'- mans, remember the way to the Becoming. We are all the children of the Anarii.*

As Morgana held her hand up to shield her eyes the Azerii suddenly departed. She blinked quickly and turned her gaze to Brealyth. Elas' Azerii still held her saddened smile.

"Brealyth, what must I do now?'

*Return to the Mirii. Go to Elas.*

Morgana reached out and touched her hand. *Why are you sad?*

Brealyth lowered her eyes briefly. *Because, through Elas, I know of the loneliness you now will face.* She raised her eyes again. *I do not know of any Hu'man who has meld with their Source.*

*I am not alone,* she felt within and gently clasped the Azerii's hand. "I am never alone," she said aloud. She stood before the three Azerii and turned her eyes to the Mirii camp on the horizon. "Do they know where I am? Or what happened?"

Kitteryth rose beside her. *No, only that which we have told them, that you are safe.* Her vibrant smile spilled across her face. *Here,* she held out a red cloth bundle, *wear this. This is your day of choosing.*

Morgana opened the bundle. It was the dress that the Vondarii Talahs had given her. She smiled suddenly and turned to look at each of the Azerii standing around her.

Moments later, dressed in the gold embroidered red dress, a resolute young woman walked back to the camp of the Mirii, while three fiery Azerii and six majestic Lii horses accompanied her.

"This is my day of choosing."

The End of Book One

# Index of Characters, Creatures & Things

**ADALA Rinon** - Dain's younger sister, Rinon LandsHold.

**ADJII RAVEN** - a large bird.

**AGELESS ONES** - Mirii term for the Kir-Latt.

**ANARII** - The Ancient Ones.

**ANCIENT ONES** - a term of reverence.

**ANRYTH** - Carda's Azerii.

**AWAKENING, The** - Mirii term for the failing of the covenant.

**AURA** - a field of energy emanating and surrounding every person, place, and thing. Can be seen or felt by those with psychic ability.

**AZA** - ancient Mirii term for warrior. Aza Har—female, Aza Tor—male warrior.

**AZERII** - the formless, sentient beings of this world, they appear in four variations; the **Unnamed Azerii**, the **wild Azerii,** the **meld or 'named' Azerii** and the **Dark Azerii.** Except for the meld Azerii, they cannot create a physical form and can only be seen by those with psychic abilities. The people call them spirits, ghosts or demons.

**BARII RING** - a garnet ring that each Mirii wears; represents the joining of all the Mirii with the Covenant.

**BREA Brejjard** - Morgana's mother, wife of Tillan, Brejjard LandsHold.

**BREALYTH** - Elas' Azerii.

**BERRANTA** - Mirii Healer, Varan's Reach Ward.

**BRIENT Brejjard** - Tagar's son by his first wife.

**CALLENT** - Mirii Aza Tor Travelaar, Mahdii Hold, Drek'h's mentor.

**CARDA** - Mirii Elder Healer, Lasah Hawk Hold.

**CEDARJINN** - a large evergreen tree.

**CHOSEN** - Mirii term for Talent prepared for meld. Vondarii term for an intimate relationship.

**CHZA** - a large deer.

**COLKENN** - Vondarii hunter, Storm-Rynnok'h clan.

**COMMUNION** - the ceremony to reaffirm the bond between the Mirii and the Azerii, held every ten years at the Te'rakk Lake in the middle of the Sumark'h Plateau.

**CONSORT** - Vondarii term for their mate. A husband or wife.

**CORRY ANATT** - Mirii Aza Tor Travelaar, Lasah Hawk Hold, past journey companion to Rejat.

**COVENANT, The** - the power that was created by the Mirii and their meld Azerii, to prevent the Dark Azerii from forcing their awareness on other humans.

**DAIN Rinon** - eldest son of the Rinons'; Kina's betrothed. Rinon LandsHold.

**DARIEL Brenan** - youngest daughter of Kaill, Brenan Lands-Hold.

**DARK AZERII** - an Unnamed Azerii that desires the meld so greatly that it would force itself on a human or any other creature to achieve the meld, risking madness and destruction of itself and its host.

**DARKNESS** - the Kir-Latt named by Morgana.

**DASKAN** - Mirii Elder Visioner, Varan's Reach Ward.

**DAYANA** - Mirii Elder Visioner, Lasah Hawk Hold. Sent Rejat to find Morgana. Elas' mother.

**DISTANCE SCANNING** - Mirii ability to 'see' with the mind over great distances.

**DREK'H** - Mirii Aza Tor Travelaar Healer, claims no Hold. Cast out from his Vondarii clan when his Lii horse died.

**EARTHKEEPER** - Mirii name for a man who cares for the land. A farmer. The Kir-Latt called Tagar this.

**EARTHSINGER** - Mirii name for a woman who cares for the land and the foliage upon it. A gardener.

**ELAA** - Elas' nickname.

**ELAS** - Mirii Travelaar Healer, Zerren's Gate Hold. Rejat's half sister. Wife to Tagar for past ten years.

**ELISSII** - name given to Morgana by the Kir-Latt.

**EYE OF THE LADY** - name of a sacred lake to the Mirii, located in the Coumar Mountains. Where Rejat and Elas joined with their Azerii and became Mirii. Morgana 'accidentally' scans the Eye while daydreaming in Elas' garden.

**FAYR HAWK** - a silver and white hawk of the plains.

**FORCED VISIONING** - Mirii term for forcing a vision, with the aid of their Azerii, on another. Rejat did this to contact Morgana at the river.

**FORESTERS** - the mountain people living alone or in small self-governed family communities in the great forests. The LandsHolders and city dwellers consider them unreliable.

**'GANA** - Morgana's nick-name.

**GUARDS** - Mirii term for palm-sized energy rings, placed around a person or object to warn of intrusion.

**HEALER** - Mirii title for one with healing abilities.

**HU'MAN** - A human of this world, the people.

**HU'MANSLAYERS** - assassins, mercenaries.

**HUNTSMEN** - Foresters working for hire as scouts or mercenaries.

**INNER-SIGHT** - the ability to 'see', or vision, with the mind, into another's body, or over distances.

**JESS** - Tagar's HorseKeeper, North Brejjard LandsHold.

**JEVEN Brenan** - Kaill's youngest son, Brenan LandsHold. Is able to see the wild Azerii. Marked and protected from the Dark Azerii in a ceremony by Elas and Rejat.

**KAHJA** - Morgana's horse, given to Elas and Tagar by Kaill Brenan.

**KAILL BRENAN** - HoldMaster, Brenan LandsHold.

**KATESH** - Lii horse, companion to Colkenn, Vondarii hunter.

**KEETHRA or KEETHRA IRONSTONE** - steel, coated with a sulfurous mixture of herbs, minerals and oils; used as a weapon or protective amulet against the Azerii and the Mirii.

**KEVASS** - a Vondarii hunter from Rejat's past.

**KERAN** - Vondarii Hunt leader, Storm-Rynnok'h clan.

**KINA Brejjard** - Morgana's younger sister, Brejjard LandsHold.

**KIR-LATT** - A sentient wolf-like creature, called the Ageless Ones by the Mirii and the Vondarii.

**KITTERYTH** - Drek'h's Azerii.

**LAA** - an endearing name.

**LADY, The** - divine figure, consort to the people's God. The Mirii and the Vondarii see her as the dominant being. The Goddess.

**LANDSHOLD** - a farming or ranching community, tenanted by several families, under the rule of the HoldMaster and his family.

**LARANN** - Vondarii, the First Healer of the Storm-Rynnok'h clan, half sister to Sarduk'h.

**LEGEND, The** - the brief history of the Mirii and the Azerii, as told by Elas to Morgana.

**LII, The** - the sentient horses of the Sumarkh Plateau.

**MADEH** - Vondarii hunter, Storm-Rynnok'h clan.

**MADNESS, The** - Mirii term for when the Dark Azerii has forced it awareness upon another.

**MAKETT** - Mirii Senior Aza Tor, Varan's Reach Ward.

**MEDICINER** - a non-Mirii name for a healer or doctor.

**MELD, MELDING** - Mirii term for the merging of awareness of an Azerii and a human.

**MARDETH** - Vondarii elder, First Mother, Storm-Rynnok'h clan.

**MELD, The, or MELD AZERII** - the Azerii that have joined with the humans. When named by their Mirii, they are able to shape-shift into physical form, and communicate with their Mirii by telepathy.

**MIA** - Elas' adopted daughter from the Southlands.

**MIND SHIELD** - Mirii term for a mental barrier to keep others from reading one's thoughts, or from sending private thoughts out to another.

**MIND TALK or MIND SPEECH** - telepathy.

**MIRII** - A human that has joined his awareness with an Azerii, creating an exchange of physical and psychic abilities. The Mirii created a society to learn of their new talents and to teach and protect others like them. The people now call them sorcerers and witches.

**MIRRYTH** - Callent's Azerii.

**MIST PONIES** - the wild Azerii.

**MORANT** - Mirii Elder Aza Tor, Zerren's Gate Hold. Elas and Rejat's father.

**MORGANA** - eldest daughter of Tillan and Brea Brejjard, of the Brejjard LandsHold, Northern Valleys.

**NAMING, The** - an important Vondarii ceremony, when a Lii horse chooses his or her rider and gives them their name.

**NIIKA** - Lii horse, companion to Tren, Vondarii hunter.

**OTHERS, The** - the Unnamed Azerii calling Morgana.

**OUTERLANDS** - Vondarii term for anyone living outside the Sumark'h Plateau, beyond the Varan and Coumar Mountain ranges.

**PEACEKEEPERS** - soldiers or the city-dwellers police.

**PEOPLE, The** - Mirii term for non-Mirii or Vondarii.

**RAKKER** - Drek'h's Lii horse, before he became Mirii.

**REJAT Tala-Lael** - Mirii Aza Har Travelaar Healer, Elas' half sister. Member of Lasah Hawk Hold.

**RICAN** - Tillan's LandsHold Steward.

**RIDASAH** - Mirii Elder Aza Har of Lasah Hawk Hold.

**RINON LANDSHOLD** - the Brejjard LandsHold's eastern neighbors.

**SALAHN Rinon** - Dain's mother, Rinon LandsHold.

**SALKINN** - a large plateau cat.

**SARDUK'H** - a Vondarii hunter of the Storm-Rynnok'h clan, older half brother to the clan Healer, Larann.

**SHADOW** - Mirii term for creating a shadow image of their body when scanning.

**SIANN Brejjard** - Morgana's younger brother, Brejjard LandsHold.

**SIGHT** - inner-sight or visioning.

**SIVA Brenan** - Kaill Brenan's wife, Brenan LandsHold. Mother to Jeven and Dariel.

**SKYRYNNAR** - the First Stallion of the Lii, mount to Morgana and Drek'h after Drek'h is injured.

**STARA** - Tagar's House Steward, North Brejjard LandsHold.

**STARRYNN** - a Lii filly, Morgana's mount after the Lii claim her horse.

**STILLYTH or STIL** - Rejat's Azerii.

**TAGAR Brejjard** - HoldMaster, North Brejjard LandsHold, younger brother of Tillan Brejjard. Husband to Elas. Morgana's uncle.

**TAJIZ** - a stimulating herbal beverage.

**TALAHS** - a Vondarii woman, assists Elas and Morgana while they are with the Storm-Rynnok'h clan. Colkenn's consort.

**TALENT** - Mirii term for psychic abilities, or a person with psychic abilities.

**TALJI** - a young Talent, Lasah Hawk Hold.

**TARNN** - Lii stallion, companion to Sarduk'h, Vondarii Hunter.

**TILLAN Brejjard** - HoldMaster, Brejjard LandsHold. Morgana's father.

**TOR** - a Huntsman, friend to Tagar.

**TORYON** - younger brother of the Hold Steward, Rican, Brejjard Hold,

**TRAVELAAR** - Mirii term for one who travels for their holds.

**TREN** - Vondarii hunter, Storm-Rynnok'h clan.

**WILD AZERII** - the Unnamed Azerii that frequent the unpopulated forests and plains. They appear as twinkling lights or imitate the animals, especially the small mountains horses, called **'mist ponies'** by children who are most attracted to their childlike behavior.

**WILDERING WAYS** - Kir-Latt term for the mountain forests.

**WILLOWARR** - a large central tree in Elas' garden, North Brejjard LandsHold.

**UNNAMED AZERII** - the Azerii who have not meld with a human. Their totality.

**VAEL** - A young Talent of Zerren's Gate Hold.

**VEIL** - Mirii term for a psychic shield that appears to make a person or object invisible.

**VISIONER** - Mirii title for one with visioning abilities; trained to experience a vision at their chosen time and place.

**VISIONING** - an altered state of awareness where one experiences another time and place, future or past.

**VOICE** - Mirii ability to use their voice to control another's emotions or actions.

**VONDARII, The** - the tribal clans of the Sumarkh Plateau that follow the Lii horses.

**YELLOWENN FRUIT** - a fist sized, round fruit.

**VREEN** - Lii horse, companion to Colkenn, Vondarii hunter.

# The Twelve Mirii Holds and Wards
(in order of size, the first being the largest)

## The Holds
Lasah Hawk
Tasken
Zerren's Gate
Adjii Raven
Sekkett
Southern Tekk
Mahdii

## The Wards
Telann
Vesska
Dolphyn's Crest
Vadamii
Varan's Reach

# The Designations of the Mirii

Talent
Chosen Talent
Travelaar
Aza Tor (male warrior)
Aza Har (female warrior)

Healer
Visioner
EarthSinger
(female)
EarthKeeper (male)

# Pronunciation

(of frequently used words & names)

**ANARII** - Ah-nar-ee
**AZA** - Ah-zah
**AZERII** - Ah-zeer-ee
**BREA** - Bree-yah
**BREJJARD** - Brej-jard
**BREALYTH** - Brea-lith
**CEDARJINN** - See-dar-gin
**CHZA** - Ch-zah
**DAYANA** - Day-yawn-ah
**DREK'H** - Drek
**ELAS** - Ee-lahs
**ELISSII** - El-ees-see
**FAYR** - Fair
**MORGANA** - Mor-gan-a
**REJAT** - Re-jat
**SARDUK'H** - Sar-duke
**SKYRYNNAR** Sky-rin-nar
**STARRYNN** - Star-rin
**STILLYTH** - Still-lith
**SUMARKH** - Sue-mark
**TAGAR** - Tay-gar
**TRAVELAAR** - Tra-vel-lar
**VONDARII** - Von-dar-ee